THE
WEDDING
DAY

BOOKS BY SUE WATSON

STANDALONES

Snow Angels, Secrets and Christmas Cake

Summer Flings and Dancing Dreams

Bella's Christmas Bake Off

The Christmas Cake Cafe

Snowflakes, Iced Cakes and Second Chances

We'll Always Have Paris

THE
WEDDING
DAY

SUE WATSON

bookouture

Published by Bookouture in 2023

An imprint of Storyfire Ltd.
Carmelite House
50 Victoria Embankment
London EC4Y 0DZ

www.bookouture.com

ISBN: 978-1-80019-951-4
eBook ISBN: 978-1-80019-950-7

This book is a work of fiction. Names, characters, businesses, organizations, places and events other than those clearly in the public domain, are either the product of the author's imagination or are used fictitiously. Any resemblance to actual persons, living or dead, events or locales is entirely coincidental.

*To my friend Ann Bresnan, who always made my books better.
I'm so sorry we never got to say goodbye...*

PROLOGUE

I lift my heavy suitcase onto the conveyor belt. It's filled with my clothes, my toiletries and my secrets. I surrender it reluctantly as the uniformed woman slaps on security stickers and points to 'Airport Security' with a sulky nod. I nod back, saying nothing, not wanting to attract attention to myself in any way.

So far, so good. I step outside for a quick vape before returning and heading for security – my tomato-red Hermes handbag on my arm, my mouth dry as sand. Stale heat gathers around the homebound tourists with sunburn and sad faces, all queueing to go home when they don't want to. I keep my eyes downwards, don't engage with anyone and after too long, I finally see Border Control.

Walking on wobbly legs towards the serious man waiting behind glass, I cast my mind back to when I first arrived here. The person who came to this paradise island is very different from the one who's leaving. I came in search of something, someone, and I found them, but now I have to go again.

I hate to leave this beautiful place, where the sun shines

all day and the cocktails flow all night. But if you look closer, there's a dark side, and friends, lovers and murder, are just a whisper apart.

The border guard is looking at me from behind glass. He doesn't smile, but I do.

'Are you going to Rio de Janeiro on business or pleasure?'

'Pleasure.' I lean forward slightly and lick my lips suggestively; straight away, his eyes are on my lips. He hands me back my passport, and I try not to look too relieved. Or too guilty...

ONE

It was Valentine's Day, and I needed a bottle of wine. Not for a romantic dinner with my partner, but to drown my sorrows.

I'd finished work as soon as I possibly could, leaving the office and walking straight into a downpour. Rain was lashing the streets, taxis skidded by, splashing the pavements and spraying my new caramel raincoat in filthy water. Nice. After a mind-numbing day answering calls from disgruntled customers, all I wanted to do was run to the station and throw myself onto the first train home, but first I *had* to pop into a nearby supermarket for that bottle of wine. Being sober always made me feel slightly prickly, and uneasy, I needed something to smooth the sharp edges and help me forget.

Through the riot of water, inconsiderate umbrellas and surprising puddles, I saw it: the Tesco Express, that one-stop shop that would make my evening bearable. Funny how, even when our lives are in turmoil we return to the places, and the rituals that comfort us.

I wearily pushed open the door of the supermarket. Coming from the dark outside, the brutal strip lighting seared my eyes and I immediately remembered Valentine's Day last year. I'd been in this very supermarket on my way home from work. It was hard to comprehend how different my life was then. My eyes alighted on the baby formula stacked in rows on the shelf and tried not to burst into tears. *I'm not mad*, I told myself. But sometimes I *felt* mad.

That morning there'd been no Valentine waiting for me, just a decree absolute informing me that I was no longer married to Dan Green. Just a year before I'd been a married woman, with a beautiful home, good friends and a decent job. My marriage wasn't perfect, in fact at times it had been hell, but I'd tried to make it work, despite all the problems. Against the odds I'd always harboured a vain hope that one day we could be completely happy, and the clouds would go away. But we didn't stand a chance because I wasn't who Dan thought I was, I'd never been honest with him, and my truth ate away at me for years. I'd kept so much hidden. I realise now I wasn't looking for a husband, I was looking for love, and security for someone who wouldn't judge me, but our relationship had failed on all counts.

I'd never been honest with my husband, there were things I hadn't told him, things he'd never understand.

Soon after the wedding I'd realised Dan wasn't perfect, but neither was I, so he was all I deserved, wasn't he? But it turned out he was as disappointed in me as I was in myself; as he'd pointed out, I was 'the woman who failed at everything.'

So that rainy night, finding myself alone again, I wandered through the shop seeking solace and comfort in something full-bodied from Italy. Red wine would be my companion that Valentine's night, it would seduce me, soften me then knock me out. This way I didn't have to endure the screams that came alive the minute my head touched the pillow.

On Valentine's night the previous year, I'd bought candles. They were pretty uninspiring, off-white with no fragrance, and designed for emergencies rather than romantic dinners. But still I'd made a fist at it and bought them, thinking, *candlelight is candlelight*. And *a marriage is a marriage*. After everything that had gone before, I still clung to the desperate hope of a life, and a family, but here I was alone again.

I negotiated a group of teenagers and an old lady shaking her brolly, adding another Jackson Pollock layer of artwork to my raincoat. *I should have bought the black one. So many regrets.*

Pushing my way over to the well-stocked wine shelves at the back of the shop, I was mesmerised by the choice of those Italian reds. As I looked at the wines, I felt an overwhelming sadness at everything that had happened in the last few years. Dan was right, I couldn't keep hold of anything, even a husband, I'd failed at something again.

I'd failed at being a mother, a wife and a sister too. Then there was my career, which had never really started. I'd had my dreams, I'd hoped to work in the police once upon a time, but life had different plans. My teenage years had changed me, I'd become an angry, disillusioned girl with a gaping hole in her heart, and took the first job I could find. I worked in Customer Relations for a telephone company, where people shouted at me down the phone most days. I took some weird, sadistic pleasure from this, it felt like the punishment I deserved, and the pay was okay. I didn't want a job that filled my mind, I had so much else to think about I needed it to be simple, mindless. I'd been troubled for years by something I couldn't talk about, something I couldn't share with anyone except my sister. Even on good days I was haunted by the past, and when Dan left, I returned to my comfort, a bottle of red in my office drawer, a bag of peppermints to hide the smell. Sometimes, when a customer was very rude, or angry, the wine won and I was rude and angry back, I didn't care. Nothing made sense anymore, I couldn't concentrate, couldn't sleep for the nightmares, and was permanently on the edge of tears. I'd had several warnings from my understanding boss, and I was about to fail at keeping my job. Dan's words rang in my ears: You never *keep* anything, Alice, you throw things away.

I could have lived with all the failure, the rude customers, the unhappy marriage if I'd succeeded in just one of those things – being a mother.

I'd spent the first years of my marriage on a loop of daily injections, hope, egg collections, hope, waiting, and crying when the hope died. Then I'd start all over again. My sister once said to me, 'Alice, your problem is, you never see the stop signs.' And she was right, I've always ploughed on against all hope and expectation in everything I do, I refuse to see the signs and live with a morbid optimism, and I can't stop myself. Just days before he walked out, I told Dan about a new treatment I'd been reading about. 'This could be it,' I said. 'I'm going to call the clinic tomorrow.'

But instead of enthusiasm and encouragement, he'd looked at me with such pity I was embarrassed.

'Alice, you need to stop chasing something you'll never have. Accept it, stop doing this, it's self-destructive.'

His words still haunt me, but he couldn't possibly understand how I felt. I've never had the joy of tucking my baby into her cot, of first words, first steps, her first day at school, all so precious – and all lost to me now.

I didn't know it then, but Dan's reluctance to continue our quest for a baby was the beginning of his goodbye. He didn't want any more madness – the uncertainties, the torture of waiting to see if it had worked and the agony of finding out.

As always, my ridiculous hope had made a fool of me. I'd really believed that everything would have been different if I'd been able to have the baby we both wanted so much.

My grief still overflowed, my mourning was raw, but it was also invisible. It lived inside me, woke me in the night, tapped me on the shoulder as I drove my car, and almost stopped my breath. It drove me to obsession. I wanted to talk forever about babies and pregnancy. I wanted to explore *why* it hadn't happened, and like a detective searching for clues, my mind went over and over and over every little thing. *Why? Why? Why?*

I kept them to myself, but I had my theories. *I* was to blame for my body denying me the one thing I craved. And because I blamed myself, I found it hard to give in, and longed for more tests, more treatment, more agony, to prove I was wrong.

I gazed at the row of green bottles on the supermarket shelf, still thinking of baby names, nursery rhymes playing in my head. After everything, was I finally going mad? *Ten green bottles sitting on a wall.*

As I ran my fingers along the cold, dark glass I chose a bottle and, holding it to me, I lingered by the shelf, wondering if one would be enough. It was Valentine's Day, and I was alone. There was no chance of seeing Dan tonight, even for old times' sake. He'd refused to meet, said it was for the best. But silly me, I always hung on to hope, even now. *Ten green bottles sitting on a wall.*

Throughout the divorce process over the past few months, I'd kept in touch with Dan by phone. That morbid optimism of mine really wouldn't let go. Sometimes I'd call him late at night sobbing into the phone. He'd try not to lose his temper, but I could hear the anger and resentment bubbling in his voice. I was finding it tough to take on any more failures and clung to the hope that we'd get back together, and he'd change and be the Dan I first married, the angry Dan who sometimes hurt me came later. Even now, as I stood aimlessly in the supermarket, wondering how many bottles I'd need to get through the night, I thought, *should I call him?*

The seed of this idea blossomed in my head. I could ask if he wanted to come over to my sister's, where I was living. We could drink this bottle of wine on my sad single bed in her spare room. It wouldn't be that crazy, would it? *But if one green bottle should accidentally fall?*

I grabbed a basket and a second bottle of Merlot and went to pay. The woman behind the counter offered me a carrier bag, but I declined, thinking I'd be able to fit them in my roomy handbag. *I could text him now, ask if he fancied a drink?* The woman stared at my mud-splashed, caramel raincoat.

'That's £14.98,' she said, unsmiling, bored. I didn't blame her, not much to smile about working the Tesco Express on a wet weeknight in February. She was young, in her thirties, but she looked tired. She probably had several kids that kept her busy, stopped her sleeping, drove her mad, sucked her dry. *Lucky cow.*

Checking my watch, I realised my train home was in

fifteen minutes, so grabbed the bottles, but I'd overestimated the size of my Louis Vuitton knock-off. I could only fit one bottle in, but the woman was now busy serving someone else and I'd have to wait and ask and... everything was becoming too complicated. So, I jammed a bottle into the handbag, held on to the other and headed for the door. It was then that I saw someone out of the corner of my eye, and I stopped, as the cat in my tummy began stretching awake. Was that Dan at the far end of the store?

It was the absolute image of him from behind. I moved away from the door to get a better look. He was wearing a similar long overcoat to one Dan had, and his hair was like my ex-husband's – very dark, but a little shorter, neater. Dan always had a big floppy fringe, it suited him, he'd never have his hair shaved up the back like that, it was far too trendy. No, it wasn't Dan, he looked different somehow, slimmer, happier.

I should have been on the train home by now, but something kept me there. I was glued to the spot. Was it fate that we were both in the same Tesco Express store on Valentine's Day – the day of our decree absolute? No, it couldn't be Dan, he never finished work before six, and besides, this was miles from the bank where he worked. But it would be funny to call him and tell him I saw his twin. Also, a good excuse to make contact?

I slowly headed up the aisle to where the guy was standing. He suddenly bent down to take something from a shelf, and I was overwhelmed as the realisation hit me. It *was* Dan! To onlookers we were strangers just passing through, but for me this was someone I'd shared my life with for over a decade, someone I'd climbed into bed with every night. The imprint of our shared intimacy was still there; like a tattoo it

might fade, but it would never be eradicated. I knew the way
he ran his hands through his hair and sometimes put his head
to one side when he was listening. How he made love, and I
could see his anger, his happiness, his love sometimes. I also
remembered as we stood close in that supermarket on Valentine's night, how he'd cried when the fertility clinic called to
say we weren't pregnant, and probably never would be.

Closer now, I felt that warm rush of familiarity. I wanted
to reach out and touch the guy standing by the breakfast
cereals in this odd little mini supermarket. It was definitely
Dan, *my* Dan.

So with tight hope in my chest, I called out, 'Dan?'

He didn't turn around, but I saw his scarf – the blue one
I'd bought him the Christmas before last. Cost me a fortune,
I'd know it anywhere. I was right behind him now, about to
tap him on the back when a woman emerged from behind
the next aisle. She stood close to him, so close their heads
were together. Who was she? I was beginning to feel disorientated, nausea creeping into my throat as the unthinkable
crept into my head. Not now, not so soon, not on Valentine's
Day. Then I saw her hand on his arm, long pink fingernails
squeezing, as I heard him call her, 'Darling.'

'Dan?' I heard myself croak.

Everything felt like slow motion, with the volume turned
right down. Dan turned to me, the look on his face one of
horror as he instinctively tried to pull away from me. I saw
the woman's hand squeeze his arm more tightly. She looked
scared, holding on to him like she might fall over if he moved.

He looked crushed. 'Alice, I...'

'Is this *her*?' I heard the woman ask, disapproval in her
voice.

I stood, frozen to the spot holding a wine bottle, the other poking out from my handbag. Proof if she needed it that Dan's ex-wife was now a lush.

'Alice, this is Della,' he announced awkwardly.

She was young, in her thirties, very pretty.

I looked uncertainly in her direction. Our eyes met fleetingly. Neither of us spoke.

In the silence, I gazed from her to him, but he couldn't meet my eyes. His jaw was clenched. Eventually he spoke; 'I wanted to tell you, I tried, but... you wouldn't listen.'

'I had no idea. Is *this* why we're divorced?' I asked, gesturing at the two of them.

'You have to let go Alice, you can't keep calling me in the middle of the night,' he replied, ignoring my question.

I turned to her questioningly, perhaps she would tell me the truth? But all I saw was fear in her eyes. Then something made me glance down at her hands, now resting on her belly. Protectively. She was pregnant.

TWO

Just after the break-up, my therapist had diagnosed me with post-traumatic stress disorder and explained that blackouts often happen after deep trauma.

'I thought that was something that happened to soldiers when they went to war?' I'd said.

'Oh, Alice, you've been to war,' she replied.

And on realising that the woman in the supermarket was having Dan's baby, I was now back in that war zone. For a while, everything seemed to go dark, I wasn't sure for how long or what happened, but emerging from the blackness I panicked, and instinctively ran out of the supermarket for the train. I was so distraught, when I got to the train I jumped on quickly, and must have twisted my ankle. Searing pain shot through the bone as the train pulled away and I limped in agony through the carriage to find a seat. I was confused and dishevelled, suddenly aware I was still holding a bottle of wine and people were staring, albeit discreetly. Everyone seemed to be on high alert at the unexpected arrival of the mad wino woman. Before I reached the first vacant seat, the man in the adjoining seat quickly put his briefcase there. I didn't want any more battles, so limped down the carriage, but approaching another vacant seat, I noticed the woman nearby pulling her child close. I wanted to cry. Did I look like someone who'd hurt a child?

The woman recoiled as I moved to the seat opposite her and plonked the bottle on the table in front of me. The pain in my ankle caused me to land heavily in my seat, causing her to jump, as if I'd pounced on her. She was looking down at her child, still clutching him, the same way I'd been clutching the wine bottle minutes before. The same way Dan's girlfriend had been holding her belly. I saw the same fear in this woman's eyes as I'd seen in Della's. Was I a monster?

I was uneasy, unsure of myself, of what had just happened. I wanted to touch the woman on the arm and explain myself, to tell her that I was a good person, and I didn't want to hurt her or her child. I just wanted to go home. I longed to tell her what had just happened to me, convinced if she listened, she'd understand, but this wasn't the time, and she was too scared to hear me.

Having been alerted to my rather messy arrival, the ticket collector was now marching towards me.

'Ticket please, madam,' he said, feigning breezy, but I could see from the way he was stood, legs apart ready for battle, that he was prepared for a fight.

I didn't want any trouble, I just wanted to escape from whatever had just happened. But where was my train ticket?

It was in my handbag. I must have dropped my handbag in the supermarket in front of Dan and that woman before taking flight. The bottle of Merlot must have smashed as the bag landed on the ground, the other bottle was in my hand. *Her* hands were on her belly.

'I *said*, can I see your *ticket* please?'

I gazed up at the man now looming over me, but all I could see in my mind were smashed glass, red wine gushing all over the supermarket floor. Then the look of sheer horror on Dan's face.

'I... I don't have my ticket,' I croaked. Was my mind playing tricks, or was there blood too?

'Well, I'm afraid you're going to have to buy a new ticket. Or leave the train at the next stop.'

'I... can't, I can't buy a new one, I lost my bag.' I looked down as if to illustrate I wasn't carrying it. My eyes alighted on the red stains on the canvas of my caramel coat.

He continued to stand over me, glaring. I was intimidated, like an animal cornered, I didn't know what to do.

'I *don't* have my purse, I *can't* buy a ticket.'

'Then you have to leave the train.'

'I can't *walk*, I've hurt my ankle. I'm five stops away – can I pay it at the other end? I can ask my sister to meet me,' I offered, knowing how well that would go down with Heather.

He was now shaking his head elaborately. 'I'm sorry, but you'll have to get off at the next stop.'

'But it's miles, it's raining... you can't just throw me off in the dark.' I started to cry.

'You can't just sit on the train to stay out of the cold either,' he snapped. 'A train is not a homeless hostel.'

I was horrified. I must have looked so messy and confused he'd assumed I was looking for somewhere to *sleep*.

'We're now approaching the next stop. If you don't get off

I'm afraid I'll have to call the transport police.' His face was like stone, he *lived* for these moments.

'No, please,' I begged.

He shrugged. 'Either get off or I get the police.'

The whole carriage was so quiet I heard someone take the lid off their coffee, and quietly open a bag of crisps. Just like the cinema, they wanted their snacks while watching the film, but were polite enough not to spoil the audience's pleasure. *Dinner and a show.*

Slowly and painfully I tried to stand. I fully intended to make my way to the door and leave the train, which was now screeching and wheezing into the station. But the minute I put weight on my right ankle, intense pain shot up through my leg. This caused me to fall back onto the seat as the collector stood watching me as my fellow passengers pretended to be engrossed in their phones, their books, their coffee. Even in my fugue state I knew they were waiting for the next line of dialogue between the crazy lady and the ticket man. Like him, the spectators assumed I was just another mad woman on the train, no one stood up for me, or offered to pay my fare, or even give me a reassuring smile. I could have been homeless, or a victim of abuse – but I wasn't their problem, they'd paid for *their* tickets, so I should pay for *mine.*

I was looking up at him beseechingly, realising my phone was also in the handbag I'd dropped in the shop before making a run for it. Even if he *had* allowed me to stay on for free, I had no way of getting home from the station. I couldn't call a taxi or my sister, Heather.

As I now had no train ticket or the means to pay for it, I was arrested by two burly transport police. The night couldn't get any worse – or so I thought.

'What are you doing, you can't do this,' I cried, as they bundled me from the train, and out onto the freezing cold platform.

'I can't get home,' I said, close to tears now.

'You're not going home,' one of them said, taking out his radio and announcing. 'We have her here, we're bringing her in.'

'What?'

'You're under arrest,' he started.

'Arrest? But...' Despite being so upset, I almost laughed. 'You can't arrest me for not having a ticket!'

'We've been looking for you ever since you ran from the Tesco Express on Crossland Road. Fleeing the scene of a crime doesn't look good, miss. We're taking you in so you can tell us exactly what happened back there tonight.'

THREE

Within the hour, I was in a cell at the local police station waiting to be questioned by detectives. The drama over the unpaid train ticket got a whole lot worse because once I'd given my name and address, turns out I was, by then a 'wanted' woman.

I was being accused of assaulting Dan, of hitting him with a bottle of wine.

'I didn't hit him. I just wouldn't *do* that,' I replied.

'But you told us you don't remember, you said you blacked out.'

'I did, I can't remember what happened. I just saw them, and the next thing I remember is I'm running out of the supermarket.'

'So *how* do you know you didn't hit him over the head with the bottle?'

'Well, I had the bottle in my hand when I left.'

'Not the bottle you hit him with, you took that from your bag.'

This conversation continued into the early hours of the

morning, until I didn't know who I was, or which wine bottle I was supposed to have hit my ex with. They clearly believed I was guilty and lying about not remembering, but I genuinely had a blackout, I'd had them before. I tried to explain this, but in my tiredness and confusion – not to mention shock – I was tongue-tied and kept tripping myself up. I fully expected to be charged with assault, they seemed so determined, but after twenty-four hours in police custody, they couldn't keep me any longer, so I was released 'under investigation,' which at the time meant little to me. All I knew was I could get out of that hell hole. I wasn't a criminal, at least I didn't see myself as one.

'Is Dan okay?' I asked the police officer as I signed my release forms.

He shrugged. 'He's still being checked over in hospital, as far as I know,' was all he said, before adding, 'you're free to leave, but under investigation.'

Confused, I looked at my solicitor who quickly explained that I'd only been released because the police didn't have enough evidence to keep me there.

'A rearrest may be 'imminent,' she warned.

My blood ran cold. 'So this isn't over?'

She shook her head. 'You're still <u>under investigation</u>. This is ongoing until they find more evidence.'

'And if they *do* find enough evidence, then what...?' I couldn't finish the sentence.

'If they can prove that the assault was committed with intent to cause GBH or wounding,' she replied solemnly, 'then the maximum sentence is life imprisonment.'

I felt the ground move under me, 'worst case scenario though?' I asked, pleading for reassurance from the only person who seemed to be remotely on my side that night.

She just shrugged.

How could something like this happen to someone like me? I'd had my problems, but never anything involving the police before.

'What if I call Dan, talk to him, tell him it's all a mistake?' I offered hopefully.

'No,' she said sharply. 'Under no circumstances are you allowed to make contact with anyone connected to the case.'

The next few days were a blur, punctuated by Heather's nagging, my two nieces arguing and my own still-vivid nightmares.

* * *

After a couple of weeks, I couldn't bear the tension. I knew something had happened that night, and Heather had heard through a friend of a friend that Dan had been kept in hospital. But I still had no idea what had happened or how he was, because I wasn't allowed to contact him. Meanwhile, there was a chance the police may find more evidence and I could be arrested without even remembering what I was supposed to have done. Every time my phone rang, or someone knocked on the door, my heart jumped, and Heather went pale. The stress for both of us was unbearable.

So I decided to give her a break, and take control of my life, and leave. But when I told her my plan, Heather was horrified.

'Corfu? You're running away to Corfu? Are you mad? You can't go abroad when you're under investigation,' she hissed. 'This hasn't gone away, Alice. It's illegal to jump bail, haven't the police confiscated your passport?' Heather was a true crime junkie, she read books, watched TV and listened to podcasts. And sometimes she made like she was starring in one.

'Oh my God, Heather, stop! As much as I enjoy your drama, the police haven't confiscated *anything*, I'm not "jumping bail." I'm not a bloody flight risk because I'm not a murderer, or a trafficker, or a danger to anyone. It was an *altercation* in a local supermarket with my ex.'

'Altercation?' she remarked, raising her eyebrows.

'Yes, that's all it was. It wasn't an assault, I didn't whack him over the head with a bottle.'

'You don't *remember* whacking him, but you can't say hand on heart that you didn't.'

'You sound like the police. I thought you were on my side?'

'I am, always but...'

'They can't prove a thing, my lawyer says the CCTV is unclear.'

'Ever heard of CCTV enhancement?' she replied. 'An expert could have those pixels sorted in minutes, then where would you be?'

'I'd be innocent,' I replied, uncertainly.

'Mmm. I'm not convinced. Look, love, someone, some-where always knows something,' she recited, a well-worn tag line from one of her favourite detective dramas. 'And if you didn't do it, who did?'

'Now you sound like the police, it's done and dusted, lock her up.'

'I'm not saying he didn't deserve it, mind,' she added as an afterthought. 'So what if you're away and the police decide you're guilty?'

'Guilty of what? *Altercating* in a mini supermarket?'

'You *know* what I mean. That... that *woman* is a lawyer

you know.' Heather couldn't say Della's name, she loathed her more than I did for being pregnant.

'Yes, I heard she's a lawyer, and she's bound to try every trick in the book to get justice for him. It's just my luck,' I sighed. I didn't like Della either, but saved the bulk of my loathing for Dan – loathing is a high-energy activity, I had to be sparing.

'I *know* why you're going to Corfu,' she said, suddenly clutching my arm.

'I don't want to talk about this now.'

'You're making a mistake. I've told you before you need to stop this craziness.'

'I'm not being crazy, I have to go, you know why.'

'I can't condone this. You need to stay here, deal with the police, and forget about what may or may not have happened in the past. You have to stop.'

'I can't stop. If I don't go now, I might end up in prison and never get the chance again.'

'You're looking for a needle in a haystack, you'll make yourself ill again,' she said, her eyes pleading for me to listen.

'I'm having the nightmares again,' I muttered, my eyes brimming with tears.

She looked concerned. 'Oh no, the same ones, like before?'

I nodded. 'I dread going to sleep, Heather.'

She put her arm around me. 'I blame myself for everything.'

'Don't, it wasn't anyone's fault, we both felt it was right at the time. And now I have to go there, see for myself. If I don't I'll never rest, Heather.'

She sighed. 'You have to do what you have to do – I suppose.'

'I've been emotionally exhausted for years.'

'I know, love,' she said, in a rare moment of sensitivity, 'and you need to follow your heart.' In that moment, I really appreciated my sister, and how much she meant to me. But then she added, 'Just as long as you do it legally, don't change your name or travel on a fake passport.'

I rolled my eyes. 'I'll try not to. I was looking into safe houses in South America working for drug barons, would that work?'

'You can joke about this, but you're still "under investigation" and if something comes to light you'll suddenly be on the wanted list with Interpol on your tail!'

I almost laughed. 'No one is "on my tail," I'm not living in an American crime movie from the 1960s. You watch too much TV.'

'Well, at least that's *all* I do, I don't get arrested for assault or refusing to buy train tickets. And your coat, have you seen the state of your coat?'

'It's red wine.'

'Are you sure? Looks like blood spatter to me. You need to get that dry cleaned before the police take it in as evidence.' 'Yeah, thanks, Miss Marple, I'll take it to the dry cleaner's, shall I? I'll say, "can you please get the wine that looks like blood spatter off this coat without going to the police?" I mean, that wouldn't alert *anyone*.'

'Don't be sarcastic. I'm just saying if you're leaving the country while under investigation it might be an idea to get rid of a bloodstained coat.'

'Who's being sarcastic now?'

'Alice, apart from the fact it might be incriminating, I don't want it here for the girls to find.'

'Okay,' I said, not wanting my nieces to ever see anything that cause them to question me.

'But when I've gone, promise me you'll explain to the girls that I'm innocent. Tell them I just got caught up in something at the Tesco Express. It could happen to anyone – even you.'

'No, it *couldn't*.' She had her arms folded tight. I saw the worry etched on her face, and it occurred to me that she'd started to look older since I'd moved in with her when Dan and I split just a year before.

During that time, Olivia and Amy, Heather's girls, were my only comfort. They were funny and laid-back in a way teenagers are, and my sister isn't. Watching *Love Island* or *Big Brother* with them was my deepest joy, it was the only time I could forget myself, the only time I felt remotely happy. I often wondered if this was what it would have been like with my own daughter.

* * *

So, I booked the flight to Corfu, a place where I might find answers to the questions that had been haunting me for some time. I was scared, desperate and unhappy, but that beautiful island in the Ionian Sea was all the hope I had left. And that's what I needed right now. Hope.

Meanwhile, I'd spoken to my boss, told her the stress of the divorce had affected me, and I needed a break. Having had several difficult but understanding 'conversations' with her the previous year about my drinking, I was aware that anything else might just lose me my job. So I told her nothing about the crime I'd been accused of, hoping to be able to return to my work once this had all blown over. She was sympathetic to my personal plight, and encouraged me to take the trip, as I emptied the tissue box in her office, soaking up my tears. 'Take all the time you need, Alice,' she said, relief in her voice. Having once been one of her best employees, I was now becoming a liability.

Leaving the country in the middle of a criminal investigation was probably not the best idea I'd ever had. I hated leaving Heather and my nieces, because they were all I had. But an unpredictable auntie with PTSD, a drink problem and a conviction hanging over her head was the last thing they needed in their spare room. I also had to protect them from the prospect of the police turning up on the doorstep and them seeing me bundled into a police car. As I hadn't had the chance to be a good mother, I could at least try to be a good aunt. So leaving for a while was my only option.

FOUR

Arriving on Corfu was exciting and scary, and I was immediately reminded of my first visit there five years before, mine and Dan's honeymoon. It was a time of happiness that turned too quickly, and though I'd chosen Corfu, had longed to go there, it didn't make me happy.

Later, as I waited by the conveyor belt for my suitcase, I watched a mum gently pull her little girl back to safety from the moving platform, feeling the familiar sting of loss and the life that had evaded me. I grabbed my suitcase and walked towards the taxi rank, pushing away my regrets and sadness, hoping that here on Corfu there might be some closure.

The owner of the Airbnb apartment that would be my home for the next few weeks had suggested an open-ended lease. This meant I could stay as long as I wanted to, which she pointed out would mean a large deposit, and a longer notice period, but it was worth it because I wasn't yet sure how long I would stay.

Martha, the owner, had assured me on email that I'd be very happy there, and as I walked in, I knew she was right.

The apartment was beautiful, and for a moment I almost forgot about the police back home, but then I realised this might be my last holiday for a long time. Slipping off my shoes, I instantly felt calmer. The stone floor was cool under foot as I wandered around my new space. *My* space. I walked across the whitewashed room to the shutters, where horizontal lines of sunshine peeped through, hinting at the promise of what was waiting for me out there. Gauze curtains shuddered either side as I opened the shutters, and heat flooded in like warm water. I had an almost physical sensation that my troubles were lifting from me and floating out into the air. Could this be the place where I finally found that longed-for peace of mind?

I stepped onto the baking hot patio and imagined myself sitting there with a glass of wine in the evening, gazing down at the street below. Corfu Town was straight from a postcard: pastel-coloured Venetian-style buildings that looked sugar-coated and good enough to eat. It may have *looked* like a film set, but every inch was lived in and utilised, from air-conditioning units teetering on windowsills, to rows of clean washing drying on high lines, colours bleached by the sun.

It was mid-morning, and busy, but not busy like home, with traffic fumes and sour-faced commuters. No, this was *Greek* busy, with people chatting on corners and waiters carrying plates to diners perched at flimsy tables on uneven pavements.

The waft of garlic and coffee danced in the air, reminding me I hadn't eaten since leaving London. I could almost taste those golden chunks of chicken kebab doused with cool tzasiki being served just metres away. But first things first. I went back inside and finished off what was left of the warm bottle of water in my hand luggage.

Martha had left a bottle of bright orange kumquat liqueur on the kitchen table with a note. *I hope you will enjoy my island*, she'd written. So once unpacked, I poured a little into a glass, and sat on the bed, enjoying the peace and quiet in my sanctuary, while outside the hustle and bustle continued. Life went on, I reminded myself, whatever happens life must go on.

After sipping on the sugary liqueur, and taking in my surroundings, I was impatient to take a walk. I thought again about Dan and our honeymoon five years before. We were both thirty-nine, and as we were both older, and had been trying for a year before we married, we started fertility treatment just after the honeymoon. We were excited about the future, and my head was filled with white lace and promises as we took long walks on the beach in the gold of beautiful sunsets. We made so many plans on those evenings, and for the first time in my adult life I thought I'd found what I was looking for, a new beginning, but in retrospect it was just optimism and blind hope wrapped up in dying sunshine.

There were pregnancies, soaring, ecstatic pockets of hope for a future I'd dreamed of, but my babies never made it through the journey. The devastation wore us down and turned out Dan wasn't the man I thought he was. It began with an angry word, a nasty remark, then graduated to a push against the wall, and a slap now and then. Afterwards he'd weep, get down on his knees and beg for my forgiveness, and at first I believed him when he said it would never happen again. But it did, it happened every few weeks or months, and in between I told myself we were fine, after all it wasn't every day, and a threatened slap with his hand almost touching my face wasn't violence, was it? I felt like it was my fault because I couldn't give him the children we wanted, I was incapable of creating a family, and a life for us. And for a while, I did what I'd always done, and adapted to him, to his behaviour. So when later I told my therapist that the anger had eased, that the physical violence was far less, she pointed out, that's because I'd changed, not Dan. I'd hidden my feelings, stopped myself from saying or doing anything I knew might trigger him, and by becoming someone else, I'd lessened the trigger points. I know now that this was stupid, naïve, weak, but throughout this time, I was still desperate to have a baby. I'd married someone who was equally desperate, I was in my late thirties, and time was running out.

I continued my walk through the streets of Corfu town, reflecting on everything that had happened, regretting my marriage, and yet still wishing we'd had that baby. I was still so mixed up and damaged from my past. I'd seen Dan as my saviour, I'd put so much hope into him, and into our marriage, I couldn't allow it to fail. It was only here, now in a different place that I could finally start to let go.

I had to stop dwelling on the past, and put it into a box, close the lid, and embrace now. So I stopped to buy an ice cream from a kiosk in the square, and crossed over the road to sit on a bench overlooking the harbour. This was what I needed right now, some peace and quiet in my head. The past had shaped me, it was part of me, I couldn't erase it, so now I had to find a way of living with the past without reliving it.

It was cooler there under the trees, and I settled down to eat my ice cream while staring at the grainy posters nailed to the tree trunks. It was difficult to work out what they were at first, but standing up to take a closer look, I could see they were faces, women's faces. I didn't know them, but having seen their photos on TV and in my newsfeeds years before, they seemed strangely familiar. Sadly, all these women had gone missing from Corfu and other Greek islands at some point over the last few years. There were theories all over the internet of course, most of them pretty gruesome, but there was also the possibility that the women had just moved on. I walked between the trees and came across more and more photos, all faded by the sun. Each woman was now an outline, a faded memory, a face holding no clue as to who she was or what had happened. There were five posters all on different trees, all of different women, and I scrutinised each one.

The dates and details had been worn away by the sun and rain and it was impossible to see much except the outline of a female face and the word MISSING.

From what I could remember, none of them had close families, they were single and all in their late thirties and forties. Heather and I talked about it a lot, we were fascinated, and gobbled up every little thing we could, but there were few crumbs. It seemed the media and the public's fascination for missing women only sustained when they were young and beautiful. Even the police seemed to have given up, suggesting a drowning for one, and another had apparently gone missing while hiking. A couple of the women were British, but with no news, and no loved ones to tie yellow ribbons around trees and put pressure on the authorities, nothing was driving the search. Heather and I were fascinated and horrified, it had become a personal quest for both of us, and like crazed amateur detectives we scoured social media for clues. But given the average age of the women, there was very little media presence so all we had were missing persons websites for any news.

'The police said they could have gone travelling?' I'd

suggested, my optimism flaring as usual. 'I mean, they had nothing and no one to tie them down, it might not be sinister, they might just have gone island hopping?'

But Heather was far more cynical than me. 'Yeah, or they've been murdered or kidnapped, *because* they're free and single. When you think about it, there's no one to miss them, or even report them missing, and no one to *look* for them.'

I felt a chill when she said this. 'If they go missing and no one is reporting them, there could be so many more.'

'Yes, but don't go imagining all kinds of stuff, love, these women are middle-aged, and they aren't all British.'

Looking now at the weathered posters pinned to trees, their memory like the pictures were fading, and as time went on and none of them were found, they'd disappear altogether.

I was so distracted by this that I only noticed my ice cream had melted when it began trickling cold down my arm. My appetite suddenly faded, and I dropped it in the nearest bin. I stood a while, going over and over the mystery of the missing women. At least five had disappeared in the last five years. That was one each year. I considered this while absently gazing at my ice cream now turning to sweet pink liquid in the bin, melting ice cream now being consumed by a swarm of seething wasps.

I walked on, but couldn't get the women's faces from my mind. Their smiles plagued me through the streets. I barely noticed the beautiful buildings, the brightly painted brick-work, the Venetian architecture, just heard the women's imaginary screams. My therapist had told me that at times like this I must distract myself, I didn't want to become obsessed again. So when I came to a small café with free tables, I sat in the sunshine and ordered a white wine. The service was, thankfully, quick, and my medication arrived cold, with a side of the salty, juicy, queen green olives as big as gobstoppers. I sipped my wine and chewed on olives telling myself *I can do this*, *I can enjoy life again*. I just had to take pleasure in the simple things and try and find some good people to share them with.

My eyes drifted across the sea of diners enjoying lunch, and I saw this good looking, older guy sitting alone just a few tables away. It's hard to define, but there was just something about him. He looked kind, which doesn't sound edgy or sexy, but I was drawn to kindness after my unkind marriage. I wasn't looking for a man, I was done with men, I just wanted me from now on, but still I noted that every time I happened to glance over, he was looking at me. Embarrassed, I turned away and distracted myself watching a table of women laughing loudly nearby. They seemed to be having a great time without a care in the world, and their laughter cheered me.

'You are kidding me? NO!' one was saying loudly. She looked to be around the same age as me, the other two younger. I smiled to myself as I watched them chatting. That was also what I needed right now, a friend, someone to gossip and laugh with, take me out of myself, and make the screaming stop.

I couldn't eat lunch, and didn't want to drink too much as it usually didn't end well, so on finishing the white wine, I ordered a coffee. I was taking a first sip, when I noticed the handsome guy had left his table, which was a shame because I liked looking at him. But minutes later, he walked past my table, having presumably been to the bathroom. But as he did, he accidentally banged into the table slightly, causing it to wobble, and some of my coffee spilled.

'I'm *so* sorry!' he exclaimed.

'It's fine,' I said, surprised at his English accent.

'What an idiot I am.'

'No, no, you're not.' I wafted away his apology with one hand, while pouring the spilled black coffee from the saucer back into the cup.

'I *have* to buy you another.' He was looking around for a waiter to order more coffee.

'No really, it's fine, look, it's back in the cup, no problem.'

He took off his sunglasses and looking directly at me, said with such sincerity, 'Thank you, you're very kind.'

His eyes were piercing blue, and I wanted to drown in them. 'It's nothing, just a few drops of coffee.'

He touched my shoulder. 'Sorry again!' he repeated and slowly walked back to his table. I watched him sit down, and was still watching when he lifted his glass up to me, in a cheers gesture. I blushed in response, then checked myself, I was a forty-four year-old divorced woman who'd given up on men.

The woman and her friends were now summoning a waiter to bring more drinks. One of the younger ones had a loud voice and I could hear her ordering cocktails which, to her audible joy, soon arrived in coupe glasses. I continued to watch from behind my coffee cup as the bright pink, foamy confections were consumed quickly. The woman around my own age was attractive, and sophisticated in a long black sundress with a halter neck. Her thick, shiny blonde hair cut into a short bob and by her feet was a tomato-red Hermes handbag. I adored designer handbags, and had several fakes at home, but had never been able to afford one – and that particular one was vintage and probably very expensive. The other two girls were dressed glamorously too, and their shared drinks and laughter reminded me that I'd never really had a group of girlfriends like that. Heather and I had stuck together when our parents died, both too concerned about making ends meet and staying safe to indulge in friendships and a social life. We had fun, and we went out, but for me it was mostly work colleagues and office nights out every now and then, not real friends like these women seemed to be. I envied their ease of conversation, their explosions of laughter, and wished I had friends like them. But reflected that perhaps any friends I may have had would have disowned me by now given the trouble I was in. Only Heather and I knew about the arrest. I couldn't bear to retell it, and unless there was a court case, no one ever needed to know. I still couldn't recall the details, I really didn't know how it happened, but if I did assault Dan, then I was scared of what I was capable of. I really had to be careful, because whatever I'd been clinging to for sanity had been kicked away like a walking stick that night. And all I could remember was running away from a tsunami of broken glass, red wine and blood.

Dragging my mind away from the horror, I reminded myself that I was somewhere else now, and there was potential here to heal. So I gazed around, taking in the colour, the clink of glasses and quiet chatter around me in an attempt to let in some light. I saw out of the corner of my eye that the handsome guy had finished his drink, and was now leaving a handful of euros on the table. But as he stood up to leave, one of the younger women in the group, the loud one, saw him and began waving and calling. At first he didn't seem to hear or perhaps he chose not to? But she was keen to make herself known, and getting up from where she was sitting, called, 'Nik, Nik!' He turned around quickly, and on seeing her, a smile lit up his face.

'I didn't know you were here. Have you been hiding from me?' She was calling in what sounded like a Greek accent. She manoeuvred herself quickly through the tables, and on reaching him, leaped into an embrace as he stood solidly, taking the impact. Holding on to him tightly, like she was afraid to let him go, she whispered something in his ear, which made him chuckle.

Watching discreetly from a distance, I could see she was very beautiful, and also at about twenty years younger than him. He must have been flattered by her enthusiastic embrace, and who could blame him? My heart tipped with disappointment. Ah well, I'd learned by now that where men were concerned, there were always younger, more beautiful women waiting in the wings. I thought again about my husband's betrayal, the way his new partner had yelled at me because I'd had the temerity to call him late at night. But I'd had no idea she was *there*, that she even *existed* – and certainly no clue that he was with someone, who was heavily pregnant with his child. Would I ever be able to think about that without hurting?

Leaving the beautiful young woman hanging off the handsome guy's arm, I paid my bill and left. I tried to think happy thoughts, but every now and then I'd see another faded poster on a tree or a lamppost. It made my heart sink, surely someone somewhere knew *something*.

FIVE

A couple of days later, I was walking through the main square, and literally bumped into the guy from the café.

'It's you!' he said, as surprised to see me as I was him. 'I'm the one who spilled your coffee.'

'Hi, yes, I remember you.' I smiled, and we both stood there awkwardly.

'Are you here on holiday?'

'Yes. I'm here for a few weeks,' I added.

'Nice. Corfu is a small island, but she has a lot to offer.'

'And you?'

'Oh, I have a lot to offer too,' he joked.

'I'm sure you do – but I was asking about you being here, are you on holiday?'

'I know, I was teasing you. No, I live here.'

With his deep tan and expensive-looking shirt, he *looked* like a resident. I wondered if perhaps he owned one of the millionaires' yachts docked in the port near the old town? I could imagine him steering a boat, his white shirt billowing behind him, the sea spray making his skin taste like salt. I realised I was staring at him, and he was staring back. We both looked away self-consciously.

'So, you live here?' I murmured, desperately trying to pick up the conversation as I dragged my eyes from his. 'Lucky you.'

'Yeah, I am lucky. I have a small vineyard, in the mountains. You should visit while you're here,' he added as an afterthought.

'I'd love to,' I said, as he put his hand in the pocket of his jeans and produced a business card.

'Kouris Estates,' I read from the card.

'Nik Kouris.' He held out his hand for me to shake it.

'Alice...' I decided not to give him my second name. As Heather had reminded me so dramatically when she dropped me off at the airport, 'You're a fugitive now, you can't trust anyone.' As always, she had a point. After all, things could change very quickly back home and someone might be looking for me.

'Lovely to meet you, Alice, and I mean it, you must visit. Call me?' he said as he walked away, a smile and something else lingering on his face.

I gave a silly little wave, immediately realising, and putting my hand down. He was gorgeous, and I was always stupid in the presence of handsome, charming men – not that I'd come across too many in my life. I put the card safely in my handbag thinking that perhaps I'd give him a call while I was there, then dismissing the idea. Who did I think I was? I'd never been confident with men, always wondered what they saw in me. I was probably a gift for Dan, a vulnerable woman with no self-confidence – men like him love women like me. Then again, I had to believe there were good men out there, because if there weren't what hope was there?

I wandered back to my apartment, thinking about Nik Kouris's blue eyes and lovely open smile. Then I reminded myself of the beautiful young woman who'd embraced him in the café. I really couldn't leave myself open to any more rejection or hurt, and from what I saw, that beautiful young woman definitely had him in her sights.

On my return, I sat on the balcony with my phone, intending to check out the places I wanted to visit while I was here. But first, I googled Kouris Estates, and discovered it was a family-owned vineyard with its own winery in the Pantokrator Mountains. It looked beautiful, but I was rather hoping for more information on (and yes, a nice photo of) Nik Kouris, but the website was more about the land and the wine. Still I managed to find out roughly where it was, and that it took about an hour to get there by car from Corfu Town.

I liked the idea, and thought I might drive over there while I was on the island. I'd planned to hire a car anyway to visit Glyfada, a beautiful coastal town on the west coast that Dan and I visited briefly on our honeymoon. I'd told him I wanted to see the spectacular sunsets there, but that wasn't the real reason. I should have told him, but something stopped me, I was scared if he found out he'd leave me, and our marriage would be over before it had really begun.

I found lots of tourist information online about Glyfada, and booked a car to go and visit later in the week. I was alarmed to discover that at least one of the missing women had been staying there when she disappeared, but there was little information available. I looked for more on the women, but as far as I could see there was currently no active investigation. After some intensive searching, and copious notes, I discovered that there were nine known missing women.

They were from different countries – Dutch, American, German, British and Irish – but looking at their photos, they were all a similar age. Physically, they looked different, but they all appeared to come from similar socio-economic backgrounds.

I checked social media, and though information was scant, I saw that one had lost a parent, another had recently divorced a millionaire, and another had taken early retirement from her job. I knew from my job that any of these life events could indicate an influx of personal wealth, in the form of an inheritance, divorce settlement or early pension payout. And from what I could gather, they seemed to have gone to Greece to start a new life, then just disappeared off the grid.

I found a news article where a spokesman for the Hellenic police had said they'd been through the island, checking caves, beaches, mountains. But as he pointed out, 'Corfu is small, but she has many hiding places, including the sea.' He refused to rule out murder, and even people trafficking. 'The women could have been taken to another country and sold,' he'd added, which made me shudder.

I continued to scroll, fascinated yet horrified, and later, as the pink dusk settled on the town, and hunger told me it was dinnertime, I sat in the pink light, soaking up what was left of the day's warmth. Only thirst dragged me away to get a glass of water, but walking back into the apartment, it suddenly felt very dark. I had to walk carefully until my eyes got used to the dim light. While pouring the water from a jug in the fridge, I thought I caught a movement in the corner of the room. My whole body tingled, and I stopped pouring, just stared into the far corner, waiting for something to move, or not. I knew it was probably just my imagination, fired by all the disturbing theories I'd been reading. This told me it was time to take a break, and rather than be alone with my scary thoughts, I decided to go out to dinner. But before I put down my phone, I checked Instagram, scrolling through pictures. Old friends, new friends, non-friends all posting their moments, their dinners, their nights out. It seemed like everyone was having a fabulous time, except me, and the usual dull ache formed in my stomach as I was reminded of my failed life.

And just when I thought it couldn't get any worse, I went back there. Della's Instagram account. And as I clicked on her page, I gave a sharp intake of breath. Della, in a close-up, no make-up, hairs stuck to her forehead with sweat. Holding her beautiful, just-born baby girl. I felt like I was looking at myself, a mirror image of mother and baby, a pixelated square of what might have been, and what was now, for me, too late.

SIX

I'd known the birth of Dan and Della's baby was imminent when I'd seen her that night. I thought I was prepared for it, and that being hundreds of miles away was the poultice I'd need for the pain. But it would take so much more than distance to ease the sheer agony of seeing my husband's new partner clutching their gorgeous baby girl.

I finally pulled myself together, and trying not to think about Della's flushed, happy face and the baby's cute little nose, I headed out into the night.

Once I'd found a table in a small restaurant in the square, I called Heather. She was fascinated by what I'd found out about the missing women, if a little freaked out.

'Don't let it take you over,' she said. 'Be careful who you speak to, don't go off with strangers, and please, please, stay in touch,' she added, like I was ten years old.

'I'm fine, no one's kidnapping me,' I assured her.

'But you fit the profile, middle-aged woman travelling alone...' she started. 'I wish you'd just come home. I'm scared, Alice.'

'I don't *want* to come home. I couldn't face it. Della's had the baby.'

Silence.

'Oh, love, I'm sorry that must be hard. How do you know?'

'Saw the photos on her Instagram. It was bad enough seeing the scans, to read about every kick, every little belch of the embryo. But to be confronted with the actual baby...' I felt tearful again.

'Why look? Why put yourself through it, you shouldn't be looking at her Instagram account, Alice.'

'I'm *compelled* to look, Dan isn't posting anymore, so I can only find out what's going on by looking at Della's posts.'

'But you don't *have* to know what's going on. It's their life, you're not part of it.'

'I know, you don't have to remind me. I'm not part of *anyone's* life,' I started to cry. 'I just wanted to see her, the baby.'

For a while neither of us spoke, then she said, 'Is it because you wanted to see if their baby looks like yours might have done?'

'No,' I lied, wiping my eyes with the back of my hand. I told her my pizza had arrived, and got off the phone quickly. I knew that when I hurt, so did Heather, and I didn't want her to know how much this had affected me.

I thought of the early baby scans Dan and I had gazed at lovingly, imagining what he or she would look like, the people they would become. It hurt that three of my babies were never born, but at the same time, I didn't begrudge Della her baby. I just wished it had been me. I'd *looked* for the photos of her scans, the first glimpse of their baby at her breast. I wanted to remember what it was like to love a human you hadn't even met.

I felt stupid and empty and alone. I wondered if Heather was right and I should just book the next flight home. What the hell was I doing here, and what the hell was I looking for?

I barely ate my pizza, but stayed at the table and ordered another drink while googling some more on my phone. I had to take my mind off Dan and Della's baby, so threw myself back into my fixation with the missing women. I felt so alone, and giving myself a purpose like this was a distraction from both my pain and my aloneness. I soon became absorbed in what I was doing, and didn't notice the blonde woman from a couple of days ago in the doorway of the restaurant. I looked up to see it had filled up quickly, and there were now no free tables. She was with the beautiful, younger woman with dark hair, they seemed to be waiting for a table to become vacant. As I'd finished, I beckoned the waiter over.

'I'm leaving now, please tell the ladies they can have my table,' I said, asking for the bill. He nodded, and before returning with the bill, sent them over to the table.

'This is very kind, thank you so much,' said the older woman. 'We thought we'd have to wait at least an hour for a table.'

'We *could* have gone somewhere else,' the younger woman remarked ungraciously, without acknowledging me or the fact I'd given up my table for them.

'Please don't leave, we can share the table with you,' the older woman said kindly, like she was desperately trying to erase her friend's rudeness with her own good manners.

'Thank you, but I have to get back,' I lied. I didn't have to get back anywhere, no one was waiting, or wondering where

I was, or missing me. I wasn't needed – just like the missing women.

'But you haven't had dessert, or coffee. You can't just go.' The woman started looking around for a waiter, and when one appeared, she said, 'Could I have a bottle of Sauvignon and *three* glasses please?' She turned to me. 'You drink white, right?'

I nodded, thinking why not? The very thought of going back to my apartment and sitting hunched over my phone looking at missing women and Dan's new baby wasn't my idea of a great night in.

'I'm Sylvie, by the way.' She smiled, as she took her seat. 'And this is Angelina, we work together.' Angelina smiled too, although clearly uninterested. But when you looked as gorgeous as she did, with her long, thick black hair and mesmerising lash-framed eyes – well, you could choose who you were nice to. I wasn't offended, just surprised at the difference between the way she'd behaved the other day with Nik Kouris, and the sulky, disinterested air she had now. But Sylvie made up for her friend's lack of conversation and the two of us were soon chatting away over the white wine.

'We've just finished work – well, a wedding actually, and we came in here for a last drink,' Sylvie said, explaining that she owned an event planning company. 'That's why we were so grateful when you offered us this table, we've been on our feet all day, haven't we?' She turned to Angelina, who nodded and took a sip of her wine.

'You okay, Angelina?' Sylvie asked.

She shrugged. 'I'm tired, I want to go home.'

'I know, I'm tired too, love, but this is nice, having a nightcap with Alice,' Sylvie replied, taking a vape pen from her beautiful Hermes handbag. 'Don't mind if I vape, do you?' she asked.

'Not at all,' I replied, and the air was suddenly filled with citrus.

'So, what about *you?*' Sylvie asked. 'What brings you to Corfu?'

A shattered wine bottle flashed in my mind, causing my stomach to tip.

'I needed a break, and I love Corfu,' I replied. She smiled expectantly, waiting for me to add more, but I wasn't going to share with a stranger, however friendly she was.

'I'm divorced. It was quite a difficult break-up.' I paused. She was still listening, nodding.

'I understand,' she said warmly. I was still feeling raw from the baby news, and very alone, so appreciated her friendliness and easy manner.

'What do you do?' she asked.

'I work in customer relations for an internet company,' I answered.

'Oh, how intriguing.'

'Not really, people usually fall asleep at Customer Relations,' I joked.

'Yeah, *I'm* falling asleep,' Angelina butt in.

I was surprised at her rudeness and immediately stopped talking.

'*Angelina,*' Sylvie reprimanded her.

'Oh, sorry, I meant it's been a busy day, I didn't mean—'

'It's fine,' I said. But it wasn't fine, it hurt, and despite her vague apology, I felt like she *had* meant it.

'Look, why don't you get a taxi and go home, charge the company,' Sylvie said, rolling her eyes subtly at me.

'Cheers.' Angelina brightened at this, and she stood up

immediately, abandoning her glass of wine, clearly eager to go. 'Nice to meet you, Alice,' she said over her shoulder as an afterthought. After hugging Sylvie, she was gone.

'I'm sorry about that,' Sylvie said. 'Angelina's a nice girl, but she has this way with her sometimes.' Her face looked pained.

'She was tired, she didn't want to hear *me* going on about my boring job,' I said, trying to be fair.

'No, she was rude,' she replied. 'She isn't usually like that, and I'm not making excuses for her, but I do allow her some leeway. She had a difficult childhood, neglect and abuse,' she said as an aside. 'I think sometimes she just gets angry and restless and looks at other people's lives and resents what they have. It's understandable, she has no money, no qualifications, no support, you know what I mean?'

'That's sad,' I said.

'Yeah, so when she turned up looking for a job, I just scooped her up, gave her work and tried to help.'

'That's kind of you.'

'Not really, I just hope I'm helping,' she added, crossing two fingers.

I suddenly felt sorry for the younger woman, and a little ashamed of the way I'd dismissed her as rude. 'We all have reasons for the way we are,' I said, thinking of my own life and how it had shaped me.

'She only started with me a few months ago.' Sylvie leaned in. 'She's still on probation, she sometimes goes AWOL, which isn't great. But I let her stay out of pity really,' she added in a quiet voice.

Her childhood went some way to explaining her brusqueness, and that brittle exterior, she was probably harbouring a lot of anger. I remembered the way she chased Nik Kouris across the restaurant a couple of days before, and it made a kind of sense now. Perhaps like a child she'd been seeking his attention, his approval? When I thought about that, my heart went out to her.

'Poor kid,' I murmured, thinking about my own childhood, and how happy and secure it had been. Despite losing both our parents when quite young, Heather and I were always there for each other. Poor Angelina probably had no one.

Sylvie poured us both a second glass of wine and asked me about my marriage and I found myself telling her all about Dan. I told her about the rainy night, the little supermarket, the smashed bottle of wine, and felt like I was talking about a different person in a different life. Having spent only a couple of warm, calm days on that beautiful island, I already felt at a safe distance from the dark night, the cold rain, and the shock of Della's swollen belly.

I didn't tell Sylvie about the assault charge, I just said I'd dropped a bottle of wine when I saw Dan and Della. Then I told her about the photo I'd seen just hours before of their perfect baby daughter, and she listened intently as my eyes filled with tears.

'Oh, love, I get it, I really do. I had a similar experience to you, but walked in on my husband with my best friend. They were in *our* bed.' The pain on her face told me this was quite recent. 'A different kind of trauma, but still a horrible betrayal,' she said, shaking her head. Despite still being upset, the drink and the talking had made me feel pleasantly woozy and we ordered more wine. I'd promised Heather I wouldn't drink too much while I was away, but for the first time in a long time, I felt good. Sylvie was funny and kind, and I enjoyed her company and the wine so much that I relaxed a little.

Before leaving the restaurant, Sylvie suggested we have drinks again and we swapped numbers. Walking home that evening through the warm, moonlit streets, I felt happier than I had in a long time. I'd loved chatting with Sylvie, and felt like she could become a friend, but got the distinct feeling Angelina didn't like me. And regardless of her youth and her past, the feeling was mutual. I couldn't put my finger on it, but there was something about her that made me feel very uneasy.

SEVEN

'Two cosmopolitans please,' Sylvie said, sounding slightly fuzzy.

It was our third night out in a row, and we were sitting on stools in a bar in the middle of town. She looked stunning in an emerald green silk dress and I lamented my own lack of style while admiring it.

'You always look so fabulous,' I said, 'this dress is to die for!' I was rather tipsy, after several cosmopolitans, and with two more on order and a fast-growing friendship, I found myself telling Sylvie about my IVF journey.

Her face filled with pain as I went through the highs and devastating lows. Reliving the trauma brought fresh tears to my eyes and made me realise how close to the surface this still was for me.

'Oh, Alice!' she cried. 'That totally puts into perspective the hurt you must have felt when you found out about his baby – with her!' I felt a rush of warmth at her loyalty, her absolute understanding of what I'd been through. I wondered then if perhaps one day I could tell her *everything*.

'I can't imagine,' she said, then hesitated. 'Actually, I can. I couldn't have children either.'

'Oh, Sylvie, I'm so sorry.'

She nodded slowly, and picked at an imaginary fleck on her bare knee. 'Miscarriage, followed by years of waiting and hoping, ending in nothing, and I still think about it every, single hour of every single day.'

As she spoke of her own experience, her words echoed down the years, as if she was telling my story. Her sadness wrapped itself around me like a blanket, and I felt a sense of relief – here was someone who *really* understood, who wouldn't dismiss my pain by suggesting I *throw* myself into my career. She wouldn't tell me how 'lucky' I was to have my freedom, my sleep, my career and so-called *me* time, as my sister and friends with children always had.

'Heather, my sister... she has no idea. She has two beautiful daughters, how could she *ever* understand?' I lamented, feeling slightly disloyal at the implied criticism of someone I loved to someone I hardly knew. 'But she means well,' I added to soothe my own conscience.

'Sisters? They *always* mean well, with their opinions, their judgement, their pronouncements on how to live life. I've got *two*,' she said, her jaw tightening. '"Count your blessings, Sylvie. You have plenty of money and a successful business,"' she growled under her breath at the memory.

'Wow. Sounds just like *my* sister,' I replied, nodding my head enthusiastically. 'She seems to think the freedom to stay out late or go on a spa weekend is adequate compensation for a baby. But there *is* no alternative to having a child, especially if it's all you've ever wanted.' I felt tears forming, but discreetly brushed them away worried that Sylvie might think I was mad. She didn't know my full story, just snapshots of my life, some of it was too precious to bring into the bright daylight and share.

'Right?' She was nodding. 'And that's what friends and sisters with kids can't get into their thick skulls.'

'Thick skulls,' I repeated, aware that the cosmopolitans were causing me to produce over-enthusiastic responses. 'God, Sylvie, sorry if I'm oversharing, I've only known you a few days,' I said, draining my glass.

'I feel like I could tell *you* anything too. I just knew you were my kind of person the minute we met. And friends for life when you told me about yelling at your husband and smashing wine bottles all over the Tesco Express,' she chuckled. Then she darted a concerned look at me. 'I'm sorry, was that insensitive?'

'No, not at all. I'd rather laugh about it.' I'd only been there for a few days, and despite everything still being really raw, I felt myself moving forward slightly.

'It's healthier to laugh about it, if you can,' she nodded, dabbing at her mouth with a cocktail napkin. 'My marriage lasted a few short years, and when the children didn't happen, I became anxious, depressed. Then one day I came home early from work and found him in our bed with Anna, my best friend. I was so devastated, I walked out and never went back. I sometimes wonder if he ever loved me,' she added sadly, her eyes watery.

'I'm so sorry, Sylvie.' I couldn't think of anything else to say, and she clearly needed a moment.

'It's fine. But I left with nothing, no husband, no money, no home, and no self-esteem.'

I sighed. 'You really did suffer, I was luckier. I lost years, but I had a roof over my head at Heather's and I also got a financial settlement. As much as I resent my sister's constant interfering, she paid for a lawyer and insisted I fight for half the house. It sold quickly, even before the decree absolute, and I repaid her as soon as I got the money.'

'You were lucky your sister could help.'

'Yeah, but I still I feel a bit guilty about the money.'

'Why *guilty*?'

'Dan earned more than me, his parents had also given him a huge deposit, so he contributed so much more. In fact, the house was almost completely paid for when we divorced.'

'Don't feel guilty, it's yours legally. Just use that money for lovely things that make you happy instead.'

'I am. That's why I'm here, on holiday, staying in a lovely apartment, drinking cocktails with new friends,' I said. She smiled and we clinked glasses, but I knew it wasn't that simple, I still had a long way to go – some things cut so deep they scar you. I'd spent most of my adult life feeling the pain from those scars and in truth doubted I could ever be truly happy again.

'Good for you, Alice!'

'Yeah, this wasn't the life I'd planned, but sitting there with bright pink drinks and a new friend is good for the soul,' I said. It also gave me a glimmer of hope after years of darkness.

I wasn't going to say any more, but after the night in the supermarket, my solicitor had told me that if I was ever convicted, Dan may have a case for compensation. If it was proven that I assaulted him, he could sue me, and as a lawyer and his partner, Della would no doubt help build the case. He'd been opposed to me having half of everything in our divorce, and this was his chance to get the money back, and knowing Dan he would go through hell and high water to do that. I'd written a will bequeathing everything I had to my two nieces, and if I was found guilty of assault, not only might I end up in prison, but Dan and Della could get everything, and there'd be nothing for the girls.

'I think we need more drinks,' Sylvie was saying, calling the waiter over and ordering more cosmopolitans.

'I promised my sister I wouldn't drink,' I said lightly, feeling a tinge of guilt.

'She's not your mother!' Sylvie chuckled at this.

I smiled at the irony, she certainly behaved like my mother. A single mum with a full-time job, along with her two teenage daughters, Heather treated me like her third child.

'She's six years older than me, and when our parents were killed in a car crash she was twenty and I was only fourteen,' I explained.

'Oh I'm sorry.'

'No, it was a lifetime ago, I'm not asking for sympathy, but just explaining the dynamic between us,' I replied. 'Back then Heather fought for us to stay together and became my legal guardian. She was only just out of her teens herself, but, if it hadn't been for her, I'd have ended up in a children's home. That's why we're so close. She's almost like a mother. I'm so grateful to her.'

'Oh I get it, that's so sad and she sounds like an amazing person,' Sylvie said with a sympathetic smile. 'But on the flip side, she still treats you like that teenager, am I right?'

Her change of gear made me laugh. 'Yep, that's it. I'm now in my forties and she still treats me like I was fourteen!'

We both laughed at this as the waiter arrived with our drinks, I handed him my empty glass from the last round, hearing Heather's warning voice in my head. 'Don't drink too much, love, you know what happens, you'll end up in a mess again.'

But I lifted my glass defiantly, and after a large, delicious sip, continued. 'She's always telling me to stop drinking, and here she calls me daily to say "come home," she thinks I'm running away from my problems, that I'm wasting my life. Thing is, she's probably right.' I rolled my eyes and took another sip. I knew I had to go back home at some point, but until I could remember what happened and defend myself, I was happy to stay out of the country and under the radar.

'I wouldn't say you're wasting your life,' Sylvie reflected. 'Look at you. You're on a beautiful Greek island drinking cocktails, and she's in chilly old blighty, probably doing the laundry having just finished a long day at work and *wishing* she could run away – so *who's* wasting their life?' She lifted up her glass, chinking it against mine, and said, 'Here's to being childless, husbandless, sisterless... and drunk!'

Sylvie reminded me of my best friend from school, seductive, playful and so much fun, and I felt a little sparkle of excitement in my throat. She made me feel young and free and rebellious, and after downing our cosmopolitans, I suggested we order two more. I was really enjoying myself, until I saw Angelina making her way towards us at the bar.

'I thought you had a hot date tonight?' Sylvie said, genuinely surprised as she approached us.

Angelina rolled her eyes and, taking a stool from further down the bar, plonked it between Sylvie and me. 'Stood me up,' she mumbled, glancing over at me. I suddenly went from being in a two-way conversation with Sylvie, to being the outsider.

'He's ghosting me now, I hate men,' she moaned.

'Oh, love, that's tough, you really liked him too, didn't you?' Sylvie said kindly.

She nodded sulkily like a child who'd lost her new bike and wouldn't be placated. 'I guess I should have known, I never have any luck. Men are just out to hurt you...' For the first time, I saw her vulnerability laid bare, and I immediately softened.

'Not *all* men, Ange,' Sylvie replied, she was clearly the mother hen in this relationship. 'You'll find your Mr Right, there's plenty of time, he just wasn't the one.'

'I'm twenty-six, I'm a spinster.'

Sylvie laughed. 'Have you heard this, Alice?' She leaned forward to address me, but Angelina made no attempt to move so I could be included in the conversation.

'You're a baby,' I tried. 'Sylvie's right, you have *plenty* of time.'

Angelina turned to me, and on that warm, summer's night, the look on her face turned my blood to ice. She couldn't hate me, because she didn't really know me, but it was clear she hated me *being* there. I don't think anyone had ever made me feel quite so unwelcome, so excluded. It wasn't something I was used to.

She turned back to Sylvie and spoke in a low voice, which was difficult to hear, especially over the music. I leaned in, but it was obvious she didn't want to share her dating disaster with anyone but Sylvie, and still sitting with her back to me, was making no attempt to include me. She was being rude, as she had been the last time I'd been in her company. Was it personal, she just didn't like me, or did she feel like I was taking Sylvie from her? Perhaps given every-thing that had happened to me recently I was more vulnera-ble, paranoid even. Suddenly we were joined by another young woman. 'This is Maria,' Sylvie said, 'she's part of the team.'

She smiled, and said hello. She was also Greek and seemed as rude as Angelina pulling up a stool to the other side of Sylvie. Once again I was completely excluded as they all began talking about a wedding they'd worked on earlier that week. But Sylvie being Sylvie was soon aware of the awkwardness of this for me.

'Could you move back just a little, Angelina?' she asked. 'I can't see Alice.'

Without looking at me, Angelina moved her stool slightly. We still hadn't said hello. I was disappointed, and confused, but as she'd moved slightly, I could at least now see the others and be part of the conversation.

'How did you become a wedding planner?' I asked Sylvie, taking advantage of a gap in the conversation.

She paused to think. 'That's a good question. It wasn't my childhood ambition, it just happened. When I left my ex I got work in a bar, and met this lovely girl who was about to get married.' She had a faraway smile on her face. 'She had no money, so I helped her to have her dream wedding on the beach, *and* on a budget. A guest at that wedding asked if I'd do the same for them, and I've been doing it for a few years now.'

'Not on a budget now though.' Angelina rolled her eyes at Maria.

'No, these days people want me to *spend* their money,' Sylvie replied. 'And I did most of it on my own until a few months ago, when this one turned up on my doorstep and asked if I needed an assistant,' she gestured towards Angelina. 'So, for my sins, I took her on, and just a couple of weeks ago, her friend Maria joined us.'

Before I could respond to this, I suddenly became aware of another person on the edge of the group. It was Nik Kouris, the handsome, coffee-spilling vineyard owner.

'So, is this the wedding planners' night out?' he remarked, smiling expectantly at us all.

Angelina immediately stood up and hugged him warmly. As I'd suspected, being sulky *wasn't* her default mode; she wasn't rude and cold to everyone – just me.

'I thought you were busy tonight?' she said, one arm still lingering around his neck from the hug.

'I was... I just fancied a drink,' he said, glancing briefly at me. 'Nice to see you again, Alice,' he nodded in my direction. At this, Angelina seemed to grip his neck tighter, drawing him to her.

'Join us, Nik?' she pleaded.

He looked hesitant. 'Thank you, but I don't want to interrupt a work meeting?' He seemed to glance at Sylvie perhaps hoping for permission, but she didn't pick up on this.

She certainly didn't encourage him to join us as I'd expected her to.

'No, it's not a work meeting at all,' Angelina insisted. 'I've just been stood up and I need a shoulder to cry on,' she said, looking up at him with big eyes.

'Oh, if it isn't work, I guess I can have a drink with you,' he said grabbing a stool, placing it between Angelina and me, but Sylvie turned to talk to Maria, and once again I was shut out.

Meanwhile, Angelina was stroking Nik's arm, looking up into his face – he didn't stand a chance. I knew I was probably being paranoid, but it seemed to be Angelina's quest to keep me away from Nik.

But eventually, he managed to extricate himself from her and turned to me. 'So, Alice, how are you enjoying Corfu?'

'I'm... I'm loving it,' I replied shyly, very much aware of the younger woman's eyes now boring into me. I couldn't blame her for feeling possessive about this guy, he was so attractive, and had this way of making me feel like he wanted to know everything about me. I wasn't stupid, he obviously made every other woman he spoke to feel the same, but still I was flattered by his attention. I guessed he was in his late forties, but could have been younger, a silver fox in waiting. And when he smiled, his cheeks dimpled and I saw something boyish under that sophisticated, older exterior.

'Nik,' Angelina was saying.

'I'm just talking to Alice,' I heard him reply firmly, but kindly like he was talking to a child.

He turned back to me, and I didn't even hear what he said as he made small talk about the places I should see while on Corfu. His face and the skin at his open-necked white shirt were bronzed, I assumed from working outdoors in the sun at his vineyard. Or perhaps as the owner he didn't need to work, and just sunbathed all day? Then I started to think about him with no top on, languishing under an olive tree on his acreage, and just responded with banality to what he was telling me while smiling into his face like a fool.

'Nik!' Angelina said loudly, impatiently grabbing at his shoulder in an attempt to turn him to face her. Sylvie had mentioned her difficult upbringing, and I was trying really hard to be sympathetic, while Nik was smiling indulgently at her. 'My apologies, Alice, but Angelina is *very* demanding.' She stuck out her tongue, and he laughed. Angelina was very beautiful, I doubted men ever refused her, and Nik was clearly no different. She snuggled up against him, and I was slightly dismayed at how comfortable he seemed, his arm now loosely slung over her shoulder, both smiling the same smile. I watched them, wondering if there was some history there, or perhaps something more current, as Angelina's eyes glared back at me, dark and threatening.

EIGHT

'Do you think Angelina and Nik are having a fling?' I asked Sylvie the next time we met. She'd invited me to spend a day on the beach with her, and we were now sitting side by side on sun loungers looking out to sea.

She lifted her sunglasses to look at me, a slight frown fighting the Botox as she attempted a doubtful face.

'No,' she said. 'I don't *know* him, but I can't think he's interested in Angelina.' Then she seemed to consider my question more deeply. 'But *she* definitely has a crush, I heard her saying to Maria that she fancied him. He's good looking and he's very rich, so why wouldn't she?' Sylvie gave a little chuckle. 'Men like Nik are catnip to pretty young girls like Angelina. I doubt she'd turn her nose up at being lady of her own vineyard. Wouldn't we all love to be chatelaine of the best winery on Corfu?'

'Sounds good to me,' I replied, then returned to the burning question. 'So you don't think there's anything actually going on between the two of them?' I wasn't sure, but after the evening in the bar I felt Nik and I had a connection.

But was I fooling myself? What could he possibly see in a pasty-faced forty-something when he had the likes of Angelina falling at his feet?

'I've met Nik Kouris a couple of times through work, and I just couldn't see him and Angelina together, they're very different,' she added, putting her glasses back on her face. She continued to stare out at the ocean, apparently not interested enough to pursue that line of thought.

'I just thought they seemed comfortable with each other...' I said, wanting to engage her, keep the conversation on Nik. I was longing for any little crumb she might have to throw in my direction.

She shrugged.

'He's really good-looking, isn't he?' I murmured.

At this, her head turned quickly towards me. 'You fancy him, don't you?'

'Yeah, who wouldn't? But I can't compete with Angelina, she's about twenty years younger than me and gorgeous.'

'You never know he might be one of those rare men who prefer attractive, older women with a story to tell?'

Then she leaned towards me, lowering her voice. 'I heard he was married once, got badly hurt. I think she left him for a billionaire or something. I don't know the details, but whenever I've seen him, he looks a bit...' She stopped to think a moment. 'Lost, yeah that's it, he looks *lost*.'

My heart ached a little at this. Sadly Sylvie didn't know any more, but she was such a 'girlie' girl, she loved the idea of playing cupid, and offered to call him for me. 'I don't know him all that well but I could probably put a word in?' she suggested.

I was horrified. 'Thank you but no, I'm not a teenager.' Then I giggled. Like a teenager.

Over the next few hours she came up with crazy ideas as to how I could 'accidentally' bump into him. We were laughing hysterically at the improbability of me hanging around his favourite haunts, even popping up from behind a grape vine at his vineyard and faking my 'surprise' at seeing him. 'Joking aside though,' she said, 'you could call the winery, pretend you're interested in a tour?'

'You mean *openly* stalk him?' I said with a chuckle. 'Actually, I do have his business card.' I told her about him spilling my coffee and how I'd bumped into him later.

'Oh my God! You're practically engaged,' she joked. 'But seriously, if he made a point of saying hi and gave you his card, that seems pretty keen to me.'

'I don't know,' I replied doubtfully, while being secretly thrilled at her assumption. I'd hoped this might be the case, but having been married for so long questioned how good my radar was regarding men who might reciprocate my feelings. 'Perhaps he was just being nice to a tourist?' I offered, wanting reassurance.

'No, it's obvious, he *fancies* you. In fact,' her face took on a mysterious look, 'I *did* wonder at him turning up in the bar the other night – he's never *out*.'

'He might have come into the bar to see Angelina?' I offered, hoping this idea was instantly rejected.

'Nah. She was all over *him*, not the other way round. I go out with her a lot, and he's never turned up before. Now I think about it, it if he'd met you before, when he spilled your coffee, he may very well have been on the lookout for you?'

'It's a nice thought, but I doubt he went into the bar to see *me*.'

'Well, I reckon he did, but we'll never know because

Angelina had him in a headlock before he had a chance to say hello.'

I laughed. 'True, and who can blame her, he's a catch. But I'm not looking for a serious relationship, even if he was interested, I just want some fun.'

'You're telling me you'd turn down someone like Nik Kouris if he asked you what you were doing for the rest of your life?'

'I didn't say I'd turn him down exactly.'

'If you want fun and no ties go on Tinder?' she suggested.

'No, I couldn't.'

'But if you don't want anything serious...?'

'I'd rather leave it to fate.'

'So you do want something serious,' she smiled. 'I'm the same. I've never even done the Tinder thing. I want more than a one-night-stand. I couldn't do Tinder either, I have this horrible feeling they might swipe right because they like the photo but hate me in the flesh. They might think I was boring or stupid or ugly.'

'God, Sylvie, you're kidding me? How could you even *think* that. You're funny and bright and clever and gorgeous,' I said, but I understood her insecurities. Like me she'd had a bad experience and that probably wasn't the only time. From the father who told me I was fat, to the first boyfriend who told me I wasn't good enough... We are shaped by the people we love.

'I understand,' I said, 'not everyone does.'

'I just sometimes don't feel enough.'

I shook my head vehemently. 'There are women who'd give their right arm to wear a bikini like that, and look as good as you do,' I stressed.

'Thanks, you're very kind.' She sat up. 'Let's have a drink?'

'I'd love to, but it's only just 3pm, and if I drink too much now I won't know when to stop,' I said lightly, but it was true.

'Just one, eh?' She was hard to say no to and within minutes, she was returning from the beach bar with two cosmopolitans, bright pink, icy, tangy and very much appreciated in the heat of the afternoon. I loved a drink, and at some points in my life that desire had verged on *need*, meaning I had to curb what could have become an addiction. I found it hard to stop at one, and by the time I'd had a few I really couldn't stop. After Dan and I split, and my drinking became worse, there were gaps of time I genuinely couldn't remember. My sister referred to it as 'Alice's *gap* year,' because I'd finish at least a bottle of wine every night to forget the pain and blot him out, but anything could happen, and I rarely remembered. That's why I was in so much trouble now, and I couldn't defend myself against the assault accusation, because I *couldn't* remember.

Sylvie was taking a long sip of her cosmopolitan. I'd never tasted one until I met Sylvie and was now hooked on the sweet-tart cocktail that started with a sugary fruit and ended on bitter lime. And like an addict, I reached for my drink.

'I'm going to miss you when you've gone,' she suddenly said.

'Me too. It makes me sad just to *think* about having to go back.' I felt tears welling in my eyes remembering the mess waiting for me at home.

'You don't *have* to go back,' she murmured, taking another sip. 'Don't go home, stay here for ever.'

'I'd love to, but I've been given time off work, so have to

go back at some point,' I explained, without mentioning why I'd been given time off work.

'Well, take it from one who knows, your boss will get over it – quicker than you think. And this time next year your only regret would be that you didn't leave work sooner.'

What she was saying was very seductive. How lovely it would be to just turn my back on all the problems piling up back home, and stay on this beautiful island sipping cocktails in the sunshine. I knew then that I should do the right thing and head back before the police realised I'd gone away. But at the same time, apart from Heather and my nieces, I had nothing left back there, no one waiting for me, no home of my own yet. Besides, I was also worried that I might be greeted at the airport by armed police waiting to rearrest me. All I could do was hope, that after a few more weeks here, everything would be cleared up and I could go home, back to work and start building a new life. I lifted my glass and Sylvie clinked hers against it.

'Let's take a selfie for Instagram.' She turned around so the sea was behind her, and pulled me in, thrusting her phone high above us both, while I pulled my sun hat low.

'What are you doing, disguising yourself?' she asked, chuckling.

'No,' I lied, pulling the hat brim lower down my face.

I doubted anyone followed Sylvie's Instagram who knew me, but I wasn't risking it.

Sylvie smiled, and rested her head back on the sunlounger, allowing the late afternoon sun to slide slowly along her body. 'I'm a great believer in fate,' she murmured, her eyes closing as she surrendered to the golden heat. 'I don't know whether it's the fact we've been through the same shit – or we just get along. But you know...' She turned her head, opening her eyes and shading them with the back of her hand to look at me. 'I think we were *meant* to be friends.'

Later, I found Sylvie's Instagram and saved a screenshot of our photo. Two happy women, sunglasses on, slightly out of focus, the sea glittering in the distance, a summer snapshot of our new friendship. But looking back, not everyone I met that summer on Corfu was my friend, and just like Instagram, real life is never quite as pretty as it seems.

NINE

I'd been in Corfu three weeks when I finally checked my work emails, and my heart sank when I saw the HR email address headed URGENT.

My finger hovered over the delete button, but I was already avoiding everything and I had to face this. So I opened the email, and read through the formal wording, which in essence told me that my work with them was now over and a final pay cheque would be sent to me.

I immediately called Sophie, my boss. I let it ring and ring, but nothing. This went on for most of the day, and by evening I was a wreck.

It wasn't until the following day after several more tries, that she picked up.

'Sophie, what is going on? I'm on compassionate leave, don't they have to have consultations with people before they just sack them?' I could hear the tears in my voice.

There were a few moments of silence at the other end.

'Sophie?'

I heard her sigh. 'Alice, it's been a nightmare. I've been

fighting tooth and nail for you here, but this isn't the first time there have been problems. I put the daytime drinking down to the divorce...'

'It *was*, I just needed a bottle in my drawer to get me through sometimes. It didn't affect how I did my job.'

'Whatever, it wasn't a good look for Customer Services, and now something else has come to light.'

'I don't understand,' I cut in, but my stomach dipped, knowing exactly what was coming next.

'I was under the impression that your recent issues were about struggling with your divorce. You didn't tell me that the *police* were involved.'

'I *was* struggling, how do you know about the police?'

'People talk, Alice, I wish you'd told me.'

'I'm so sorry.'

'Me too.'

Her voice sounded cold and clipped. 'I'm sorry we have to let you go. I know this is a bad time, but you left us no choice.'

'But, Sophie, I'm not guilty of anything. I haven't been charged, it's just an investigation. I need my job – it's all I have left—'

'I'm so sorry, Alice, it's out of my hands. Your final pay cheque will be put through at the end of the month. Hope things turn out for you.' Then the phone went dead.

Devastated, I threw my phone across the room and cried angry tears and lay on my bed looking up at the ceiling as my life continued to spiral out of control. No marriage, no family, and now no job. I had to pull myself together, only I could solve my problems and I conjured up some of that blind optimism, tried to find my phone.

I eventually found it in the corner of the room where it

had landed. It was, apparently fine, and still in working order, and this had been tested by Heather who'd left at least three messages asking what flight I'd booked.

So I called Heather, who answered straight away.

'I'd take full responsibility if I'd done something wrong, but I haven't,' I started. This was an ongoing conversation between us, and despite her being so annoying, I found it comforting to just call someone and not even have to say 'hi'.

'You can't *remember* doing something wrong,' she reminded me. 'But you might have – Alice you're being investigated for assault.'

'I know, but my solicitor said that according to police reports he walked away that night, so I couldn't have hurt him that much even if it *was* me!' I cried down the phone.

'Surely there needs to be some proof it was me. There are two of them, and Dan and Della are both saying the same thing, can't you see, Heather, they want me to be convicted so they can then go for compensation.'

She sighed. 'I know, love, and it's infuriating. *He's* the one that walked out on you. He's the one that wrecked *your* life – and even if you did assault him, in my view it's his fault because he drove you to it,' she replied, angrily.

In my heart I knew I hadn't assaulted my ex-husband, but my head kept telling me that I might have. I could be impulsive, and my default reaction to most things was emotional, I didn't think I jumped. That's why I was there on Corfu, I'd just gone there without thinking, driven by my emotions and my fears.

I took full responsibility for my situation, but Heather was right, Dan was the catalyst, my marriage and divorce and everything that happened in between had shaped the life I now had.

'You're right,' I said. 'Not happy with ending the marriage, he's now dismantling my life, piece by piece, I have no home, and now no job. I'm so angry I could, I could...'

'Now, now calm down. He's not worth it,' Heather said in a voice she used for her girls. 'Getting angry isn't the answer. It's never been the answer, love.'

I knew what she was saying. I'd sometimes found it hard to quell my anger, always had. And since I was a teenager I'd sat on my pain, my loss and my grief had turned to rage. Mum and Dad died when I was fourteen, and I still hadn't dealt with that, and the stuff that came after, and it bubbled away like a pressure cooker. By day I seemed fine, but it was only superficial, the agony lived inside me, and revealed itself through the nightmares, filled with screams.

'Come home, Alice. We can sort this out, running away isn't the answer.'

'I will. Soon.'

'Your lawyer left another message on our landline. You told me you'd get back to her.'

'Shit. I will, sorry.' After that awful night, I'd changed my phone number. I hadn't wanted to talk to anyone that knew me ever again.

'I take it you didn't give your lawyer your new phone number?' Heather said, sounding disappointed, but like she expected it, which stung.

'Yes, I gave it to her, she must have lost it.' This wasn't true. I'd meant to give her my new number but was putting it off, subconsciously hoping if my lawyer couldn't contact me, then it would go away.

'So you're coming home?' Heather was saying.

'Yes,' I answered weakly, not meaning it.

'Okay, book your flight *now*.'

'I will,' I muttered, and put down the phone. Then I found a bottle of wine in the cupboard. It was sweet, Greek wine with that woody retsina tang that wasn't exactly pleasant, but I downed it through my tears. It calmed my rage and sent me to sleep, where I relived the nightmare of everything that had happened that night. Then continued into the past, my marriage, infertility, my difficult teenage years, then straight back to now, waking with a start, my first thought the same as always. Is it *her* screaming in my dreams?

I lay there for a long time, trying to remember her smile, but as the years faded, so had her face. Sometimes I couldn't even remember what she looked like, and it broke my heart. I'd hoped that going there to Corfu my mind would allow me to see her face again, but the only difference here was that the screams in my nightmares were louder.

I staggered to the bathroom and threw cold water on my face.

As much as I loved her, I couldn't countenance another lecture from Heather, so just texted Sylvie to let her know what had happened. I knew she was busy with meetings all day, so didn't expect a response straight away, I just felt the need to tell someone I'd lost my job – but obviously not the reason why.

Still in a kind of shock, I walked out onto the balcony to feel sun on my face, and tell myself it was all going to be okay. Glancing down onto the street below, I saw him, and my heart jumped a little. Nik Kouris was sitting alone having a beer at a pavement café. Should I go and say hi? I stood for a while just watching him, then realised he only had to look up to see me hanging over my balcony staring like a psycho. In fact he might already have spotted me. So I decided to take my chances. I had a lot on my mind, and a chat with a handsome guy who didn't know me was just what I needed. Ten minutes later, after a slick of sunscreen, make-up and a change of clothes, I was sauntering past him, then doing a double-take with a surprised look on my face when he called my name. *Bingo!* I walked over to him, still feigning surprise. 'Hey, what are you doing here?' I said stupidly, like the chances of seeing him in a small town we were both staying in was the most amazing coincidence ever.

'Waiting for you, obviously,' he joked.

I stood at his table a few seconds, talking rubbish about the weather, and then he asked if I'd like to join him.

I looked around as if I had somewhere else to be, then decided that I could spare the time and sat down.

He ordered himself another beer, and I said I'd have the same. I told myself the beer would simply quench my thirst but it tasted good, and when my thirst was quenched, he ordered two more. I didn't object. By the third beer, I was feeling very relaxed, and Nik seemed so nice, I found myself telling him my life story – well, the edited one. He listened intently. 'Alice, that's so sad,' he sighed when I told him the true part about my parents dying young and how my sister was like a mum to me.

Then I told him about bumping into my ex-husband with his new, pregnant girlfriend, I didn't mention any super-market 'altercations' involving smashed bottles of wine, just told him how hurt I'd been.

'That must have been very hard,' he said. I knew his empathy was probably informed by his own experiences as Sylvie had said he was divorced and had been hurt himself.

'Are you married?' I asked, but he just shook his head. 'I'm married to my job,' he replied, presumably not wanting to talk about his former marriage. He obviously wasn't comfortable sharing with someone he hardly knew, but now on my fourth beer, I was totally oversharing. But somehow, even in an inebriated state, my self-editing kicked in, like when I told him I'd lost my job because of 'cuts,' rather than the fact I was involved in a police investigation.

'What will you do for money?' he asked tentatively, as we finished our drinks.

'I'm okay for now,' I replied. 'There was a divorce settlement, I can use that. I'd hoped to buy somewhere to live with that one day, when I go back to the UK.'

'You don't have a place back home?'

I shook my head. 'I lived with my sister, but that won't work long term.'

'I don't want to embarrass you, or sound flash or anything, but don't struggle while you're here, will you? If you need money, I can always lend you money to tide you over?'

'That's very kind,' I said, touched but a little embarrassed by his offer. 'But I'll be fine.' I had this compulsion to hug him. This man hardly knew me, yet was offering to lend me money to help me out of a hole. I felt guilty not telling him the truth, but I didn't want to test him that far, it made me sound like a psycho. I liked Nik, and didn't want to ruin the chance of a friendship, or anything more with him.

I was about to suggest another drink, when he looked at his watch. 'This has been lovely,' he said, 'but I have to get back to work now.'

'At the vineyard?' I asked, trying to hide my disappointment. I'd hoped we'd go on into the evening, perhaps even have dinner.

'Yes, we're right in the middle of the grape harvest,' he

replied, while picking up the paper receipts on the table and wafting my hand away when I offered to pay.

'I thought the grape harvest here was September to October?' I remembered reading it on the Kouris website.

'Depends on various different things,' he said vaguely. 'We're busy all the time at Kouris Estates, you must come over.'

'Yes, I'd love to,' I replied expectantly, thinking he'd suggest a date I could visit and we would part knowing we'd meet again. But he didn't, and after saying our goodbyes I watched him wander away, feeling rather deflated. Perhaps he wasn't interested in me even as a friend? He disappeared into the crowd, and I thought how men like Nik didn't stay single for long, however hurt they might be. Even if it wasn't Angelina, I was sure someone would be waiting for him in the wings. Still, I'd enjoyed chatting with him, and for a while it had taken my mind off the darkness that closed in whenever I was alone.

TEN

Later that evening, when I was back at the apartment, Sylvie called me.

'Sorry I didn't text you back sooner, I am *so* sorry about your job,' she said. 'You must be at your wits' end.'

'I'm fine, really. I need to process it, that's all.'

'I was thinking, you might need some work?'

'I'll survive until I get home.'

'But now you don't *have* to go home, Alice. The reason you were going back was your work.'

'My sister would—'

'Your sister would *what*? Nag you about losing your job, tell you how to live your life?'

I was going to say my sister would be upset if I didn't go home, but Sylvie's words cut through and hung on the line. She had a point; did I really have to go home? Did I even want to? I was used to Heather's nagging, it came from a good place, but there was the small matter of the police investigation. What if I stayed here indefinitely? I still needed to find some answers, and I could give myself the time to do that in a place where no one knew me, and no one could find me.

'Are you still there, Alice?' Sylvie's voice on the other end of my phone dragged me back into the present.

'Yeah, yeah I'm here.'

'Okay. I have a proposition for you.'

'Oh?' I was puzzled.

'The wedding business is doing well. As you know I'm incredibly busy, and only have Maria and Angelina but they've only been working with me for a few months, and they're young, they don't have your maturity, your life experience. Your customer service experience too...'

'I don't know...' I started, I hadn't planned to do any kind of work, and I certainly had no intention of applying for work visas and alerting anyone of my whereabouts.

'All I'm saying is, if you need some work for just a few weeks, you can stay here in the sunshine rather than head back to rainy Britain. And don't worry about tax and permits,' she added like she'd read my mind. 'We can work around the red tape. The offer's there.'

Now I was tempted. I could lay low there for a while until everything back home had blown over. There was something else too – I couldn't help thinking about Nik Kouris and those blue eyes.

'I'd love to help out, but there's no need to pay me for now. I'll come along to a wedding or two and see how I do.'

'Brilliant, but you aren't doing it for free. You don't have a job anymore. Hope I'm not being tactless, but you'll need the money.'

'I'll be okay for money, it's other stuff that keeps me awake at night,' I half-joked.

'Want to talk?' she asked softly.

I immediately regretted saying anything, even in jest. 'No, it's all so complicated.'

'I'm worried about you... are you okay?'

I didn't want to lay my troubles on Sylvie, we were new friends, so I played it down. 'I'm fine.

'Actually, I had a lovely afternoon with a very nice man,' I said, moving to something more light-hearted.

'Oh, really?' She was intrigued.

'He's a great listener too,' I said.

'That's interesting, I didn't have Nik down as a listener. Good-looking people usually only listen to themselves.'

'How did you know it was Nik?' I asked with a smile on my face. 'Did you see us in town?'

'No, I've got better things to do than follow you around town,' she laughed.

'Did Nik tell you?' I asked, aware that I couldn't take the smile off my face.

'No. Angelina told me.'

'How did *she* know?' Now the smile was off my face. *Wiped* off.

'I guess *Nik* told her?'

ELEVEN

The following Saturday, Sylvie turned up at my apartment at 9am to collect me for a wedding. I was grateful to her for offering me work, even though I didn't know what I was going to do going forward. But I was keen to learn the ropes, and even more intrigued when she told me the wedding was going to be at the Kouris Estates vineyard. I was dying to see it, and also quite keen to see Nik again, if only to find out his story. He'd seemed so friendly, flirtatious even when we'd drunk beer together in the square a few days before, and I still wondered why he'd left so quickly. I understood he had to be at work, but he *owned* the vineyard, surely he had workers who did the harvest, if that's what it was? My concern was that one too many beers had made me talk too much and he'd made excuses and left. If I had scared him off, working the wedding was the perfect opportunity to bump into him to show my calm and sober side.

Sylvie arrived earlier than I'd expected, and drinking coffee on the balcony, still in my dressing gown, when I heard her calling me.

'Come on, lazy bones, you've got work to do,' she yelled from the street below. I hung over the balcony laughing. I felt eighteen again, being with her made me feel free and happy and silly.

I opened the door to my apartment and she wandered in, looked around then took a seat on the bed. She had with her a large beach bag style bag made of straw and leather, probably very expensive. She opened it, took out something wrapped in tissue, and handed it to me.

'What's this?' I asked, puzzled, as I took it from her.

'Just a little something from me to you.' She took out her vape pen, walked to the balcony opening, and started breathing in the fruity citrus scented vapour.

I laid the tissue-wrapped gift on the bed, opening it very carefully, and as I parted the tissue, which had been wrapped loosely, I saw a flash of green silk. I knew immediately what it was, and unfolding the soft, silky fabric, I could feel myself flushing with pleasure. 'It's a dress just like the one you were wearing the other night.'

'It *is* the one I was wearing the other night,' she beamed.

I gasped slightly in disbelief. 'It's a lovely gesture, really kind of you, but I can't have it – it's *yours*.'

'Don't be a silly billy,' she said sweetly. 'I *want* you to have it.'

I looked up from the dress, saw her delight, and in that moment, I could see the little girl whose only desire was for her friend to be happy. Despite the gorgeous clothes and the vivacious personality there was a little girl in there who'd give you her sweets at playtime – she just wanted me to like her. This was a kind gesture but I realised that she'd likely give me anything I wanted if I could, and made a mental note not to compliment her on anything ever again. If I did, there was a strong chance it would be handed to me wrapped in tissue.

'You really shouldn't have, you can't give your things away, Sylvie. But I love it,' I added, clutching the soft, silky dress.

She was smiling broadly between puffs on her vape, and breathing the scent of a million lemons into the room.

I walked towards the rather marked old mirror hanging on the wall, and held the dress against me. The fabric was pure silk, I could tell by its feel; it must have cost a fortune.

'I knew it would suit you,' she murmured, standing behind me to look at my image in the mirror. 'We're the same colouring and size, except for the fact you have a tinier waist.' She gently grabbed some of the fabric that draped slightly, tightening it around my middle, and told me I simply had to wear it for the wedding. How could I refuse? Just holding it against me I felt a million dollars. A few minutes later, I was walking across the square with her feeling like a supermodel, which was only slightly better than climbing into her peppermint-green, open-topped sports car parked in the square. I was surprised, I didn't know about cars, but this one looked very shiny and very expensive. 'She's pretty, isn't she?' Sylvie climbed into the driver's seat and opened the passenger door.

'Wow! I didn't realise the wedding business was so lucrative,' I murmured, clipping my seat belt on and running my fingers along the dashboard.

She just laughed and started the car. We were soon climbing the high coastal road to the vineyard. The further we went, the steeper it became. We weaved up through the rocks, and the view below was more breathtaking with each mile. As we drove along, Sylvie gave me a guided tour of the beautiful scenery. The endless blue ocean, glittering in the distance, golden beaches appearing and disappearing beneath us, while whitewashed villas studded the mountainside. I felt like we were in a movie, just two girls flying along, the sun shining down on us as we headed off on an adventure. We were Thelma and Louise, Grace Kelly and Cary Grant, the beautiful car, the unreal setting. Music played in my head as the salty breeze ruffled my hair. Then suddenly, Sylvie's car hit a pothole right on the edge of the road.

We both screamed, and as we came to a shuddering halt, looked at each other.

'Are you okay?' she asked.

I nodded. 'You?'

'Yeah, just need to get away from the edge,' she said through gritted teeth.

In an attempt not to look beneath us as she started up the car, I turned away. At the side of the road was a small, decorated shrine. I'd seen these roadside shrines before in Greece, and this was similar, made of white stone, with rosary beads and a small statue of Jesus behind a small pane of arched glass. Pinned to a wooden cross to the left of the white stone structure was a picture. It was yet another one of the missing posters, as ragged and faded as all the others, but I hadn't seen this particular one before. It took me completely by surprise, and I had to hold on to the edge of the car seat as I stared at the woman's face in the poster. My heart pounded so loudly I was sure Sylvie could hear it. The woman in the missing poster looked exactly like me.

'Do you see that poster up there?' I asked Sylvie, gesticulating towards it with my head, unable to drag my eyes from the young woman looking back at me.

'Yeah,' Sylvie muttered, as she tried to manoeuvre the car off the cliff edge. We were on a dangerous precipice and yet I couldn't take my eyes from the poster. It was as if the world had stopped. I wasn't aware of anything else around me.

'Do you think she looks like me?' I heard myself say the words out loud, fear trickling slowly through me like sweat.

'Alice, can you help me please?' She sounded irritated, confused, then her eyes slowly followed mine to the poster. She was distracted by the car situation, but even so, I could see she was genuinely shaken. She looked from the poster back to me, clearly trying to compose herself.

'You see it, don't you?' I said, gazing up at the faded face, 'she looks a bit like me. Do you think he has a type?' I asked, seeing the ghost of a familiar smile. I grabbed my phone and zoomed in, blindly clicking, hoping to capture her, just in case.

'Oh God, Alice, what are you *doing*? I need you to help me get this car off the edge.'

I heard her, but wasn't listening. Nothing else mattered.

I was vaguely aware of Sylvie struggling with the ignition, and for a moment I thought she might burst into tears. But she finally started the car, setting off more slowly this time along the rubbly coastal road.

'You okay?' I asked.

'Yeah, just a bit freaked out by almost coming off the cliff,' she snapped.

'Sorry, I was completely distracted,' I said, and stopped looking at my phone for a moment, while still holding it tight, wanting to protect the image, keep her safe.

We drove a little further in silence, I wanted to say something, make small talk, but couldn't think of anything else. So I opened up the photo app on my phone again and enlarged the photo.

'It's faded, but I think this woman's definitely younger

than the others, she looks like a teenager,' I murmured, enlarging it even more. 'I think she has flowers in her hair. Wonder what happened to her.'

'She probably went island-hopping,' Sylvie offered absently.

'Do you think so?' I asked hopefully.

'Yeah, I mean where else could any of them be? No one's ever found them. I bet they *all* left the island to pursue a man or a dream or a better life.'

'Yeah,' I said, smiling. 'I hope they're all living in a commune somewhere sunny with lots of kids.'

'Everyone's got different theories, and perhaps we'll never know, so let's talk about something else,' she said. 'We could drive ourselves mad wondering what happened.'

'My sister and I are always trying to solve mysteries, we are both addicted to true crime shows, I always wanted to be a detective,' I said.

She briefly turned her head away from the road to look at me.

'I can't see you as a detective.'

I shrugged. 'I'd rather do that than work in customer services.'

'So why did you do that instead of solving crime?'

'I just didn't,' I replied, unwilling to share any more.

'Well, it's never too late, Alice.'

I didn't respond, I'd given up my dreams a long time ago. And anyway, it *was* too late, especially if the police found evidence and decided to charge me.

We continued in silence, and after about twenty minutes we left the hot, dusty road and approached the vineyard. It was only then that my anxiety lifted.

'This is *nice*,' I murmured, as the scenery changed from

white hot road meeting bright blue sky, to rows of shady green cypress, orange and olive trees. The lush canopy of cool green gave respite from the scorching, dry heat and, moving slowly through the dappled light, I lay my head back, my eyes half-closed to the twinkly slivers of sun penetrating through branches.

'Lovely, isn't it?' she said, as we drove up the long, wide gravel drive to an enormous white villa standing in acres of land. 'Mature, gorgeous and worth a fortune,' Sylvie announced.

'Just how I like my men,' I joked.

'Me too!' she said, smiling as she parked the car. 'It's also the best wedding venue on the island in this wedding planner's opinion.'

The villa had been beautifully preserved, bleached white by the sun, sea-blue paintwork on the shutters, pale olive trees positioned meticulously either side of the big, wooden door.

'If I had to paint a picture of Greece, this would be it,' I said, climbing from the car and taking it all in.

'Yeah, it's special,' she said admiringly. 'And all that land behind eventually leads to the sea. Apparently the salt air gives the grapes a tangy flavour, makes the wine taste of the sea.'

'Does Nik Kouris own all this?' I asked.

'Yep, been in his family for centuries, I believe.'

'And his wife left him... and this for some rich guy?' I asked, feigning vague interest, when I was dying to know more.

She shrugged. 'Apparently. Madness if you ask me, and worse than that, I mean money is money but when she left

Nik Kouris she walked out on one of the biggest wine cellars on the island.'

I giggled, as she knocked on the big, wooden door and waited for someone to answer. I fully expected to be greeted at the door by a butler, maid or whatever the Greek equivalent was. But suddenly the door opened and an older man probably in his sixties, was standing in front of us. He was huge, over six feet tall, with enormous, muscular arms and this really creepy stare.

'Oh hi, Dimitris,' Sylvie said, visibly tensing. 'We're here for another wedding.' She didn't introduce me, just rolled her eyes slightly, while the man just looked down at us both. 'He doesn't speak any English, it's always *so* difficult,' Sylvie muttered, as I looked up into his face, heavily weathered after a lifetime working in the sun. Grime and sweat had collected in the crevices. He maintained his stare without smiling, which made me feel very uncomfortable.

'Is Nik Kouris around – you know, your boss?' He stared at her blankly.

She seemed nervous, and stepped back a little as he leaned forward to try and understand what she wanted.

He continued to glare at her until she spoke a few words in Greek which he finally responded to in guttural, one-word answers.

Sylvie turned to me. 'It's okay,' she offered, 'Nik's here, I think.'

We both turned back to Dimitris, who stepped aside for us to walk in. I stared at Sylvie, who looked anxiously back at me before cautiously stepping forward into the house. We followed him, at a safe distance, through a long, cool hall, covered in framed pictures of the vineyard from several hundred years before. This was old money, with high, vaulted ceilings, and as we walked through to the back of the house, I glimpsed huge rooms filled with beautiful pieces of art. Once at the back of the house, a more contemporary living/dining room opened out onto a terrace with an outdoor lounge. I could imagine sitting there in the evenings, with a glass of wine, watching the sun set over the vineyard, which stretched for miles.

Sylvie gestured awkwardly for me to sit down on a sofa where she joined me.

'We'll wait here for him,' she said, in a subtle attempt to dismiss Dimitris, but as he didn't seem to understand, he loitered nearby. The faint stench of his body odour wafted over us, his rasping breath filling the silence until he eventually lumbered slowly into the kitchen. I watched him leave, and after initial relief, became aware of a shadow on the wall – he was still watching us from behind the door. I felt so uneasy. There was only Sylvie and me, two women of average build. We wouldn't stand a chance against a man of his stature. I shivered slightly; the house felt cold despite the day being so warm.

What had looked so beautiful from the outside, was quite different inside. It smelled old and damp, the soft furnishings were threadbare, and the furniture was dark and ugly. I was strangely fascinated by the old-fashioned wallpaper, long tendrils emerging from dark flowers and birds with sharp claws. It was obviously as old as the furniture. I was surprised that Nik or his ex-wife hadn't given the place a makeover.

I glanced at Sylvie, who was looking through into the kitchen. 'He's gone now,' she said under her breath.

'Good, that was weird.'

'*He's* weird!' Sylvie whispered.

'Who is he?'

'I heard he's Nik's cousin, been there for years. He works in the vineyard, I think Nik made a promise to his father to look after him or something, but I guess he's now stuck with him for life. He speaks some Greek, but you probably noticed, he isn't exactly chatty.'

My mouth was dry. I had this feeling that wherever he was, he might be listening to us. But Sylvie kept on talking.

'I worry about the brides and grooms who sometimes take the option to stay the night in the honeymoon suite. They could wake up one night and find Dimitris standing over them with a kitchen knife.' She shuddered, then looked at me. 'Don't look so scared, he's gone, besides he doesn't speak a word of English.'

'That explains why he didn't say hello, why is he here?'

'I think Nik feels sorry for him.'

My heart swelled slightly at this. 'He's obviously very kind.'

'Yeah, I guess.' She stared ahead, in her own world, and added, 'But Nik's trying to build his business – it can't be easy when there all these weird *rumours* about Dimitris.'

Her words hung in the silence.

'*Rumours?*'

She nodded slowly, seemingly reluctant to go into detail. 'The missing posters all over town, like the one you saw on the way here?'

'Yes...' I felt my heart thudding through my body, vibrating through the sofa where I sat.

'There have been a few over the years.'

'I know, they're women who came here for a holiday, or work – and never went home.'

'That's right. And as I said, I really hope there's a happy reason they left Corfu, but...'

'But what?'

She leaned towards me, despite saying he didn't under-stand English, she was as scared as me that he was still within earshot. 'There are some people who think he knows *exactly* what happened to those missing women.'

'Do you think *he* did something?'

She raised her eyebrows. 'Look, I don't know, it's only what I've heard – just don't ever be alone with him.'

Her words hung over us like a dark cloud. I felt the chill in the room, and the faint echo of his body odour, still with us even after he'd gone. I'd felt unsettled earlier by the poster by the roadside shrine, and now I was freaked out to think I'd been in the presence of – a kidnapper? A killer? Was I making a connection where there wasn't one? *Was* Dimitris involved in the missing women, or was it just gossip, and that's why the police had dismissed it?

'What do the police think?' I asked.

'No one knows what they think, they haven't a clue,' she added dismissively.

'My sis and I have followed the story of the missing women, we've looked online, a few TikTokkers have covered it...'

'Really? I find it so distasteful that kids do that, play armchair detectives.'

'Yeah, but someone, somewhere knows something. And sometimes it's about getting the information out there. Apart from the odd tiny news report there's been nothing.'

'No, the police don't put out information because it's not good for tourism for women to go missing on a paradise holiday island,' she scoffed. 'Come on, enough of Dimitris the serial killer,' she said, shaking me from my dark thoughts. 'The florist will be here any moment.' She marched into the kitchen, and I followed, unable to shake off the sound of women screaming. It terrified me, but at the same time I was compelled to be here on the island, where they were last seen. I was driven to try and save them, to stop the screaming in my head. But over the next few months my life turned into a game of hide and seek. I was warmer, then hotter as I came closer to what I *thought* was the truth, but all the time, the truth was hiding from me. I was soon cold again, with no clues, and no answers, and the screaming in my head got louder.

TWELVE

Much later, when the smell of mint and freshly cut cucumber filled the kitchen, and the flowers had turned into frothy explosions on beautifully curated table-scapes, Nik Kouris appeared.

'Alice, you finally came to visit?' he said, as he walked into the kitchen where I stood with Sylvie. He was wearing a pale linen jacket that made his tan look even deeper, and my heart beat faster.

'Yes, but this isn't just pleasure, I'm with the wedding planners,' I said, not wanting him to think I'd taken his invite seriously and randomly turned up in his kitchen.

Ignoring everyone else, including Sylvie, he wandered over to me, arms outstretched, and as he hugged me, he smelled delicious.

'Lovely,' I murmured, giving myself away at the prospect of being in his arms. After we'd hugged, and kissed on both cheeks like old friends, he asked if he could show me around.

'I'm working actually,' I replied rather awkwardly.

'It's all part of the job,' Sylvie said. 'You go with Nik, let him show you the place, it will be good to have a working knowledge of this building, I got lost last time,' she said with a reassuring smile.

'Hi,' Nik said, holding out a hand. 'Good to see you again, Sylvie. You're well?'

'I'm great thanks,' she replied. She took his hand. 'I see you two already know each other?'

'Yes, Alice and I are old friends,' he teased, but before she could respond, he guided me gently through the door and up the stairs, where more exposed brick was painted bright white. At the top of the stairs, he guided me outside onto an upper terrace, pointing out the olive press, the winery, and even a shop that sold the wines to visitors.

I didn't say too much. I felt strangely shy, like a teenager with her first crush, I watched him as he stood next to me on a high terrace. In the sunshine, his skin was smooth-shaven and the colour of honey, and he smelled expensive.

'How wonderful to be married in a place like this,' I said, recalling my own late summer wedding with Dan, how it rained all day and the bar ran out of wine and we argued about everything. I should have known then.

'I got married here,' Nik said, but didn't offer any more.

'Are you... still married?' Sylvie had mentioned he was divorced, but I wanted to hear Nik's story from his own lips.

'No, we're not together anymore,' he said sadly. 'She left me, she's with someone else now. And I thought marriage was for ever.'

'Nothing is for ever,' I said.

Suddenly I was back in the brightly lit supermarket, the smashed bottle, red wine and something else... blood. Blood, followed by silence. *Deafening* silence.

We were both now leaning on a wall, looking over the

vineyard, in our own worlds, yet together. I breathed him in, feeling the warmth of his body next to mine, and wondering if *he* might be able to save me? Could Nik Kouris take away the sound of screaming women and blood on a supermarket floor?

I was suddenly ripped away from my train of thought by a loud obtrusive buzz.

'My phone, sorry, I have to get this,' Nik said, walking back inside to take the call. I could hear him talking, but not what he said, then I heard laughter, and a tone of gentle teasing. In that instant, I just knew who had called him and as I peered over the edge of the terrace, I saw her. Angelina on her phone. Laughing. More disturbingly, she was looking straight up at me, like she *expected* me to be on the terrace looking down. Our eyes met, and though my instinct was to look away, I didn't. She continued to stare, and laugh.

Was she laughing *at* me? Was Nik laughing *at* me too? I'd been introduced to several kinds of paranoia courtesy of my time with Dan. He'd managed to make me feel self-conscious, disliked, and suspicious of most people and their motives. My low self-esteem had been compounded by everything he did until I found salvation in a glass, which led to all kinds of problems. I watched Angelina watching me from below and wondered if what I was seeing was the truth. Was I hot or cold? Or was I *still* suffering from some kind of delusion? Had my brain anaesthetised everything so much that as my therapist had suggested, I didn't know what was real or imagined?

As for Nik, was I being delusional about him? I'd been so attracted to him, and so overwhelmed by who he was, had I lost all perspective? I could hear Dan's voice asking why would someone like him even *look* at someone like me? He was gorgeous, and he *owned* a vineyard. I was a very lack-lustre forty-something divorcee with no job, who was being investigated by the police, not exactly an immediate swipe right for anyone. Who was I to move in on Angelina who was beautiful, keen, confident and so much younger?

I was suddenly distracted by something moving on the terrace – the light breeze coming from the ocean, a bird or my rather untrustworthy imagination? It wasn't Nik because I could still hear him talking on the phone, and as I looked back over the wall, I could see Angelina was also still on the phone. She was also *still* staring back up at me. Was it malice or indifference in her eyes?

Turning away from her I was aware of something moving in the doorway that led out from the hall. 'Hello?' I called. When no one responded, I slowly walked towards the opening. It was dark, and I couldn't see properly.

I gasped and stopped in my tracks. Dimitris was lurking in the doorway of the terrace. He stepped out and I moved back as he started saying something in Greek that I didn't understand.

'Hello,' I croaked, horrified to find myself alone up here, caught between this weird man on one side, and a laughing Angelina below.

He walked heavily towards me while pointing to the little wall around the terrace.

My instinct was to walk backwards, so I could keep a distance while having him in my eyeline. Sylvie's warning, 'Don't be alone with him,' rang in my ears as I inched back.

I moved slowly, uncertain of what to do. Dimitris seemed angry, troubled, and I had to be very careful. Now wasn't the time for anything to be lost in translation. From where I stood, the nearest exit was over the wall, a drop of about twenty feet, where Angelina stood chatting to Nik on her phone.

I approached, my intention being to pass by Dimitris politely and calmly, and leave the terrace. But he was huge, he filled the only exit, and I soon realised he wasn't going to let me pass. He stood very still, with apparently no intention of moving. The terrace was high and I was alone with a man who might or might not be responsible for the disappearance or even murder of nine women, ten if the younger girl was missing, and hadn't just gone off grid. I thought she looked like me, but again, was my fevered imagination taking over? Even if there was a resemblance, it didn't mean anything, I had something in common with most of those women. But what if he had a type? What if that type was me? And what if *he* was standing on this isolated terrace with me now, where no-one could hear me scream?

'Dimitris, can I get through the door please?'

He was looking at me. He didn't understand me, or was he *choosing* not to? We stood for endless seconds staring at each other, then suddenly, to my deep relief, I saw someone move behind him.

'Sorry, that was a supplier on the phone,' Nik said, gently pushing past the older man, giving him a nod and a smile. Suddenly the tension disappeared. Dimitris was gone, and Nik was here. Relief flooded through my veins. I put my hand on the wall, to help me stay upright. I'd been scared for my safety, but after what had happened with Dan that night, I was now concerned about my own reaction to fight or flight. I'd always assumed I would fly, but it seemed there was a chance I'd stayed and fought. Is that what I'd done to Dan that night, for the first time ever had I stayed and fought? That's what the police seemed to think. So if I *had* assaulted

Dan, who's to say I wouldn't lash out again if I was backed into a corner?

'Sorry, where were we?' Nik seemed oblivious to the tension his presence had diffused just seconds earlier. Dimitris had now disappeared, and I wondered if I should say something, but what could I say? That Dimitris was scaring me? That I might have been overreacting to a man who was perhaps just confused and misunderstood? Though I doubted it.

'So, you've seen the upstairs, let me show you the wine cellar,' Nik offered.

'I'd love to, but I wonder if I should be helping Sylvie. I think today's a sort of trial and I don't want to let her down on my first day.'

'Sylvie is fine. Let me give you one of my famous master-classes in wine,' he said, flashing a beautiful smile. 'Anyway, I'm doing your boss a favour, it's good for wedding staff to have a working knowledge of wine.'

'Oh, in that case then great, let the masterclass begin,' I replied, following him downstairs, into the kitchen where there was a lot going on. I saw a couple of chefs hats, some shouting, some laughing and a lot of food, piles of jewel-coloured vegetables, enormous crates of salad. The butcher had just arrived and over the sound of crashing plates and glasses, was yelling at one of the chefs. Nik raised his eyebrows at me as he opened a heavy wooden door and led me down more stairs into a cool dark room.

'That was a *lot!*' I remarked, following him down the stairs.

'Yes, I sometimes wonder at the wisdom of letting strangers into my home,' he said wistfully. 'They tend to take over, and forget it isn't theirs.' He shrugged slightly like he had no say in these things. He was standing at the bottom of the stairs now, holding out his hand to me, and in the dimly lit cellar I was glad to have someone to guide me.

I knew nothing about wine, but Nik was a professional who talked me through temperatures, acidity, tannins, maceration and other words that were pretty meaningless to me, but I liked to hear him talk. I was just watching his mouth move, loving his knowledge and passion. He was standing by a barrel, his long, slim fingers caressing the dark, aged wood. 'And then you have the angel's share,' he said.

'What's that?' I liked the sound of it.

'It's the portion of wine left in an ageing barrel that's lost to evaporation.'

'I like the idea that there are angels around, sipping wine from barrels,' I said, and my mind took me back to the women. I hoped wherever they were they were sipping wine and getting the angel's share.

'Yes, it's a rather nice idea, isn't it?' He was smiling at me. It felt nice.

We stood in that cold dark cellar for at least an hour, and by the time we walked out into the sunshine, I'd fallen just a little bit in love with Nik.

Walking onto the bright patio where tables were being set, was quite a shock to the senses. Nik was now dealing with queries from the caterer about wine. I looked around for Sylvie, who seemed to be having a few intense words with Angelina. I only caught the tail end of the conversation, but there was obviously some tension between them. 'We can't go to the police, there's no *evidence*,' Sylvie was hissing under her breath. Both women looked angry.

'But I saw him with that woman, I did. I'm not mistaken, Sylvie.'

'Yes, but it doesn't mean he did anything *wrong*? Angelina, you can't just go around saying things like that, you'll get yourself into trouble.'

Was this about Dimitris? Had Angelina seen him with one of the missing women? If I'd been part of the conversation I'd have encouraged her to go to the police, but Sylvie didn't want any trouble, she was sometimes too kind for her own good.

'Sorry, I didn't mean to interrupt—' I started.

'You're not, we're just talking about a lairy guest,' Sylvie said, putting her arm loosely around Angelina, who looked at me sulkily.

'Are you okay?' I asked.

'Yes, why wouldn't I be?' she snapped.

'No reason,' I snapped back, unwilling to start a battle with her. What was her problem?

'So tell me what I need to do?' I asked, shaking off the tightness in my chest, and the feeling that I wasn't the only one at the wedding with secrets to hide.

THIRTEEN

A week after that trial wedding, there was another wedding, again at the vineyard. Sylvie asked me if I'd work, and was due to pick me up outside my apartment, where I waited for her on a bench in the sunshine. As I was early, I called Heather, and after her usual inquisition, I mentioned the poster I'd seen of the young girl.

'I'm worried about you, Alice,' she said with a sigh. 'You fit the profile of these women.'

'Yeah, it looks like he might have a type, but don't worry I won't do anything stupid and put myself in danger.'

'You? Danger?' She laughed. 'Why don't I believe that?'

'I'm... things are changing for me, Heather, I'm good, honestly. I don't feel so low now I'm here. I've met some nice friends and I'm not *obsessing* so much.'

'Good, I'm glad you've got a network of support, we all need people around us.'

'One of my friends owns a vineyard and—'

'Oh, I hope you aren't taking advantage of her produce, your drinking...'

'No, actually it's a man who owns the vineyard, and I'm cutting down on my drinking too,' I lied, so she wouldn't worry. Heather didn't need to know about my regular cocktail sessions with Sylvie.

'You sound happier.' She paused, I knew what was coming next. 'This guy, is he a friend?'

'For now, but who knows?'

'Take it gently, you're still fragile, Alice. I know you think I'm a killjoy, but you fall easily. You fell for Dan quickly and look how that turned out.'

'I'm not going to rush into anything, he's just nice to be around.'

'That sounds good, all I want is for you to be safe and happy, Alice, it's all I've ever wanted.'

'I know.'

'But this photo... the missing women, it worries me. Promise me you won't start looking too hard.'

'Oh I won't, don't worry, I'm not going to start obsessing again.'

'You said that after Dan left, but you did start obsessing, and drinking too much and then you'd be calling him in the middle of the night.'

'How do you know I called him in the night?'

'I heard you, these walls are thin. I heard you crying too, and now you're talking about these missing women and it's a concern. Come home, Alice, we can work through all this together.'

'You're the best sister ever, but I've relied on you too long. You've got your own girls to look after now, I can't be your third teenager,' I added, in a vain attempt at a joke. 'And I promise I'm not obsessing. It might be nothing. My friend Sylvie says the missing women could all have had a legitimate reason to leave the island,' I offered, not actually believing this myself, but hoping it would go some way to convincing my sister I *hadn't* become consumed by this.

'Let's hope they have, but until one of those women turn up, you don't know who you can trust, so steer clear and come home as soon as you can.'

'I will.'

'Alice...' She paused. 'I don't want to add to your worries, but things seem to be moving fast here, Dan and Della only live down the road so I hear stuff.'

'What like?' I tried not to let her hear the terror in my voice. What now?

'Yesterday I overheard a woman in the hairdresser's talking about Dan and Della. She doesn't know me, but she knows them and she said the police are getting closer to *charging* you, Alice.'

I took a breath. I found it hard to form words, this had never been far from my mind, but I didn't expect it so soon.

'Shit, have they found something? Some proof?'

'I don't know, but if they decide to charge you it doesn't matter where you are, they'll find you,' she said into the silence. 'I understand what you're looking for out there, love, but at the moment it feels like a distraction. You've got something far more important to deal with here.'

'How can you say that? How can anything be *more* important, Heather?'

'I know, I know, but it is – I'm really worried, Alice. You're going to end up in prison. Or a victim of whatever's going on there. If he *does* have a type, you might be next.'

'Don't say that.' I shivered, only too aware that she could be right. 'Look, I have to go, Heather, I'm working today and I'm late,' I lied. 'Love you, talk soon.'

The women's faded faces were a constant montage in my head, and as I put down the phone they came back to the fore. But now one of them was haunting me more than the others. She was central to my thoughts, and it was seeing her face that had triggered me to find out more. All I had was a photo of the poster, and if it had been a photograph it would have been well-thumbed by now. I kept opening the photo app to look at her. Even in the middle of the night I'd wake up and look, like I might catch her by surprise and see a clue, something I hadn't noticed before.

I thought she looked young, but as Sylvie had said, you couldn't be sure of her age as the picture had deteriorated so much. The only information on the poster was a telephone number for the Greek police, and even that was incomplete.

I was dragged from the photo by Sylvie yelling my name from her car, just feet away.

'I must have called you ten times,' she was saying as I climbed into the car. 'I thought you'd gone deaf.'

I smiled, putting on my seat belt. Heather was right, I was already becoming obsessed.

But Sylvie's happiness had a way of distracting me. She never seemed moody or low, and always saw the bright side of things, which I found to be very therapeutic. Even her clothes were happy, and that day as I climbed into her car she was wearing bright orange palazzo pants, a white halter-neck top and the gorgeous tomato-red Hermes handbag was by my feet in the footwell. I didn't compliment her on the outfit or handbag for fear she'd strip off there and then, and give it all to me. The outfit alone must have cost a fortune, not to mention the bag. She'd come so far since her relationship breakdown, she told me she'd walked out with nothing, yet here she was embracing life in the sunshine, and making a fortune to boot. I hoped one day I could leave my past behind, push forward as she had and find that happiness; she was my inspiration.

'What kind of wedding is it today?' I asked.

We were now sitting at traffic lights, so she turned to me, and pushed her sunglasses onto her head.

'A millionaire and a Victoria's Secret model,' she winked. 'It's the biggest wedding so far, nothing is too much for them.'

'Shit, now I feel *really* dowdy. How will they feel about a member of the Amish community turning up at their million-dollar wedding?' I said, plucking at my rather shapeless pink linen dress.

'You're not happy with it, are you?' she said, clicking the left indicator, turning the car round and ploughing into tourist traffic heading for town. 'Let's go to mine, we have plenty of time. I have just the outfit for you to wear today.'

'No. I wasn't saying that so you'd offer to lend me some-thing...' I started, knowing I shouldn't have said anything, and at the same time knowing there was no point arguing with her.

Minutes later, we were pulling up outside a very expen-sive-looking apartment block. 'Come on, Miss Amish,' she said, turning off the engine. 'Let's get you dressed up!' I followed her through huge double doors, and she gave a little wave to the concierge on reception then pressed the lift button for the third floor.

'Penthouse apartment,' she murmured. And she wasn't joking, it really was a penthouse, floor-to-ceiling glass, warm wood floors and an acreage of the palest sofas.

'To think I felt sorry for you because your ex walked away with everything,' I said, gasping at the view overlooking the harbour, all whites and blues and sea and sails.

'You've heard of revenge porn? Well this was my revenge property,' she said, with a smile. 'I guess you could say he did me a favour. When he cheated, I was determined to make a success out of my life, and I started the business.'

'Your home is like *you*.' I was gazing around at the soft white leather sofas, the cool marble floor.

'What do you mean?'

'Well, it's clean lines, comfy sofas, lovely views, tasteful, expensive, exactly as one would expect. Then there's *that*.' I pointed to a huge spiky chandelier light suspended from the high ceiling. 'It's a total surprise, and sometimes you are a total surprise.'

'What do you mean?'

'I sometimes feel I know you really well, and then I don't.'

'Are you going to say something horrible about me?' She looked genuinely hurt.

'Never, you're perfect – just surprising.' I felt bad, Sylvie had once made a passing comment about being bullied at school, then she had the bad experience with her ex. Despite appearing to be confident and happy, she had a vulnerable side, and I needed to be more careful, and not feed into those insecurities, even if it was unintentional. So I changed the subject, moving away from Sylvie, and towards my new obsession. I wasn't letting this go, and like an addict was driven to find out more.

'The other day I asked you if the woman in the poster looked like me,' I started. 'I expected you to brush it off, tell me I was being silly. But you were as scared as I was, is that because you think he has a type, and *you* might fit the profile too?'

She looked at me for just a moment like she was going to

admit to this, but then launched into a denial. 'No, I wasn't scared about the woman in the poster looking like you *or* me, I was scared I'd damaged the car,' she replied abruptly. 'I don't like talking about it, I just find the whole thing...' She stopped to think, and taking out her vape pen, she said; 'Okay, here's what I think. Living here is wonderful, I've never been happier, but however great my life is, there are always shadows. I've never lived without shadows, Alice, so I've learned to live *with* them, and that means not looking too closely into dark corners. And if you don't mind me saying, you would be happier if you did the same.'

She looked away, facing the window, absorbing the view. It was her way of telling me the conversation was over, that she found it too painful to even speak of. I wondered what lurked in her dark corners, had she'd lost someone too? My grieving began with my parents' death, and I understood what she meant by the constant shadows. But where she wanted to ignore them, leave them alone, I wanted to open up those dark corners and let the light in. Make the screaming stop.

'That woman you saw in the poster, it looked like a faded photo of someone from years ago, and there's nothing we can do now to save her.' She sucked at her vape, then concluded: 'And nor do I think the killer – whoever he may be – has a type.'

'I guess not, but...' I stopped myself. It wasn't fair to lay my dark thoughts and theories on Sylvie. She'd made her point, she'd chosen how to live her life. Who was I to bring my darkness into our friendship?

'Do you like the room scent?' I envied her ability to switch off, to embrace the pretty things, to feel the sunshine on her face despite those shadows.

'It's lovely,' I replied, as a waft of acidic lemon hit my nose.

'I like everything to smell clean and fresh,' she said, as we moved through the apartment.

Her bedroom was stunning, and as she slid open one of the wall-to-wall wardrobes, in mirrors and glass, she stepped through. 'A walk-in wardrobe?' I exclaimed. 'You have a dressing room like the Kardashians.'

'Yeah, I figure if you're going to have designer clothes, they need a decent place to live,' she smiled proudly. The room was stacked with so many clothes, everything and anything for a woman to wear – in every shade and length. Each section was shades of one colour, like ombre, going from the lightest to the darkest, and trust me there was *every* colour. But the shoes, oh the shoes.

'Jimmy Choo?' I breathed, bending down to see the transparent storage boxes all containing designer footwear, from full-length boots (which Sylvie lamented were rarely justified to wear in that climate), to the tiniest little straps of leather.

'Do you have someone to dust and clean all this?'

'No.' She laughed at the absurdity of my question. 'I clean my *own* shit,' she added. 'I love cleaning, I find it therapeutic. I'm actually a bit OCD, everything *has* to be spotless. Sometimes I'll be lying in bed at night, really tired, and if I start to think about the kitchen surfaces or the shower, I end up getting out of bed and scrubbing everywhere,' she chuckled. 'My ex was always complaining, said I could never relax. I couldn't let anyone else go through my stuff either, it's personal. I'd feel *invaded*, you know?'

She delved in one of the compartments and brought out a

pink trouser suit with a white camisole top, and handed them to me.

'Try these on.' She was standing back, waiting for me to strip off, but I asked where the bathroom was. I wasn't as body confident as Sylvie. She pointed me in the direction, and I opened the door on a cool, black onyx-tiled jewel box of a bathroom, it was gorgeous. Ultra modern, all sleek and shiny, with a shower head the size of the moon. The minimalist design concealed bathroom cupboards in the walls, and I couldn't resist sliding one open. It slid, smooth as butter, and automatic lights flickered on to reveal the contents – everything I would expect from Sylvie, expensive perfumes, high-end make-up, a whole area devoted to Chanel skin care. I opened the one next to it, and was surprised to see a men's shaving brush, a bottle of aftershave and combs. I wondered if Sylvie had a partner, or if she just kept those things in case she had a man stay over. I didn't get a chance to look anymore because she was anxious to see me.

'Come on, let's have a look,' she called from outside the door.

I'd pulled on the trousers and top, and looked at myself in the full-length mirror, delighted at the result, and emerged, my hand to my mouth in elated surprise. I'd never realised I could look that good, and Sylvie obviously approved. 'I *like* it,' she said, standing back, then stepping forward to adjust the camisole under the jacket.

'We can't let you upstage the bride obviously,' she said with a wink, taking out the candy pink mules I'd been clutching earlier. 'But these will look great.'

'But they're Jimmy Choos.'

'I'm sure he won't mind,' she replied with a giggle.

I slipped my feet into the most expensive, most beautiful shoes I'd ever seen, and standing before her, felt like a model.

* * *

'Wow, you look lovely, Alice, really lovely,' Nik said, hugging me as I arrived at the vineyard for the wedding. I breathed in that delicious aftershave smelling of sea air and expensive resorts.

Sylvie led me out beyond the patio to the vineyard, where the wedding ceremony would take place later that day. We walked on together through rows and rows of old tables, dressed in acres of blush pink roses, and huge satin bows. The crockery was off-white, the edges a little uneven. 'Are these handmade?' I asked, picking up a large dinner plate.

Sylvie smiled. 'That's what the guests are *supposed* to think.' She was holding an etched wine glass, with a ribbon tied around the stem.

'This wedding is what I call "traditional light,"' she said quietly, for my ears only. 'The bride *thinks* she wants authentic, she *thinks* she wants traditional, but a *traditional* Greek wedding would involve the priest slapping the groom, a baby being thrown on the marital bed, and plates being hurled around like frisbees. Trust me, she doesn't want what she thinks she wants – I know what she wants. It's all smoke and mirrors, Alice,' she chuckled.

Sylvie asked me to help check each table and being concerned that my standards weren't as high as hers, I took this very seriously, scrutinising every single piece of cutlery. I was concentrating so hard, that I jumped when a loud voice nearby shouted, 'Oh my God!'

I turned around and wasn't surprised to see Angelina staring at me, her mouth wide open.

'What?' I asked, irritated by her sudden loudness.

'You're wearing Sylvie's trouser suit!'

'Er... yes,' I replied, a little embarrassed.

'I thought it was her. I was coming over to ask you what needed doing.' She put her hand over her mouth and giggled.

'Well, I'm flattered, but as I'm new here I'm clueless, I have no *idea* what needs doing,' I joked. 'Sylvie asked me to check these tables.'

'Well, you'd better be on top of it, she always finds something wrong. Have you seen her apartment? You can eat off the floor.'

I nodded. 'It's beautiful.'

'Oh, so you've been there?' Her face dropped.

'Yeah, earlier today,' I replied.

'I've stayed over at the apartment. If she asks you to stay over, say no. You won't get a wink of sleep,' she lisped in her Greek accent. 'I was woken up at 4am to this racket coming from the bathroom, freaked me out. So I picked up a heavy object ready to whack someone over the head – and there she was in the bathroom, in her pyjamas and rubber gloves, singing and cleaning. She is *insane.*'

This story was no doubt true, but why was she telling me? I heard a spike of jealousy, and vague threat hovering in her voice. It was as if she didn't want me to get close to Sylvie, and was warning me not to stay over, that Sylvie was Angelina's friend first. I was surprised into silence by this. I didn't feel comfortable with a response she might take out of context and use against me later. We both stood in silence for a little while and I went back to checking the cutlery, without being able to concentrate, just going over what she'd said, but more importantly, how she'd said it. Whatever her motive for speaking to me, she was certainly chattier than she'd ever been, and so I took advantage of this and moving away from Sylvie and any friendship issues, I said, 'I hope you don't mind me asking, but a few days ago, I heard you and Sylvie talking about calling the police on someone?'

She'd been standing with her arms folded, watching me check the table, and suddenly looked very uncomfortable. She reached for a vase of flowers and started to mess with the blooms like she needed something to do with her hands. I hadn't expected such a strong reaction.

'Yeah, and Sylvie *told* you, it was about a guest,' she said slowly, unable to look at me, irritation dancing in her voice.

'She did, but I just wondered if I needed to be aware of anyone?'

'Like she said, it was a guest at a wedding weeks ago,' she replied, then looked up. 'But if you want my advice – don't trust *anyone.*'

She was obviously trying to scare me off, I could hear the threat lingering in her voice, but tried not to react. 'That doesn't sound good.'

'It *isn't* good.' She was deadly serious, her face pale, black, winged eyeliner framing green eyes now boring into me.

Her demeanour made me uneasy, as she continued to glare, implicit threat hanging between us. I knew I should probably leave it there, but being me, continued to push. 'I asked because I'm going to be doing more weddings, and I wondered if it was Dimitris you were talking about to Sylvie? I don't want to add to the gossip, but—'

'More *weddings*?' Her face flushed with what looked like fury.

'Yeah, Sylvie asked me if I'd like to join the team. She needed extra staff, and I want to stay here a little longer and—'

'Sylvie hasn't said anything to me,' she said, clearly doubting my news, sulkiness forming in her chin.

'She only asked me to help out so I can take some of the burden off you and Maria,' I offered, trying to take the unexpected heat out of this.

'I heard my name, is someone talking about me?' Maria's Mediterranean singsong voice teased through the trees. She soon appeared and stood beside us, smiling, looking from me to Angelina and back again.

'Meet our new colleague,' Angelina replied, giving Maria a knowing look.

Maria immediately bristled. 'You? But why would *you* want to take work off us? You have a good job back home, don't you?' This was sharp and to the point, laced with panic.

I felt awkward, I didn't expect this reaction from Maria.

Perhaps they assumed I'd come in and usurp them, that I'd be Sylvie's favourite and take all the work. 'I'll only be doing weddings when Sylvie's short-staffed. I wouldn't take work off you, I've no long-term plans,' I said, in an attempt to reassure them.

'You *can't* have long-term plans, you're only here on a tourist visa, aren't you?' Angelina said coldly, waiting for my reaction.

'I have a working visa,' I lied.

Before we could say anything else, Sylvie was back with two waiters and was now bustling around the tables.

'You *need* to go through each table setting with a fine-tooth comb, everything has to be perfect,' she was saying. Given that neither of the waiters appeared to speak English,

I doubted they understood the comb reference, and they looked rather bemused.

'Okay,' she said, walking towards us, 'I don't know the Greek for fine-tooth comb.'

'You don't know the Greek for *anything*,' Angelina said.

Sylvie smiled at her. 'I know enough.'

Angelina just giggled at Maria, obviously an in-joke between them. I could see now why Sylvie was keen to have me around. Those two were a tag team, both in their twenties, both fluent in Greek so it must have been quite alienating for Sylvie, whose command of the language was limited. I understood how that felt. Not understanding the language was frustrating, and I vowed to take lessons if I ever decided to stay there permanently. I'd heard Nik talking to the catering staff in Greek earlier. Perhaps if I stuck around, he might teach me some useful words and phrases? I'd rather learn Greek from him than from Angelina. If I were Sylvie, I wouldn't trust her with anything.

A little later, I watched Angelina from across the room. I pretended I hadn't noticed, but she was draping herself around Sylvie and whispering in her ear, while looking over at me. I saw Sylvie smiling at what she'd just said, and she batted her away affectionately. I was curious, what was Angelina up to? And just who was she fighting me for – Nik or Sylvie?

FOURTEEN

At 5pm, the bride and groom exchanged rings and vows under the trees. Under the dappled light of olive and cypress trees, with the waft of sea salt and thyme dancing in the air, I watched as a gorgeous model married a millionaire. The ceremony was in Greek, and I hadn't understood a word of it, and apparently neither had the groom, but everyone agreed it was beautiful. Halfway through the vows, I was aware of someone standing close, and turning my head slightly, saw Nik moving through the olive trees. I was looking ahead at the couple, but very much aware that he was now standing next to me. He was close, but not too close, just enough to take my breath a little as we watched in silence.

'Beautiful setting,' I whispered as the rings were exchanged, but he couldn't hear me, so came closer, bending down so his face was almost touching mine. I felt an unexpected rush of warmth run through me, and my heart was beating in a way it hadn't done for a long time. I remembered Heather's words about how I always fell too quickly, and reminded myself not to get carried away. He was a nice guy, just being *nice*. But when I leaned towards him to repeat the whisper, my lips brushed his ear accidentally, and he didn't flinch or move away. Neither did I.

After the wedding ceremony, the catering team stepped in to serve champagne and canapés, and the guests passed us by. They were following the couple back to the sunlit patio, tramping through the forest of vines and olive trees.

'It must feel weird to have all these strangers in your home?' I said.

'It is, but I have to move with the times. And this kind of wedding brings in money.'

'I can imagine, I suppose it's the only way to survive, to keep the vineyard going – tourists and weddings?'

'Yes, when my father handed it down to me, I promised I'd take care of it. Kouris Estates has been in my family for years. My father and his father before him.'

'You must have some very happy childhood memories here?'

'Not really.' He shook his head, finally raising his eyes from the ground as the last of the guests left the vineyard. It was as if he didn't want to look at them, or for them to see him. I'm sure they would have been surprised to know this unassuming man who stayed in the shadows was the owner of the beautiful venue. Nik was so modest, and I liked that about him.

'No, not many happy memories,' he said wistfully.

We were alone now, and it was quiet save the bubbling distant murmur of the wedding guests sipping on champagne and contemplating dinner.

'My parents split up when I was very young,' he continued. 'And as my mother was English, she took me back to the UK with her, so this place didn't really feature in my childhood at all. The divorce wasn't pretty, I think the writing was on the wall early on, when they couldn't even agree on a name for me,' he added regretfully. 'Dad wanted to call me Achilles or Adonis, but Mum said she couldn't call me something that was associated with a heel or a love God.'

'So they compromised with Nik?' I asked.

'Yeah, it could be Greek or English, Nikolas with a K – Dad won on the Greek spelling, I guess.'

'So you spent your childhood in England?'

'Yeah. I didn't come back here until I was an adult. My mum refused to let Dad see me, especially when he met someone else,' he added as an aside. He took a deep breath, then continued. 'So, when Dad was sick a few years back I finally came back here to see him. Mum had already died, so I wouldn't be hurting her, and I wanted to say hello and goodbye to my father. I had no intention of staying, but on his deathbed he begged me to take the vineyard on for him.'

'And your own son will do the same one day, I suppose?'

'A son? I don't have one, and I don't plan to,' he replied, still gazing out onto his acres. 'Mum and Dad made such a mess of it, why would I be any different as a parent? I guess *these* are my children,' he murmured, gesturing towards the trees and the vines beyond.

'That's a lovely thought,' I replied.

'It may sound romantic, being the owner of a vineyard, but this life isn't for the fainthearted,' he said. 'There are many early mornings, late nights, the constant worry about pests, floods and the climate. It's all so delicate, and there's such a fine line between surviving and losing everything in one bad winter.'

'God, your whole livelihood hanging on a grape vine, literally.'

'Yes, olives too, we have an olive press, our oil is just amazing. And of course, the citrus... We have an orange grove here. Come, I'll show you,' he said, and was suddenly heading off through the trees. I wanted to follow him, but at the same time felt guilty. I was supposed to be working, and Angelina and Maria would make such a fuss if I disappeared. But he was now marching off into the distance, I could hardly just turn around and head back to the house. The ground was dry and dusty, and call me superficial, but all I could think of was how this would impact Sylvie's gorgeous Jimmy Choos. I stood there helplessly watching him forge ahead, keen to show me his orange grove, completely unaware of my dilemma. So I took off the shoes and carried them, teetering on my tiptoes through the vineyard, hoping there weren't any thorns or sharp stones around. I kept walking in the direction he'd gone, but after a while, I couldn't see him for trees, and found myself alone in what felt like a very dark forest. It was early evening, and still light, but the canopy of leaves blocked out the sunshine.

I called Nik a few times, but no answer. The area around was so vast he could be anywhere. I began to feel slightly disorientated; everything was green and leafy, and whichever way I turned it all looked the same. There was no path leading anywhere, no clearing, I couldn't see what was ahead or behind me. A sliver of panic cut through me. This was like a maze, how the hell was I going to get out of here? I had no choice but to keep going, not knowing if it was right or wrong, and the deeper I went into the trees, the darker it seemed. I called Nik again, then louder, standing still and waiting in the echoing silence for a response. But nothing. I couldn't even hear the wedding party anymore, just an eerie hush, the gentle rustle of leaves as the warm, evening breeze ruffled through.

I called out, 'Is anyone there?' And suddenly, I saw a movement, swift, lurching between the trees. Was it an animal? Or was someone following me? I found the broken branch from a cypress tree and picked it up, holding it out like a weapon. I stayed very still. If someone was hiding, they couldn't stay there forever, they'd have to move. If they did, I might see them, and if they came towards me, I'd whack them over the head with the branch. I scrutinised the bark on every tree from where I was, staring to try and make out a shape, something tangible. I continued to gaze around. A rustle made me jump and move. Turning around and around, I looked up into almost darkness, the fading light curtained by the canopy of trees. I looked down at my feet, black with soil and dust, a little blood where I'd caught my heel on something sharp. I raised my head slowly, and what I saw chilled me. Dark working boots, a man's boots; whoever they belonged to was now standing merely feet away from me.

'Who are you? Why are you following me?' I yelled into the trees.

Then suddenly, a movement, someone coming from a different direction. Nik.

'Are you okay, I've been waiting for you in the orange grove?'

'I... I was lost,' I croaked, jerking my head in the direction of the boots.

'What? What is it, are you okay?'

'There's someone over there,' I hissed, still wielding the tree branch.

'Where?' He looked alarmed.

'Over there,' I insisted, taking my eyes away from the

boots for just a few seconds, as Nik tramped past me, calling, 'Hello? Hello?'

But as soon as I looked back, the boots had gone. 'He must have run off,' I said.

'So you saw someone, you actually saw a person?'

'I saw someone move, then I saw boots – someone was hiding behind the tree.'

He searched for a few minutes, calling and shaking the trees, but whoever it was had left.

'I wonder who it was?' I said. 'I was so scared.'

'It was probably just a guest who'd wandered too far,' he suggested, obviously trying to placate me, but I saw the fear on his face too, and the way his eyes darted between the trees. By now I was shivering with fear and adrenalin, and just wanted to go back as quickly as we could.

'I'm sorry, it was all my fault,' he said, seeing my fear and pulling me towards him protectively. He wrapped both his arms around me which was so comforting I began to cry and couldn't stop. I cried for everything that had happened, for everything I'd done, and for the fear that I'd never find what I was looking for, and would spend my life wondering what if?

'No, it's my fault,' I said, emerging from our hug. 'I wasn't behind you, I was taking my shoes off and then once I started walking, realised that I wasn't fast enough to catch you on bare feet.'

He looked down, clearly appalled at the state of my feet. 'Have you hurt yourself?'

'No, I'm fine, must have stood on a branch or some gravelly stones,' I said, trying not to grimace with pain.

'We might as well continue on to the orange grove,' he said. 'We aren't far now. From there we can go back a different route where there are fewer trees and it's more open.'

Along the way, we talked about everything and nothing, and I mentioned Angelina.

'I think I've upset her by starting work with Sylvie,' I said.

'Really? Why?'

'I don't know, I think she's pretty insecure, probably worried I'll take her job, but I'm only here for a while.'

'Only for a while?' To my deep joy he seemed rather dismayed at this.

'I haven't decided yet what I'll do. My life has always been planned, quite restrictive really. For the first time I have the freedom to decide,' I lied. 'Some days I could stay here for ever, but I have stuff to deal with back home.'

'I hope you decide to stay, at least a little while,' he said quietly. 'I'd love to show you more of the island.'

'I'd like that. But can I ask you something?'

'Of course.'

'I just wondered if... if you and Angelina are an item? I'd hate to upset her, or cause any problems by being friends with you.'

'No, not at all. She's just a friend.'

'Thing is,' I hesitated for a moment before adding, 'I think she likes you.'

He smiled at this. 'I'm sure Angelina has plenty of suitors younger and far more handsome than me. She's a lovely girl, but she's just friendly and likes to have fun, nothing more.'

I was relieved, she always seemed so pleased to see him, and was rather territorial with the way she touched and hugged him. Sylvie reckoned Angelina had an unrequited crush, but the other day, when I saw her talking to him on the phone, it occurred to me that there might actually be something between them. I really didn't want to step on her toes, it wouldn't be fair – besides, I was in no doubt that Angelina would be a formidable enemy.

Now I knew there was nothing between them, I didn't feel so guilty about pursuing this, if it was an option. I still thought he was too handsome, too worldly, and probably too rich to even look at someone like me. But as we walked on, I turned to say something to him, and caught him looking at me, and hope bloomed in my chest like spring flowers.

We walked into the orange grove just as the sun was setting. The sky was deep apricot, and unlike the dense darkness and shadows of the vineyard, the orange grove was fused with golden light. The sunset was flooding orange through the trees, and the pretty white blossom seemed luminous. 'Like the petals look like fairy lights,' I murmured.

'And the fallen petals are nature's confetti,' he said, not taking his eyes from mine.

'Can I smell oranges on the air, or is that my imagination?' I asked.

'Yes you can. I often come down here at sunset this time of year, just to breathe in the aroma.'

The air was laced with sea salt and the tang of citrus, and I suddenly felt warm and fearless, the dark corners were illuminated, and my fears were lifting. And when Nik put his arms around my waist, and leaned in to kiss me, I melted into his arms, just as the sun melted into the sea.

A little later, we wandered back through rows of olive trees that glittered in the moonlight, and my heart was so full I thought I might burst with happiness. Until we got closer to the house and saw Angelina marching towards us. 'Where the *hell* have you been?' Her voice rang out loud and clear in the darkness of the vineyard.

'We were... Nik was showing me the orange grove,' I said, stunned at the way she was storming towards us.

'We've been looking for you everywhere,' she spat. 'You're covered in dust, where are your shoes?'

I felt humiliated, it was none of her business where I'd been, and I was tempted to say that, but knew it would just start an argument which wouldn't help.

'It's all fine, Angelina,' Nik said calmly.

'Yes, no need for you to be concerned, Nik was showing me the orange grove and I got lost.'

'No need for me to be concerned?' she scoffed. 'You can't just disappear like that!' She was genuinely furious. I could also see how upset she was, and though I had an inkling as to why she was so openly distressed, her emotional response surprised me.

'I was on my break,' I replied firmly.

'We don't *get* a break until the wedding is over and all the guests are gone,' she hissed. 'Even *then* we can't just go off into the woods, we have to assist with clear-up.'

'And I'm here to do that,' I said calmly, unsmiling.

Angelina wasn't angry that I'd disappeared for an hour, she was angry I'd disappeared with Nik. Realising I'd just spent time alone with him had obviously upset her and she wasn't being very subtle about it.

This was embarrassing in front of Nik, but I couldn't let her speak to me like that, it was humiliating. 'Angelina, do you have a problem with me?' I asked.

'I don't have a *problem*.' Her eyes slid over to Nik, who looked very uncomfortable, standing on one leg then the other.

'Good,' I replied, and she defaulted to what seemed to be her usual sulky child mode. I was tired and didn't want a stupid argument with this stroppy, jealous girl to spoil the wonderful moments I'd just had with Nik.

'Okay,' I said. 'Let's start again. Is there anything I can do to help you?'

'No, Maria and I have done *everything*.'

'Oh, so you don't need me. Okay, I'll go and find Sylvie and see if there's anything I can do for *her*.'

'I told you, we've done *everything*. Look, it's been a long day. I'm going to get a cold drink from the kitchen. Do you want to come with me? You look hot and tired.' I saw her glance quickly over at Nik again as she said this. Was this her not-so-subtle way of pointing out my flaws to him?

Nik saw that as his cue to escape, and discreetly touching the back of my arm, murmured that he'd see me later and walked away.

I watched Angelina watch him walk away, and wondered what game she was playing. One minute she was expressing her annoyance that I'd been missing, yet couldn't find me anything to do. And now she was suggesting I go with her for a drink.

She probably did see me as a threat, that's why she'd called him when she saw us together on the terrace that day, at the first wedding I worked. This was all about keeping us apart. And she was very determined. I didn't trust Angelina, I didn't trust her at all. She followed me to the kitchen and she started asking me questions.

'Is something going on with you and Nik, I mean are you seeing him? Or screwing him?'

I was horrified. 'It's none of your business, and please don't speak to me like that,' I said.

'I was only joking.' She faked a smile. 'I just wonder what you see in him, I mean he's so old.'

And you're so obvious, I thought, unable to believe her lack of subtlety. 'I like him, I take it you don't?'

'Me? I'm not interested in Nik Kouris.'

'Good, then you won't mind if I am.'

With that, I put down my drink and headed off towards Sylvie, who was chatting animatedly to Magda, the bride. Sylvie immediately brought me into the conversation, introducing me as her friend, and making me feel included. It was a gift; she had this generous, trusting nature that made her open and warm but at the same time her naïvety made her vulnerable. As her friend I felt this responsibility to protect her, and despite her meanness, I knew that Angelina felt the same. She seemed to look out for her. She translated for her and laughed affectionately at her confusion with social media while helping her. I still felt that was part of the tension between me and the younger woman, that Angelina wanted to protect Sylvie from new people, aware Sylvie was easy to take in. Perhaps in time, when she got over Nik, she wouldn't see me as a threat and we might be friends?

'Thank you for making everything so special,' Magda said to me in a soft Greek accent, as I congratulated her.

'I really can't take any credit. I'm new and only just learning the ropes.'

She smiled. 'Well thank you anyway. It's not my first wedding, and it probably won't be my last,' she added with a giggle, 'but it's my most expensive!'

Sylvie chuckled at this, but I could see Magda's comment had made her uncomfortable. She went to such trouble to make her weddings perfect, I think she wanted the couple's relationship to be perfect too. In fact, she'd told me only that morning that she wouldn't work with a couple she didn't believe were genuinely in love.

'You shouldn't tease,' she gently reprimanded Magda. 'I happen to know you two are *crazy* in love, so just go and enjoy the rest of your lives,' Sylvie said. Magda walked away, blowing her a kiss. Sylvie then turned to me. 'So, have you enjoyed your second wedding?' she asked, a faint pleading in her voice.

How could I disappoint her? My kind, and generous friend who'd opened up her world to me deserved more than just a yes.

'I've loved every minute,' I said, as we watched Magda wobble off on high heels. 'They *seem* happy, and in love, but I wonder if she'd love him that much if he didn't have any money?' I murmured to Sylvie.

She turned to me. 'I know what it looks like, but honestly money has nothing to do with this relationship,' she said. 'Magda adores him,' she gestured with her head towards the patio dance floor where the beautiful woman was now looking into the millionaire's eyes like he was the only man – or bank – in the world.

'Honestly, people can be so cynical,' she said, more softly now. 'I'm a wedding planner, I believe in love.'

'You still hold out hope, don't you?'

'Don't *you*?'

I nodded, wanting to tell her all about Nik and I kissing in the orange grove, but deciding to save it for another time.

I did believe in love, but later, I spotted Magda flirting wildly with a handsome young waiter, she was touching his chest, and he was laughing. It made me wonder if I was right, and Sylvie was being naïve?

I turned away from Magda and the waiter, my eyes

alighting on Dimitris. I hadn't seen him all evening, and the kiss with Nik had erased all my concerns and fears until now. I felt that prickle of anxiety return at the sight of him standing by the bar, talking to Angelina. It was late and dark, but the sky was alive with moonlight and stars. But even in the glittering dimness I could see the fear on Angelina's face as Dimitris leaned in close and whispered something in her ear.

FIFTEEN

The following day, Sylvie called sounding even happier than usual and asked if I'd like to meet for lunch.

I immediately agreed, and later found myself sipping chilled white wine down by the harbour as she talked excitedly about the previous day's wedding. The sun was warm on my arms, and our table was perfect, a view of big white yachts sitting on calm, turquoise water.

'Ideally I need more couples like Magda and Mike...' she was saying, as we sipped on our cold white wine, and gazed out onto paradise.

'You mean you want to attract more millionaires?'

'No,' she said, pretending to be slightly offended. 'God, you make me sound like some wedding planner gold digger,' she replied, laughter in her voice. 'Are you ready for the next wedding on Saturday?'

I was dreading this conversation. 'I loved the wedding day, Sylvie,' I started, 'but I don't feel I can commit to working with you. My sister, she wants me to go home... and...'

'You can't go home.' She looked genuinely surprised and upset at this.

'I won't go immediately, but I do need to be realistic, I can't stay here for ever,' I said truthfully. Since I'd arrived, Heather had been calling and begging me to return to the UK, and she was right, I was running away.

'Well, don't you dare just go back home without letting me know.'

'As if. But if it's okay with you, I won't work next week, I'd like to do some exploring and take some time for myself, you know?' In truth I wasn't keen on another combative working day with Angelina. I was also concerned about the conversation we had regarding work permits, where the hell did she get that from? I was worried that if she thought I was a threat in some way she might report me, and I didn't need that. I could manage financially for a while, I didn't want to use too much of the money from my divorce, but for now I would have to live off that and my final pay cheque. It was safer than risking any kind of trouble via Angelina, that one had trouble-maker written all over her.

'I almost forgot,' Sylvie said. 'The groom gave all the staff a bonus, I'll put yours in your account with your wages for yesterday.'

'Thank you, but I don't deserve a *bonus*. Split my bonus between Angelina and Maria,' I said, hoping this would endear me to Angelina and she'd call off the dogs.

'I'm not giving your money to the girls.'

'But they worked so hard.'

'So did *you*!'

She put down her glass, and looked at me. 'Did Angelina say something?'

'Yes, but she had a point. I took a break, I didn't ask, just went off for an hour during the wedding. The girls had to do my share of the work, it wasn't fair – Angelina was right to say something.'

'Everyone works differently...' she replied. 'Please don't take any notice of her, she can be difficult, but don't let that put you off.' She called the waitress over and ordered two cocktails. 'I know it's early for cocktails,' she said to me, 'but it's Sunday, and we're alive under this beautiful sky.'

I smiled.

'So, Angelina,' she continued, 'ignore her, she was probably just in a bad mood.'

Clearly Sylvie had never seen Angelina's rage, she saved that for me.

'She was angry because I left them to do all the work while I went for a walk with Nik Kouris.'

'Ah, that explains it. Look, Alice, I *love* that you spent time with Nik Kouris, he's a nice guy, and selfishly, he's good for my business. And if you have a friendship with him then...' She paused, and looked at me, intrigued. 'Is it *more* than just a friendship?' She leaned forward slightly to hear what I had to say.

'Perhaps. I mean it *could* be.'

Her face broke into a big, beaming smile. 'So, go on... you went for a walk?'

I could feel my face flushing. 'Yes, and we talked and—'

'What? What?' Typical Sylvie, she was excited, encouraging me to go on.

'We were gone for about an hour.'

She rested her chin on one hand, her eyes were smiling. 'And?' Sylvie was like my best friend at school, on my side, eager to hear my news and cheerlead me on.

'And... he showed me the orange grove, it's beautiful, the blossoms were falling...'

'Nature's confetti!' she said with a sigh.

'That's so weird, that's just what Nik said,' I giggled.

'Sounds like both of us have weddings on our mind,' she was still beaming, 'but perhaps he was thinking of his own?'

'I think we're getting ahead of ourselves there,' I replied, enjoying the silly, schoolgirl talk. This was the kind of conversation Heather would put a stop to, no dreams, no building our expectations, everything based in reality and dread. Sylvie was such a breath of fresh air. She never wanted to talk about failed marriages or danger or sadness or death. She loved talking handbags and shoes and flowers and falling in love. As she'd said, she liked everything clean and sweet-smelling, and what the hell was wrong with that? I needed this escape, this time of sunshine and cocktails and white sandy beaches. I needed a break from my own thoughts and the darkness lurking there.

Our salads arrived, and we stopped talking for a moment to eat salty feta, sweet tomatoes and juicy olives. But it didn't distract Sylvie for long and she was soon asking me more.

'So, you and Nik?' she asked, and lowered her eyes as she lifted her fork. 'Did anything *happen* on this walk?'

I had to tell her, I was dying to tell *someone*, it made it more real. 'A kiss,' I said.

'Yesss!' Her face was flushed with excitement.

'Perhaps don't mention it to Angelina yet?' I suggested.

'Okay, perhaps not, but don't let Angelina get in the way of something wonderful. If you like him, Alice, go for it. I'm sure he'd much prefer a woman like you than a *girl* like Angelina. You do like him, don't you?'

I nodded. 'Yes, he seems lovely, he's interesting and intelligent, he knows all about wine, and I... yes I *do* like him.'

'Did he ask to see you again, or make any plans to meet up?'

'No.' I shook my head sadly. 'He might not want to take it any further, it might have been just a spur of the moment thing?'

'He doesn't strike me as a spur of the moment kind of guy. Angelina says he hasn't been with a woman since his wife left, and I think that was a while ago now. I mean, he kissed you, Alice, he *must* be interested in you.'

'I hope so, I just don't know how Angelina would be if we did get together.'

'Who cares how she'd be?' she said, taking a large sip of her cosmopolitan.

I just picked up my drink, but in truth I cared about how Angelina would be. I couldn't forget the hate on her face, the fury as she yelled at me, 'Where the hell have you been?'

'Whatever happens with you and Nik, Angelina will get over it,' Sylvie continued. 'There are loads of handsome young guys out there just itching to take her out, she'll soon forget about Nik Kouris,' she added between mouthfuls of feta and cucumber.

'Angelina was upset about something, or someone last week. She wanted you to call the police,' I said. 'Was it *really* a guest who'd upset her?'

She rolled her eyes. 'Yeah, I told you it was. She's easily offended, you know, someone makes a remark, or says something she doesn't like and she wants the police called.'

I lifted my head in acknowledgement of her explanation. Sylvie obviously didn't see it as an issue, but I wondered again if it might be Dimitris. And after seeing the way he was talking to Angelina at the wedding, the look of fear on her face meant it would continue to play on a loop in my mind.

'Let's talk about something more fun, like does Nik Kouris have any friends for me?' she chuckled.

'If he does, you'll be the first to know.'

'Double date?'

'Absolutely.'

'For what it's worth, I think he's perfect for you, he seems kind and trustworthy – we all need someone we can trust.' She sat back and considered what she'd just said, nodding slowly. 'Yeah, Nik Kouris strikes me as the kind of guy you could trust with your darkest secrets.'

I raised my eyebrows at this. *Could* Nik be trusted with *my* darkest secrets?

I hoped so, but the real question was, could he trust me with *his*?

SIXTEEN

The day after my lunch with Sylvie, Nik called. As soon as I heard his voice my heart quickened, and like a Jane Austen heroine, I thought I might faint.

'I hope you don't mind me calling you, I got your number from the wedding contacts list.'

'Oh...'

'I know I shouldn't have, but... but I enjoyed chatting the other evening, and I wanted to get in touch,' he said, sounding as awkward as a teenage boy.

I wasn't used to this either. The kiss had moved our blossoming friendship into different territory and having been able to chat quite freely to him, it now felt clumsy, every word loaded.

As a teenager I'd gone off the rails through my early teens, causing Heather no end of trouble. But that stopped when I was older, and I just got on with life, staying single, not really embracing my youth as perhaps I should have. I was resolutely single throughout my late teens and twenties; meeting Dan and falling in love in my thirties had been quite a surprise. Dan was the only real relationship I'd ever had, so this – whatever it was, with Nik – felt very new and strange, and I wasn't sure how to read it.

There was a horrible silence, and eventually he spoke. 'Forgive me, I'm not used to this kind of thing – it's been a while,' he started.

'It's the same for me, as you know,' I said. 'I basically told you my life story sitting outside a café on our second meeting.'

'Yes, you did, I appreciated your openness.'

'Thanks, I tend to overshare, but I do understand, it isn't easy to reach out, especially as an older person,' I added into the silence, feeling his agony over the phone.

I heard him take a breath. 'Yes, it's true, I'm rusty when it comes to the opposite sex,' I heard the laughter in his voice. 'Thing is, I understand if you'd rather not, and don't want to put you on the spot.'

My heart soared expectantly at this.

'But... I wanted to ask if you'd like to perhaps come to the vineyard one evening, I could cook for us, and this time you could properly *taste* the wine?'

'Yes.' I was so thrilled, this was unexpected, and I had no intention of playing hard to get. 'I'd love to.'

'When are you free?' I could tell by the hesitation in his voice this wasn't easy for him.

'Most evenings,' I replied honestly. The only friend I'd made here so far was Sylvie, so unless I'd made plans with her I was totally free.

'Okay, tomorrow?' He wasn't implying he had to fit me into a busy diary, he was free the next day and was honest about that. I found it refreshing, so was honest back.

'I'm free tomorrow. That would be great.'

We agreed on 6pm at the vineyard. I didn't sleep that night, I was kept awake by excitement and nervous energy, unsure what to expect, but delighted to be asked, and hoping I didn't disappoint.

* * *

The next morning, I texted Sylvie to tell her all about it, and she responded in capital letters and exclamation marks. Then she called me. 'Oh my God! I'm so excited for you, Alice. Let's go shopping for something for you to wear.'

I was forty-four years old, but because of my family situation I'd never really been able to enjoy the freedom of youth. Going shopping with a girlfriend, drinking, and spending money, were not things that Heather and I could afford when we were younger. Besides, being the oldest, and responsible for me, it had been up to Heather to make sure we were both safe. All this was on her shoulders, along with having enough money to live and eat and keep a roof over our heads.

When I'd eventually married Dan, Heather welcomed this. I think it was a relief, she finally felt she could pass on the responsibility to someone else. I didn't tell her, because I didn't want to worry her, but he hadn't cared for me, he hadn't kept me safe, and on top of this, I became swallowed up by baby grief.

Sylvie had coped with her childlessness in a far more positive way. 'It wasn't meant to be,' she'd said, 'and I have to find out how to make my life into a different shape than what I thought it would be.' Where I'd seen infertility as an ending, she'd seen it as a beginning, a new adventure. I still had vague hopes for the future, and knew I'd never completely accept my childless state. I hoped that one day I could be more accepting, but my story was very different to Sylvie's, and I hadn't told her everything.

So after all the sadness, all the smashed expectations in my life, here was someone telling me to go shopping, get excited, to move on and embrace what life had to offer. Instead of doubting my judgement and filling my head with fear that I might be going down the same dark road, Sylvie wanted to talk about what to wear and what lipstick to choose. And we arranged to meet within the hour at a boutique she knew just off the square.

'I am so proud of you,' she said, as she rifled through designer dresses in what turned out to be a very expensive dress shop.

'It's just dinner at his place,' I kept reminding her. 'I don't want to raise my expectations too high, we never know what can happen, it's very early days,' I said, hearing Heather's words in my voice. Funny how we sometimes change depending on the people we're with. I was the optimist with Heather, the pessimist with Sylvie, and the pleaser with Dan. I really hoped Nik would be different, perhaps I could even be myself with him?

Sylvie nodded absently from behind a pile of sun hats. She wasn't listening, didn't want to talk expectations and early days, she wanted the full-blown excitement of a first date. And I loved her for that.

'Now try this on with some of these.' She thrust a teal silk top at me then bustled over to some white trousers and handed them to me. The boutique seemed plush and expensive, and once in the changing room, I checked for price tags. There were none. But still, I dutifully tried them on, hoping against hope this outfit wasn't going to set me back a month's wage.

'How are you doing in there?' she was calling excitedly, before I'd even taken my clothes off, but eventually I stepped out from behind the curtain to her gasps. She was holding a gold pendant with a huge turquoise stone, placing it over my head and around my neck, then she stood back and smiled.

'You look amazing, you have to get these for tonight, and the pendant just finishes it all off.'

I'd seen myself in the changing room mirror, and loved what I saw, but she was right, with that pendant the whole outfit just came together. 'You're a great personal shopper,' I murmured, admiring myself in the big shop mirror.

'Is she a model?' I heard in a Greek accent, and I turned to see the shop owner, a very glamorous, brittle woman with coiffed hair and too much make-up.

'No, she's not a model, but I can see why you'd think that,' Sylvie said kindly.

I shook my head, wishing they'd stop. They were being kind but it was too much, I was no model, but clearly the woman was after a sale.

'She'll take the top, the trousers and the pendant,' Sylvie said.

'Hang on, I don't know how much they cost.'

Sylvie leaned in, and whispered, 'And you don't ask in places like this.'

'Well in that case,' I started, going back into the changing room.

'In that case,' she continued my sentence, 'I will buy them if you can't afford them.'

I popped my head out between the curtains. 'No, you won't.'

'I will. They look fabulous on you, and if you can't afford to treat yourself, then I'll treat you.'

'No, no, I can *afford* it, I just wonder if I should spend the money. I'm jobless after all,' I said, looking at myself again in the privacy of the changing room. Sylvie had selected an outfit I'd never have chosen for myself, and it looked great. 'Yes, I can afford to treat myself,' I announced, pleased with my reflection.

'That's the spirit, dip into that nest egg, my darling, life is for living!'

'You're right about that,' I murmured, looking in the mirror, imagining myself sauntering around the gorgeous house and vineyard in that outfit later. And it was only the thought of his gorgeous eyes, and the way he might just slip off the teal silk top later, that walked me to the till.

The woman slowly folded the trousers, wrapping them in tissue paper, then she put them carefully and slowly in a big, fancy carrier bag before starting on the silk top. Again agonisingly slowly, she folded and tissued the beautiful slippery silk, and though I wanted these things, I also desperately wanted to know how much they cost.

Eventually, she started making notes, and looking up said, 'That comes to 600 euros.' She smiled widely, with matte peach lips. But she was dead behind the eyes.

I had to grip the counter, and tried not to show my horror as I reached into my handbag for my card.

'You okay, Alice? I can use *my* card?' Sylvie whispered as the woman pretended to busy herself with nothing, while she eagerly awaited my credit card. I didn't even know what the limit was and putting it into the machine she was now proffering, I held my breath, unsure what would be the best outcome; that I paid more than I ever had for a couple of items of clothing and a paste pendant, or that the machine rejected it, and I'd save myself a fortune. But Sylvie was right next to me and I knew if there was a problem with my card, she'd insist on paying, which I couldn't let her do. So either way I was having this outfit.

'Wow,' I said, once we'd stopped in a little café for a sandwich and coffee. *I just spent six hundred euros on clothes?*

'Let me buy some of it, I feel bad, like I forced you somehow?' She really didn't understand. Sylvie's business was obviously successful, and she didn't even have to think about what treats she bought for herself and assumed everyone else was the same.

'No, I can afford it, honestly. I just didn't expect it to be quite so much.'

'You paid by credit card – do you really have enough to cover it, babe, because I don't want you getting a huge bill next month and—'

'No, no. I can take it from my savings.' I had over £500,000 from the divorce settlement, a huge amount really, but without a job, or any prospect of getting my old one back, I couldn't just blow that money on whatever I fancied. I needed to keep some of it to buy somewhere to live. Heather and I had always said if we had a roof over our heads we could survive anything. I'd also hoped to put some of it in trust funds for my nieces. I didn't want to tell Sylvie this because it meant revealing that I was under police investigation, but my biggest fear was that within a few months, Dan – or his lawyer baby-mother, to be precise – intended to wipe me out financially.

'You looked gorgeous in that teal blue,' Sylvie offered, like that justified the cost. She was clearly seeing the buyer's remorse on my face.

'Yeah, I loved it, and I love nice clothes – handbags too.

But I've never had designer stuff, 600 euros,' I gasped, 'I didn't pay that much for my *wedding* dress.'

Her mouth was wide open. 'You are kidding me?'

'Yes, the bill was 600 euros, in pounds that's—'

'No, I mean you're *kidding* me that you didn't even pay that for your wedding dress. Where did you get it from, a charity shop?'

I smiled. 'Oh, Sylvie, we aren't all rich like you. I bet *your* wedding dress would cost as much as my house!' I joked.

'How much was your house worth?'

'About £600,000 when we bought it ten years ago,' I replied. She didn't flinch; to her that was just pocket change. I could only imagine how much she had in *her* bank account.

'Well I might not pay quite *that* much for my wedding dress,' she said with a giggle, 'but it would have to be in the thousands.'

'I really don't want to think about my wedding day today,' I said sadly.

'Oh I know it's hard, but you have to let go, Alice. And something tells me you still haven't. Is it because you love him?'

I just smiled, and she touched my arm comfortingly. I didn't still love Dan, but it was easier to pretend than to try and explain the truth, that I wished he was dead.

SEVENTEEN

That first evening with Nik was magical. I took a taxi to the vineyard, the taxi driver spoke good English, and during the long, rather mountainous route, we chatted.

'So you have friends at the vineyard?' he asked.

'Yes, I know the guy that owns it.'

'Ahh he's a nice guy, nice guy,' he said, talking with his eyes on the rearview mirror.

'He is, and he knows a lot about wine,' I added.

'Well it's been in his family for many years, many years, wine must run through his veins.' He nodded at me.

'Yes, he's shown me round, talked about his family, he wants to continue building what his grandfather and father started.'

'It's good for tourists, you understand? They like the wine, you English, you love it.'

I smiled. 'Yes we do.'

As the taxi pulled up on the gravel drive, the sky was beginning to fade to pale orange, setting off the brickwork, and pale green paintwork of the substantial house. Rows of pretty olive trees provided a leafy, shaded pathway, and I climbed out of the car, and paid the driver.

'Say yassas to Dimitris for me,' he called, as he drove off in a cloud of chalky white gravel. My stomach dropped. In all the excitement, I'd almost forgotten about Dimitris. I hoped he wouldn't be there, so I didn't have to even pass on a friendly 'hello' in Greek from a local taxi driver.

Approaching the front door, I banged the knocker, and within seconds Nik was standing there. He looked so handsome in a crisp white linen shirt and chinos. I had wondered if I might be a little overdressed in designer silk and white trousers, but my clothes felt just right.

'You look lovely, Alice,' he said, his lips brushing my cheek. 'Come through,' he put his hand on my lower back as I walked through the door. 'I thought we might sit outside?'

His aftershave wafted me in as I followed him through to the huge French windows at the back of the house, where we slipped through onto the patio. I hadn't really appreciated this space at the wedding, it had been cleared for eating and dancing, but now there was just one large table, simply but beautifully dressed with vine leaves, foliage and fairy lights.

'This is lovely,' I said, as he pulled out a chair for me at the table. 'Did you do this,' I gestured to the table setting.

He nodded, it was almost a shrug, and I saw again that understated man. No showing off, no macho posing, just a gentle, unassuming man.

The back of the house, the kitchen and this beautiful patio were in complete contrast to the dark, foreboding front room. It was as if the past and the present were colliding under one roof, uncomfortably so.

'Did you design the exterior yourself, it's so different from the front of the house?' I asked, wondering if perhaps his previous wife, or even a professional, had created the extended rear, which was contemporary, with clean lines, modern lighting, with a nod to its origins in the exposed brickwork and scrubbed oak table.

'My... my own work,' he said, again a little shrug, he didn't want a fuss.

'Can I get you a drink?' he asked. I'd been very anxious about the evening, but I'd already had two glasses of wine at home, which had soothed me. Another would be good.

He returned from the kitchen with a bottle and two glasses and went on to describe the delicious pink rosé from his own vineyard.

'Wow, that must be so satisfying, wine from grapes you've grown yourself, on your land.' I took a sip, 'this is delicious,' I said.

He smiled. 'I thought you'd like it. Dimitris is cooking supper, it won't be long.'

No. 'Oh, I didn't realise he was here.'

'Yes, he's in the kitchen. I hope you don't mind, but I invited him to join us for supper. He's... he was very keen to cook for us. I couldn't *not* ask him.'

What the hell? 'It's fine, absolutely fine with me,' I lied. I suddenly didn't want to eat a thing. I hadn't expected this at all, had I misunderstood the evening. Was this not actually a date? Who would invite their weird cousin to a romantic dinner for two?

'I'll go and give him a hand,' he said, standing up from the table. 'Once he's eaten, I'm sure he'll leave, he goes to bed early,' he added, like that made a difference.

'It's fine, Nik, *really*,' I lied again, and he wandered off to the kitchen, leaving me sitting alone wondering what the hell I'd got myself into. I took a large slurp of wine, I needed to chill, there were just two plates on the table, so Nik *had* planned for this just to be the two of us. I just didn't understand why he didn't explain this to Dimitris and say he wanted to be alone with me? I could hear them in the kitchen speaking in Greek. It seemed pretty amiable, Nik even laughed at one point.

'You may need to bring an extra setting,' I called to him. He put his thumb up in the air in response. As weird as it was having three for dinner, he'd probably invited Dimitris at the last minute because he felt sorry for him. I realised I was being rather closed off, and a little selfish, Dimitris was obviously lonely and Nik was being kind. Perhaps it was time for me to be the same and rather than resent Dimitris, I should welcome him. So when Nik returned to the table, followed by his rather dour cousin, I smiled broadly and said, 'Yassas, Dimitris.'

Without meeting my eyes he mumbled, 'Yassas,' under his breath, and plonked a big pan in the middle of the table.

'Lamb kleftiko,' Nik announced, as he dished it up. 'Dimitris' speciality.' He nodded over at his cousin, who didn't respond. He sat down, but as we put food on our plates, he just watched us, which I found quite distracting. Before eating, I waited for Dimitris to put food on his own plate, out of politeness but also to make sure it was safe to eat. But the sweet, slow-cooked lamb with the spike of salty feta was absolutely delicious, and I smiled to myself as I ate, realising I'd watched too many true crime documentaries with Heather where the murderer laces a tasty dinner with antifreeze.

'Please tell Dimitris this is delicious,' I said, and Nik repeated this in Greek, with little response from Dimitris. I just continued to enjoy the food, it certainly took my mind off this weird tableau of the three of us sitting under the stars eating dinner by candlelight.

We ate in silence, and desperate to start a conversation, I mentioned to Nik that the taxi driver who'd brought me there had said hello to Dimitris. Nik passed this on to Dimitris in Greek, as I looked on, smiling, expecting very little response, but this time, his reaction was a rather unexpected nod. For the rest of the meal I felt on edge, he was pretty unreachable, except to Nik who seemed to have some kind of connection, but even that was stilted. For the rest of the meal, Dimitris just stared and ate while Nik said the odd sentence to him in Greek, while looking at me apologetically.

Once Dimitris had eaten, he took the empty pan away, leaving all the dirty plates behind, so I started to gather them together.

'No, please don't, I'll do that later,' Nik said softly. 'I wanted to spend time with you tonight, and already you've been here a while and we haven't had a chance to talk. I'm sorry about Dimitris.'

'Don't be, I understand. I guess he's lonely.'

He nodded slowly. 'He's my cousin, and I'm the only one he really communicates with, if you could call it that,' he added, sadly. 'Dimitris is socially reticent, he's unable to understand people or engage with their emotions. Sometimes, I wish I could find the key to unlock him, but then he's happy in his world, so who am I to turn it upside down because society expects something from him that he can't give?'

'That's so true, and I'm guilty of that. I feel slightly uncomfortable around him, but that's my fault, not his.'

'I know but it isn't easy to like him. I won't deny his

behaviour can be difficult and at times quite alarming, but on the whole, I think he's harmless.'

The fact he only thought he was harmless and couldn't absolutely vouch for him waved red flags for me. I took another sip of wine, I'd been drinking nervously throughout the meal and knew I should have stopped two glasses ago, but I couldn't.

'I think you see a lonely man who needs your help, and you seem so kind, Nik, but are you being too kind?'

He looked puzzled, his brow furrowed.

'What I'm trying to say is, I really, really, *really*, think you need to keep an eye on Dimitris,' I slurred. 'I think he might be dangerous,' I heard myself say. I was in that in-between bridge where I wasn't yet drunk, and my sobriety was horrified at the unedited thoughts tumbling from my mouth.

'I don't believe he's dangerous,' he replied. 'He just needs support, and kindness.'

Even in my tipsy state I could see Nik was trying hard not to let this escalate and smiled benignly at me as I spoke. Aware my voice was raised a little more than necessary for a quiet romantic drink, I ploughed on, knowing I should drop this, but compelled to go on. The Kouris rosé wine was potent.

'Dimitris is *dangerous!*' I repeated, too loudly.

In that moment Dimitris returned to the patio and said something to Nik in Greek.

Nik replied without turning to look at him, and Dimitris nodded once and went back inside.

'Is he okay?' I asked, hoping he hadn't heard me mention his name.

'Yeah, he just wanted me to know he's going to bed now.'

'Has he always lived with you, in the house?' I asked.

'Yes, he likes it here, he could stay in one of the cottages on the estate, and sometimes he does, but he says he's more comfortable in the house.'

Again I was touched by Nik's kindness, but wondered if he was perhaps being too kind, and putting himself or his guests in danger.

'He doesn't have much, Alice. And if a nice big bed and air-conditioning on a hot night is all he needs, then I'm happy to provide.'

I felt guilty now. 'Sorry, I shouldn't have said anything.'

'You're only thinking what everyone else is on this small island,' he said with a shrug.

'I just think it's best to be careful' I started, but before I could continue, he put his fingers to my lips so gently I wasn't sure if this was a romantic gesture, or a sign for me to stop talking.

'Let's not discuss my cousin any more tonight,' he said in a whisper. Then to my amazement, he leaned across the table, and kissed me. He was tentative at first, polite even, but then he put his arms around me. I could feel the pressure of his hands on my back, around my waist, and just as I thought things might develop, I opened my eyes. And there, in the darkness of the kitchen I saw a shadow standing in the doorway.

As I pulled away from Nik, I saw them dart away quickly. Goose bumps danced along my spine.

'What? Was I being too forward?' Nik asked, confusion etched on his face.

'No, it isn't you,' I said, staring through into the kitchen. 'Someone was there, I saw them, watching us in the dark.' I shuddered. 'They were there,' I nodded in the direction of the kitchen.

Nik turned around to look. 'I can't *see* anyone,' he murmured, standing up.

'Someone was *definitely* in there. I think it was Dimitris,' I said.

'Are you sure, he's just gone to bed?'

'Who else could it be, there's only him here, apart from us. Isn't there?'

'Yeah, of course. Perhaps he was just getting some water, or checking we were still here – he likes to turn the outside lights off before he goes to bed.'

I felt really uneasy now. 'He knew we were still here. He was standing in the shadows, he was *watching* us, Nik.'

'Alice, I'm sorry he makes you feel anxious, but he just gets a bit disorientated sometimes.'

'Do you feel safe with him around the house?' I asked. 'I guess you've heard the rumours?' I heard Heather's voice telling me to stop drinking.

'You mean the missing women? Yes.'

'What do you think? Is that all they are, just rumours?' I tried to ask this gently, aware it wasn't really a first date conversation, but I had to know.

He paused for a moment before answering. 'Yeah, Dimitris has been here pretty much all his life. He isn't like everyone else, and people have prejudices about men like Dimitris, they assume he's not to be trusted, they're suspicious of him. It suits everyone's narrative to think he's predatory. He's just misunderstood. He wouldn't hurt a fly, and I know there's been talk about stuff happening here at the vineyard, but trust me, nothing happens here that I don't know about.'

'I hadn't heard anything about the vineyard,' I said, 'just Dimitris.'

'Well, people say all kinds of things that aren't true, I don't listen to the rumours,' he replied testily.

I wondered if he didn't want to listen because he didn't believe the rumours, or because he couldn't bear to think they might be true. Sometimes we only hear what we want to hear and tell ourselves the things we want to believe. My mind suddenly alighted on Dan on the floor of the supermarket. Blood and rainwater in rivulets on the floor, a scream in the silence, Della yelling and jumping in to save him, to stop *me*. The image was becoming clearer each day, and I tried not to let it in, let the film develop into the full picture. I didn't want to *see* my own crime, didn't want to discover what horror I was capable of. Was Nik the same, and didn't want to *know* what Dimitris might have done, and might continue to do?

'I don't listen to rumours either, Nik, but there are some weird things going on. Like last Saturday, when you took me to the orange grove, and someone was hiding behind the trees. I saw their feet, I heard them rustling through the trees. What if it was Dimitris, what if it was *his* feet I saw? They were workman-type boots just like he wears,' I said.

'Every worker in this *vineyard* has a pair of workman-type boots,' he replied gently. 'They hang around here all the time, even during the weddings and corporate events we hold, and any one of them could have followed you that night.' He moved the table. 'Look, I wear the same kind of boots, it could have been me,' he smiled at this.

'But you were with me?'

'Not when you saw the boots, and I was wearing them too.'

I giggled. 'I never noticed. You wore workman's boots at a lavish wedding? You weirdo.'

'Yep, I'm the winery weirdo, it's me!'

We both laughed at this, but as always, my obsession wouldn't let go, and I pushed on down the track.

'Okay, I accept it could have been *any* of the workers, even you. But my money's on your cousin. And let's face it, I wouldn't be the only single woman of a certain age to feel threatened here, the others have already gone missing.'

'I think the whole missing women thing is pure hysteria. This is rural Greece, nothing ever happens here, so people make things up for entertainment, so gossip – and coincidences – become big stories. The last woman who'd supposedly "gone missing" turned up on Skiathos three years later.'

'Yes, there are always going to be those stories about missing people. Back home my sister and I used to check the missing persons websites, and often people had just chosen to leave their lives for their own reasons. But that still leaves nine women unaccounted for.'

'Why did you and your sister check missing persons' websites?' he asked with a curious smile.

'We're just interested,' I lied. 'We follow true crime podcasts, and documentaries. We're fascinated by missing people, why have they gone, where are they, did they run away or were they taken? People go missing for a reason.'

'They could all just be somewhere else,' he said. 'Like these so-called missing women, they may have gone travelling, be off grid, escaping some jealous lover, who knows what goes on in people's lives?'

'Yeah, but these women were all single, they had no apparent reason to escape *anyone* or *anything*. They were alone, or estranged from their families and partners. That's why it's hard to know when exactly they went missing, because in most cases, no one reported them missing immediately. Some of them had been on social media and if you look closely at their friends and the places they go to, you can build a vague picture of who they were. Some of the accounts have been deleted, but some are still there, and they suddenly stopped posting.'

'You've really looked into this, haven't you?' He looked slightly horrified. I realised I sounded obsessed.

I'd said too much, the drink had loosened my tongue. All I could hear was the sound of crickets, louder and louder, reaching a crescendo, like the screaming, it filled my head. So I took another sip of wine to turn down the volume.

'Alice, why are you so troubled by the fate of these women?' he asked, sitting back in his seat, a look of concern on his face.

'Because I'm a woman, and I care about other women.'

'I care *too*. I just don't believe anything *bad* happened to them, and they're probably living different lives now.'

I heard a frisson of irritation in his voice, and under different circumstances I'd have backed off, aware this wasn't the ideal subject matter for a first date and it wasn't really fair of me to lay this on him. But this was my obsession and I'd had a few too many drinks, so instead of letting it go until I knew him better, I leaned forward, keen to press the point, and said, 'I know you probably think I'm mad at this point, but I think this is just the beginning, this isn't just about nine or ten women, I think it's bigger.'

'In what way?' I could tell by the amusement in his eyes that he was humouring me now, but I didn't care.

I picked up my phone, and clicked on it, finding the information I'd been going over only the night before. 'It says here that there have been unexplained disappearances of women travelling alone on Kefalonia, and Zakynthos, both nearby islands. I reckon it's connected, the islands are close by, it would be easy for someone to move around. I wonder if there's a serial killer hopping between islands and targeting lone, female travellers?' As soon as I said it I wished I hadn't. His face told me that saying something like this out loud to someone other than Heather made me seem overdramatic and rather silly.

'I think you're getting carried away, Alice.'

'Probably,' I murmured, missing Heather, who instead of dismissing it always wanted to explore crazy ideas like this. It used to annoy me the way she took a simple idea and imagined a terrible crime, but I missed that now, because I didn't believe this was imagined. But his reaction told me Nik felt I was making a big fuss about nothing. He was a business owner, he wanted to believe it was all village rumours, because anything otherwise would be bad for business.

I really didn't want Nik to think I was silly, and longed to understand why this mattered so much to me, but I couldn't. I should have stopped drinking then, but I kept talking and sipping. Then Nik brought a fresh bottle and poured more wine. It tasted good and as always it stopped the sound of women screaming.

EIGHTEEN

The morning after my dinner with Nik I woke up feeling terrible. I had the worst hangover, and all I could remember was eating dinner, talking too much and Nik helping me into a taxi. Everything else was a blur, apart from Dimitris. I couldn't recall the details, just a dark presence. I really hadn't drunk that much, I'd usually be able to handle four or five glasses over an evening, but the lovely rosé wine went down far too well, and along with my anxiousness about the date, I turned into a hot mess very quickly. One thing I did vaguely remember, as I came to, was the kiss – witnessed by Dimitris. I climbed out of bed and grabbed my phone to see several missed calls from Heather, so took it out onto the balcony with a cup of coffee, and told my sister all about the night before, in the misguided hope of sympathy.

'Alice, you have to stop drinking,' she sighed, 'you're a disaster.'

'I only had a couple of glasses,' I lied, almost tearful wondering what on earth Nik must have thought of me. I'd ruined something potentially good with my drinking and my obsession with the women and Dimitris. 'As far as I remember, he didn't ask to see me again, and he hasn't called or texted.'

'I'm not surprised he hasn't been in touch. You say you had two glasses, but I know you too well Alice. You get stressed, you drink, you get tired, you drink, you get upset, you *drink*. And every time you do that, you just piss people off and make everything worse. I'm sorry, Alice, but you can't pick up a bottle every time you're hurting.'

'I *didn't*,' I snapped, irritated. 'Okay, I had more than two glasses, but the amount I'd had wouldn't normally get me drunk.'

'It would *me*.'

'I know, but you don't drink, so your tolerance is low,' I said. 'But last night I was anxious, and Dimitris was there, he freaked me out.'

'He sounds really dodgy.'

'Nik says he's harmless, he's his cousin.'

'So he would say that.'

I filled Heather in on everything I'd found out, about the missing women and the rumours about Dimitris. I also shared with her my theory that the same 'someone' might be responsible for women going missing on the other islands.

'A serial killer you mean?' My sister could be a pain, but she never judged my mad hypotheses when it came to stuff like this, in fact she embraced them.

'You need to tell the police.'

'I will, when I have something to tell them, but at the moment it's just me flailing wildly around.'

'And talking of which, why are you getting involved with another guy when you're still dealing with the fallout from Dan?'

'I'm not getting *involved*, he asked me over for dinner. And just because Dan was a selfish, abusive dick, it doesn't mean all men are,' I heard my voice trail off.

'So he lives out in the woods with his serial killer cousin, and you just went out there alone? *And what happened to his first wife? Does anyone know where she is?*'

'With her new beau, the billionaire apparently.'

'Wow, she moved on, didn't she? Do you know anything about this billionaire?' she asked, like she didn't believe a word of it. 'Are you sure she's not just gone missing too?'

As much as I missed my sister's enthusiasm on these matters, now wasn't the time. The pain on his face when he talked about his ex-wife was enough to tell me how real her betrayal had been. But more worryingly, I may have ended things with Nik before they'd begun and I now had to work out my damage limitation strategy. It was clear that Nik thought I was slightly unhinged the previous evening when I'd shared my theory on the missing women, but my sis was way ahead of me on the armchair detective madness scale.

Heather and I both loved watching true crime shows and detective dramas on TV, but she saw murder and mayhem where it wasn't.

I said goodbye to my sis, then sat for a little while in the sunshine contemplating my latest emotional mess, and called Sylvie. 'How was your evening, I want to know *everything*!' she said as soon as she picked up.

And I wanted to *tell* her everything. So I told her about the stars, the wine, the kiss, the weirdness of Dimitris being around, and how I'd told Nik his beloved cousin was dangerous and there was a serial killer at large in the Ionian Islands.

I heard her gasp a couple of times during this account,

which I concluded by saying, 'And he hasn't called because he thinks I'm an idiot and doesn't find me in any way attractive.'

There were a few seconds of silence on the line, then she spoke. 'Wow, there's a lot to unpack. First of all, how could he not find you attractive? He obviously likes you, or he wouldn't have invited you over and kissed you, so please stop beating yourself up. Secondly, let's look at this objectively – you weren't the *only* one who messed up a beautiful evening. Yes, you drank a lot and ended up tipsy, and perhaps you were more open than you might have chosen to be—'

'That's an understatement.'

'But,' she continued, '*he* invited his creepy cousin to a romantic, candlelit dinner.' She chuckled to herself.

'Yeah, perhaps it wasn't *all* my fault?' I conceded.

'Exactly, now just relax, enjoy the sunshine, and I'm sure he'll be on the phone begging to see you very soon. Trust me, I know men, and I've got a good feeling about you and Nik Kouris.'

And she was right, because the very next day, he called.

'So sorry I haven't been in touch, but we had a disaster,' he said.

'Yes we did, didn't we? I drank too much and—'

'Oh I wasn't talking about the other evening, I enjoyed spending time with you. No, a pipe burst and we lost *gallons* of water.'

'Oh no.'

'But with the help of Dimitris and the rest of the staff, we managed to salvage some of the water and repair the pipe.'

'Thank God,' I said, more in response to the fact that his lack of communication had been about a faulty pipe rather than me.

'I was worried about the harvest, and how we might lose everything. One bad harvest can ruin a vineyard.'

'I wish you'd told me, I could have come over and helped, or at least made cups of tea.'

He laughed. 'Ahh tea is not the palliative for all things here as it is at home. Greek brandy does the job instead.'

'I can serve brandy too,' I said with a smile. I was just pleased he'd called. He obviously hadn't been offended by my comments after dinner, nor was he judgemental about my drinking. I liked him even more.

'So, now things are cool, can I make it up to you and take you out to dinner?' he asked.

'I'd love to... Will it just be the two of us this time?'

'No, I invited Dimitris, I hope that's okay?'

I didn't know what to say, I couldn't actually speak.

'I'm joking, Alice.'

I laughed, with relief rather than mirth. 'No offence to Dimitris, but I think two on a date is enough.'

* * *

The following evening, I found myself in a rooftop restaurant under a canopy of stars with Nik. This time we were alone, and we talked and talked. We discussed everything and anything, from art to wine to music, and all the time we laughed and drank retsina. We ate chicken souvlaki on skewers, golden and tasty with cool, zesty yogurt dressing and crisp salad. The night air was infused with thyme and rosemary, and my arms tingled from that day's sun as we gazed into each other's eyes.

His marriage story was as Sylvie had been told; he'd met

his wife on the island, been completely besotted by her, and after just a couple of years she'd met someone else.

'I'm not sure she ever did love me,' he said. 'I think she loved the idea of the vineyard, and presumed I was rich, which compared to the other guy I'm definitely not. He's a billionaire.'

'Wow!' I feigned surprise, didn't want him to think I'd done any research. 'How did he make his money?' I asked, which was probably a question too far, because Nik shrugged, he clearly didn't want to talk about it anymore. I remembered Heather's comments about where his wife was now, and I wondered if he didn't want to talk because it was painful, or because he was hiding something.

'Where is she now, your wife?' I asked, as casually as I could.

'On a yacht somewhere in the Indian Ocean I guess,' he said with a faraway look in his eyes.

'Married to a fortune, but she still wanted her share from our marriage, and demanded half the vineyard.'

'But it's been in your family for centuries, how could she?' I murmured. 'Is that even legal, that someone can take half of a family business when they divorce?'

He nodded. 'Well she did.'

'So does she own half?'

'She was awarded half in the divorce settlement, but fortunately I was able to buy it back from her. I sold everything I had, took out a mortgage and now I'm the sole owner again. Kouris Estates is worth a lot of money, but everything I had went into buying her half, so if I need new equipment or have a bad season, I have nothing put by to see me through.'

I just shook my head at this. He'd really been through it,

emotionally and financially. His life's work, his home, his future, were all on such shaky foundations.

'I bought her a beautiful apartment, a car, lovely clothes, but it wasn't enough – I wasn't enough,' he added sadly.

'She came from a wealthy family, had a lot of her own money too,' he continued. 'But when I was struggling to pay the bills at the vineyard, she refused to help me. After she left, I was so devastated I seriously considered taking my own life...' He paused. 'I haven't told anyone that before – it's not something I'm proud of.'

I saw the deep sadness in his eyes, and related so much. That night we left the restaurant and crossed the road to walk along the beach. We wandered along, almost aimlessly, neither of us in any rush for the evening to end. Now and then we'd stop and look out at the black, endless ocean, and the midnight stars. At some point, I remember him putting his arm around me, and despite being unable to trust anyone, I allowed myself to lean in. I was stronger now, and ready for a relationship, but was Nik someone I could rely on? I hardly knew him, and there were still some doubts on my part, but later, when he drove me home, and pulled up outside my apartment, we kissed. He ran his hands around my back, and I felt from his breathing and the way he was touching me that this might lead to more, and I was ready. I told myself this didn't have to be a lifetime, it could just be a night, someone to hold for a while. But when we stopped kissing, he abruptly pulled away, and started the car. 'I have to go now,' he said, like nothing had happened.

Confused and disappointed, I instinctively reached for the car door, wondering what had just happened. Was he unsure of me, or afraid of going too far and regretting it? In those few seconds I tried to process everything and came to the quick conclusion that perhaps he was waiting for me, that the ball was in my court. That was it, I was rusty, things had changed since I last dated anyone, he needed me to let him know *I* wanted him too.

So I took a breath and heard myself say, 'Would you like to come up to my apartment?'

I waited, expecting him to say yes, not because I'm an arrogant person, but this felt like a natural next step. We were both grown-ups, both single, and we knew what we were doing, so I waited for his confirmation. But I was greeted with a hesitant silence, a horrible awkwardness exuded from him, I could sense his unease in the darkness. Mortified, I didn't move as he stared ahead, not moving, or looking in my direction. This was quite unnerving. Had he heard me? My hand was on the passenger door, which was open, I was ready to climb out. But I didn't know what to do. Should I stay and wait or just save myself and go? His silence was deafening, and eventually he turned to me and said, 'I ... I have an early start.'

I couldn't make out his expression, and suddenly felt foolish. I'd obviously misread the situation, and was filled with doubts again.

'Of course,' I muttered, and before he could say any more, I climbed from the car. We each blew a kiss to each other as he drove away, and though I smiled and waved and skipped up the steps to my apartment, I was totally crushed.

* * *

The next morning I woke with such a heaviness I didn't even want to talk to Sylvie. Was Nik unsure of me? If so why did he keep inviting me on dates? Was he playing games? If he was I didn't want him in my life. But then just ten minutes later, he called, and I felt myself being swept up again in his warmth and old-fashioned charm.

'Sorry I was so tired last night, after all the problems with the pipes I haven't slept for days, I nearly fell asleep at the wheel.'

That still didn't really explain why he didn't want to come up to my apartment. 'I wouldn't have minded if you'd crashed at mine,' I offered.

'No, I had to get back,' he said, without apparently feeling the need to say why. His tone felt like a brush-off, so when he suggested we go for a drive to the mountains that afternoon, I was glad, but irritated that he assumed I'd be free.

'I'd have loved to, but I'm busy,' I said, without saying why. *Two can play at that game.*

'I'm sorry, I was being presumptuous, wasn't I?' he said, like he'd read my mind. 'I made a picnic but I should have checked with you. No worries, when are you free again? I could take tomorrow afternoon off, or the day after – or the day after that?'

I softened, feeling mean, he wasn't playing games, he was probably as vulnerable as I was. We were both walking a tightrope, and I felt like I should be more trusting, he was like me, just a bit clumsy and out of practice.

'Do you think the picnic will keep until tomorrow?' I asked.

'Most definitely,' he replied.

So the next day we drove up into the mountains where it was so different from the town and the beaches. Up there it was cool and very green, the air heavy with the scent of pine. We parked up on the edge of a mountain, where we could see for miles. We just sat and took it all in, our hands entwined. He'd packed a picnic and laid it on a blanket, hummus and flat breads, olives, grapes and orange juice that tasted of sunshine.

And after we'd eaten, we lay down on the blanket looking up through the matrix of leaves above us.

He told me the names of the trees, and wildflowers, and I knew then I wanted to be around him always. I wanted to listen and learn, I was intoxicated by this handsome, kind, clever man who was so in tune with nature. We lay side by side, in the shade of the Judas tree, where it was only us, the birds, the tiny little sprigs flowering between craggy rocks, and the sound of the ocean.

A salty sea breeze rustled through the Judas tree above us, and I snuggled up to Nik. After a while, I slowly ran my hand down from his chest to his belt buckle. I let my fingers linger a while, then began to undo his belt, my heart racing, knowing this could finally be the next step for us. I felt his warm hand on mine, taking it gently – and to my surprise, he lifted my hand, moved it away from his belt. Then he gently patted my hand. It felt like a reprimand. I was fragile, I had put myself out there and felt foolish – again. Tears sprung to my eyes. I was amazed at my own reaction, and looked up at him questioningly. But he didn't say or do anything, just lay there silently gazing up at the sky, as the sun went behind a cloud, turning everything grey and cold.

NINETEEN

I didn't try to make the first move again. I hoped that perhaps I'd misinterpreted him moving my hand from his belt that day in the mountains. I'd felt rejected, but told myself this was all new to me and I shouldn't overthink it, so I tried to push it away. And over the next few weeks, Nik and I saw a lot of each other, it was fun, and the early insecurities began to disappear the more we got to know each other. But, in spite of the talking, the kisses and the warmth of our relationship, there was still no intimacy. I didn't want to talk to him about it and turn it into an issue, some people took longer to trust, and after what he'd been through with his ex-wife, he might not feel ready for a full-on relationship. But as much as I tried to resist, Heather's doubts as always penetrated my brain. *And what happened to his first wife? Does anyone know where she is?* she'd asked suspiciously. Her imagination was overactive, but it seemed to me that she thought something might have happened to her. I would have dismissed this, but when I'd asked Nik if he had any photos of his wife, he shook his head, 'When she left I deleted them,' he said, clearly not wanting to talk about her.

'Every single one? But she was part of your life.'

He shrugged.

'What's her name?' I asked.

'Elizabeth... Elizabeth Brown.'

'As you met her here, I assumed she was Greek?' I replied.

'Half-Greek, like me, she had family here, she was on holiday, she lived in the UK.'

The past tense bothered me slightly, and later I googled her name along with 'billionaire' and 'Corfu' and even 'Kouris Wines,' but nothing. I told Heather, who did her own online research and couldn't find her on social media either. I mentioned this to Sylvie who seemed surprised that I was even concerned about his former wife.

'I don't understand why you're so bothered. Loads of people don't have social media accounts, and unless she's famous, or her husband is, nothing will come up on Google,' she said. This was true, but at the risk of sounding paranoid, I decided to talk to Nik about my concerns, and asked him more questions about her. Unfortunately, he didn't seem to understand why this was important to me.

'Alice, I know you were lied to, you've been hurt and you find it hard to trust, but if you're ever going to move on you *have* to trust me.'

'I do,' I replied uncertainly, 'I just find it hard to understand how you were married to someone for years...'

'Two years, only *two*,' he said, gently. 'Look, I don't have her photos on my phone any more, and I don't have pictures of her on the walls as I once did.'

'You can't blame me for wanting to see the woman you

married, I just think it's part of who you are. I'm not being needy, or nosy, it's just part of your history. I have pictures of Dan if you want to see them?' I offered, wondering why he'd never asked me much about my ex-husband.

He then stood up and walked over to his phone on the kitchen table, clicked on a couple of things, then placed it before me like an open book.

'Here she is, this is the Instagram account of my ex-wife Elizabeth Brown, now known as Elizabeth Kyriocou. She calls herself an interior designer now, she doesn't do it for the money, she just does it for her rich friends. Take a look, she's here, she even mentions the fact that she was once married to me in an earlier post.'

I felt my face burn with embarrassment as my eyes skimmed the beautiful photos. Nik's former wife was alive and well and living in Cannes. I blamed my sister for even planting the seed, and so much for her online detective work. Later that night when I called her with the good news, she actually sounded disappointed that Nik hadn't murdered her in her sleep.

I looked up from the Instagram page and he was laughing.

'What?' I asked.

'You are impossible. You're crazy, you wanted proof that I was married,' he said, shaking his head. I didn't doubt his marriage, I had worse doubts than that, but didn't want to offend him or appear to be even more paranoid.

He was looking at me now, his eyes soft and glittery. 'I think that's why I love you Alice.'

I was surprised, this was the first time love had been mentioned, and it felt nice. From that moment I stopped fretting about his ex-wife. As long as we were happy, that was enough for me for the time being.

Meanwhile, the weddings had gone a bit quiet, but Sylvie said it was always quiet midsummer, the heat and tourists put people off. She didn't seem too bothered, it wasn't like she needed the money, and I didn't want the work, I was enjoying spending time with Nik. My sister wasn't too happy about that, she was still convinced he was a wife killer and called me regularly telling me to pack and go home immediately.

Some of Heather's calls were worse than others. I naïvely hoped that if I stayed on Corfu, the assault investigation would start to fade and be forgotten, but one of Heather's calls revealed that Della and Dan were still pushing this.

'They think they can make money off you, take back your divorce settlement if you're convicted. Apparently she's harassing the police about it,' Heather said. 'She wants the investigation to stay open, says there are new witnesses. And I don't want to worry you...'

'Oh?' I was now worried, of course.

'But they call her the Rottweiler in court.'

'What witnesses?' I asked, ignoring the Rottweiler remark.

'Who knows? But someone, somewhere always knows something,' she said, in that dramatic way she always did.

I'd realised the only way not to get upset and anxious about this, was to try and pretend none of this was happening. Unfortunately, Heather had a different approach, and if she couldn't get me on the phone, would send texts that began with 'URGENT!' What she didn't realise was that anything in capitals from her produced a Pavlovian response in me to press delete.

'Come home,' she'd say whenever she called me. And it would have been the sensible thing to do, but how could I leave now? I couldn't face what might be waiting for me at home, besides I was compelled to stay and find out more about the women. On a lighter note, I'd found the most wonderful friend in Sylvie, and something like love with Nik. He'd become part of my life, we saw each other most days now. We'd meet for dinner, and if he was working late into the evening, we'd meet for a morning coffee or a walk on the beach.

I was happy for the first time in a long time. Heather was right when she said I was being irresponsible and stupid and making everything so much worse for myself, but back home everything was a mess. Here, there were problems I might be able to *solve*. I was drawn to Corfu, and couldn't get the missing women out of my head.

I'd spend hours googling, making notes, making lists of the women, trying to find out more about them – who were they, why were they here, did they have anything in common? Had someone taken them, hurt them, killed them? Were they chosen at random, or did they all share something? Was there a reason why someone would hurt them? I looked at potential suspects online, and was grateful for the translation tool on Facebook that enabled me to read the latest local news and theories. But even in the short time I'd been looking, it was clear interest was fading. These women were middle-aged, they weren't young and pretty and vital – except one, and I wasn't even sure she was part of this. Hopefully there was no connection, she just happened to be here, then left.

The last woman who'd disappeared had been gone for

over a year, and people soon moved on. I sometimes wished I could too – but I could never move on.

Then one night, when Dimitris wasn't around, and Nik and I were alone, I told him about some of the comments I'd seen online. I didn't want to repeat gossip, but I felt Nik should know what was being said about his cousin and the missing women. He'd previously fobbed me off when I expressed concern, but he had to take this seriously for his own good.

'Most of the comments don't name Dimitris, but some do, and they're accusing him of *horrible* things,' I said.

'You're talking about the missing women again?' Nik turned to look at me, concern etched around his eyes.

'Yeah, it's well-documented on Facebook, there's a whole page dedicated to it.'

'Really? People are ghouls, aren't they?'

I guessed he included me in that, perhaps he was right, but I had my reasons. 'I've looked back on the page over the past few years, and though at first other men were in the frame, it looks like local people are pointing the finger at Dimitris.'

'So who *was* in the frame?' he asked absently. He still wasn't really taking this on.

'Well, the first few women seemed to have a connection with a bar... They'd either visited regularly or worked there. It was called The Aphrodite Bar in town, apparently it's not there anymore. No one is actually named, but it seems there were a couple of guys who worked there who went out with some of the women.'

'God, that doesn't look good for them,' he said.

'Did you ever go in the bar?'

'No. Never heard of it. Does it say who the bar men were?'

I shook my head. 'No one seems to know, the bar closed down about four years ago.'

'As you know, I'm usually here, I don't stray too often into the bright lights of Corfu Town.'

'Do you know if Dimitris ever worked in a bar?'

Nik shook his head. 'Not as far as I know.'

'Something you should know,' I started, 'is that someone said they'd seen Dimitris loitering by the trees near the harbour. Apparently, he was looking at the missing posters.'

'That's not illegal, is it?'

'No, but he was loitering, and... and panting.'

He looked doubtful. 'What the hell? He has limited lung capacity, sometimes he breathes like that.'

'Another comment said the police had found photos of some of the missing women on his phone, but can't prove anything so can't arrest him.'

Nik groaned quietly as he raised his head from his chest, then looked up to the ceiling.

'Another woman who's apparently known him since they were kids called him a "frikio," which means weird.'

'I know what frikio means,' he murmured, his head still gazing up at the ceiling.

'I'm not saying this to hurt you, Nik. If you genuinely think he's not guilty of anything, I think you should try to get the posts taken down. They're defamatory,' I added, wondering just how much he was prepared to do to prove his cousin's innocence.

He brought his head down, and nodded very slowly, without looking at me.

'It may all be rumour of course,' I continued, 'but about a

year ago, when the last woman went missing, there was a comment about Dimitris hanging around a search area and asking the police too many questions.'

'I remember that,' he said with a sigh. 'I was with him. I told him to stop bothering them, he was agitated... but that doesn't mean he *knows* something.'

I shrugged. Had the misunderstood loner turned to killer, kidnapper, rapist? Or was it something else, was he just an easy target for what Nik referred to as 'the ghouls'? I was trying to be fair, but the more I read, the more convinced I was that Dimitris was somehow involved.

'Has Angelina ever said anything to you about Dimitris?' I asked.

'No. Why?'

'Because I heard her complaining to Sylvie about a man, she seemed quite upset. I don't know what happened, but she was saying Sylvie should tell the police. Then later I saw him talking to her and she looked worried, scared even.'

Nik's demeanour suddenly seemed to change completely at this, and sliding his arm around my shoulder protectively, he said, 'Angelina scared?' He shook his head. 'Nothing scares her.'

'Do you know what upset her?'

'Yeah, she made some accusations, but it was just Angelina being... Angelina.'

'And what the hell does that mean?' I felt a flush of anger; if Angelina had complained and Nik wasn't taking her seriously, then he wasn't who I thought he was.

He seemed flustered, I think he was surprised at my reaction, but this was serious. I pulled away to face him.

'What *happened*?' I urged.

'She said Dimitris was cosying up to her and she felt uncomfortable. I told her I'd have a word with him.'

'And that's Angelina being... *Angelina*, is it?' I snapped.

'I didn't mean it like that. She can be a handful, you know what she's like. She has a colourful imagination. And I'm certainly not going to accuse him of something Angelina says he did. I don't know what happened, I wasn't there.'

'No one knows what happened to those women either because no one was there,' I said angrily. 'And if we all keep pretending nothing is happening, something *will* happen?'

'Look, I promised Dad I'd look after him, and I promise *you*, he's harmless.'

'Do me a favour, Nik, and take Angelina seriously, or the next woman who goes missing won't be on his conscience, she'll be on *yours*.'

'If I thought he was in any way dangerous, Alice, I'd have gone straight to the police.'

I had to accept his decision, it wasn't in my hands, but I planned to talk to Angelina the first chance I got. If she told me anything that concerned me about Dimitris, I would offer to go with her myself to the police. The irony wasn't lost on me. I was being investigated for a minor crime I didn't think I'd committed, meanwhile someone on this island *had* possibly committed murder, several times, and no one was doing anything about it. But if Angelina's complaint was anything to go by, it looked like the answer might be closer than I thought.

Looking at the fragments of information I couldn't find much, just the odd newspaper article. Because most of the women were middle-aged, not stunningly beautiful, with no sexy backstories, the media had moved on quickly, no-one wanted to read about invisible older women. So far, I'd worked out that the women were mostly middle-aged and travelling alone, it didn't look like they had family back home or friends on Corfu. That was probably the reason there wasn't much information or urgency to find these women. No one was missing them. No one cared, except me.

It might be too late to save them, but I had to find them, to save myself.

TWENTY

Since I started seeing Nik, I hadn't seen as much of Sylvie, but we'd stayed in touch. I'd kept her abreast of the developing relationship in texts and calls, and we both kept promising to find time to get together, and finally decided on a day and a time that suited us both. I'd been on Corfu for 3 months now, and despite not having the right visas, or much work, felt like I belonged. The police had Heather's number and address, but she'd heard nothing from them for weeks. I was daring to hope that things had died down, that Dan and Della were busy with their lives and they'd moved on. Surely the police had enough to do without worrying about a minor marital bust-up in a supermarket? So if my ex and his fragrant new woman had stopped agitating, the investigation may well be on a back burner by now. I could only hope, and didn't have any immediate plans to go home and find out, I had enough money to live on, and at first I wasn't too worried, but having no pay cheque was making quite a dent in my savings/divorce settlement. Sylvie of course had no such issues, and insisted we meet at the rather expensive yacht club, which overlooked the harbour.

She'd ordered cosmopolitans for both of us, and mine was waiting on the table when I arrived. It was great to finally catch up properly, not just the odd call and text. She told me about her latest wedding, and a guest who'd asked her out. We both giggled at the idea we were dating. 'Two forty-somethings,' she said, 'and we're behaving like teenagers.'

'So I want to know everything,' she squealed, and I told her all about Nik, how I was falling for him and all about life at the vineyard.

'He sounds just perfect, all that and a bloody big vineyard? You always said you had to go back, but sounds like this guy could tempt you to stay?'

'I don't know,' I replied, brushing it away. 'It's a gorgeous place, and sometimes in the evenings we walk through the olive groves, and you can hear the crickets and the sky is pink. I love it.'

'Sounds like bliss, and Nik hasn't invited Dimitris along to any of your romantic dinners lately?' She was still holding the menu, and her eyes flickered over the pages then back on me.

I raised my eyebrows. 'Well, he doesn't actually *invite* him, but he does seem to turn up wherever I am. I'm probably being paranoid.'

'You're *not*. You should be on your guard, trust your instinct.'

'I find Dimitris' presence intimidating. Like a big, dark shadow following me around.'

'I know what you mean.'

'Yeah, and he has that effect on lots of other people too,' I said and went on to tell her about some of the stuff I'd seen online. She found it all quite uncomfortable, so I just gave her the basic outline of some of the comments on social media.

'Honestly, don't tell me any more,' she said, holding her hands up and pulling a horrified face. 'You know what I'm like about that kind of thing, it makes my skin crawl. I just hope the police are reading those comments, because the sooner they lock him up, the better,' she added, with a shudder.

'Yeah, he's *odd*, but does that make him a killer?' I said, echoing Nik's words. 'No one can actually *prove* anything.'

'What do they need to *prove*? If what they are saying online is true, that he's hanging around the police search areas, asking too many questions, it's enough to charge him as far as I'm concerned.'

I smiled. 'Don't ever join the police, will you, Sylvie?' I said. 'There's such a thing as innocent until proven guilty.'

She pulled a disgusted face. 'Yeah but I've seen the way he looks at women at the weddings, I'd never forgive myself if something happened. I'd never forgive the police either – they have a responsibility to keep people safe from men like him.'

I shrugged. 'I've said the same to Nik, but he's family. I think it was difficult to hear, and unless the police have evidence, no one can say for certain it *is* Dimitris.'

'Apart from the fact that he lurks around the place and turns up wherever women are.' She made a face. 'Look, when you're at the vineyard, just make sure you're never alone with that freak. *Never*, you hear me, I'm not joking?'

I nodded, feeling a shiver of fear at the tone in her voice.

Sylvie rarely got serious, or even discussed horrible things, but now she sounded like Heather.

She must have seen the concern on my face, because good old Sylvie was soon back to her usual light-hearted self.

'So, let's talk about something nice, you and Nik.' She put down her menu, and leaned forward conspiratorially. 'I want to know *everything*,' she whispered, with an expectant smile.

'It's lovely, *he's* lovely,' I started.

She beamed. 'I'm assuming you two are an item now?'

'I *think* so.'

'Why do you only *think* so?' she asked, concerned for me.

'Oh I don't know, it's just... It's probably me overthinking things; it's nothing.'

'Something's bothering you, so it's *something*.'

I hesitated, then told her. 'You know I've been seeing Nik now for almost three months?'

'Yeah?' She was smiling at me uncertainly.

'Well, several times now I've tried to take it further, and he doesn't seem interested.'

'You mean sexually?'

'Yeah, it's odd. Like if we're kissing and things get heated, he moves away, pretends he needs a drink or has to check his phone or something.'

She looked vaguely surprised, but not shocked. 'Okay, and you've talked about this?'

'No, I do need to speak to him about it, I just keep hoping it will happen by itself. I don't want to make a big thing about it, don't want him to feel like I'm pressuring him. Thing is, Sylvie, I haven't been in a relationship for a long time and I don't know the rules any more. I'm beginning to wonder if it's me – is he not attracted to me?'

She began shaking her head vigorously, but I knew she was just being nice.

'I'm not stupid, he's really good-looking, and I've seen a photo of his ex-wife, she was gorgeous. It's affecting my confidence and I just – I just think I'm not *good* enough for him.'

'Wow! How can you *think* that? You *are* good enough, *more* than good enough,' she replied reassuringly.

'But you can understand why I might *feel* that, can't you?'

'I can, but there's bound to be an explanation.'

'Well have *you* ever been out with a guy for almost *three* months and not had sex?'

She tilted her head to one side, and paused a while. 'I have actually.'

'Oh?'

'Yeah, a Greek guy I met here,' she said. 'I'd been seeing him for at least three months, couldn't understand why we weren't "progressing." I felt ready, and tried everything, virtually offered myself up like a banquet, and he just never took it on. I couldn't understand it! Anyway, when I began questioning my own worth, I decided to have it out with him.'

More drinks arrived, and I wanted the waiter to leave quickly, I was dying to know what happened.

'And?' I said, eventually.

'Well, turns out, he'd been in a horrible relationship, and didn't feel ready to go the whole way. He told me I was special, and he wanted to marry me – he *wanted* to sleep with me but was worried about falling too deeply.'

I considered this for a moment. 'Nik was in a horrible *marriage*, perhaps he feels the same?' I suggested.

'Totally. And what you describe is *exactly* what

happened to me. I'd put money on it that Nik is seeing this thing you have together as something special, he wants to get involved, but he's scared the same thing will happen with you as happened with his wife.'

'I wonder. Thing is, I have this habit of burying my head in the sand sometimes, and instead of facing it, dealing with the issue, I close my eyes and hope it will sort itself.' I rolled my eyes. 'I know, I know I'm an idiot.'

'Hey, you aren't, you just do things your way. And there's no judgement here,' she offered gently. 'Your sister has been telling you you're an idiot for years, not in so many words, but if someone says it long enough, a person starts to believe it.'

I'd never thought about it like that before, but I blamed myself for everything, and even now, when every fibre of my being knew I didn't attack Dan that night, Heather was still introducing doubts. 'No, Heather doesn't trust me, she doesn't believe in me, and so I don't believe in myself.'

'Exactly, and she's probably putting doubts in your head about your relationship with Nik too. But it sounds to me like you guys have a great thing together, you just need to be open and honest. And if you haven't, then it isn't your fault, sometimes it's about timing. And perhaps the time to have a proper chat with him is now?'

I smiled. 'You're right.'

'And I really wouldn't worry about it, love, he's crazy about you.' She lifted her glass to mine. 'Here's to love!'

Sylvie had given me hope, she'd eradicated my self-doubts, and though I wasn't good at facing up to anything, I was ready to talk to him.

As the afternoon wore on, we drank more cocktails and

ate a delicious Greek mezze of creamy dips, vine leaves, olives and flatbreads.

After we'd eaten, Sylvie vaped, and I breathed in the lemony citrus as it hit the salty sea air, and I wondered if I could ever go home.

It's such a strong memory, imprinted on all my senses, the lingering warmth of the dying sun, the sound of rippling water and the fresh scent of lemons. But now, the waft of citrus takes me back to that time, that place, and makes me want to be sick.

TWENTY-ONE

Buoyed by my evening with Sylvie, and her theory about why Nik didn't want to sleep with me, I decided to do something about it.

The day after I'd talked with Sylvie, I arrived at the vineyard for an early dinner around 6pm. I found Nik outside on the terrace, where he always sat, and stood for a moment watching him engrossed on his phone. He looked so handsome under the pergola cloaked in bright pink bougainvillea. I loved the orange sun-soaked evenings there, when day became night, and everything cooled down. Later as we watched the orange turn to navy blue, I said, 'Nik, what do you want from this, from us?'

He turned to me, his face puzzled, perhaps trying to fathom yet another of my many questions.

'I want too much probably,' he murmured looking up at the night sky. He often looked up when faced with difficult conversations, like he thought the answer might be in heaven.

'It's just that...' I hesitated. 'I don't feel like we're a couple, not in *every* sense of the word.'

He paused a while, it was seconds, but to me it seemed like hours.

Eventually he started to say something, then mumbled, 'I guess I'm scared, I don't want to get hurt.'

'I feel the same. Is that why you and I haven't... why we haven't *slept* together? Is it your fear of becoming too involved and the same thing happening again?'

He sighed, put his head in his hands. 'Alice, you have to understand that for me this isn't a fling, or a "hook-up" as they call it. What I have with you is forever.'

I hadn't expected him to say anything like this and I reached out and touched his face. Immediately, he took my hand and kissed my palm, his mouth warm and damp and delicious.

When he looked up, he said, 'I'm worried that you might leave at any time. Your sister calls you all the time telling you to go home, you hint at stuff you have to "deal with" back in the UK. I guess what I'm saying is I love you, and I want to be with you, but don't feel like you're committed to me, or to Corfu, so how can we take this any further?'

I took a long breath. 'There *are* some things back home that draw me, but there are things here *too*. And yes, Heather is desperate for me to go home and be safe and sort my life out. But I don't always do what she says.'

He put both hands behind his neck, resting his head as he looked up into the night sky. 'I'm glad you don't do everything she says, because... I don't want to be alone anymore.' He dropped his head, so his eyes were now on mine. 'Stay here on Corfu with me.' He reached out his hand and took mine. 'Forget everything back home, it's the past. I'm offering you the future.'

Nik stood up, and still holding my hand, slowly led me

inside the house and up the stairs. I'd never stayed overnight before, but at some point, while sitting under the stars, we'd both agreed to something. And when we reached the bedroom, *his* bedroom I presumed, I went inside, and heard the distinct click of the lock as he closed the door. I turned to see the dark outline of his shape. He wasn't moving, just standing feet away, his back against the door. And it occurred to me, that even if I wanted to leave, I couldn't.

'Take off your clothes, Alice.' His voice came out of the darkness.

In the thick silence, this didn't feel real. I stared back unable to see his expression, just the outline of his face. I slowly pulled my dress over my head, and stood facing him, feeling exposed and vulnerable in my underwear. I could just see the outline of him leaning with his back against the closed door, watching silently, waiting for me to unwrap that final layer. Everything was so still, so warm and quiet, as if a blanket had been thrown over the world. Then I saw his outline move, felt the air stir as he came close to me, I could feel his breath on my face. I shivered in anticipation. What was he going to do? I waited, and waited, aware he was standing close, then he touched me, featherlight fingers down my arms sent a shimmer of lust through me. I reached out my arms; 'No,' he said quietly, and moving away he walked towards the bed, turning on the small lamp, illuminating my vulnerability, my almost nakedness.

Without looking at me, he walked back to the wall and stood against it, several metres away from me. It was too far, I wanted him close, against me. The longing was unbearable.

'Take everything off.' He spoke quietly, without any emotion, without movement. Just watching.

Despite the lamplight, he was standing in shadows and I

still couldn't see his face clearly. Wordlessly, I loosened the catch on my bra, let it fall to the ground then pulled down my underwear and stepped out of it. Now completely naked I felt strangely vulnerable, defenceless. I was excited, aroused, but a frisson of fear edged through me. I didn't know this Nik, he was like a stranger, and I suddenly felt exposed. And all the time he stood in the dimness, staring.

'Now go and sit on the bed,' he said, and I stepped backwards, climbing onto the bed which was big and high. I felt the cool bed linen against my skin. And only after he'd watched me for several more minutes, did he walk towards the bed.

'Now imagine I'm not here, but you're thinking about me,' he said.

I knew what he meant, and despite my arousal felt crushing disappointment. We weren't going to make love after all.

'Go on then, do it, touch yourself. I want to watch,' he said huskily. I could hear the lust in his voice as I put my hand between my legs and began to touch myself. He stood over me, seemingly emotionless, and as fireworks exploded through me, I lost control and cried out. I didn't want to be anything or anywhere else but there with him. Watching me. He did nothing, just stood, fully clothed and very still.

Eventually, I sat up, and tried to speak, but was unable to form words.

He continued to watch me, saying nothing, doing nothing, like he was in a trance.

Finally, I said, 'What about you?'

'That was all I needed,' he whispered, then leaned down, and kissed my lips like I *belonged* to him.

We must have both fallen asleep for several hours, and I

woke to the pale early morning light easing through the shutters, hinting at the day's heat to come. I now wanted to avoid real life and just live in that beautiful room with the long, shuttered windows for ever. The cool white walls now emerged in the morning light, and I saw the room for the first time, touching the pastel blue satin eiderdown, soft and cold on my fingertips. I looked into his eyes, and saw us wandering through the orange grove, walking out towards the sea, hand in hand. Somewhere in the night there'd been a shift. I couldn't put my finger on it but the dynamic had changed, I felt less in control, more willing to be wafted along by life, by him, and by whatever happened next.

As if he'd read my mind, I heard him say into the silence, 'Marry me, Alice.'

'Do you mean it?'

'Of course I mean it.'

There was so much he didn't know about me, and I couldn't live a lie with the man I married. I had to tell him everything, but how could I? He might decide he didn't love me after all.

'Can I have some time to think?' I asked, and he looked crestfallen, almost as if he might cry. 'I do want to be with you, I just need to *think* about it.' This had been so unexpected I didn't know what to do. 'In the meantime, why don't we just keep that door locked and stay here forever?' I said, looking over at the bedroom door and suddenly feeling very uneasy.

'Nik, when did you open the door?'

He glanced over. 'I didn't.'

'But the door's open,' I gasped, pulling the covers around me, fear tingling at my finger ends. I was now sitting up, ready to run.

'Oh, I wonder what...?' he muttered. 'I mustn't have closed it,' he said, almost to himself as he climbed out of bed, and walked cautiously to the door.

'You *did*, I remember, I heard it click, you were leaning against it.' I pulled the covers up over me. 'You don't think—'

'What?' He seemed genuinely puzzled.

'You don't think Dimitris opened it, unlocked it by mistake?' I asked, imagining him standing in the shadows watching me.

'No, he wouldn't do that.' He looked at me, and I went cold. Nik *knew* it was him. Dimitris had been watching from the darkened doorway.

'Nik, someone was there, and I think we both know who it was. I think you're in denial because you don't want to scare me, and you don't want to believe it of your cousin. But there's something very wrong.'

'It may have been him, perhaps he's home late and just came looking for me? Whatever it is, he isn't dangerous, and you need to believe that. Alice, please don't let this stop you from being with me. I need to know you're going to be here,' Nik murmured. 'To know that when we go to bed together at night, you'll still be there in the morning. I can't go through someone I love leaving me again.'

I heard the desperation in his words, the pain of betrayal and loss, and knowing that we wanted the same thing, it seemed crazy not to just give in to that. I think Nik saw Dimitris like a confused child. Perhaps that's all he was, and I had to think of him in the same way. I was probably seeing danger where there was none. After all, Nik really didn't see Dimitris as a threat. If he did he'd have thrown him out, and called the police. Even now the only thing that concerned him about his cousin was that he might be a reason for me to leave him, but in the optimism of a sunny morning, I forgot Dimitris, and all the other problems and assured Nik I'd never leave. 'I'll be here,' I whispered, 'forever.'

'Will you marry me?' he murmured, sleepily.

And I heard my own voice respond, 'Yes. I'll marry you.'

He leaned over and kissed me, and I was elated and happy and so very sure in that moment. But he was soon asleep and I lay there confused and unsure of what I might be letting into my life. This was crazy, wasn't it? My feelings for Nik were strong, but did that justify me turning into some kind of fugitive, and never going home? This was balanced by the fear that I could be on borrowed time, and might have to go back to the UK at any moment if the police said so. If that happened, I'd be forced to leave Corfu and lose Nik anyway, so did I just grab what happiness I could now, and leave tomorrow to look after itself?

Now, I look back and wonder at my madness, to think I could hide there on Corfu, and live happily ever after with Nik. But on that cool, blue morning, early sunshine flooding the room and a beautiful man sleeping beside me, it made a kind of sense. I was prepared to leave everything behind for good and take my chances here, in the hope that I'd found love, and no one would ever find me. But I should have known that blue mornings, sunshine and beautiful men are a lethal cocktail. To be taken with caution.

TWENTY-TWO

Over the next few weeks, Nik and I talked about getting married, and even planned a date.

I loved him, and wanted to be with him, but there were other, less romantic reasons that made me feel it was the right thing to do. A call from Heather early one morning made me realise that marrying Nik might also be the logical answer to my problems.

Nik was out in the vineyard, and I was still in bed when she called. I was feeling very groggy after a few glasses of super-strength Kouris wine the previous evening.

'What the fuck, Alice?' was her opening gambit as was often the case. I breathed deeply and reminded myself that she was thousands of miles away, and I could put the phone down at any time.

'Where were you? I called you late last night, *and* early this morning.'

I took another deep breath. 'So don't call me at those times because I'm *obviously* asleep.'

'Not necessarily. When you don't answer your phone, you could be being mugged, raped, or *murdered*.'

'It's possible, but I don't usually do any of the above on a Wednesday evening. My night for being mugged, raped and murdered is saved for Tuesdays, you *know* that.'

'You think everything's so funny, don't you?'

'If I didn't laugh, I'd cry.'

'You told me you were coming home, but you're still not here. You're messing around there while all the problems keep piling up here.'

'Heather, do you call me just to lecture me? I'm a grown woman. I know how mad this is, but it's my choice to stay here. I'm living in a Greek idyll with its own wine cellar overlooking an olive grove. Why do you have to ruin it by telling me the problems are piling up?'

'It's ridiculous,' she sighed. 'You've already stayed longer than legally allowed.'

Trust Heather to do her visa homework. I didn't answer, now wasn't the time to get into this.

'There's a letter here saying the police need to speak to you.'

I felt like I'd been punched. They were closing in.

'Heather, have you been opening my bloody mail again?'

'Okay, yes. I have. Apparently there are new witnesses,' she continued. 'Your ex-husband's girlfriend is making a huge fuss, and the police say they want to question you again with a view to charging you.'

I felt nauseous. 'I need some time. If the police turn up, just say you don't know where I am.'

'You're under investigation, in case you'd forgotten – and this is the address I kindly allowed you to give to the police as your permanent residence. But you're not *resident* here, you're in bloody Greece and if I lie for you I'll be committing perjury.'

'I'm not asking you to *lie*, just say you don't know where I am.'

'Do you realise how serious this is, Alice? You *have* to talk to the police. If you don't they'll turn up here at 4am in a dawn raid looking for you.'

I heard the anxiety in her voice. It wasn't fair of me to put her through this, but sometimes I just wished she'd let go a little. 'Look, I'm sorry you had to be involved. Just forward the letter to me, and I'll sort it.'

'Yeah, okay, so I'll send it to your flat in Corfu Town, and tell the police I don't know where you are. Oh hang on, I'm not sure that would stand up in court when I'm in the witness box being cross-questioned by your ex-husband's cunning lawyer girlfriend.'

'*Don't* forward it then, send me a photo of it, and if anyone asks tell them the last time you heard from me I was in East Timor.'

'Hilarious.'

'Ooh that's my bus. Sorry, Heather, got to go, love to the girls.'

I put down my phone. It broke my heart to think I didn't know when I'd next see my sister and nieces, and couldn't even countenance the fact I might never see them. I wasn't surprised there were witnesses, the supermarket was full that night with people buying last minute valentine's flowers and chocolates. My only surprise was they hadn't found the witnesses sooner, but what difference did it make? I could go back and try to clear my name, but the stakes were too high,

because if I failed I would lose everything, and might even
end up in prison. I couldn't go back home now even if I
wanted to. Not happy with taking my husband, my house
and my life, Della now wanted even more of me, and if they
managed to get me convicted, they could then go for the
money I had from the divorce settlement in compensation.
And it looked like they were prepared to move heaven and
earth to make that happen.

This really focused my mind, and things began to crystal-
lize for me. Nik was a Greek citizen, and if I married him, I'd
be able to stay on Corfu. I was currently staying in Greece
illegally, but being married meant I could stay without fear of
being arrested or deported as an illegal alien. Plus, I would
change my surname to Kouris, and give Della and the UK
authorities even less chance of finding me.

Nik still lived with the residue of hurt from his previous
marriage and once we'd set a date, he seemed keen for me to
stay at the vineyard. 'Now I know we're going to be together,
you might as well move in,' he'd suggested.

I wanted to spend more time with him, and it made no
sense me paying for the apartment in town, so I moved in.
Being there, I was also less visible, as the vineyard was miles
from anywhere, and given my current situation, it was better
for me to live somewhere remote.

Dimitris was still there, which wasn't ideal, but as Sylvie
said, 'Everything has its price.'

Nik and I talked, and he told me he'd prefer to save our
ultimate intimacy until the wedding night. I respected this,
even if it did make me feel a little uneasy. Who in this day
and age puts that kind of price on their wedding night? It
wasn't as if he was religious. Still, if it was important to him
then I was okay with that. I still had self-doubts left from my

former marriage, but he assured me that he wanted me. He just needed this time to be different, and didn't want echoes of either of our previous relationships.

'I want to come into this marriage like it's the first time,' he told me, saying he wanted it to be special, and to feel safe. I found this disarmingly honest and vulnerable, but again couldn't help but feel a little unsure. For me it wasn't about the sex, it was about the relationship, and I was slightly concerned that there'd be a part of him that I didn't know until the wedding night. What if his sexual desires were different to mine? What if he wanted something I didn't?

But Nik was keen to get married as soon as possible. 'Why wait?' he'd said. 'We know what we want, no point in letting it drag on, why don't we just go for it? You know a wedding planner, I have the venue, let's book it now!'

I was excited, encouraged by his keenness, and I'll admit I was still very flattered that someone like Nik wanted me so much. We'd sleep in his big bed, and I lay close, half-hoping he'd be overcome with desire, but nothing ever happened. One night, as he slept, I reached out and gently ran my fingertips across his chest, then touched his stubbly cheeks, breathing in his delicious, exotic, expensive smell. I usually loved his smell, but that night I'd been feeling a little sick, and what was usually delicious, suddenly made me want to vomit. So I climbed from the bed to fetch a glass of water. But as I walked across the bedroom, I thought I heard a noise outside, so went to the window, opening the curtains a little.

As I looked out onto the dark vineyard, I saw movement through the trees. *Someone was in the vineyard.* I felt my finger ends tingling as I opened the curtain wider to see what was happening. There was definitely someone there, but I could just see their movement, and a dark shape, nothing to identify them at all. Still verging on nausea, I walked carefully back to my nightstand, picked up my phone and zoomed in on whoever it was. But in the dark distance, it was almost impossible to see everything, so I zoomed and stared until I thought I could see the outline of a hunched figure. 'Christ!' I murmured to myself. It looked like they were *digging*. My legs almost buckled beneath me. Who the hell was digging in the vineyard at four in the morning – and why?

Whoever it was, was now wandering back through the distant acreage with the shovel over his shoulder, carrying a torch. And then, in the moonlight, I saw his shape, the gaited, lopsided walk. Dimitris.

'Are you okay, darling? You're not feeling sick again, are you?' Nik muttered from the bed, half asleep, I'd obviously disturbed him.

'I'm okay but, Nik, I think your cousin is out there with a shovel, digging in the vineyard,' I said.

Nik shot up out of bed. 'What, now? He's out there *now*?'

'Yeah.'

'I can't see anyone, whereabouts?' he said, screwing up his eyes.

'I think he's gone now. But he was definitely there.'

'Are you sure?' He looked at me like he didn't believe me, and started walking back to bed.

'I'm not making it up, Nik.' I raised my voice, angry at his dismissal.

'I'm not saying you are.' He climbed back into bed. 'But I think you're mistaken, it's probably a fox.'

'No, a man digging and a fox are two quite different sightings, even in the dark,' I snapped.

'Sorry, I'm tired,' he muttered, 'come to bed.'

'Do you think it's Dimitris, and he can't remember where he buried the bodies?' I half-joked.

'That's not funny, Alice,' he said, his voice edged with fear.

'No. It's not funny, it's not funny at all,' I murmured, as the hairs on the back of my neck rose.

TWENTY-THREE

I was terrified of what was happening back home, but the more scared I was, the more I tried to push it away and distract myself with what may have happened on Corfu. My upcoming wedding was now a far nicer distraction, and whatever had happened there in the past, and whatever might happen to me in the future had to be put on hold. So for just a little while I put my ex-husband and the missing women in imaginary boxes in my head and locked them away, just as the therapist had suggested when Mum and Dad died. I now had something positive, a flower growing out from the dark craggy rocks of my life – and his name was Nik Kouris.

So once I'd locked the horrors away, I allowed myself to be a little excited about getting married and hopefully putting everything to rest. This was everything and more that I could have hoped for, and to be on Corfu was the icing on the cake. With every fibre in my body I'd longed to stay there, drawn to it like a moth to a flame, the only place I could really find peace, and who knew, one day I might find answers too.

Nik was brilliant and left no stone unturned in all the practical and legal stuff for the marriage. 'I know a good lawyer,' he'd said. 'His company specialises in citizenship, and he's solid on property ownership too, which we'll need.'

'I don't *have* any property,' I said, wondering if he'd assumed I was coming into the marriage with some property dowry.

'I know, but I do, and as my wife you should have a stake in this place.'

'God no, I couldn't do that, Nik,' I said, knowing how much he'd already been burned. 'The vineyard is yours, it's your family's.'

'You're my family now. And you're giving up everything to stay here in Greece with me. On a practical note, I also want to make sure that if anything happens to me you'll be okay – you have nothing, Alice.'

'I do, I would be okay – I have some money, but the bulk of it's in the UK.'

'That's *your* money. I just know that I want you to share this with me, in every sense, I don't want my wife feeling like a lodger in my home. I want this to be *our* home, I want us to be a team, Alice.'

I was touched by his gesture, he wanted to give me what was his, but expected nothing in return. I did feel like it was Nik's home, and it would make me secure and complete my happiness for this to be *ours*. But now I could see how easy he'd made it for his first wife to take advantage of his kindness, some might even say naïve. Nik was clearly one of those people who fell totally in love and wanted to give everything.

I was too, but I wasn't his ex-wife and had to give something back.

'I would love to share the vineyard with you, but I'm not a passenger, and I would want to contribute,' I said.

'You just being here is enough—' he started.

'No, I want to share this properly, and I'd like to help with repairs on the property,' I said, trying not to think of Dan and Della who had their own plans for my money. I know you've struggled since the flood, and you were saying only the other day that the outhouse is leaking?'

'No, that's my responsibility.'

'Our responsibility. Remember? You don't want me to feel like a lodger, and neither do I. We are a team,' I stressed. 'And if I could get hold of my money we could use it for the vineyard, and perhaps invest some of it?'

He shrugged slightly, looked doubtful. 'I don't know. I haven't a clue if you could even get your money from the UK. You could talk it over with the lawyer when we go and see him? As for investing, it's your money, Alice, and I'm not good with money, but again the lawyer might have some ideas?'

'That would be great,' I said, then paused a moment before asking, 'Will Dimitris stay here – after we're married, I mean?'

He looked uncomfortable at this, and I felt bad putting him in such a difficult position, but I had to know.

'I'm not sure, Alice, it's complicated.'

'I understand. But I wonder if perhaps we could make his cottage on the estate more comfortable for him? I could pay to have it done up and he might want to spend more time there?' I offered gently, recalling the open door the night I lay naked on the bed while Nik watched.

'Yeah. I'll broach it with him, but he *thinks* he's in charge, thinks the place is his – and I've never really told him any different.'

'That's sweet of you, but perhaps you need to be clear with him. It isn't fair on him to let him think one thing when actually...'

He smiled. 'I get it, I really do. But I feel guilty, to be honest. By rights, he *should* have inherited half the vineyard, but our grandfather left everything to his son, who left it all to me. Dimitris' mother, being female, missed out – she inherited a few trinkets, some jewellery of my grandma's, but Dad got the lion's share.'

'Oh I see.' Now I understood why Nik kept him on there. 'But still, I didn't want three of us in the marriage.'

'I'd love to buy him a nice home somewhere by the sea where he could retire to. But I'd just worry about him.'

'So you can't ever see him living independently?' I tried not to sound too disappointed.

'I don't know,' he hesitated. 'I mean if you and I married, and it was a problem for you, then we'd have to work something out. *Your* feelings would take priority.'

I was slightly reassured by this, but then felt mean for even bringing it up. When we married Dimitris would be my family too, so I might need to be kinder, and more tolerant like Nik.

'But he's so alone in the world,' he continued. 'He's never married, has no children, and there won't be any down the line for him.'

It was now my turn to feel uncomfortable. 'If we married, *we* wouldn't have children either, Nik,' I said gently.

'I understand, and it's not an issue.' He put his hand on my knee, and kissed me on the mouth. I melted.

Then he pulled away. 'Besides, if I'd wanted children...' He smiled and reached for my hand. 'I'd be marrying Angelina.'

This felt like such a slap in the face, I wondered for a moment if I'd misheard or misunderstood.

'Why would you say that?' I snatched my hand away.

'What?' He looked up from his coffee cup, the comment already forgotten. It may have been a throwaway remark, but it stung and I wasn't letting it go.

'What? You don't realise that what you just said about marrying Angelina might hurt me?'

He seemed genuinely puzzled.

'The implication was that she's younger, therefore fertile and you could choose her over me if you *felt* like it. What a hurtful and arrogant thing to say.'

His face dropped. 'I'm sorry. I didn't mean anything by it, I just meant if I wanted children, I'd have probably looked for someone younger. It was a joke.'

'It wasn't funny.'

'I'm so sorry, darling, I really meant nothing by it, I feel terrible.' He dropped his head, and we both sat in silence for a few seconds. I was still stinging, and felt tears at the back of my throat. I'd had so much worse than this from Dan, but it came out of the blue, and I realised I'd put Nik on a pedestal, and my expectations were too high.

'I don't know what to say to make it up to you, all I can do is apologise.'

'It hurt, but I may have overreacted. I'm sensitive about the infertility and growing old, I guess.'

'I'm such an idiot. I shouldn't have said it, after all you've been through. I'm so, so sorry. How can I make it up to you?'

'It's fine, really,' I backtracked.

'No, anything, please?'

'No, Nik,' I said, concerned at how easily he was struck down, how desperate he was to please. I hadn't seen that in him before; he'd always seemed like his own person with his own opinions, and he wasn't afraid to argue for what he believed in. Funny how our perception of someone can change as we get to know them – I thought he was strong yet sensitive, kind but assertive, yet all the time I had been imposing my ideals onto this man who might never live up to my expectations.

And turns out, he was as flawed as the rest of us, perhaps even more so...

TWENTY-FOUR

Sylvie was so excited about my wedding news, she insisted we have a girls' night to celebrate. I took a taxi to a bar in the town where I was slightly disappointed to see she'd brought along Angelina and Maria.

I arrived at the table and before I could say a word, Sylvie yelled, 'Congratulations!' Then she held my hand and turned to the girls, and said, 'Our lovely Alice is getting married!' She immediately called for champagne, while Angelina's face dropped visibly. She'd clearly had no idea.

'Who are you marrying?' Her face was stern, her voice hard.

'Nik Kouris, of course,' Sylvie replied on my behalf, laughter in her voice.

She obviously hadn't realised just how uncomfortable Angelina and I were together, and in her excitement hadn't thought how the girl might take this news.

'So, talk me through the proposal, did he go down on one knee?' Sylvie asked, pulling out the chair right next to her, and ushering me into it.

'I think I need a drink first,' I said, smiling, not wanting to dampen Sylvie's lovely enthusiasm for my wedding. How could I possibly tell her all this with Angelina glowering across the table. It spoiled the moment, and I wished it had just been Sylvie and me celebrating. It was hard to drink champagne and listen to Sylvie saying what a beautiful couple we made, with Angelina smirking and rolling her eyes to Maria. I was used to her anger, her meanness, but when she got up from the table, I saw something like defeat in her eyes, and it made me feel sad for her. So I followed her to the toilet and once inside waited for her to come out from the cubicle. When she did, I opened my arms, hoping she'd come in for a hug. But she swerved and went to the sink.

'Angelina,' I groaned softly. 'What is it? Why are you always so angry with me?'

She looked up from washing her hands, and stopped for a moment. Her eyes bored into mine for a few long seconds, and the fear and hate in those eyes was visceral, she was like a wild animal. 'Alice...' she started, through gritted teeth, as I held my breath, waiting for the abuse, the vile, stinging insults she was about to hurl at me. But something in her face changed, that defeated look again. It cloaked her sharpness and her anger, and she clearly decided not to say anything.

'What?' I asked. 'Just say it and let's get this over.'

She shook her head and went back to washing her hands angrily.

'I do understand.' I tried gently to diffuse her hurt and anger. 'I know you don't want to hear this from me, but Nik's too old for you. There are loads of guys out there your age who would die to go out with someone as pretty as you.'

She dried her hands. Her mouth was set tight. I saw her

jaw muscle move, her anger so contained I worried she might burst.

'Nik and I just want to be happy, and I hate that this seems to make you unhappy. I want you to be pleased for us.'

She spun round. 'Is that what you *really* want? For me to be *pleased*? Well, little miss Alice in Wonderland, I hope you'll be very happy. But a word of warning,' she spat, moving right up into my face. 'You are playing with fire. And if you don't fuck off back home ASAP, you are gonna get burned!'

With that, she pushed past me, and stormed out through the door and back into the bar, leaving me breathless and shocked. I knew she was angry but I had no idea it went so deep. She was *threatening* me. I was seriously concerned now. This girl was dangerous, and out of control, and I worried for me and for Nik, because the way she'd just behaved made me feel like she might cause harm, to herself or one of us.

I went back into the bar feeling like I'd been punched. Where had all that venom come from? Her anger genuinely scared me. But as I rejoined the table, I was shocked to see her chatting away to Maria and Sylvie as if she hadn't a care in the world. And weirdly, when I sat down, she smiled at me, and said in the sweetest voice, 'Have you chosen your dress yet, Alice?'

I shook my head, unable to speak to her. I felt like she'd beaten me up, and was now saying sorry. But it was too late, I wasn't ever going to be treated like that again by anyone. It reminded of the time Dan gave me a black eye then a Tiffany bracelet.

I didn't tell Sylvie about Angelina's outburst, it was too raw to relive, but I also didn't want to cause trouble between them. This was my fight, and her words hung over me like a bad, cloying smell. Every time I looked over at her that night, she seemed to be telling funny stories, making the others laugh. I found this hard to reconcile with the snarling, hate-fuelled girl who'd threatened me in the toilets, and couldn't join in. Later, when I got home, I was still playing it over and over in my head on a loop. So I told Nik, who seemed surprised, but as he hadn't been there, he didn't really get how scary she was, how threatening.

'She's just some twenty-something kid,' he said, 'don't take any notice of her.'

'She told me to fuck off back home,' I told him. 'She said I was going to get burned, what the hell was she talking about? Did she mean because I was with you?'

At that he looked up from his phone. 'Did she say that?'

'No, not directly, but that's what it was all about.'

'I think you're overreacting,' he said, and went back to his phone. He clearly had no idea of just how much she liked him.

'You must have noticed the way she is around you?' I asked.

He looked up again. 'I barely know her, she's friendly with everyone.'

'No she isn't, just friendly with you. She's constantly seeking your attention, she fawns over you and laughs at everything you say and finds excuses to touch you.'

His lips slowly formed into a big smile. 'You're jealous, aren't you?'

'No, I'm not – I'm threatened and I don't like how she makes me feel. Sexual jealousy is something quite different, I feel like you're belittling my concerns, Nik.'

'Sorry, I don't mean to.' He put down his phone. I finally

had all his attention. 'I just think she's a friendly, sometimes flirty girl – she isn't interested in an old man like me.'

'And you aren't interested in her?'

'So you are jealous.' He leaned back, smiling, clearly getting a kick out of this.

'No, I'm not at all,' I replied, irritated at the way he was making this fit into a narrative that flattered his ego. It was the same with Dimitris, he wasn't really listening to my concerns, just telling me how things were from his perspective. I reminded myself once more to take him down from that pedestal. He never said he was perfect, and at that point I loved him so much I wasn't looking too hard for flaws. Or seeing red flags.

So I threw myself into the wedding and tried to be like Sylvie, think only of pleasant things and leave the darkness behind.

* * *

'I'm loving the orange blossom in the bouquet,' Sylvie said, the night before the wedding, when I stayed over at her apartment. 'It was the right decision. Did you know that orange blossom is a symbol of good luck, wealth, health and fertility?'

'That last one might be a bit of an ask,' I said.

'Sorry, I didn't mean to rub salt in the wound. How about cocktails made from Cointreau and oranges?' she said, moving swiftly on.

'I love a theme,' I smiled. We were at a comfortable point in our friendship when nothing in our lives was taboo, and now I had this wonderful new life I was even beginning to accept there'd be no more children for me. Meeting someone who'd been through the same had been like therapy for me, and she was so giving I often felt she was a better friend to me than I was to her. But giving was her joy, and she had given us the wedding planning as our gift and was just getting so much pleasure from making it the best she could.

I'd insisted on paying for the wedding itself, and being Sylvie, she had spent a lot – much more than I anticipated. I still had plenty left to contribute to the repairs for the vineyard, as long as nothing bad happened back home and I found myself in the middle of a costly court case followed by Dan and Della doing a smash and grab compensation. I'd wanted to pay for the wedding, and though he'd offered, didn't feel Nik should have to pay for everything. He was already providing the venue, not to mention gifting me half of his home.

'Just think,' Sylvie was saying, 'tomorrow night you two will sleep together as man and wife.'

'Yeah, I can't wait.'

'How is everything between you?' she asked.

Sylvie saw her role as wedding planner as a sort of crossover between that and relationship counsellor. I'd seen that at the wedding of Magda and Mike, as much as she'd fussed about the flowers and guests and drinks, she'd been keen to make sure *they* were okay as a couple too.

'Things are wonderful, and I love him, and he loves me, he tells me all the time,' I said.

She folded the laptop. 'But? I know there's a but coming?'

I sighed. 'Oh, he seems a bit stressed, always on his phone, and Angelina's been hanging around him. She's been working at the vineyard recently. I shouldn't even give it a second thought – but it makes me feel uneasy.'

'Have you told Nik how it makes you feel?'

'Sort of, but he doesn't really take it very seriously.'

'You mean he doesn't take *her* very seriously,' she said with a smile. 'I really wouldn't worry about her, he's asked *you* to marry him.'

'I know, but she seems so angry with me.'

'I know she can be a bit stroppy, but Angelina's a sweetheart, you just have to get to know her.'

In the same way Nik saw her as a harmless 'twenty-something kid,' Sylvie didn't see the same girl I did. So there was no point in me telling her, because that was my experience, not hers and it just made it seem like I was trying to persuade Sylvie to dislike her, which I wasn't. 'Yeah you're probably right, I do overthink things,' I conceded. 'I guess I just want everything to be perfect, and everyone to be happy for me.'

'And they are!' she said, like there'd never been any doubt that everyone on Corfu, especially Angelina, was happy for me. Sometimes I would have loved to escape into Sylvie's fragrant world of nice people where everyone loved each other and no one ever did anything evil.

'So, you need a good night's sleep to prepare you for tomorrow,' she said. 'I put lavender on your pillow, and I'm setting my alarm for seven. Who knows what snags we may encounter before we get you down that orange blossom aisle?'

'Indeed,' I murmured.

TWENTY-FIVE

Sylvie's words proved to be prophetic, as on the morning of the wedding, Heather called. I ignored the first few voice-mails, all a variation on the theme of, 'Do NOT ignore this message! You *have* to call me, Alice, you can't hide from this. Please, *please* call me.'

She had no idea it was my wedding day. I'd decided not to tell her as she might have tried to fly over and celebrate with me, or more likely stop me. Besides, as the police now wanted to question me I didn't want to compromise her by telling her where I was or what I was doing. I didn't know at that point just how keen the police were to have that chat, but if they questioned Heather, I couldn't risk her unwittingly leading the police to me.

I was still at Sylvie's, and about to get ready, but this sounded serious, so I ducked into the bathroom, and quietly called her back.

'Oh thank God,' she said. 'FaceTime me.'

'I can't, I'm in the bathroom,' I whispered.

'Alice? It is you, isn't it, Alice? Speak!'

'For God's sake, Heather,' I said quietly. 'What's so urgent?'

'Why are you whispering?' she hissed.

'I told you I'm in a bathroom. I'm at work, I'm working on a wedding, I shouldn't even be on the phone.' The lies came easily by then.

'You shouldn't even be in the *country*!' she replied.

'Okay, okay, you aren't helping. What is it, Heather?'

'The police have been here, turned up yesterday wanting to know where you are. Apparently there's another witness, more evidence and your lawyer says there's every chance they're going to freeze your bank accounts.'

'Shit... no, no. You didn't tell them where I am, did you?'

'No, because I don't *know* where you are. I'm not even sure you're still on Corfu.'

'Good, keep it like that, for now.'

'Thing is, what are you going to do for money if they freeze your building society account? That's where the house money is. It's all you've got to live on, and you've been going through it, haven't you?'

'How do *you* know what I've been spending? I've told you about opening my post. My bank statements are none of your business Heather.' I was horrified. God knows what she'd make of the two-grand wedding dress Sylvie said I just *had* to have, from the posh boutique in Corfu where we'd previously shopped. But more importantly, if the police froze my account, *nothing* would be paid, and I'd have *nothing* to live on. I had to find some way of getting that money out of my account before the police swooped.

'Are you okay in there?' Sylvie was asking. 'It's okay to be nervous on your wedding day, do you need to take something?'

'I'm... I'm fine,' I croaked, sitting on the toilet in my wedding dress, my head in my hands, my life in tatters. 'I've got to go, Heather, don't worry I'll sort this,' I said and turned off my phone. I left the bathroom and walked into Sylvie's bedroom where she was sitting with her laptop. She looked up, concerned, and just seeing her expression made me want to cry.

'What is it?' She put down her laptop.

'Nothing, I'm okay.'

'No you're not.'

'That was Heather, she gave me some bad news.'

'Oh. Nothing to do with the wedding?' Now she looked really worried.

'No, it's stuff back home, a bit of a problem. It's my ex-husband's girlfriend, she's got it in for me.' I still couldn't tell her about the police wanting to question me and that they might freeze my bank account. It made me look so guilty, when I *knew* in my heart I wasn't.

'Oh, babe, is there anything I can do to help?'

'No... it's nothing,' I said, smiling broadly.

She stood up and hugged me, then started straightening my dress. 'I'll leave you to have a few minutes on your own,' she said, and blew me a kiss as she closed the bedroom door. Still sitting on the bed, I caught my reflection in the dressing table and saw an air-brushed version of me wearing my beautiful, pearl-encrusted wedding gown, my hair curled, coiffed and stiff with hairspray. But tears coursed down my cheeks, and the make-up that Sylvie said made me look like a model began to look stained and cracked. My mask was breaking.

In just two hours, I would walk down a flower-strewn

vineyard, to the orange grove, where I would marry the man of my dreams. I'd never been so scared and unhappy in my life and looking down at my beautiful wedding dress prompted fresh tears. It wasn't meant to be like this, it was meant to be light and lovely, filled with friends and family and the buzz of wedding day happiness. But instead I was alone and anxious, and it was all my fault. How foolish I'd been. From a very young age, I'd made some bad decisions, and if I'd learned nothing else, I should have learned that there were always consequences to the things we did. And now, instead of facing the whole, horrible mess back home, I'd run away, convincing myself the investigation would fizzle out. But it hadn't, if anything it seemed to be gaining momentum.

'Right, now come on, let's get your face repaired, we have a wedding to go to.' Sylvie was opening the door, and walking over to the bed, she took both my hands in hers. And as she wiped my tears, retouched my face, and later helped me into her convertible, I felt protected, cherished even.

'Thank you for looking after me, and for not asking too many questions,' I said, as she started the car. 'The truth is, my life is total carnage. I'm wanted by the police in the UK and once those cheques start bouncing the Greek police will be on my tail,' I said.

'Police? Dodgy cheques?'

'No, it's just that the police might freeze my bank accounts.'

She almost went off the road.

'Alice, what the hell?'

'I know, I know. It's a long story, but I'm hoping I can work things out.'

'I don't understand stuff like that, have you told Nik?'

I shook my head.

'Talk to him, Nik has money, he can help you, at least advise you.'

I really had a bad feeling about all this, but she was right, I had Nik now, and he would help me. He was my knight in shining armour and wouldn't let me come to any harm.

I glanced over at her, smiling, then looked back at the sea beneath us, swirling, waiting. One slip on the accelerator, one swerve of the wheel and it would take us. Danger was everywhere, but life was about risks, and you have to take risks and step out of your comfort zone to feel alive. And that day, as we drove along the winding coastal road to my wedding, I'd never felt more alive. Sylvie driving too fast, my veil blowing behind me, and my future ahead. The police would never find me. I'd be safe at the vineyard and live there happily ever after with Nik. But as I soon found out, fairy tales aren't just about princesses marrying their princes, they're cautionary tales, warnings of danger.

TWENTY-SIX

It was mid-August, I'd been on Corfu for almost six months, and still hadn't got used to the intense summer weather. When Sylvie slowed the car down, the heat landed like a huge blanket.

'Come on, let's sort your hair out, it's pretty wind-blown.'

'I like it like this, it's more natural,' I said, I'd hated the feel of hairspray, it felt like someone else's hair.

'Okay, but we need to get you inside with some air-con, we don't want a sweaty bride,' she chuckled to herself at this.

'But I can't go inside, Nik can't see me before the wedding, it's bad luck.'

'It's okay, Angelina's taken him down to the orange grove.'

'Oh?' My stomach flipped, but being an intuitive friend, Sylvie picked up on my anxiousness at this news.

'All the guests are down there too, they aren't alone, love.'

'I didn't... I'm being paranoid, I wasn't thinking—'

'It's perfectly understandable. It's your wedding day, you're allowed to be paranoid – it's a pre-requisite.' She smiled at this. 'Now, I'm going to take you into the sitting room. The heat's done your hair no favours, so we're going to fix it, get a cold drink and chill – literally.'

'I'm so nervous, I feel jittery.'

'It's fine, calm thoughts, think of cool running water. I'll get us a drink,' she said, wandering off, a vision in powder blue heading to the kitchen where the catering staff were preparing the wedding breakfast. The ceremony was just an hour away, and as much as I wanted this, I also wanted it to be over, and be alone with Nik.

I was anxious, and though she was trying to seem calm for me, Sylvie was just as stressed. She was desperate for everything to be perfect and had said to me that morning that mine was the most important wedding she'd ever worked on. 'You're my friend, it's everything to me,' she'd said. 'I feel a huge weight of responsibility, but I welcome it. This is going to be the best day of your life, and I'm privileged to be the one to make it happen.'

Mine and Sylvie's was a sisterly friendship, but unlike Heather, Sylvie gave me all the good vibes and none of the bossy disapproving ones that came from my big sister. I was just pondering this and checking my face in the hand mirror, when I saw something move behind me. As the mirror was small I hadn't seen what it was, so turned the mirror, to see Angelina standing in the open doorway glaring at me.

'Where's Sylvie?' she asked, unsmiling.

'Gone for cold drinks,' I replied.

'Why are you *doing* this, Alice?'

I spun round, and the mirror slipped from my hands, smashing onto the floor.

'I *told* you, go home, leave Corfu. If you don't I promise you—'

'Look, I'm sorry, but you are not doing this on my wedding day.'

'Wedding day?' she smirked. 'That's a joke. You two don't even *know* each other.'

'*Hey!*' Sylvie's voice bellowed behind her. 'What are you girls talking about?' Sylvie was smiling and holding two large glasses.

The younger woman flushed. 'I could have brought you those drinks.'

'Oh that's sweet, but I've got them now.' She handed one to me which I took gratefully.

'So, what were you saying?' Sylvie was smiling expectantly. It wasn't a trap for Angelina, it was a genuine desire from my friend to join in our conversation.

'I was just saying that Alice has seven years' bad luck,' she said, gazing down at the smashed shards of mirror.

'Oh no.' Sylvie's hand went to her mouth.

'You don't want years of bad luck, Alice, especially on your wedding day,' Angelina added slyly.

I glared at her.

'No worries, I'll sweep it up and then I'll throw some salt over my left shoulder to cancel out the evil,' she sneered.

'That's so sweet of you, Angelina,' Sylvie beamed.

I took a large swig of what I thought was cold water that Sylvie had given me, but it turned out to be wine. I hoped after today Angelina would finally accept this marriage and realise that it didn't matter how many threats she made, I wasn't going anywhere. I was home.

'You okay, love, you're a bit pale?' Sylvie said.

I nodded, my mind now racing and nerves jangling. Angelina just seemed to be able to push my buttons. I took another sip, and then another, in the vain hope of calming the raging voices in my head. The wine wasn't exactly thirst-quenching, but it was refreshing, and I needed it. 'This Kouris wine is super strong,' I said, reluctantly putting down the glass.

'Yeah it knocks you out doesn't it, something to do with the tannin and the sea,' Sylvie said.

'Yeah it's lovely but I think I might just forego the wine for the moment. I don't want to fall over at my own wedding, and I'm thirsty from the heat. I need some water.' I went to get up, but she as my self-appointed lady in waiting, stopped me.

'You will not move, I will get your water, madam,' she said, and popped through to the kitchen, returning with a large glass of water, that I downed very quickly.

It was a few minutes before 5pm when Sylvie looked at her watch and stood up. I knew what that meant, and my stomach lurched, causing the wine to make a return trip into my throat. The acidity made me cough. 'Oh you poor thing,' Sylvie was saying, as she bustled around straightening the back of my dress, puffing out the delicate veil around my shoulders.

'I feel a bit sick,' I confessed.

'I'd be worried if you *didn't* – every bride feels sick,' she said with a sympathetic smile. 'Did you feel sick at your first wedding?'

'I don't remember, it's all a blur,' I said, which was true. I tried not to let Dan into my head these days.

'Okay, stand over by the light of the window,' she said, positioning me like a doll, and snapping photos with her phone. Angelina was supposed to have booked the wedding photographer, but apparently he hadn't turned up. Later, I learned from Sylvie that when she finally tracked him down days after the wedding, he told her he'd *never* been booked.

After Sylvie took my photo, she poured us another glass of wine, which I didn't ask for, but knocked back anyway. And then we set out, arm in arm to the orange grove where Nik and our guests were waiting. If only I could turn back time, if only I'd known what was ahead of me, I'd have run that day and never stopped running. But the dress was bought, the tables were laid, the guests had arrived, and I was madly in love. By then it was all too late.

TWENTY-SEVEN

As I walked through to the orange grove, what greeted me was beyond anything I'd imagined. The light was fading slightly, but turning gold, just as it had that first time I'd been there with Nik. The late sun was burnishing the leaves, and transforming the blossom into white clouds in the now dimming orange light that melted over the clearing like marmalade. There was a wistful breeze rippling through the trees as we approached the wooded area, where Angelina and Maria were lighting candles in glass jars.

They both smiled, which was a relief to me because it seemed that however Angelina felt, Maria would come out in sympathy. I didn't need *two* of them sending bad vibes and evil spells my way today.

We just needed to get through the ceremony and Sylvie was with me all the way. This day was as important to her as it was to me, and seeing the carpet of blossoms that she'd had Angelina and Maria lay before me, I took off my shoes. The feel of cool blossoms under my feet soothed me, as I stepped forward into the clearing, kept cool by the canopy of trees. The guests stirred, and turned to look at me, a gentle murmur of approval rising from Nik's family and friends who'd come to celebrate with us. They were all sitting on rustic chairs lined up in rows. Each chair was tied with a huge white satin bow, and a sprig of orange blossom.

Nik was at the pergola – a cloud of white blossom, dotted with oranges and twisting vines. On hearing the guests' murmured approval, he turned around and saw me. His eyes opening wide, the relief evident on his face as he smiled the biggest smile. The celebrant announced my arrival, and asked that everyone stand. I then began what felt like a very long walk towards Nik and marriage, clutching my bouquet of fragrant blossoms, the fine veil over my face the traditional way. The fragrance of citrus was heavy and sweet, and I breathed it in as I walked past the guests smiling benignly. Every single one of them was a stranger. I felt a pang of homesickness for Heather, my nieces and my friends. As I walked slowly past everyone, hoping to work out quickly who was who, they seemed to glance away as I walked by. I was wearing a veil, they couldn't see me, they were probably distracted by the beautiful setting and taking it all in before the ceremony began. I looked forward to meeting them all properly very soon, I loved Nik, I *wanted* to be his wife, and these strangers at my wedding were the family I was yet to meet.

I finally joined him at the pergola, lifting my face to his, waiting for that magical moment when our eyes met. But as I gazed longingly into his eyes, my heart sank. He wasn't looking at me, but through me, his face had barely registered my presence, and the look on his face wasn't admiration for his bride, or love, it was tension. I didn't understand, and suddenly had the awful feeling that I didn't know the man I was marrying.

As the celebrant began the service, we both said our vows, his words didn't sound heartfelt, they sounded scripted, like he couldn't wait to get it over. Was it nerves, or something else? Eventually the celebrant declared us 'husband and wife,' I lifted my veil, and we kissed under a cascade of weeping blossom.

As the photographer still hadn't arrived, Sylvie suggested she take some pictures. 'We have to capture all this,' she was saying, directing us both in different poses. But during this time, the wine and heat were reacting with the mouthfuls of syrupy air I'd been breathing. Nik's demeanour had disturbed me, and I'd begun to feel nauseous again, but tried to put on a brave face. I wanted photos to remember this day and everyone watched in silence as I smiled wanly for the pictures.

'We need to get the guests up for a photo,' I said to Nik, trying to dismiss feelings of doubt about my groom. 'I want to meet them all,' I said. I didn't particularly want Dimitris in the photo, and it seemed the feeling was mutual. Despite being at his cousin's wedding, he'd stayed at the back, lurking in the trees throughout the ceremony looking uncomfortable in a shirt and tie. 'We must have everyone here, where are your mum and sister? I must meet them.'

'Later, darling, we need to get pictures of us first,' Nik replied.

'But, Nik, we need them in the photos.'

I'd bought his mother and sister gifts, and was excited to meet them.

'Us first,' he said with a smile, putting his arm around my waist and posing for Sylvie.

I really wished I felt better for meeting his family, but just kept smiling for Sylvie's camera as she clicked away, and hoping when the nerves died down my nausea would too.

'Kiss each other,' Sylvie called, so I turned to Nik, but he was staring beyond the trees in Dimitris' direction. 'There are cars, people arriving,' he said, puzzled.

'More guests?' I asked, confused. But he didn't answer, just stared, his face white as my veil.

I glanced over at Sylvie who also looked concerned, and was staring at the opening of the grove, where we came in, her hand over mouth.

I heard one of the guests murmur something like, 'Astynomia.' I hadn't a clue what that meant, until I saw a group of police officers emerging through the trees. 'Shit,' Nik said under his breath.

But I gasped. They'd found me. The UK police had sent local officers to arrest me and force me to return to the UK where they would put me straight in a cell. I'd have to leave my new husband, and whatever I'd hoped to find here, I'd run out of time. I stood, frozen to the spot, my head down waiting for them to handcuff me, at my own wedding, in front of everyone. But instead, they said something in Greek, grabbed Nik and put handcuffs on him.

He turned to me, his face white. 'Don't worry, it's all a mistake,' he said. 'I'll be back soon, I'll get my lawyer.'

'You've made a mistake,' I said to the policemen now surrounding him.

I looked at Sylvie who marched over shouting, 'What's going on?' But by then Nik was being pulled away, arguing loudly with them in Greek. I had no idea what he was saying, or why they were taking him.

'Nik, Nik,' I called frantically, as he was manhandled

through the trees. I was close to tears, my guilty conscience about my own police issues caused me to think this was my fault, that there'd been a mistake and they were arresting Nik instead of me. Sylvie was now standing at my side, her arm around me protectively. We both watched helplessly as my new husband disappeared into the trees.

I was sobbing, and looking out at the guests, who seemed more bemused than concerned by what had just happened. They all seemed to be looking back to where Nik had disappeared, like he might suddenly reappear and say it was all a joke. Perhaps they thought it was one of those pranks at a wedding where 'the waiter' suddenly and deliberately, drops his tray of glasses to break the ice and make the guests laugh. But no one was laughing.

'This must be a mistake, it's inhuman. Why would the police arrest an innocent man at his own wedding?' Sylvie said, clutching me.

I couldn't believe what had just happened. 'I don't know. It doesn't make any sense,' I said, scanning the orange grove looking for Nik's family. 'I need to find Nik's mother, and explain that it's all a mistake, she must be distraught.' Nik had a photo of his mother and sister in the bedroom, it's all I had to go on, and I couldn't see any likeness in the guests present. Then suddenly out of the corner of my eye, I became aware of someone standing near the pagoda watching me. It was Angelina, staring over at me like a brooding watchdog, her eyes burning into me as I frantically looked around. I caught her eye, and stared defiantly back at her. I realised that the person I was dealing with was far, far worse than I could have imagined. She was looking right at me, and she was smiling.

TWENTY-EIGHT

In the aftermath of Nik's arrest, I was an absolute mess, but Sylvie was amazing. She was calm, practical and took over in the crisis, and asked the girls to look after the guests while she got me back to the house. I was desperate. What happened had made no sense.

'I reckon it's something to do with his bloody cousin,' she said, guiding me into the sitting room, where she grabbed her phone.

'Could you make out anything the police said?'

'No, not really, but I definitely heard Dimitris' name, and something about the missing women – and another word, "dolofonia"?'

'What does that mean?'

'Murder,' she said absently, releasing a lungful of vape, while punching numbers into her phone.

I felt so helpless sitting opposite her, watching intensely as she desperately tried to communicate with some switch-board. 'Astynomia?' she kept saying, hoping to speak to someone in the police department. It was agonising, my hopes lifted and dashed at each facial expression, the sound of each meaningless word. She seemed to be getting nowhere, as I now paced backwards and forwards like a caged animal, still unable to believe, or understand what had happened.

She was now tapping her fingers on the coffee table, and rolling her eyes at having to wait for someone to come back to her. I couldn't bear it a moment longer.

'Shall I go and find Angelina, she's fluent, she can talk to them in Greek and find out—'

Sylvie just looked at me blankly. 'Angelina? Really?'

'Yeah, we can tell her what to say and she can relay it back.'

'Angelina who's obsessed with the man you just married? You want *her* to translate for us?'

'Okay, you're right,' I said. This intrigued me; so it turned out Sylvie didn't trust her either, she'd just avoided any conflict by pretending everything was fine.

She was clutching the phone, flushed and upset. She'd worked so hard for my day to be special, and it sounds mad, but despite me being the bride, I felt sorry for *her*.

Apparently, someone on the other end of the phone spoke a little English, and with Sylvie's bits of Greek and lots of hand gestures she came off the phone with information, but it was sketchy.

She took a deep breath. 'Okay, he's been questioned, but he isn't a suspect. They can't tell me anything else, they're hoping to release him later today.'

'Oh, thank goodness. Have they arrested Dimitris now?'

She shrugged. 'Not sure, but I imagine they're asking him about Dimitris, what he knows?'

'He doesn't *know* anything. I told you Nik thinks he's

innocent, but said if he ever saw anything that worried him, he'd go straight to the police.'

'It will all be fine, trust me he'll be back here in a couple of hours, like nothing happened,' she added, sounding more like the usual Sylvie, who dusted doubts away like cobwebs. 'I'm so sorry about all this, my darling,' she said, 'we had the perfect wedding day planned, everything was so beautiful – including the bride.'

I couldn't even think about my wedding, it was too painful, and it still didn't make any sense. 'Why would they turn up at someone's wedding, and arrest the groom without any real evidence?'

She rolled her eyes. 'Remember we're not in the UK now, we're in Greece, and anything can happen. Their laws are quite different.' She paused a moment then said, 'I hate to say this, but if you ask me, the real mystery is that someone, somewhere called the police on Nik today.'

'Who would do *that*?' I asked, knowing the answer already.

'Someone who didn't want him to get *married*?' She raised her eyebrows.

I nodded slowly, recalling Angelina's twisted smile after Nik had been dragged away from our beautiful wedding, and we both sat in silence for a few moments digesting this.

'Well, all we can do now is wait,' Sylvie said, standing up. 'I'm now going to do what us English always do at times like this and make us both a cup of tea,' she said, heading off for the kitchen.

In the few minutes she was gone, I relived the arrest, clenching my fists, angry at the police, devastated that our wedding had been ruined. I thought again about Nik's friends and family, and when Sylvie came back in the room with two cups of tea I told her I had to see them.

'Where are all the guests?' I asked. 'I haven't even met his mum or his sister, and they've travelled so far, I have presents for them, in the middle of all this I'd like to offer them some comfort,' I said, as she handed me my cup of tea, which I sipped gratefully.

'Yes, I agree, that would be lovely, but for now the guests have had to leave.'

'Why?' I was upset at this news. 'Who sent them away? Seeing his family and friends would have helped *all* of us, they must be as confused as we are, and we might have been able to explain to them and... I don't know, *feed* them. We have plenty of food, all paid for, all very expensive,' I said, sounding like my sister.

'Yeah, but you wouldn't want a wedding breakfast without the groom,' she offered, looking uncomfortable.

'I assumed they'd be taken to the winery for refreshments, I thought the girls would look after them?'

She was standing in front of me holding her cup, like a little girl who was about to be told off by a teacher.

'I... I'm sorry. Angelina reckoned the police might search the place and I just thought how humiliating it would be for you if the guests were all here. It would be an awful experience for them too.'

I sighed and told myself I was being unreasonable, Sylvie had done what she thought best, and perhaps it was for the best. 'Sorry, I was just disappointed. You're right it would have been mortifying for the police to be trampling through with people here. Thank you,' I said, and in the silence and horrible aftermath, we did what British people often do at times like that: we drank more tea.

Much later, when the house was dark and quiet, Sylvie and I sat outside on the terrace. She'd suggested wine, but I didn't want to be any more confused and out of touch than I already felt and was already groggy from the day.

'Let's have a nice cup of tea instead,' I said, trying to rally.

She smiled at this and went to make us some tea, and then called the police again. I had a faint glimmer of hope that they might say Nik was being released, or that he was on his way home even. 'The good news,' Sylvie said as she clicked off her phone, 'is that Dimitris is now with the police – looks like he's been arrested.'

'Wow! That was quick, I never saw them.'

'I don't know where they arrested him, he may have run off?'

'Well hopefully they'll now get to the bottom of things and find out just what he's been up to,' I said, but Sylvie was looking at me like she had some bad news. 'That is good news, *isn't it?*' I asked, wanting her reassurance, and not quite ready for what she may have to say.

'Yeah, it means they have their man,' she replied uncertainly. 'But I am sorry, love, they're keeping Nik overnight.'

'Christ, what do you think that means?'

'I think it just means they have more questions to ask, and now the *real* suspect's been arrested it makes sense, they can ask Nik about him, can't they?' she said, smiling hopefully. I didn't think she believed this herself, and was just trying to make me feel better.

I wasn't so sure, none of it made sense to me. And I reckoned Sylvie had sugar-coated her police calls when relaying them back to me.

'I'm so sorry.' She put her arm around me. 'Would you like some supper?'

I shook my head. 'Thanks, but I'm not feeling great. I think I'll go to bed,' I replied. The nausea that had hit me at the wedding had returned with a vengeance, and all I wanted to do was be sick or lie down. 'I think I'll go to bed now,' I said, standing up on wobbly legs, 'I just need to rest.'

'Of course,' she said, and walked with me upstairs, her hand on my back, my friend for life.

'Will you stay?' I asked.

'Sure,' she said. 'I'll stay in one of the guest rooms, shall I?'

She came with me into mine and Nik's bedroom, closed the curtains, turned on the lamp, and like a mother, she tucked me in and told me everything would work out. 'You'll see, he'll be back in the morning, with a story to tell, and you guys can spend time together and—'

'Angelina said I was like Alice in Wonderland,' I said. 'I certainly feel like that now, I feel all woozy, like I'm too big for the room.'

She smiled, and putting her hand on my forehead, said, 'Just look out for a grinning Cheshire cat.'

'Thank you for today, you've been amazing,' I murmured, as my head sunk deeper into the pillow. I felt safe knowing she'd be around that night, and hoped sleep would overpower the terrible nausea.

'By morning, you'll feel much better,' she said soothingly, as I drifted off.

* * *

I was woken in the middle of the night with a terrible urge to vomit, and clambering out of bed, only just managed to get to the bathroom in time. I have never been so sick in my life, and afterwards I lay on the bathroom floor, exhausted. After some time lying flat on my back, I managed to get up and stagger back into my room, but now I was wide awake, and with the previous day flooding back like a torrent, there was no way I was going back to sleep. I checked my phone; it was six thirty. Nik should be back today, I thought, hope blossoming in the darkness. I wondered if Sylvie had heard anything from the police. They had her number as a contact, so she'd be first to know. She was always up early, and I was sure, like me, she wouldn't be sleeping in, wanting to start the day and get Nik back home. So I got out of bed, and padded out into the hallway, unsure of which room she'd slept in. There were eight altogether and I opened every door slowly, quietly so as not to wake her in case she *was* still sleeping. Each time, I half expected to see her sitting up in bed, on her phone, vaping – or both. But as I walked into the final room, the bed was still made and there was no sign of her. I realised she may have gone home for a change of clothes and was annoyed with myself for not offering her some of mine, we were the same size after all. But surely she'd have asked if she'd needed a change of clothes?

The only door I hadn't tried was the room where Dimitris slept when he was there. I'd never been in, nor did I want to, but this time, knowing he was with the police, I knew it was safe to check if Sylvie had slept there. After all she wouldn't know it was where he slept. So I went in, and though there was no sign of Sylvie, the first thing I noticed was the bedside drawer, slightly open. Instead of closing it, I took this as an invitation, and walked over to the bed and slowly opened it. I knew it wasn't right to do this. Even Dimitris deserved his privacy, and in truth, I didn't expect to find anything. This wasn't one of Heather's detective shows where the answer was to be found in the open drawer, life was far more random than that.

Inside the drawer were two books in Greek, which from the covers, looked like they were about wine. But tucked underneath them was a beer mat, and what was written on the beer mat made me tremble, the picture of a naked female statue, and the words, 'Aphrodite Bar.' I could almost feel him in the room, and looked behind me, to see if he was there, hiding behind the door waiting to grab me. Even if Dimitris didn't work there, he had been at the bar. The bar where some of the women had visited. I was really scared now and felt so shaky I stood up and was about to close the drawer, when something told me to pick up one of the books. I had no reason to look through either of the books. I wouldn't understand them, even if he'd made notes in the margins. It wasn't random. She was with me that morning in the cool dawn, guiding my hand, begging me to find her. And as I opened the first book, something fluttered from between the pages and fell to the floor. A photograph. It landed face down, and as I kneeled I was afraid to pick it up, dreading what it might be, but knowing in the depths of my soul that this was significant. So I picked it up, and when I turned it around, I heard myself groan. There she was, the original photo, and this time her face wasn't so faded. She was young, with flowers in her hair, and sunshine in her eyes, and the ghost of a familiar smile.

TWENTY-NINE

Later that morning, Sylvie called to tell me she'd left the vineyard at dawn and gone home.

'Yes, sorry I should have offered you something to wear, you had no change of clothes.'

'No you had enough to think about. I had to change out of my wedding suit, so thought I'd go back, get changed and call the police. I have great news, your husband is being released this morning.'

'Oh thanks so much for letting me know.' Relief flooded through me and I felt like sobbing.

'Yeah, I don't know anything, but it seems his lawyer turned up eventually, and it's all been sorted.'

'My legal knowledge is limited, and UK only, but still I felt the Greek police had taken liberties to ambush a wedding and arrest an innocent man.'

She sighed. 'Well, just be glad he's coming home and you can finally have some quality time together.'

'Thanks, Sylvie, you've been amazing,' I said. 'Why don't you come over later once Nik's home? I'm sure he'll want to thank you himself for calling the police and translating, and for looking after me too.'

'I'd love to, but I have back-to-back meetings today – besides, you guys will definitely want some alone time.'

'Okay, tomorrow then, I'll call you?'

'It's a deal.'

I put down the phone, relieved that Nik was coming home. I wanted to see him, but also wanted to tell him about the beer mat and photo I'd found. I'd put them in my own bedside drawer, under my make-up bag, knowing they would be safe there, especially while Dimitris was at the station. I wondered now if we'd ever see him again. I certainly wouldn't be visiting him in prison. Once the police saw the photo surely that would help to convict him? What the hell was he doing with it in his bedside drawer? The Aphrodite Bar was obviously also significant because that's where he'd met some of his victims. I felt tearful at the thought of him touching that young girl. I knew that in drawing the police's attention to the photo, we might be drawing their attention to the vineyard, and therefore to me. But it was worth risking my own freedom to put Dimitris behind bars. I wondered if he *had* killed them, he might tell the police where the women were? I hoped so, the women deserved a headstone, a proper burial, their lives and deaths to be acknowledged.

* * *

Despite all the sadness and fear, I reminded myself that only the day before, I'd got married. And I didn't want to lose sight of the joy of Nik's return. We had something to celebrate, and I was thinking about trying to reconvene with his family and friends. I was particularly keen to meet his mum and sister, and invite them over once he was home. I was lifted slightly by this prospect, telling myself I had to be more Sylvie, and be positive, and celebrate the good things I had in my life. At least we'd got through the ceremony. We were now married, and there was nothing to stop us celebrating that.

But as the day wore on and there was no news, no call from Nik to say he was on his way, I started to feel anxious. All the optimism and hope of earlier began to diminish by the hour. By 6pm that evening, my rather naïve belief that we could build something from the ashes of our wedding day, had died. I really didn't want to spend another night in that house without Nik. Finding the beer mat and photo had been distressing enough, but thinking about what Dimitris might have done, and where he'd done it was making me very nervous. The implications had been twisting around my brain all day, and it was now obvious that Dimitris was involved in the disappearances. So in my despair I decided that instead of waiting for Nik to get home and telling him about the photograph, I would call the police myself. So I found the number and made the call. To my amazement, when I asked the person on the line if anyone spoke English they responded immediately in English.

Relieved, I explained about finding the photograph of one of the missing women in Dimitris' drawer. But instead of the police officer responding with surprise, he said. 'Yeah, yeah, we know about the vineyard.'

'Okay, so in Dimitris Kouris's bedroom, he had the photo hidden in a book.'

'It's not exactly evidence though, is it?'

'Well you have him there now at the police station, he's being questioned, isn't he?'

'I can't discuss that.'

'Well, ask him about the photo, he's the main suspect, surely this is significant?'

'Look, I shouldn't be discussing this at all with you, but Dimitris Kouris isn't a suspect.'

'But you arrested him.'

'Look, I'm sorry I can't discuss this with you.' He was clearly winding this up and about to put down the phone.

'Before you go... Nik Kouris. Is Nik Kouris still there? Have you released him?'

'I'm sorry, I can't discuss someone in custody.'

I knew this must be a lie, they'd told Sylvie earlier that Nik was about to be released.

'I'm his wife, he was arrested yesterday. He was being questioned as a witness,' I pushed.

'Look, lady, I'm sorry, but this is all getting a bit crazy. We get people calling us all the time about the missing women, and unless you have something concrete...'

'I do, a photograph!'

'A photo isn't evidence of *anything*.' He paused. 'Look, everyone on the island, including us – wants to find these women, but people calling in with random theories, trying to pin the disappearances to certain men, pretending to be someone's wife to get information on suspects – well, it isn't helpful.'

'I'm not *pretending*—' I started, but he'd gone.

I wanted to cry with frustration. No wonder they'd never found those women with an attitude like that. Seeing that photo had been so emotive, so distressing I'd had to do something, but had I made things worse? He obviously thought I was just a gossip from Facebook who was trying to get Dimitris arrested. But there was the beer mat, and her photo was hidden between the leaves of one of his books, in his bedside table. There was no other explanation – *was* there?

I was about to call Sylvie and run it by her, when I heard the front door open, and to my deep joy, Nik appeared.

I dropped my phone and just ran into his arms.

'Darling, I'm so sorry, so sorry,' he was saying into my neck as we held on to each other.

'I was so worried. I didn't understand what happened?' I said as we walked together into the kitchen.

'I'll tell you. But first, I need a glass of Kouris Cabernet,' he said with a long sigh.

'Of course.' I took a bottle from the side and poured it into two glasses. It tasted so good, and we both looked at each other in relief.

'So, come and tell me,' I said, and we walked into the sitting room and sat together on the huge corner sofa. As he talked, I thought, *this is all I need. I can get through all the other mess as long as he's here.*

'They arrested me because someone had called them and said I had something to do with the missing women. It was only after I'd accounted for the last five years of my life, they let me go,' he said with a sigh.

'Did they ask about Dimitris?'

He nodded. 'Of course, they wanted to know everything about him, they asked if he ever leaves the vineyard unexpectedly, and if I knew where he was on those occasions.'

'And does he?'

He nodded slowly. 'He goes away for days on end sometimes. Told me he stays with his brother, perhaps he does, but I'm doubting everything now.'

'Christ,' my hand flew to my mouth. 'Do you think they're in it together, him and his brother?'

He shrugged. 'Who knows? I wouldn't be surprised at anything now. I thought I knew him, and all the time I tried to save him, but in the end I was the one who betrayed him. He'll never survive in prison...' He broke down, sobbing into his hands like a child.

'You had no choice, if you hadn't they might still have thought *you* had something to do with the missing women.'

'What are you saying?' He lifted his head from his hands. 'Are you saying I threw my own cousin under the bus?' He said this slowly, like he couldn't believe it.

'No, God no. I wasn't suggesting for a minute that you told the police about him to get yourself off a charge. You simply told the truth, you did the right thing.'

'I feel so bad about snitching on my own flesh and blood. I'm finding that hard.'

'I know, I know,' I replied. He was tearful and exhausted having been questioned by police for twenty-four hours. I knew exactly how that felt.

'I'm so sorry about the wedding,' he was saying. 'You'd been planning it for weeks, it was your special day, and I let you down.'

'You *didn't* let me down. Whoever called the police and told lies about you was the person who let us *both* down,' I said.

'Yes, I'd like to get my hands on whoever did that.'

'Sylvie and I reckon it was Angelina.' I hadn't planned to tell him. After all, we didn't know – it was just an educated guess. But I couldn't help it, all I could see was her smug face beaming at the carnage of my wedding day.

I expected him to be surprised, and probably agree that she was the likely culprit, but he was now looking at me with incredulity.

'Angelina wouldn't do that.'

'She *would*, she's the *only* one who would, she hated the fact we were getting married, she actually *smiled* at me after you were arrested.'

'Not *this* again.' He gazed up to the ceiling like he was trying to stay calm, stop himself from saying too much.

'What do you mean?' I asked, confused.

'You have a real problem with her, don't you?'

'No I don't have a *problem* with Angelina,' I snapped. 'She's the one who has the *problem*. She's jealous, she hated that you were marrying me and tried to throw a grenade at it. I don't trust her, and neither does Sylvie.'

He leaned back and looked at me for a few seconds, a smile slowly forming on his face. '*She's* not jealous. *You're* the ones who are jealous, you and Sylvie.'

'How can you *say* that? I can't believe you *see* me like that,' I said, hurt at his remark.

'What I *see*, is you being insecure and taking it out on Angelina. I also *see* the way you look at her.'

This made me so angry. 'You see *what*?' I stood up and walked towards him. He'd moved to an armchair and I stood over him.

'How dare you make assumptions about me and my feelings. You say I'm treating Angelina badly because you don't see her, you can't see what's going on, but I can. All you *see* is a pretty young girl making eyes at you. I might be insecure, but you're a *fool!*' I was close to tears, rage and hurt swirling through me.

Instead of placating me, and apologising for what he'd said, he just stared through me. 'Go to bed, Alice,' he said dismissively, before taking another mouthful of wine, then reaching for the bottle and pouring himself a second glass. It was as if I wasn't even there, like I was insignificant. And that hurt far more than anything he'd said to me.

I stood there, helpless, tearful, looking at his emotionless face. Then I saw the wine bottle, and thought of Dan. I had to leave the room, take myself away from the confrontation.

'I *will* go to bed,' I hissed. 'Our wedding was ruined because of that girl, but I'm not even going to dignify your ignorant and uninformed comment with a response.' With that, I walked towards the door. Turning back, I realised he hadn't even looked up from his glass.

'Oh and by the way – your cousin is keeping trophies from missing women in his bedside drawer.'

At this he visibly paled. 'Trophies?' he croaked.

'Yes and don't worry, the police know all about it. I phoned them earlier.'

I walked through the door and as he called my name I turned around. He looked like I'd just punched him.

'The police? You talked to the *police*? What... what trophies? Alice, don't be like this. Please come back, you're overreacting.'

'I'm sleeping in the master bedroom tonight, alone, with a chair under the door handle. I don't want you *or* – if the police release him – your cousin trying to get in.'

'Alice, *please*, what trophies?' he called after me again, but I ignored him and ran up the stairs. I was tired and traumatised by everything that had gone on. Once in our room, I propped a chair under the door handle, then lay on the bed, still fully clothed, and cried.

Later, much later, I heard him come up the stairs, there was a gentle knocking on the door. 'Alice, please, I love you,' he tried. I could tell he was drunk by the way he said my name. I didn't respond.

'*Talk* to me, Alice, *please* don't lock me out. I'm your husband now and you're my wife.'

I didn't reply. I didn't move, just continued to lie there staring at the ceiling.

'Tell me about the trophies, I don't know what you're talking about, what did the police say?'

There was a shuffling at the door, and then eventually I heard him padding off to another room and closing the door. I was relieved, but it was tinged with sadness. This was the man I loved, the man I married only yesterday. Was what happened downstairs the result of two tired, stressed people simply bickering over nothing? Or did Nik want a fight, did he mean the nasty things he said? Had I just made another big mistake, only this time a long way from home?

I lay there for a long time, and as daylight slid surreptitiously through the shutters, I eventually closed my eyes, but now the screams were louder than ever.

THIRTY

The morning after I'd stormed to bed, I was awoken by Nik knocking on our bedroom door.

'Darling, it's me, please let me in.'

I checked my phone. It was 9am. I'd had about three hours' sleep, and felt terrible. But keeping Nik out of our room wasn't going to help anything. We had to talk. So I removed the chair from the door, opened it, and went back to bed.

He walked in cautiously and sat on the bed, his hand on the cover, where my leg was.

'I don't know what to say. I am *so* sorry. I'd had a terrible time with the police, and having a couple of glasses of wine on an empty stomach was a mistake. I know I became argumentative. There are no excuses, and you'd be absolutely right not to forgive me.'

'I don't,' I said, glancing at my phone which was buzzing – it was Heather. After a sleepless night, I'd texted her at 5am to tell her I'd got married. I was uneasy about everything, and wanted her to know. It was stupid of me to tell her like that, it was insensitive too. I should have known it would worry her. And now she was texting and calling in full-on stalker mode.

'Your sister?' he asked with a wry smile.

'Yeah, she's probably responding to my text telling her I got married,' I said, before adding, 'but now I'm considering divorce.'

He raised his eyebrows. 'Do you *mean* that?'

'Well, things have been weird, haven't they?'

'Yes, I don't suppose many grooms get arrested at their own wedding.'

'What are the chances?' I mused, leaving out my theory about Angelina. It clearly triggered us both – but in different ways.

'It's just a blip, and I'm sorry, Alice, last night should never have happened, I don't want you to even joke about divorcing me after two days of marriage.'

'Who says I was joking?'

He half-smiled, not sure how to take it. We were husband and wife, but barely knew each other. We'd both seen different sides of each other and were wondering if we could live with that for the rest of our lives.

'I'm sorry,' he repeated, getting up from the bed, and leaving the room. I felt the same abandonment as I had the night before, when he gazed into his glass. Then I read Heather's texts, they were everything I'd expected, negative, warning, no congratulations, just panic. This was topped by the final text though that had arrived just seconds before.

'Just found out from my friend who knows Della that Dan's injuries are worse than we thought. A fractured skull from the bottle, and now a bleed on the brain.'

I never expected that, my heart was in my mouth, I didn't know what to do, and was about to call Heather when Nik returned to the bedroom, kicking the door open with his foot, carrying a tray.

'I want to make it up to you,' he was saying as he walked across the room and placed the tray on the bed in front of me. I wanted to tell him about Dan, I had to, but for now I decided to wait a while, to let him bring me breakfast, to give our marriage a chance.

'Let's put last night behind us,' he said. 'Can we start again? Can this be the first day of the rest of our lives?'

I softened at this. He'd made such an effort with the breakfast tray: strawberries, sliced oranges, croissants and tea, and a sprig of orange blossom in a bud vase. I desperately tried to push the news of Dan away.

'I don't know how to say I'm sorry, but I'll just keep saying it until you forgive me,' he continued. 'I know I was out of order, and I'm not making excuses, but the police interrogation aside – if I'm honest I'm scared of being married.'

As worried as I was about what was going on with Dan, I had to be in the present with Nik. 'So if you're scared of marriage, why did you beg me to marry you?'

'Hear me out. What I mean is, I'm scared of being married, but I do *want* it. After what happened with my first marriage, I can't bear to lose you. This has to work, Alice, because I – I can't live without you.'

I saw tears in his eyes as he stroked my hand, and my heart went out to him.

'Perhaps we're both scared?' I suggested. 'We both desperately want this marriage to work, and last night was just us regrouping, feeling spiky and upset about the police, disappointed about the wedding.'

'Yeah, and that thing you mentioned about Dimitris? That freaked me out too.'

I nodded slowly. 'I'm sorry to lay it on you like that, I was saving it for the right moment, I shouldn't have told you in anger,' I said, and explained about finding the beer mat and the photo.

'Well, if I needed proof, needed to face the truth, then that seems pretty definitive,' he said with a sigh.

'Do you know the girl I'm talking about?' I asked. 'The one in the photo?'

He shook his head. 'No, I haven't really followed the missing women, I don't even like looking at those posters in the street. I find it upsetting,' he said.

'Me too, I find it distressing, and this girl particularly, she was so young.'

'Do you have the photo?' he asked. 'Or have you left it in the drawer?'

I climbed out of bed, and leaned over and opened the bedside drawer where I'd hidden the photo and beer mat under my make-up bag. I returned to the room and showed him the beer mat first.

'Why did you take this?' he asked.

'Don't you remember, the women went to that bar, The Aphrodite – it was closed a few years ago, but it's significant.'

He looked doubtful as he handed it back to me. 'I know there are some unanswered questions, Alice, but going to the police with a beer mat could do more harm than good, they'd think we were mad.'

'Okay, well here's the photo, and I don't care what you say, this is significant.' I held it out to him. At first he seemed reluctant to even touch it, but he took it and looked at it, then handed it back.

'She was pretty,' was all he said.

'*Was?*' I queried. 'She might *still* be pretty?'

'Yeah, you know what I meant.'

We sat in silence for a few moments, both with our own thoughts, then he touched my arm.

'So, Dimitris is still with the police, and who knows what the fallout will be from that, so while we have some peace between police visits,' he half-joked, 'let's just concentrate on me and you for today.'

I agreed, and put the photo under my pillow, and tried not to think about Dan. He was in hospital, presumably he'd recover, but I wondered what that would look like? How much permanent damage might the head injury leave?

'That sounds like a plan,' I said, 'and thank you. This looks like a lovely, if belated, wedding day breakfast.'

He settled on the bed next to me, and I took a slice of orange. It tasted cool and bittersweet. 'Delicious,' I said, pouring myself some tea from the little teapot. It was really thoughtful the way he'd included the single stem of orange blossom, and a little napkin, I was so touched. I leaned over and kissed his cheek. He beamed. We'd both accepted that the previous evening was a blip, and he seemed relieved that I'd forgiven him, which to me meant he cared after all, and that mattered.

'So what shall we do today?' he said. 'Do you fancy going into town and meeting Christos, the lawyer I told you about? Now we're married we need to get our lives in order.'

'Yeah, I would like that, it's just that first, I have a few issues back home that I need to sort as soon as possible,' I said, sighing.

'Okay, anything I can help with?'

'I don't know, but now we're married, I need to tell you.'

'What?'

'It's hard to explain, I'm not sure where to start.'

'Okay.' He looked puzzled, moved further onto the bed, and settled down to listen.

'Thing is – basically, I'm being accused of something, and the police are involved.'

He didn't say anything, just waited for me to continue.

'I don't remember what actually happened. My therapist said that sometimes the brain shuts down painful memories, and she thinks that's what's happened with me. I did the same when my parents died – it was a car crash, and I think I've had PTSD from that, then I had a difficult time as a teenager, then more recently with Dan.'

'Right,' he said slowly. 'What did you *do*, Alice?'

At this point I had to make a decision – did I fob him off with some minor injuries, or tell him the truth?

'It's not good,' I warned him.

'We're married now, and your problems are mine. I need to know what we're dealing with so I can help you.'

It was just what I needed to hear, and what made me decide to tell him the truth. 'The police are calling it assault,' I added uncertainly. 'I told you about bumping into Dan in a supermarket and being faced with his pregnant girlfriend?'

'Yeah, you told me that early on, and it was awful, but what has that got to do with...'

'Hear me out. I saw Dan, then Della, I had a wine bottle in my hand and one in my bag, and somehow the one in my bag ended up smashed, the theory is that I smashed it over his head.'

Nik let out a low groan.

'But I don't remember doing it, I *really* don't. And if I did, why didn't I just hit him with the one in my hand? I was still holding that when I ran from the supermarket.'

He was just looking at me, no doubt confused by all this information being flung at him.

'Thing is,' I continued, 'the "assault" as they're referring to it, can't be seen on the CCTV, because when he'd fallen, he'd grabbed a shelf and brought that down with him, and it hid us from the camera. That's why they couldn't charge me at the time, they have no proof.'

'So what they're saying is you pushed him, then smashed the bottle over his head?'

I cringed again, hearing this. 'That's what the *police* are *surmising*. Problem is, it was *my* wine bottle, I'd just bought it, it's clearly in my bag on the CCTV – I had the receipt.'

He was nodding slowly as I talked. I couldn't guess what he was thinking, but just continued.

'I saw blood and I was probably scared that Dan would retaliate.'

'You were scared he'd *retaliate*?'

I hadn't wanted to get into this, but I'd told him almost everything else. 'He sometimes... he had anger issues.'

'He hit you?'

I nodded. 'Sometimes,' I said, not wanting to dwell on this. 'And that's why I was scared, the last thing I remember that night is him bearing down on me. I waited for him to hit me, and blacked out, it had happened a few times when we were married; it's a post-traumatic stress thing.'

'I had no idea.' He looked so concerned tears sprung to my eyes. Sometimes seeing our own stories through someone else's lens is harder.

'Anyway, I was going to tell you, but now it's looking even worse. I just had a text from Heather, and looks like the bottle I'd *apparently* smashed on his head fractured his skull and caused a bleed on his brain.' Hearing my own words, I could feel the tears forming in my eyes. 'He's a father, he has a baby, Nik.' Tears were now falling down my cheeks.

I thought of the baby scans Dan and I had, along with the dreams that died. I didn't begrudge Della her baby, I'd *looked* for the photos of her scans, the first glimpse of their baby at her breast. I wanted to remember what it was like to love a human you hadn't even met.

Nik reached out and embraced me, and I fell into his arms, resting my head on his chest as he stroked my hair.

'It sounds like whatever happened you were mixed up, confused. You've been through so much, and if you smashed a bottle over his head, surely it was extenuating circumstances, it wouldn't stand up in court.'

'My solicitor reckons it would, Dan's girlfriend is a lawyer, he resented me having half the money from our marriage in the divorce settlement...'

'Oh I see, so if you're convicted, they can apply for compensation?'

'Yes, I believe that's the end game here, but who knows, and I wouldn't blame them if they did.' I pulled away slightly, wiped my eyes and sat up. 'If I did hurt Dan, and he can't work again as a result of what happened, perhaps I should give back my half of the divorce settlement anyway?'

'You'd give your ex your divorce money?' he asked questioningly.

'Yes, I'd hold some back for my two nieces, but I don't need it. I'm staying here, I can earn enough to live on if I do the odd job, help Sylvie out with weddings, help out here at the vineyard?'

He nodded. 'Yeah, that would work. But if it does ever go

to court, that might look like an admission of guilt... a bribe even?'

'Yeah, I hadn't thought of that, and perhaps if he is permanently injured they'll want more than money anyway? Heather reckons they won't rest until I'm in prison?'

He sighed, then got up from the bed, began pacing the room.

'So, do you *still* want to be married to me? There's a hell of a lot of baggage,' I said, as he continued to pace the floor. 'I should have told you all this before. I'm sorry.'

At first, he didn't respond, then I realised he'd been thinking.

'Okay,' he said, walking back to the bed. 'First, you need to get the money out of your account ASAP because the police could freeze your accounts at any time.'

'Okay.'

'I just need to think this through,' he murmured, still pacing.

'I've been *thinking* for days, weeks, months, I can't *think* anymore...' I was tense, a headache was forming right above my eyes. The stress was making me feel nauseous again.

'Let me call Christos, the lawyer I told you about. He deals in financial and corporate stuff. I'll call him now,' he said, as he wandered from the bedroom, clicking out a number and calling.

'Christos, hi there, long time no see? How are you, how's Marina... the kids...?' I heard him say, as he went down the stairs. 'Yeah, yeah good. Look, I have a little favour to ask...' I didn't hear the rest. I went into the bathroom and had a long, hot shower. When I came out of the en suite, he was lying on our bed with a notebook, pen and iPad.

'So, I've spoken to Christos, and made an appointment for us to see him later today. Is that okay?'

I nodded, unable to speak. I was so grateful. Seeing my tears, he immediately climbed off the bed and walked towards me, putting both arms around me.

'Hey, hey,' he said softly. 'We *can* sort this. It probably seems like a really big deal right now, but trust me Christos is the best in the business, and whatever it is we will make it go away... I promise.'

'Can we? Can we *really* make it go away?'

'Yeah. Christos said the key thing is to keep you here, and if you're a resident with a Greek passport, the police can't touch you.'

'That's what I thought. But there's a chance I could be extradited?'

'It would be harder for them to do that if you're a Greek citizen, and we can start that ball rolling today.'

I was so relieved, I suddenly felt my appetite return, and wandered over to the tray on the bed. I ate some orange, then took a sip of tea. 'This tea tastes funny,' I said. 'I didn't notice it before, but it's got a really weird flavour.'

'Perhaps it's because you're eating oranges, that can affect the taste?'

'Maybe.'

'It's Earl Grey, isn't it?'

'I don't think so.' He rolled his eyes. 'I *told* her to make it with Earl Grey leaves.'

I was suddenly prickly again, I thought he'd made the breakfast himself. 'Told *who*?'

'Angelina,' he replied, continuing to scroll through the iPad.

'Was Angelina here?'

'Yeah, she was here earlier to clean. She said it was her wedding present to you, that you needed a break from domesticity. And she insisted on making you breakfast. Even *you* have to admit that was *kind* of her, wasn't it?' He was looking up at me, and I couldn't decide if he was offering me an olive branch or trying to start another fight. Surely he knew how this would make me feel? But I gave him the benefit of the doubt, and putting down the cup of the now lukewarm, weird tea, I smiled and said, '*Very* kind,' as the bile rose up in my throat.

THIRTY-ONE

Before I had a chance to leave the house to go and meet with Nik's lawyer friend, Heather had called and texted me several times. As I suspected, she wasn't texting to congratulate me on my nuptials. No, her various messages were based in and around the core belief that the only reason my new husband had married me was for a passport. It didn't do much for my self-esteem.

'Am I so repulsive that someone would only marry me for a British passport?' I said to Nik, as we drove into town later.

'Why do you say that?'

'Heather is and I quote "highly suspicious" of any Greek man who marries a woman over forty in a rush. She thinks you want dual nationality.'

He laughed at this. 'I already *have* it.'

'I know, and I'll take great pleasure in letting *her* know that when I call her.'

He smiled, and glanced over at me. 'Anyway, you should say to your sister that perhaps it's *Nik* who's being taken for a ride.'

'What do you mean?'

'Well, *I'm* the one with property, the business. *You* might only want me for dual nationality – and a vineyard?'

'Nik, you know I would never—'

'I know. I'm only joking,' he said, but I wasn't so sure. I wondered if, by telling him the truth about the police and Dan's injuries, he now saw me in a different light. Did he not trust me anymore? We drove the rest of the journey in silence, until we arrived outside Christos's office in Corfu Town.

Stepping into the searing heat of a Greek afternoon, we headed for a small, white office block set back from the road. Once inside we were directed upstairs to Christos's office, where he greeted us at the top of the stairs.

'Hey, good to see you, Nik,' he said, smiling and hugging him. 'And the new bride,' he said, alighting on me. 'Congratulations, both of you, I hope you'll be very happy.' He shook my hand and led us to his office.

He took the seat behind his desk, and we sat opposite. I was nervous. Christos seemed warm and welcoming, but I dreaded his reaction when we told him why we were there. I explained about the charge, the possible court case, and the freezing of my accounts while Christos listened intently, his chin resting on the back of his hands. His only reaction to my story was a raising of his eyebrows now and then, so I just kept talking uninterrupted, and when I'd finished, he took a deep breath.

'Well, we have some issues here, but nothing we can't overcome,' he said, in a thick Greek accent. He made some notes, while I glanced nervously at Nik, who gave me a reassuring wink.

'Okay,' Christos said slowly, lifting his head from the

notes. 'So, the main issue here is the investigation by the UK police.' He stood up, pushed back his chair and walked towards the window. 'I have several contacts in the UK police force...' he began, while staring out of the window.

I was a little concerned by the man's demeanour, that he might not be completely above board, and this didn't sit right with me, I was already in enough trouble. Was he suggesting a bribe? 'I just want to stay here with Nik and live happily ever after,' I said. 'But I don't want to break the law,' I added, which was probably hilarious to him given the mess I was in.

'Of course, of course. It's all legal, that's why you need me, a lawyer.'

'Exactly,' Nik said. 'She needs the proper, legal paperwork, and I know you can get that for us Christos.'

'I can, I can.' He nodded. 'I can also get a Greek passport.'

'Great, and can I apply in my *married* name to avoid anyone finding me?'

'So yes, the paperwork, the passport, it will help to keep you here, and make you harder to find – but no guarantees.'

'No guarantees?' I asked, dismayed.

'No guarantees,' he repeated, with a warning voice, while shaking his chubby index finger at me.

'I can't stress enough how much Alice needs to stay here,' Nik cut in. 'I want her here with me, she's my wife and I love her—'

Before he could finish, Christos cut in. 'Buy property.'

Puzzled, I glanced at Nik, who looked equally surprised at this suggestion.

Christos wandered back to his desk and made some more notes.

'If you're foreign but own property here, there's less

chance of extradition.' He gave a knowing wink at this. 'The Golden Visa scheme grants a five-year residency permit to foreigners investing in property in Greece.'

'Okay.'

'I can't stress how important it is to get that money out of your account as soon as possible,' he urged. 'But the *other* criteria... is *no* criminal record.'

I groaned.

'However,' he wagged his fat finger at me again, 'there is, as yet *no* criminal record, you've not been convicted.'

'Oh, right.'

'Yes right, I'm a clever lawyer, I know how it works,' he said, moving back into the centre of the room, dropping his pen on the desk like he was dropping the mic. 'So, my advice to you is to buy property, anything above €250,000 as *soon* as possible. This will free the money from your bank, if the police freeze your accounts, you'll be safe to stay here for ever and ever.'

'And that's it, no red tape, no hoops to jump through?' Nik asked.

He shook his head. 'We will do it all, health insurance, passport and visas – all fast-tracked. I may have to pay a little extra here and there, if you know what I mean?' Another wink.

I didn't care how much we had to pay him, I wanted to kiss him on the face right there and then. This man was offering to take away all my problems and making it possible to stay in the place I loved with Nik Kouris. I looked across at Nik and we smiled at each other.

'So how much would your fee be for doing this?' I asked.

'For keeping you here, processing the visas – doing the legal work for the property purchase – saving you from a prison sentence?' He chuckled at this. 'I would say a ballpark figure of... Remember I have to pay some high-ranking people in the embassy to get these fast-tracked?'

My instinct was correct, this was dodgy, but was it actually illegal? Probably – but what else could I do?

'So how much?' I heard myself ask.

'Ballpark we're looking at about €50,000 – up front as I may have to smooth the way with officials at the embassy.'

I gasped. I hadn't expected it to cost so much, and glanced over at Nik who shrugged.

'Up to you, darling,' he said. 'It's a lot of money.'

What choice did I have? I was likely to lose everything if I didn't do *something*. I wasn't one hundred per cent sure the police hadn't already frozen my account and they were waiting for me to try and access it. If so, they would know where I was. Again, I had little choice, so I didn't waste any more time, and paid by direct transfer from my phone, holding my breath as I did.

'Well, everything seems to have gone through,' I announced, wiping the sweat off my upper lip after a few tense minutes.

We all shook on it, and left Christos's office, walking back into the sunshine. I felt like the weight of the world had been lifted from my shoulders and suddenly it felt like I'd bought back my future. But at what price?

THIRTY-TWO

Having handed Nik a car crash, he'd really helped me out, and now everything seemed to be going smoothly. I still wasn't convinced the passport and papers were completely above board, but if it cost a bit extra for someone to push the application through quicker, then it was worth it.

So, with Christos's promise of all the necessary documents within thirty-six hours, a desperate need to get my money out of my bank ASAP, and a guarantee that I could stay, Nik and I set off for the nearest estate agent's.

Nik suggested Adonis Estate Agent's on the high street, which was a family business. 'I trust them, known the family for years,' he said, walking through the door. Once inside we were greeted by Clio, a very beautiful Greek estate agent who Nik greeted like a long-lost friend. Her make-up was thick, lashes black and luscious and her hair incredibly long and shiny. Her eyebrows looked painted, and didn't move when she spoke. Clio had the kind of beauty I'd only seen on Instagram with a filter, almost too perfect to be real.

'How's your dad?' he asked.

'My father is well, thank you,' she replied, in an accent as thick as her brows. 'And yours?'

'Oh, he isn't with us anymore,' he replied awkwardly. I was surprised she didn't know that his father had died six years before, and felt sorry for Nik having to explain.

'A beautiful seafront villa in Agni,' Clio started, reeling off the list of properties available to buy. 'A beachfront estate in northeast Corfu, a seafront property in Dassia... erm, a unique and rare opportunity to purchase luxury seafront property with access to a secluded bay...'

I'd been devastated just hours before, but Christos's advice had turned my life around. 'We could divide our time between here and the vineyard?' I said, resting my finger on a white domed villa overlooking an impossibly blue sea.

'That would be great,' Nik replied. 'I could take the paperwork there, now we're married we should spend more time alone together,' he added quietly in my ear.

We continued to sift through the stunning, glossy photos of beautiful farmhouses, enormous villas perched on the side of mountains, beautiful town houses with ornate Greek interiors. I would have happily bought any one of them to live happily ever after with Nik.

'I need to buy one that's over €250,000,' I said.

'Okay,' she answered slowly, her plump lips curving as she spread out the photos of properties around the price I'd mentioned. I was amazed at how much I could afford. 'Wow, something like that would be millions in the UK,' I exclaimed, looking at a large, contemporary home by the beach, all white stone and glass.

'Without the weather too,' Nik murmured, as he read through the small print. Then, I saw it – and it looked like a home to me. A gorgeous, traditional house in Corfu Town,

Venetian style, pastel pink, with high ceilings, big pictures on the walls, a contemporary look, but not cold and minimalist like some of the homes by the sea.

'This one would be lovely,' I said to Nik.

He nodded. 'Yeah, that would be nice. We could enjoy a social life there too. I worry that after a while you might feel cut off in the mountains.'

'Yes, I love the rural life, but once I have Greek citizenship, I won't need to worry too much about lying low,' I murmured to him. 'How much is this one?' I asked.

'These is five,' Clio said in broken English and held up five fingers.

'Oh, €500,000?' I asked, a little dismayed.

'Yes,' she said like I was being stupid.

'I only wanted to pay €250,000.'

'Ahh. You said over?'

'Yes, sorry, I meant above, but not too much more.'

'Okay,' she said slowly, 'I have the two-fifty,' she replied, laying down a few photos of other houses out in the wilds of Corfu.

'That's not quite what we're looking for,' I said with a smile. 'Do you have anything in the town?'

'Sorry, no we don't,' she replied, pulling her mouth down at both sides, while making eyes at Nik.

Another customer walked in, and she excused herself, so with her out of earshot, I turned to Nik. 'Shall we go and look somewhere else?'

'There isn't anywhere else I'd *trust* to be honest. Clio's grandfather sold my grandfather the vineyard, that's how long this company have been here, and I feel like anywhere else you'd be ripped off because you're British. They'd see you coming.'

Once she'd finished with her customer, Nik turned to Clio. 'Would you give us a reduction for cash on the house in the town, Clio?'

She pulled a doubtful face, and shrugging slightly, punched some numbers into her phone with bejewelled fingernails, and had a long conversation in Greek with someone on the other end.

'How much is your maximum?' Nik asked me quietly.

'I don't want to spend everything from the settlement, I need to give my nieces some money, and would still like to offer something to Della for the baby if I can.'

'Up to you, darling, but like I said, you will probably be incriminating yourself if you do.'

'Perhaps I could do it anonymously?'

He raised his eyebrows. 'You're very sweet, but be very careful, you don't even remember hitting him with the bottle,' he said under his breath.

'You're right but...'

'Look, even if you put *all* your money into a property here, it's not like you're losing it, this is an investment. And if you decide you want some money a few years down the line for Della or your nieces, you just sell. And at a profit – so don't see this as a spend, see it as a savings scheme.'

He had a point, everything was happening so quickly I wasn't seeing things clearly.

'It's such a lot of money to spend in one go though...'

'Yes, it's a lot of money for the police to freeze too,' he warned.

'You're right.'

'How much do you have in your account?'

'About £480,000,' I replied, realising how much the

wedding and living expenses had made a dent in the settlement.

'That's about €550,000 in euros,' Nik said to Clio.

'Okay, so you can go a lot higher than €250,000?' she asked.

I thought for a little while. 'Yes I can, but €450,000 is the maximum I can afford to pay. I've already paid Christos €50,000 so if I spend that much on a property, I'd have almost nothing left. But I guess I could find a full-time job.'

'We already talked about that, you can work some of the weddings and help at the vineyard. You could take tours, do wine tastings, at the moment we all muck in, but that could be *your* job.'

'I'd love that,' I said.

'I think it's wise decision you're making, to spend the maximum amount you can,' Clio remarked. She seemed to appear from nowhere. 'Would you like to visit the town house?' she asked.

'It's €500,000, I can't afford that,' I said.

'Don't worry, if you like it, we can haggle, and if they won't budge, I'll see if I can contribute, after all it's going to be *ours*,' Nik reminded me.

Fifteen minutes later, we were wandering around the beautiful town house, seduced by its Greek splendour. The interior was as fabulous as the marketing photos suggested, and I was totally in love with the idea of living there.

'I have to have it, Nik,' I murmured, running my palms along the smooth walls, admiring the furniture, and the way the current owners had decorated.

So we called Clio together, and put in an opening offer of €450,000.

* * *

I didn't sleep that night worrying about the visas, the passport, and if the vendors of the town house would accept our offer. Clio had said it was low, but she would certainly make the offer on our behalf and get back to us as soon as she could. But it had been late when we called and she hadn't got back by 11pm, so we'd gone to bed, and Nik slept silently beside me seemingly untroubled by the maelstrom in my head. But it was just after midnight when I heard a noise downstairs. Scared, I lay there for a few minutes just listening, and when I realised someone was definitely downstairs, I shook Nik awake.

Still half asleep, he staggered from the room and down the stairs to see what was going on. I went to the top of the stairs, prepared to go down and support Nik if there was some trouble. After a few minutes I heard raised voices. It seemed that Dimitris was back from the police station, and was standing in the doorway talking very loudly in Greek, until eventually Nik let him in. I went back to our room, where Nik joined me ten minutes later.

'Why have they released him?' I asked, my heart sinking.

'Not enough evidence I guess.'

'Where is he going to sleep?'

'In his room.'

'No, Nik, he can't.'

'He refused to leave, says he's going nowhere.'

I groaned, and pulled the covers over me. I was in hell. Just when things had started to look up, and everything was working out, Dimitris was free again. Free to roam the island looking for women, defenceless women who had no one to protect them, no one to look for them. I was back on my quest to find out their fate, and reaching under the pillow, I took out her photo. It was dark, I couldn't see her, but it was enough to hold her close to my chest, to keep her safe, even though in my heart I knew it was too late. Then I fell asleep, as always, to the sound of women screaming.

THIRTY-THREE

The next day, I woke up to find Dimitris gone from the villa.

'He was a bit of a mess to be honest,' Nik said over coffee and toast. 'I think the police gave him a hard time so he's gone to spend a few days on the coast with his brother.' I remembered Nik telling me that it was quite isolated there, and I wondered again if his brother was part of this.

'I know you told the police that he visits his brother, did you give them his address, I just have this feeling that his brother's house might have some answers?'

'Yeah, they have all the details. They said they'd be paying him a visit.'

'Good. I can't believe they just released him like that,' I said.

He took a long breath. 'Look, if and when he *does* come back, I don't think you should be on your own with him.'

'Sylvie said the same,' I murmured, chewing on my toast, a shiver snaking through me.

'Well, on this occasion, *Sylvie* might just be right. I don't *know* anything, I've had my doubts, but everything seems to be pointing to one thing. And now, you finding that photograph, it's just made me realise that at best he's disturbed and has erotic fantasies about young women. Well, *women*. And at worst, he's... well at worst he's responsible for the disappearance of at least nine – possibly ten.'

'Those are just the ones we *know* are missing, I think there are probably more than that,' I said, pouring us both a second coffee from the cafetière.

'Yeah well, I don't want to think about it.'

'I know, it's horrible.'

'So, what do you say about us getting someone to stay here with you when I have to go away?'

'I'll be fine, you're here most of the time.'

'Yeah but if I'm out in the vineyard or away on wine business it would be good to have someone here, and you won't ever be alone with him. We could bring someone in, a sort of live-in cleaner?'

'Live-in?' I suddenly guessed where this might be going, while desperately wanting to be wrong. 'Did you have anyone in mind?'

'Not really, but I know Angelina would be keen.'

'Oh, *do* you?'

He rolled his eyes. 'Don't be like that. She's having a few issues with her landlord at the moment, and she asked if I knew of any rooms to rent. I just thought...'

My face was burning, every fibre of my being was against this. 'No, no, oh and... no.'

'Okay, calm down, it was just a suggestion.'

'Well forget it. I'm perfectly fine here on my own, and if Dimitris is here and you aren't I'll stay in our new place in town.'

'That may take a few weeks before we can move in, what about just letting her stay here for now?'

'Oh, you mean she'd move in today? Why didn't you say?' I said sarcastically, before adding, 'No thanks.'

'She's offered, she's as worried about you as I am.'

'I can imagine.' I rolled my eyes. 'So the two of you have been having cosy little chats, have you?' I asked, knowing I sounded like a psycho.

'Don't start, Alice,' he groaned.

'Nik, I don't appreciate you discussing me with... with *her*, and I certainly don't appreciate her offer to come and babysit me. Quite frankly of the two of them, I'd rather take my chances with Dimitris, he has the sweeter nature!' I stood up and began clearing the table, slamming our breakfast plates on top of each other, to confirm my fury.

Nik didn't answer. I hoped this meant he was getting to know me, and learning which buttons *not* to push. I stomped into the kitchen with the breakfast things, banging pots and pans and slamming cupboard doors. I think he got the message and was soon locked away in his office while I cleaned the kitchen with vigour and waited for the phone to ring.

I didn't have to wait long. I had a call from Christos later that day to say everything was now being fast-tracked; the passport and paperwork was coming from Athens and would be with me in a couple of days. He gave me a confirmation number that I could use with the estate agent to prove I had all the relevant paperwork, and the house purchase could go through.

Then Clio called and said the vendor had accepted my offer, apparently they were moving with work to Athens and needed a quick sale. She said that despite slightly higher offers being made by other buyers, they'd chosen me because I was paying with cash, and it would be a quick exchange. She then congratulated me and gave me the details to pay directly to the estate agent's. They would take their commission then pass on to the owners once the deeds and contracts were all with us. Meanwhile, Christos was waiting at his end to do the legal checks and make sure the sale and transfer went through smoothly.

I wasted no time, every day that went by was another day closer to the police freezing my account, and then it was game over for my life on Corfu. So, I perched on a stool at the kitchen island, held my breath, and dialled the bank.

After lots of number pressing and waiting in queues and listening to awful music, someone answered.

I nervously asked if I could transfer the €450,000 from my account to the estate agent's account. 'Then I'd like to withdraw whatever's left and close my account,' I said.

I was expecting some resistance, some deep discussion about why I wanted to leave the bank, and what could they offer me to stay, but to my deep relief, the guy on the line just agreed to do everything I asked. I wanted this done instantly, time was of the essence.

'Okay,' he said very slowly, 'can I just check that again?'

'Yes,' I almost snapped.

'Right, so you want €450,000 transferred directly to account number...' he reeled off the number while my heart thudded.

I just kept saying, 'Yes please,' and 'yes thank you,' when what I really wanted to do was scream down the phone. 'JUST DO IT!'

Eventually, he seemed to have made the transfer, despite taking an achingly long time, but just as I was about to thank him and collapse on the kitchen floor, he suddenly said, 'Oh hang on a minute, I just need to check something.'

I wanted to be sick. I'd got this far, please God there wasn't some red flag on there. What if the police had been waiting for me to call the bank and my number was now being traced? What if they'd told all the bank tellers to call them if I phoned? I started to shake, and just when I was about to click the phone off and run for the hills, he came back.

'Oh there seems to be something...' he said very slowly.

Christ no! If I hadn't been sitting down, my legs would have given way.

'Yes?' I croaked.

'Did you say you'd like me to *close* your account?'

'Yes,' I said weakly, it was almost inaudible.

'Your final balance is £44,000, so you'd like to transfer that too?'

'Okay, thanks,' I tried not to cry with relief.

I'd miscalculated the pounds to euros, so was better off than I'd thought.

I gave him the details of Heather's savings account, and asked that he transfer it there.

Later that day, we drove back to the estate agent's in Corfu Town, my heart was in my chest. The guy at the bank had seemed so laid-back, had he actually *done* it? Had the money been transferred? Was it safely invested in the new property? I couldn't rest until we had absolute confirmation everything was going through. There was always the outside chance that the vendors had changed their minds, or had the police got to my account in the interim.

My chest was tight, and I was too warm, even with the car air-con at full blast.

'It'll be fine,' Nik was saying, but I wasn't going to rest until I knew the money had landed with Adonis Estate Agent. By the time we pulled up outside the office, I thought I was going to throw up. Nik had to help me from the car, and held my hand as we walked to the office.

We walked in, and there was Clio standing in front of her desk, with a solemn look on her face. My legs were weak, and I thought I might collapse from stress. This didn't look promising at all. Then, just when I couldn't take another second of suspense, she moved aside, to reveal a bottle of champagne and three glasses. 'It's yours, Mrs Kouris,' she announced. I could have kissed her.

We left with me clutching the details of the property and Nik delighted that his wife was now securely on the island.

'I'm so happy,' he said. 'I can now relax knowing I'll be waking up with you for the rest of my life.' And in the middle of the street, the sun blazing down, my life opening out before me, he kissed me. When he finally pulled away, he said, 'Alice Kouris, you are now a resident, a property owner and my wife. You are never going back to the UK ever!'

Little did I know then how true those words turned out to be, but not in the way I'd ever imagined.

THIRTY-FOUR

In my excitement and relief about the money transfer, I felt I could allow myself to relax a little now everything was going through. As Nik drove us back to the vineyard, I called Sylvie to tell her my news.

'Oh my God that's amazing!' she said, which is exactly what I expected. 'A little place in town? Handy for our girls' nights out – or in? So, we need to celebrate, let's meet up in town and have some fizz?'

I glanced over at Nik. 'Oh I'm sorry, we're heading back now, that would have been great. What about tomorrow?'

'Oh no worries, just call me when you're free, I miss you!'

'I miss you too,' I said, aware that Nik was listening, and feeling a bit teenage. 'Hey, I just had a thought,' I said, glancing over at Nik again. 'Why don't you come over for supper tonight?'

'Oh, I'd *love* to, but are you sure? I don't want to be a gooseberry.'

'You wouldn't be, it'll be lovely to see you.'

'Well, if you're absolutely sure?'

'Yes, absolutely. Shall we say 8pm?'

I clicked off the phone and turned to Nik. 'You don't mind, do you? She wanted to meet up and celebrate.'

'*Celebrate*? Why, it's not *her* house purchase?'

'No, but she's *pleased* for me, for *us*,' I added, glimpsing his irrational resentment for Sylvie again. 'You really need to meet her socially,' I said. 'She's lovely and she's been a good friend to me since I came here.'

'Yeah I know, I just think she's a bit of a gossip.'

'She's no more of a gossip than I am,' I said.

'That's my point,' he joked.

'If it wasn't for Sylvie, we wouldn't have *met*,' I reminded him.

'Okay, I forgive her, she can't be all that bad if she's the reason I met you,' he chuckled.

Returning home that afternoon, I felt like nothing could bring me down. Even Heather's persistent texting wasn't as annoying as usual. I just responded by saying, 'Everything is under control this end, stop worrying.'

I was in such a good mood, knowing we'd soon have a bolthole to escape to that if Dimitris had been hanging around scowling, I would have smiled at him. I couldn't stop thinking about that gorgeous house, how I'd furnish it, the shades I'd paint the walls. The ways I could reflect the Venetian heritage in the colours and furniture.

Later, Nik and I sat in the kitchen drinking cold white wine and eating salty olives from our own olive press. 'Thanks for everything, Nik,' I said.

'Why are you thanking me?'

'For understanding my situation, not judging, for finding someone to help me... for marrying me, and letting me live in this beautiful house.' I kissed him.

'I'm your husband, I told you we're a team. Besides, you'd do all those things for me,' he said, kissing me back.

With everything that had happened, his arrest, then me locking him out of the bedroom the night he came home, and me being exhausted and slightly nauseous with stress most of the time, we still hadn't had sex, and we'd been married for four days now. I knew that nothing would happen if I put him under any kind of pressure, so had just trusted in the process and the fact that we were two people who were in love, and attracted to each other. Surely that was the place to start and at some point, something would happen? And now, as the kissing became more passionate, I started to believe that this was the moment. Our lives were back on track, Dimitris wasn't here and the stars were aligning.

I could barely take in how much my life had changed, and this had crystallized for me the night when Nik told me to take off my clothes. Dan would also tell me to take off my clothes, and sometimes we'd make love and he'd be kind. But sometimes, after I'd taken off my clothes he'd look at me, and walk away, leaving me humiliated and naked in the middle of a room. And when Nik stood in the dark, watching me, I instinctively expected this to lead to humiliation and abandonment. But Nik didn't hurt me or abandon me, he just watched. He didn't even *touch* me, and yet it was thrilling, it was wonderful. And afterwards there was no sting in the tail, no passing, devastating comment about my body.

I'd lived far too long with Dan, and been poisoned by his quiet, unseen cruelty. But here was Nik, the antidote who could heal me, who thrilled me more than Dan ever had, without even touching me. And I wanted him to excite me again, but this time, I wanted *all* of him, and it was clear he felt the same. Just then, the front door opened, and in walked Dimitris.

'Fuck,' Nik murmured under his breath.

I quickly grabbed our dirty cups and plates, and headed for the kitchen, out of sight of Dimitris. Suddenly sex was the last thing on my mind.

Minutes later, Nik joined me in the kitchen. 'His brother wasn't well, so he came back,' he said quietly. 'He's okay, not manic, just a bit low.'

Unsmiling, I raised my head in acknowledgement of what he'd just said. 'Shit timing.'

'Sorry, I'm really sorry, Alice.'

'Not your fault.'

'I know but... can we finish what we started later?'

'Only if we put a chair under the door handle,' I said, half-smiling. 'There are three of us in this bloody marriage.'

He smiled back, kissed me on the back of my neck, and left. 'Off to check the vines,' he called to me and waved, as I watched from the kitchen window, lifting my hand like a wave. He and Dimitris wandered off together, through the garden and on through to the vineyard, and I tried to be positive and look forward to Sylvie coming over.

Once I'd stacked the dishwasher I checked the fridge, something I should have done *before* I'd invited her to supper. I found hummus and pitta, a plate of moussaka, some cold chicken and all the ingredients for a Greek salad. There was even a jar of mandolato on the side, that I would serve with coffee afterwards.

I gathered the salad vegetables, thinking how this now felt like home. This was me living my life, I wasn't a tourist or a visitor, I belonged. Clutching the vegetables to my chest, I turned away from the fridge and he was there, right behind me. Dimitris.

I gave a surprised yelp, and a tomato fell from the salad pile in my arms. We both watched it fall and splatter to the ground, and I was instantly reminded of that cold wet, February night when my life changed. I saw the red wine running in rivulets along the floor, mixing with the rainwater and wine and smashed glass. And now I was scared to pick up the smashed tomato, like a shattered head on the stone floor, seeds and pulp smatterings of brain. I thought fleetingly of Dan, and wanted to cry.

Dimitris was now looking at me intently. I'd never seen him this close up before. His face was sun-beaten, rows and rows of wrinkles criss-crossing his cheeks, and forehead. His brows were bushy and unkempt, his hands brown and gnarled. I couldn't stop staring. The screaming was loud in my head now.

Where the hell was Nik, had he done something to him?

He was glaring into my face, his gnarled hand reaching out towards me. I instinctively stepped back, I couldn't translate what he was trying to say into words or language of any kind. The sounds were forced out, as if they were coming from his stomach, not his throat. Only one side of his face seemed to move. He was trying to scare me off, but when I stood there, rooted to the spot, he heaved out again. 'Go... go.'

'Nik,' I called, then louder, '*NIK!*'

My instinct was to run right out of there, but things were different now. Dimitris was still some creepy guy hanging around the kitchen, but he was also my husband's cousin. He'd just been released by the police, and he wasn't going anywhere. I had to live with this.

'No. I'm not leaving,' I said as firmly as I could. 'I'm Nik's wife now.' I smiled nervously, thinking of the women, and the photograph of the young girl in his bedside drawer, and wanting to scratch his eyes out.

He put his head to one side and turned slightly like he hadn't quite heard.

'I want us to be friends,' I offered, smiling while holding my breath. I don't know why I did it, perhaps I wanted to test him, but I moved forward to bend down and pick up the tomato. I knew if he was going to hit me with a hammer, or jump on me, now would *be* that time, but I thought perhaps if I showed him kindness, not just fear, it would endear me to him, and I'd be safe. He might even trust me enough to tell me things. I cupped my hands, gathering the tomato pulp, seeds and skin, and standing up, still holding the mess, I said, 'I need to clean the floor now, so if you don't mind moving?'

He stepped towards me, and I tried not to recoil, especially when he moved closer, all the time eyes unblinking and wide, staring at me. Then in silence, he slowly reached out his left hand, towards the contents of my hands. Assuming he was going to take the ruined fruit from me and put it in a bin, I offered him my still cupped hands. Without taking his eyes from mine, he retrieved the bulk of the tomato in one hand and squeezed, raising his fist for me to see the red dribble oozing through his clenched fingers. In the silence, I gasped.

'Why are you doing this?' I heard myself cry. He was clearly threatening me.

I could see the glint of a kitchen knife in the block, and took a step towards it. But as I did, he stepped towards me.

'Don't come any closer!' I said, moving backwards, keeping my eye on him while dropping the salad vegetables onto the counter, and pulling the knife from the block. Then I held it, the pointed tip in his direction.

'I *will* protect myself,' I said.

At this, he seemed to get the message that I was scared and angry and if he took one more step towards me, I would use the knife. He stopped moving forward, and we stood facing each other, frozen in a tableau, until I slowly manoeuvred myself to behind the kitchen island, which was now between us.

Just then the front doorbell rang, and I moved out of the room backwards, watching him and holding the knife as a threat. I stopped in the kitchen doorway. 'I will use this,' I yelled, waving the knife, and in that moment, he seemed to realise he was defeated, and slowly lumbered away through the patio door and out towards the vineyard.

I took a moment to get my breath, my heart was beating wildly, and when the doorbell chimed again, I jumped. I was still clutching the kitchen knife, when I opened the door to a very excited Sylvie, whose face dropped when she saw it.

'Oh my *God*, what are you doing with that?'

'Come in,' I said, hugging her, tears rolling down my cheeks. I was so angry with Dimitris for making me feel like this.

She handed me two bottles of expensive white wine. 'Looks like you might need to open one of those immediately!'

'Thank you. I'm sorry, I'd wanted to welcome you like the chatelaine of the house, sweeping through the lovely rooms, supper ready, a glass of chilled white waiting,' I said. As she followed me through the long hall, I glanced around quickly to make sure he hadn't returned, before entering the kitchen at the back of the house.

'Sorry!' I said anxiously. 'It's been a bit of a day.'

'Stop apologising. But please put the knife down, unless

you're planning to stab me? If you are, can you please wait until I've had the grand tour and a nice glass of that Chablis,' she said, putting both bottles on the island, while I tried to find the glasses. 'So much for chatelaine – you don't even know the way around the kitchen.'

'There are so many options, this kitchen's enormous, it'll be years before I know where everything is.'

'So, can we talk about the knife?' she asked, putting her beautiful tomato-red Hermes handbag on the kitchen island and climbing elegantly onto a stool.

I rolled my eyes. 'Oh, it was Dimitris—'

'You don't say?' she rolled her eyes.

I found the glasses and poured two large ones, taking a large mouthful before continuing. 'He was out in the vineyard with Nik, or so I thought, but he obviously crept back. So I tried to reach out to him.'

'Gross,' she curled her lip.

'Yeah well I wanted to make him feel like he could trust me or something. Oh whatever – it works in Disney films.'

'Ugh! Ten out of ten for effort though, I get what you were doing, a sort of Esmeralda to his Quasimodo?'

I had to laugh. 'Oh I've missed you. You always make me smile and relieve all my tension.'

'Sexual tension?' She immediately leaped on that.

'No, sadly – well, yes, earlier...'

'Go on?'

'But Dimitris turned up.'

'You're really not having any luck on that front, are you?'

'No, but I might be on a promise later.'

'Finally! So, where *is* Nik, I wanted to congratulate him, haven't seen him since the wedding.' She then realised *what* she'd said. 'I won't say that to *him*, obviously.' She made a throat-cutting gesture with her fingers and took the glass of wine I'd now filled.

'I'm not sure *where* Nik is, the last time I saw him he was heading out to the vineyard with Dimitris, but I think he must be back,' I remarked, seeing the light on in his office. 'He's probably still working, so it might be just a girls' night after all.'

'What, no Dimitris?' she joked.

'No, I think he's busy upstairs tonight, going through everyone's underwear drawers.'

'Oh how delightful.'

'Yes, both Dimitris and Angelina both seem keen for me to go home, it's a recurring theme. But apparently she's offered to move in here and look after me. Wouldn't that be nice?'

'What the *hell*? When did she offer to do that?'

'Today, yesterday, I can't remember, my memory is shot these days. I think it's my age.'

'Perimenopause.'

'Great, something else to look forward to.' I started to prepare the food. It was lovely just having her there, chatting away as I laid the contents of the fridge on plates and called it mezze.

Once I'd put everything out, I left Sylvie for a moment and went over to Nik's office which was just across the courtyard. I could see him through the window on the phone, so popped my head round the door. 'Sylvie's here, are you going to join us?'

He immediately put down his phone and clicked off whatever he was doing on his computer screen. 'I'm really busy, Alice, something's come up,' he said. I didn't believe him, he just didn't want to socialise with my friend. I was pissed off, and something about the way he was putting his phone face down on the desk made me uneasy. I walked further into the office, and leaned over to kiss his cheek, and watched him slip his phone from the desk and into his pocket. This bothered me, but it wasn't the first time he'd been a bit secretive with his phone. He never left it around, and always had it with him. I was happy and not prepared to fall out with him so didn't mention it. 'Okay, don't work too late,' I said, and closing the door behind me, walked back across the courtyard. Glancing back, I could see he was back talking on the phone. It occurred to me it was late to be doing business, and I realised I didn't trust my new husband. I wondered if I ever would.

THIRTY-FIVE

The following morning, I was woken to several missed calls from Heather, who'd probably been bingeing true crime again on Netflix and was convinced I'd been murdered. So to prove that someone else wasn't using my phone and pretending to be me, she'd sent a text requesting I texted her back three answers to her questions.

Tell me your favourite colour?

Favourite coffee from Starbucks?

Favourite film ever?

I started to respond by text to put her out of her misery. Nik was still sleeping next to me, he hadn't come to bed until about 3am. So once again there'd been no alone time. And when he came to bed I was half asleep, and he just went to sleep as soon as his head hit the pillow.

And now, it was morning, and I could hear the grape-pickers arriving outside, and no doubt Dimitris was lurking. I was feeling nauseous again from the previous night's wine, and sex was the last thing on my mind, not that Nik was even suggesting it. He was now getting out of bed.

'Who are you texting?' he asked, checking his phone, his back to me.

'My sister's just asking me what's my favourite Starbucks coffee,' I said, without looking up.

'Of course she is,' he murmured, scratching his head, as he wandered off to the bathroom.

I texted Heather back to put her out of her misery and promised to call her later. I didn't see Nik for the rest of the morning, he was out working the vines with the grape-pickers. I felt slightly in limbo around that time. We were now waiting for the property in town to be vacated by the current owners, and also for my paperwork to come from Athens. Both were imminent, but as Nik said, the postal service was rubbish, everything took ages to arrive, and like all house buyers we had to wait for the seller to move.

The stress had made me even more nauseous than usual, and I felt permanently on edge over everything. Nik said he felt like he was walking on eggshells with me, and took himself off into the vineyard then his office for hours. I couldn't wait until we had the house in town, it would be our sanctuary – no Dimitris, no Angelina, just me and Nik. Hopefully, the peace and the privacy was all we needed to begin married life and make a go of it?

So, while I waited for news of the house, and post from Athens, I kept myself busy cleaning the house. I didn't want to take work from Angelina, but I didn't think it was healthy for her to be working for us there if she still held a torch for Nik. So, that morning, I did all the bedrooms, even Dimitris', obviously checking all the drawers, the wardrobe and under his bed. I found nothing this time, which was a relief, but it made me realise I was becoming obsessed, and needed to perhaps take a step back.

Standing in our bedroom later that morning, I took out the photo and stared at her. I had this feeling that just looking closely I might see clues, that in her own way she might tell me something. But it was a tight shot, no clues in the background; it was like she was preserved forever on Corfu, in the sunshine, but where on Corfu? I looked up, and gazed out of the window, suddenly aware of voices on the terrace below.

It was lunchtime, and a few of Nik's grape-pickers were taking their break, sitting at the table hunched over fruit and bottled water. I glanced across them, and my eyes stopped on one: slim, long dark hair... No it couldn't be? But it was – Angelina. I was angry with Nik. How could he continue to employ her knowing there was a problem, and knowing how I felt?

I moved closer to the window, trying to stay out of sight. Angelina always had eyes everywhere and it was weird and disturbing how she always seemed to find me. Her eyes were always watching me, threatening, glaring. I was anxiously expecting her to look up any minute and smile at me in that secret sinister way I was sure she saved just for me. But she seemed lethargic. She wasn't talking to the others or attempting to be the centre of attention as usual. As it was a hot day, and grape-picking is manual work, I thought she must be tired, she seemed disinterested in those around her. Alone. But suddenly that changed, and she appeared to be more alert, agitated even, her movements quicker. Her whole body now tensed as she sat up straight. Then Nik came into view; it was his presence that had caused such an abrupt change, and she smiled perkily as he wandered over to the bench nearby. He was sitting alone, but within seconds she had left the table of grape-pickers and was walking towards him. He looked up and I saw the smile on his face. It cut me.

They talked for a couple of minutes, their voices low. It was agony but I couldn't hear a word, I didn't even know if it was in English or Greek. Then, he slowly stood up and walked towards the kitchen. I was relieved he wasn't staying with her, he *had* listened to me, and realised he shouldn't lead her on. He disappeared into the kitchen and I breathed a sigh of relief, and watched as she sat alone on the bench, like her battery had died. But within minutes he was back on the decking, walking out into the sunshine with two cups, and she was clapping her hands like an excited child. I'd never found Angelina easy. From our first meeting, when she'd been with Sylvie and I'd offered them my table in the restaurant, she was sulky and rude. And since the night in the ladies' bathroom when she'd threatened me, I felt genuinely scared of her. She'd shown me that she didn't care what she said or how she looked, she was driven by hate.

But now, she was sitting on my patio with my husband drinking coffee and giggling at everything he said, and I saw for the first time what he and others saw. Angelina seemed like a perfectly nice girl. No wonder he thought Sylvie and I were being mean when I'd said we blamed Angelina for his arrest. And no wonder he looked at me in disbelief when I told him she'd threatened me, because from my bedroom window I was watching the smiling, worryingly flirty conversation she was having with him right now. I could tell by the tone of his voice that he was teasing her, and enjoying it as much as she was. As his new wife, this was difficult to watch, but what came next almost had me flinging open the window and screaming at him. I watched transfixed with horror as he gently reached up to her face, and moved a few strands of her long, dark hair. From where I was standing, I could see his fingertips touching her cheek, moving slowly down to her lips, where they stayed for a few, tortuous seconds. I gasped, my hand over my mouth, tears filling my eyes. It was a moment, it was very discreet, and no one else around seemed to be aware of the erotically charged gesture happening in front of them. Except Nik, Angelina – and me.

I couldn't watch anymore, and moved away from the window, but the heavy feeling inside didn't go away. My throat felt tight, my heart thudded with jealousy and hurt. I hated him with every fibre of my being, but loved him the same way. It was agony.

I had to regroup and locked myself in the bathroom. I didn't want him or anyone else suddenly appearing upstairs, I had to think this through. I tried to convince myself that perhaps I'd been mistaken, and he hadn't touched her like that, but seeing it had burned the image into my head and it was now playing on a loop. It happened. Now I had to look at my own perspective on this – I'd seen Angelina's jealousy as unfounded, pathological, like an obsessive who couldn't see the difference between the real and imagined. But I'd been wrong, very wrong, because apparently her feelings were being fuelled and encouraged by him. I couldn't blame her for feeling hurt and devastated and angry with me about being with Nik. She'd genuinely believed he liked her, Nik had made her think she stood a chance. Or was it more than that? Did Nik feel the same about her, and I had been the mistake, the fling, the woman on the side? Was it me who'd been the obsessive who hadn't been able to see the real from the imagined?

I kept this inside me all day, like a dying animal in pain I clutched it to me, unable to let go. By evening, I couldn't eat, I was feeling tired, sick and headachy and didn't have the strength to say anything, but nor did I have the strength to keep this inside. So after he'd eaten supper, and I'd toyed with some food on my plate, I said, 'How was Angelina today?'

He looked up from his glass of wine. 'I've no idea.'

'Haven't you seen her?'

'No. Why would I?'

'Because she was working here today?'

'Was she?'

'Nik, you *know* she was. I saw her on the patio, she was drinking coffee with you.'

'Do I have to run everything by you now? Am I not allowed to speak to women anymore, or drink coffee with my employees?'

'You know that's *not* what I'm saying, Nik,' I groaned inwardly. I was tense and tired, and Nik was easily triggered, which led to a lot of tension which often developed into rows. 'Surely you can see it isn't a good idea to let her work here because she has feelings for you.'

'Alice, this is too much. I'm so over your incessant whingeing about Angelina.'

'And *I'm* so over you touching her face and whispering sweet nothings to her on the terrace!' I hissed.

He looked at me open-mouthed. 'Oh, my God. Really? Now you're spying on me, at *work*? Were you hiding behind the trees watching me?'

'I didn't need to, I could see the whole performance from

the upstairs window.' I leaned in close to him. 'You were both under my nose. Literally!' I spat, feeling some of the old Alice fight rising through my nausea.

'I bet you got quite a *thrill*.' The disgust on his face was hard to bear, as he went back to his glass of wine and picked up his phone.

I stood up from the table. 'I'm going to bed,' I said, trying to dampen down the rage and the hurt swirling around my head.

I staggered upstairs, exhausted, tears streaming down my face. I didn't think I could fight anymore. What was happening to me? I suddenly felt dizzy so sat down on the bed for a moment until it subsided. While sitting there, I took out her photo. It always soothed me, despite knowing in my heart she didn't have a happy ending, I liked the way she was smiling. At least she seemed happy when the photo was taken, it was good to know she'd had sunshine on her face and good times in her life, however fleeting. I put it under my pillow, and knowing Nik would stay down there for hours drinking, pulled my phone from my pocket to speak with Heather. I was keen to tell her what just happened and get her take on it. She was always fair, and was happy to point out my flaws. She might see where I was wrong, or confirm that Nik was a bastard. Either way, she would present me with a rational, objective view of what was beginning to feel like a very messy marriage.

I'd been driven by love, but I'd also been driven by Nik's keenness, and not forgetting my own financial/legal problems which had all been eradicated by getting married. So there was a silver lining, even if we weren't getting along and he had the hots for someone else. I wondered now if Angelina was the reason we still hadn't had sex. I was probably overthinking as usual and it was simply the fact that we hadn't managed to be happy together for long enough to actually have sex. Something or somebody always seemed to get in the way. No wonder he was touching Angelina, he was probably very frustrated, this should have been our honeymoon time. Then there was my health, which was putting me off even *thinking* about sex, and that in itself was becoming a concern. I'd assumed my constant tiredness and nausea was the wine, the wedding nerves, but even giving up wine wasn't easing it. I was beginning to worry I had something seriously wrong with me.

Just as I started to click on Heather's name to call her as I'd promised, my phone buzzed. She was calling me.

'You're psychic,' I monotoned.

'I wish. Thank *God* you've picked up. The police have just been – again!'

What now? I hadn't wanted to talk about any of that, I just wanted marriage guidance and to tell her how ill I was. She was my surrogate mum after all.

'The police are looking for you, they came to find you, Alice.' She sounded tearful, on the edge of panic, it wasn't like her.

'You didn't *tell* them, did you?' I was immediately on full alert.

'No, because I don't know where you are, do I?'

'What did you say to them?'

'I said I thought you were in South America.'

'What?' I said, wondering where Nik was, how he was feeling, and picking at my nails. 'Heather, running away to South America's such a cliché, you really have to stop watching crime dramas.'

'Thanks to you, I'll be bloody *starring* in one soon.'

I rolled my eyes; she could be *so* dramatic.

'So what did they *want*? The police...'

'Love... I don't know how to tell you this, but they said to let you know, you aren't under investigation anymore – they have an arrest warrant. Alice, you're wanted for *murder*.'

THIRTY-SIX

I sat on the bed holding the phone. In shock.

'Say that again, Heather?'

'Dan's died.'

Tears sprang to my eyes. 'Are you kidding me, is this a joke?'

'No, it bloody isn't.'

'What happened... and why am I wanted for murder?'

'The bleed on the brain,' she started, 'it killed him love.'

Tears sprung to my eyes as I remembered more fragments of that night, the way he'd looked at me with such hate, the sudden move he made that scared me, made me think he was going to hit me. The move I'd seen so many times late at night when he'd had a drink and I'd said something he didn't agree with. I fled from the supermarket without looking back. I'd run away, like I always do. *Had I killed him?*

'Turns out he's been in hospital since that night, he was knocked out in the supermarket, but then rallied in hospital.

He was the one instructing Della to push for you to be rear-rested, everyone thought he'd just pull through.'

I took a long breath. 'If I am responsible,' I said, 'I know it's not an excuse, but I was probably defending myself.'

She didn't answer.

'He sometimes hurt me, you know?'

She stayed silent for a while, then spoke: 'I guessed he did. I asked you once, you had a bruise around your left eye, you told me you'd walked into a door,' she said. 'I never liked him.'

'Heather, I don't actually remember doing it, but I've not been on Instagram for a few days and earlier I saw that I must have messaged Della. I haven't been very well, I've been feeling sick and exhausted and I must have had a blackout like I did that night because I don't remember. But I asked if Dan hurt her too.'

'I know,' she said.

'How?'

'It wasn't you, Alice, it was me. I sent those messages on Instagram.'

'Heather?'

'I know, I *shouldn't* have. But she was saying you hit him with a bottle of wine, and I didn't think you'd ever *do* that, love. Then I realised, if you did anything at all, it was probably in self-defence or fear, and in order to prove that, I thought it would help if Della confessed he'd hit her too. I'd watched this crime drama where this man abused his wife, but then his wife and mistress got together and took their revenge. I had this crazy idea if I could get her onside telling her story, then you and her could fight him together, and it might get you off in court.'

'I can't believe you went into my Instagram account and

pretended to be me,' I murmured, trying to stop thinking of Della, and how I'd killed her baby's father.

'I know, and I'm sorry. But that message I sent to Della, asking if he ever hurt her?'

'Yes her response was that I was breaking the law by making contact, and threatened me with the police. Heather you could have got me into so much trouble.'

She may have threatened legal action about contacting her... but before she deleted it, the first reply was "yes."'

I wasn't surprised. Men who hurt women don't usually stop at one.

'I took a screen shot of her admitting he hurt her before she deleted it,' she said, 'might be useful in court love?'

'Yeah, thanks Heather.'

I told her I loved her but had to go, and clicked off the phone. I sat on the bed in silence thinking of Della, who'd just begun to live my old life. As sad as I was that someone had lost their life, I couldn't help but think what a lucky escape she'd had, even if I was wanted for murder. There really was no choice, I could never go home now.

A strong breeze blew in the distant darkness, and I was reminded that autumn would be here soon. This one wouldn't be like the autumns at home, chilly round the edges, with crisp mornings of woolly jumpers and long, golden walks. This year I'd miss the dark afternoons eating crumpets and drinking tea while watching an old film with Heather and the girls.

My homesickness dragged me into the past. I wondered how I'd ended up in this foreign place with people I didn't really know. It was incredibly sad to think how I'd said goodbye to everything, the good and the bad – just to stay out of prison. I opened up my Instagram, going straight to Della's account, and seeing a new post. It was a photo of Dan with his daughter. She was a few days old and had been placed on his hospital bed.

Daddy never woke up, never got to meet you darling, but he'll always be with you.

Tears rolled down my face. Whatever he'd done, he didn't deserve to die like that. Was I responsible for this terrible, terrible thing?

I looked back over her tiny squares, her personal history, and saw a photo from two Christmases before. She was with Dan, there was a Christmas tree in the background, both in pyjamas drinking champagne – Dan and I had still been together that Christmas. It was then we'd just found out the final round of IVF hadn't worked. I was no doubt crying at home, while they drank champagne in their pyjamas. I'd find it hard to ever truly grieve for Dan.

THIRTY-SEVEN

I waited for the passport and paperwork, checking the post each morning, and calling Christos, who said there were postal delays and to be patient. But I'd been told they'd be ready in thirty-six hours, it was now three days and I was starting to worry, but as Nik and I were barely speaking, I didn't share my concerns with him. I didn't tell him about Dan's death either, I kept it to myself, couldn't go there. I also didn't feel safe telling him, he'd probably add 'murderer,' to his list of insults the next time we argued. So we both went through each day being polite, making small talk, but not really *talking*, and when one morning I woke up and realised he hadn't come to bed, I wasn't surprised. It felt to me like the end of something that had barely begun. Our marriage had been dying before it had been born, and instead of trying to save it, he'd killed it.

Cleaning the bedrooms that morning, I saw that he'd slept in another room. He'd even moved some of his clothes in there. I looked through the drawers, and when it came to the bedside drawer, I opened that too, wondering if I'd find a cute little love note from Angelina. But instead, I found exactly the same two books I'd found in Dimitris' drawer days before when I'd discovered the photograph. I opened both books, and checked them thoroughly to see if there were any more photos, but I couldn't find any. Then as I was closing the newer one, I saw an inscription on the first page.

To Nik. Let's drink, for tomorrow we die. Love A xxx

I couldn't think straight, but while trying to process this I immediately returned to the room where I'd found the photo in the book, the room I *thought* Dimitris slept in. Were there several copies of the book, were they in both rooms? But when I opened the drawers, they were empty. The books belonged to Nik, which presumably meant the picture of the girl was Nik's too.

I went downstairs and found him on his phone in the kitchen. For the past few days he hadn't even gone out to the vineyard as far as I could see. He was rarely in his office, he just paced the floor, never off his phone.

'I feel like you're waiting for bad news?' I said as I joined him at the kitchen table.

'I'm not waiting for any news,' he said between his teeth. 'It's called working.'

'Your default position is irritation these days, everything I say seems to annoy you.' I tried not to make this too challenging in tone, more of an observation. Equally, I wasn't turning into some weak little person scared of his anger. I'd lived through much worse.

'Nik,' I started. 'You know the photo that I found in Dimitris' books?'

He didn't speak, just looked up from his phone enquiringly.

'They were *your* books, weren't they?' I said, just going for it, expecting him to deny this.

He put down his phone. There was something about his silence that unnerved me. Was he confused – or was he trying to come up with an explanation?

'Yes, they're my books, but I'm not the only one who's read them,' he said. Which of course was true, perhaps Dimitris had also read them and put the photo inside after all? But still, something was niggling at the back of my head.

'So the photo wasn't yours?'

'Of course not, I don't keep photos of young girls,' he snapped.

'One of the books,' I hesitated, aware I might sound psycho and start something with him. 'There's an inscription...'

'Yeah, something about, let's drink, for tomorrow we die.'

I nodded; 'Yeah, it was signed A.'

'Anthony was one of the grape pickers we had here last summer, he gave it to me, a sort of thank you when he left.'

What could I say? I didn't believe him, but was that because it wasn't true, or I was simply paranoid.

'What's wrong with you Alice, you really are so insecure, it isn't attractive,' he went back to his phone, while I stood there stinging.

'And what happened to the Nik I met?' I snapped. 'He used to be funny and kind and caring. You seem to jump down my throat at everything I say.'

'Sorry,' he replied. 'I just have some issues, work issues, and it's making me a bit stressed. I don't mean to take it out on you. But when you get needy and jealous I find it really difficult.'

'I'm not needy, Nik, or jealous. I just want a proper marriage, I want us to be honest with each other, to be able to talk without biting each other's heads off.'

'Me too.'

'Talking of honest,' I started, hesitantly. 'Heather called me, and Dan – my ex – he died.'

'What? Of the injuries you gave him?'

I knew he'd say that, but then again, on the surface this would appear to be the case.

'Well, that's what the police think.'

'Shit Alice, where does that leave you?'

I wondered if he was really wondering where that left him.

'I don't know, the police in the UK are looking at a murder charge.'

He whistled under his breath, all the colour had left his cheeks.

'I know, it's horrible and I would understand if you simply wanted a divorce, but I have a defence.'

'I'm sure you do,' he murmured. I thought I detected a note of sarcasm in his voice, it hurt, I could almost feel him pulling away.

'Look, I'm Alice Kouris now, I live in rural Greece, until they actually find me, nothing's going to happen. And if they do, then I will say I did it in self-defence.'

He nodded, slowly, 'you could do that, but let's not worry too much at this stage, as you say, they don't know where you are. So let's just carry on as normal until we hear anything?'

I was so relieved, here was someone who, like me, was happy to keep on and not live in fear of the police knocking on the door. 'I want to live this life married to you, here on the island until I can't,' I said, and in the madness it all made a kind of sense to me.

'Let's not give up yet, Nik, why don't we start tonight? You come back to our room and we can at least wake up together. You always said that's what you wanted most?'

'Yeah, let's do that. As for sleeping together, I don't ever want you to think I don't love you, or find you attractive,' he said gently. 'It's just this work stress is affecting me so much, I can't even think about sex.'

'I understand, and it's not just down to you. I've been having these bouts of sickness, and feel permanently exhausted, so I haven't exactly been jumping on you either.'

He smiled and reached for my hand. 'Let's start again, put everything behind us?'

'That sounds good,' I replied. 'And I'm starting by calling a doctor, I need to have some tests, find out what's wrong with me.'

'I know just the woman, she's brilliant, looked after my family for years. She's good, so you sometimes have to wait a week or two to see her as she gets booked up. I'll call later and get you an appointment.' He touched my face tenderly. 'I worry about you, darling, you always look so pale.'

'Nik, I'm worried it's something serious.'

'Probably just the stress of the wedding and everything else, you have a lot back home to worry about too. But soon all that will be sorted, and I'll call Dr Samaras and she can check you over just to be sure.'

That night, he joined me in our bed, but the pains in my stomach, and nausea were so strong I could barely lie down.

'Darling, I had no idea you were this bad,' he said, clearly concerned, and through the night he looked after me, bringing water, an extra pillow, massaging my stomach. I was touched at how he cared for me, and even fell asleep for a little while in spite of the pain. But at about 4am, I woke with nausea again. I couldn't lie down, it made me feel worse, so I quietly padded around the room, and naturally was drawn to the window, where I opened the curtains. I was greeted by a flood of silvery moonlight. It washed over me soothingly as I gazed out onto the terrace and the vineyard beyond. And with a jolt, I suddenly realised, he was out there. Dimitris was in the vineyard, at a different spot than the one where I'd last seen him digging. But he was still digging nevertheless.

What was he looking for? Last time I couldn't be a hundred per cent sure it was a man out there. But this time the area was flooded with moonlight, and I didn't even need to zoom my phone to see it was Dimitris.

And yes, he was definitely digging, so when I'd half-joked that he'd forgotten where he buried the bodies, it looked like I might be correct.

'You okay, Alice?' Nik asked, half asleep.

'Nik, I'm scared,' I said.

He sat up in bed. 'Why?'

'Dimitris is digging out there, again. This time I'm sure it's him, and he is digging.'

Sighing, he clambered out of bed, and staggered over to where I stood.

'It's four o'clock in the morning, Nik, what the hell is he *doing*?' He followed my eyes as I looked out through the window, both of us now staring at Dimitris digging for his life. 'What if he's put them in the ground – out there?' I wrapped my arms around myself protectively. We were both silenced by this horrific thought.

'I would *know*, Alice,' Nik said authoritatively.

'Would you?' I replied doubtfully.

'I know every inch of my vineyard, if someone were burying women's bodies in the vines, there'd be large banks of fresh soil, it would be obvious.'

'It might *not* be bodies. He might be hiding more trophies? Remember the photograph I found?'

He raised his eyebrows. 'I'm beginning to realise you might be right about him. Perhaps my cousin isn't the poor, beleaguered old guy I thought he was after all?'

I was surprised, he'd finally realised. Nik had been adamant for so long that Dimitris was innocent.

'I'm going to go and talk to him, find out what he's up to.'

'He seems to have gone now,' I said, still peering out of the window. 'Don't go out there now, he might hit you over the head with the shovel.'

'I'm calling the police,' he said. With that he grabbed his phone and talked in Greek to the police, and when he'd finished, he put his arm around me. I was shivering with fear. 'What did you say, that Dimitris was digging in the vineyard?'

'I told them that, I also told them that we suspect he knows *something* about the missing women, and there may be some trophies here in the grounds. But what they're looking for isn't here, the place to search could be my other cousin's – his brother's place along the coast. I wondered why he's been staying there – it's just the place to bury bodies, one huge expanse of beach wilderness.'

'And a great big sea,' I said, with a shiver, climbing back into bed, imagining a dark, watery grave, and hearing the women scream.

THIRTY-EIGHT

The police never came to the vineyard, probably because Nik had told them to go and search at his other cousin's place. But I couldn't take much more of Dimitris' nocturnal wanderings and the next day I called Clio at the estate agent's to see if there was any news on the current occupiers moving out.

'Any day now, Alice,' she replied brightly. 'I have the contracts, and the family are moving out – let me check – yes, next Saturday.'

That was a week away. I was so disappointed. Nik and Clio had both said that things moved very quickly when buying a property in Greece. I couldn't bear the prospect of another night in that house. But I stayed another week, and we didn't see much of Dimitris. Nik said he'd stay around and keep an eye, and he had the police on speed dial, so I didn't feel too anxious. But when, on the following Saturday, we hadn't heard from Clio I was becoming very agitated.

'It's fine, darling,' Nik said. 'You know what buying a house is like, it can take a week, it can take a year.'

'I can't wait much longer,' I said, stressed, anxious to move in and get away from the vineyard.

By the following Monday, after much reassurance from Clio, and reminders to 'be patient,' from Nik, I was still waiting for the keys. I was still poorly, and feeling very, very tense.

Nik was being kinder, more reassuring, and I could see he was consciously trying not to be irritable, but there was still tension there. I was convinced that the town house was the answer. If we could just get away and be alone it would be the sanctuary we needed.

During this time, I felt overwhelmed, all my worries were intensified: Dan's death, Dimitris' digging, and Angelina's constant presence. She seemed to be hanging around at the vineyard most days. My sightings of her were fleeting as she was out picking grapes, but it was getting to me. So I called Sylvie, who obviously heard the distress in my voice, and invited me over for lunch.

'When?' I said.

'Now?'

'I'd love to,' I said, jumping at the chance to do something nice, and normal that didn't involve death and arguments, nocturnal terrors or women's screams. Nik had gone north that day to Sidari to check out a new olive press, and wouldn't be home until late. I needed a distraction from my bag full of worries and from waiting for the keys to our new place, which still hadn't materialised. So I put on some lipstick and took a taxi to Sylvie's apartment.

'Hey!' she said, opening the door and hugging me. 'I missed you!'

'I missed you too,' I replied, relieved at her warmth. 'I worried we might lose touch, that you'd think I'd abandoned you for married life,' I said, following her through to the lounge.

'No, I didn't for a minute think that you'd rather be with your rich, handsome vineyard owner than me.' She smiled to herself at this and gestured towards the balcony. 'Take a seat, madam, lunch is ready.'

I sat down at the table on her huge balcony overlooking the sea. Having looked at properties like this at the estate agent's, I realised now how much something like this must have cost.

'This place is so gorgeous,' I said, as she stepped out onto the decking with a large platter of charcuterie and cheese.

She placed it carefully down on the table. 'Thought we'd nibble,' she said, then joined me to stare at the aqua water, the mountains in the distance, the pale gold sand underneath. 'Yeah, I'm lucky to live here. I have to pinch myself every day,' she said, not taking her eyes from the horizon. 'And in the evening, that sunset...' She pinched her fingers and kissed them. 'So, how is married life?' she asked, like she'd suddenly remembered.

I sighed. 'Difficult. We're just having a few teething troubles at the moment.'

'But buying this house and staying here is a good thing?' she asked.

I told her about some of our arguments, his stress, the way he'd changed. 'That's not the only problem,' I said. 'Dimitris has become nocturnal.'

'Oh shit. I'd steer well away from that. The stuff I'm hearing—'

'I can guess,' I replied, 'and bloody Angelina's hanging around, supposedly picking grapes, but I think she thinks her job description is flirting with Nik.'

'Oh yeah she mentioned that – not the flirting obvs – but that she's picking grapes. Thing is I'm really quiet at the moment wedding-wise, I can't offer her any more work.'

'You must worry being quiet. I imagine the mortgage on this place is huge?'

'Oh property's cheap here, as you know.'

I smiled. Sylvie's idea of 'cheap' and mine were obviously very different.

'And talking about property, how's the purchase coming along?'

'Not great. Clio, the estate agent, said the house would be empty by Saturday, but it's now Monday and I'm still waiting.'

'Yeah, I know Clio, she's fab, sold me this place.'

'Right?'

'It took weeks, no, months for me to move into this place, and I paid for it almost as soon as I saw it.'

'Same here, it's all paid for, I'm just waiting.'

'It'll happen, just a bit frustrating.'

Talking to Sylvie made me feel so much better, as I knew it would.

'I'll call Clio later, she might be able to hurry them along?'

Later that afternoon, after a lovely long lunch with Sylvie, I took a taxi back to the vineyard, but as I was passing Corfu Town, I asked the driver to drop me off at the estate agent's. I wasn't rushing to go back to the vineyard. Nik would still be in Sidari, and I didn't relish the prospect of being alone with Dimitris.

But when the driver dropped me off, I was disappointed to see Adonis was closed, then realised they probably closed in the afternoon and would open early evening. No point calling Clio, she'd be having an afternoon nap like the rest of the town, so I would call another taxi and head home. But then I remembered Nik wasn't around, so decided to take a walk to our new house on the edge of town.

Despite being late September, it was still warm, and the walk along the harbour was fresh and pleasant, I would walk this way when we lived here. At that point I could see myself spending more time at the house there in the town than the vineyard. And approaching the house, I felt a lovely sense of relief. This would be my sanctuary, I just knew I'd be happy there. As it was on a quiet street, with no gate or front garden, I walked right up to the house, and glancing up at the windows, saw a woman looking down at me. Our eyes met and I felt rather embarrassed. She probably didn't realise who I was and I wondered if I should perhaps introduce myself. I'll admit, I was hoping to be invited in so I could see my new home again. And while I was there, I could ask about their moving date. As good as Clio was, she hadn't pinned them down, and she wasn't even at the office that afternoon. I felt she'd lost momentum for the sale. So, feeling a little nervous, I knocked on the door, and eventually it was opened.

'Hello, do you speak English?' I asked, and the woman nodded.

'Great, I'm Alice, Alice Kouris from Kouris Estates.'

She looked confused.

'Sorry, I thought you might be aware that it's me who bought your house?'

She looked even more confused now. 'Bought?'

She was obviously having problems with my English, I was definitely going to take Greek lessons soon, I'd relied too long on Nik for translation.

So I tried to explain some more, but she just kept shaking her head, then held up her hand as if to say, 'I'll be back.' I stood on the doorstep, and from where I stood, I could see into one of the sitting rooms. Nothing had been packed yet. Eventually the woman returned with a much younger man, who she introduced as, 'My son, Michalis.'

'Can I help you? I think my mother is confused, she says you want to buy our house? But I think you are enquiring about our Airbnb option. Would you like to rent the whole house or just a room?' He smiled at me expectantly.

My unease blossomed. 'No I don't want Airbnb, I've already *bought* your house. I bought it several weeks ago through Adonis Estate Agent's, and I'm now just waiting for you to move out.'

He looked from me to his mother, puzzled. 'But we *live* here, this is our home, we aren't moving out. I'm so sorry, you must be mistaken, this house is not for sale.'

Devastated and very confused, I ran back to Adonis Estate Agent's, and this time, I banged on the door. But still no one was there, so I called Clio, whose phone went straight to voicemail as my heart clanged to the ground. I needed to know what was happening, some explanation, anything – not knowing was driving me mad. Surely this was just a mistake, but how could it be?

I called Nik, who didn't answer; he'd said he might not have a signal in Sidari, so I just left a message for him to get back to me straight away.

I called Sylvie, and told her about my conversation with the people at the house. 'Have you ever heard of anything like this happening before?' I asked.

'No, that sounds weird,' she said. 'Are you sure the house owners understood what you meant?'

'I *think* so – I mean the boy I spoke to seemed to under-stand English,' I replied, 'but I don't know, perhaps he *didn't*. He kept offering it to rent?'

'That can sometimes be a bit confusing over here,' she said, 'renting and buying can mean the same. Where are you?'

'I'm in Corfu Town, about to head back to the vineyard.'

'But you said Nik was in Sidari and won't be back until late, you can't go back there alone, not with Dimitris loitering around. Look I'm ten minutes away, why don't I drive over to the town, pick you up and I'll take you back to the vineyard?'

'That's kind, but I wouldn't dream of—'

'Are you outside Adonis now?'

'Not far,' I said, grateful for her offer of a lift.

'Well, wait near there, grab a coffee and I'll come and get you. And no arguments, I'll stay with you until Nik gets back, I can't believe he's just gone off for the day and left you alone with Dimitris. Why didn't he take you with him to Sidari? It's a lovely little place. Fabulous beach, lovely restaurants, you could have had a romantic dinner there...' She stopped, probably realising I might not want to hear that. 'I'll see you in ten.'

I was desperate to get to the bottom of this and knew that until Clio returned I wouldn't. And all my doubts about Nik were now crystallizing, so I called Heather. I sat on the doorstep of Adonis Estate Agent's waiting for Sylvie and for once told my sister everything. I told her about Nik, and Clio, and Christos and the house, and I cried a little.

'I don't know who I can trust anymore,' I said. 'Something here is really, really wrong, Heather.'

'Yes it is, and I'm really worried about you, I think your husband and that Dimitris guy are in it together.'

'Do you?' I replied, the thought had occurred to me that Nik was involved, but I'd tried not to listen to the sane voice in my head telling me that.

'Yeah, I do. And I can't let this go on, I have a plan, and I want you to listen carefully, and don't tell a soul.'

So, as the late afternoon sun beat down on my bare shoulders, I sat on a dusty pavement, my eyes searching the road for Sylvie to come to my rescue. And as my life bled out slowly, I listened to my sister, and tried not to cry.

THIRTY-NINE

I put the phone down to Heather, nervous and upset to have it confirmed that she didn't trust Nik either. I'd half-hoped she'd tell me I was overthinking everything, but after I'd told her about the photo, the beer mat, his behaviour after we were married, she was convinced that Dimitris wasn't acting alone. As I waited for Sylvie, still sitting on the pavement, my mind drifted back to what *she'd* said about Nik not taking me with him to Sidari that day. More proof if I needed it that he was not what I thought he was, and our marriage was a sham. Why *hadn't* he taken me along? If nothing else, surely he wouldn't want to leave me alone with Dimitris? He'd apparently been so worried about me *not* being alone, he'd wanted Angelina to move in! I hadn't seen her around – she was probably with him now about to enjoy a romantic dinner on the beach.

After about half an hour, Sylvie turned up. I was so relieved to see her, I almost cried. 'Sorry, the traffic was awful getting here.' She was as smiley as usual.

'I'm so sorry to mess you about, Sylvie... I know I said I'd be okay, but...'

'Will you *stop* apologising? You're my friend, and I love you, there's nothing I wouldn't do for you,' she said, clicking on her indicator, and pulling away from the kerb.

'I don't deserve you,' I said, and I meant it.

'That's enough of that, you're getting really sickly now,' she joked, as we sped out of the town, heading along the coastal road, the wind in our hair.

'Like old times,' I said, feeling like I'd known her forever as she drove so fast we were soon at the vineyard.

'Tea or wine?' I asked once we were in the house. There was no sign of Dimitris, for which we were both relieved and grateful, as we sat together on the terrace watching the sun go down.

'Wine,' she said, 'but just the one glass, I'm driving.'

She went to sit on the upper terrace while I made our drinks.

'Sylvie, can I stay with you tonight?' I asked as I walked up the metal steps with the tray. She was sitting on a lounger, her face raised to the sun. I was glad she was there, I might need some support when Nik returned.

'Yeah, sure. I thought you said Nik was coming back?'

'He is, but I don't know what time, and...'

She didn't seem to pick up on this. 'Are you drinking tea?' she asked. 'You're not pregnant, are you?'

'What? Oh no, of course not. It's just that my head gets so foggy with Kouris wine.' I handed her a glass of white. 'It makes me feel sick too – at least I think that's what it is. Nik's made me an appointment for next week with a doctor.'

'Good,' she said, 'you need some blood tests if you're feeling sick.'

'To be honest, it's the least of my problems. First of all, the property,' I said, my stomach sinking, as I checked my phone. Nothing from Nik or Clio, I'd left messages for both. It was now after 8pm. 'I don't know what's going on, Sylvie, and I don't know *where* Nik is.'

'You said he was in Sidari?' she murmured absently, probably thinking of the wedding she was currently working on.

I saw him in my mind's eye, Angelina sitting opposite him in a rooftop restaurant, their eyes glittering in the candle-light. 'Don't worry about the property, love. Everything takes longer here,' Sylvie said, relieving me of the romantic dinner I was torturing myself with. 'I had loads of delays when I bought the apartment, but Clio is wonderful, she'll call you back. It might be tomorrow though, like I say she's good, but there's a real laid-back vibe here that extends to business too.'

'Yes, I've noticed. Nik's one of the worst, he hasn't done his accounts for weeks, and he says he's stressed, but the papers are piling up, I don't know what he does in that office all day.'

She smiled. 'Well he is half-Greek. Have you heard from him today?'

'No, I've left messages, he'll get back when he gets them,' I said, 'but I'm worried. I just googled the distance from the vineyard to Sidari, and it's less than ten miles – he told me the journey would be at least two hours.'

She looked puzzled. 'Really?'

'I don't think I trust him, Sylvie.'

She looked at me doubtfully. 'Nik Kouris? I reckon he's the most trustworthy—'

'I know he seems that way,' I cut in, 'but he's not what I thought he was. I found a photo of that young girl who'd gone missing. It was placed between the pages of a book in one of the bedrooms. I thought it was Dimitris' book, but it was Nik's.'

She shrugged. 'What are you saying?'

'I don't know. But the girl in the photo was the one I saw up on the coast road, she was quite young, she went missing about five years ago. I wonder now if Nik was seeing her?'

'No, surely not? She was only young, in her twenties, Nik would have been in his forties then.'

'Angelina's in her twenties, and he's in his fifties now, perhaps he likes much younger women? I don't know, but he seemed bothered that I had the photo, kept asking me where it was. In the end I lied, said I couldn't find it, but something told me to keep it hidden from him.' I didn't tell Sylvie but in truth I wanted to protect her from him.

'I mean for what it's worth, I've never heard anything at all bad about Nik Kouris, and I've been here a few years now,' she offered.

'But I *know* him, and Nik – he's erratic, inconsistent. Sometimes he's caring and loving, other times he's cold and absent, he can say quite hurtful things – he's not what he seems.'

Her eyebrows raised slowly, this was news to her. 'Well, as you say, *you* know him. Bloody hell I didn't have him down as a nasty piece of work.' Being Sylvie, she insisted on making me feel better, and this took the form of another cup of tea. 'You know my motto, a cup of tea cures everything,' she said with a smile, as she went downstairs and into the kitchen.

'Not everything,' I murmured to myself.

I guessed her rush to the kitchen was probably more about her pouring herself another glass of wine than making me more tea, but to be fair, she returned with a steaming mug, and no more wine for herself.

'I'm just so worried, Sylvie, and then there's the property – what if something's gone wrong and the money's gone missing?' I said as she put the steaming mug down in front of me, then took her seat at the table. 'Has the money cleared from your bank?' she asked.

'Yes, it's definitely gone.'

She pulled a sad face, then composed herself. 'Like I say, things are slower here, but I'm sure it's all good. Clio is amazing.'

At this point my phone buzzed, and thinking it might be Nik, I checked it. 'Heather!' I breathed.

'She loves checking in on you, doesn't she?' Sylvie said with a chuckle.

'She loves *harassing* me,' I said, feeling disloyal. I read the text quickly, my heart beating, then clicked it off and put the phone back in my jeans pocket.

'What does she want?'

'Oh just asking if I'm okay,' I lied.

Sylvie rolled her eyes. 'She's hilarious,' she said.

I nodded, then tried to change the subject, but I couldn't concentrate. All the time my worries were gnawing away – Nik, then the money, then the murder charge, and back again in a loop. My head was like a tumble dryer going round and round and round as Sylvie talked, and throughout the whole time, my phone was constantly buzzing, and it was always, *always* Heather.

When Sylvie went to make more tea, I called Nik, but he didn't pick up, so I left a message, telling him again there'd been a mix-up about the house. '*Please* call me back as soon as you get this!' I urged, close to tears. Then I tried Clio again, but it went straight to voicemail. I kept telling myself this would all be sorted the following day, I just had to stay calm.

Sylvie was walking back over the decking this time with two mugs of tea, when into the silence came a loud slam of the door downstairs. We both looked at each other. The colour drained from Sylvie's face. I was so shocked at the sudden loudness, I thought my heart had stopped.

'Is it Nik?' I said, hopefully, getting up from my seat.

But instead of Nik's voice, there was just an ominous silence. My stomach was now twisting, I looked at Sylvie. '*Dimitris!*'

Terrified, she looked over the edge to see if she could see him. 'He's coming up the stairs,' she screamed.

I could hear the clank of his big boots stomping up the metal staircase on the side of the building, each step making my heart beat faster.

We were both frozen to the spot, until eventually he appeared, the sunset behind him, a dark silhouette standing before us.

He was wheezing from the exertion, and leaning on the wall of the terrace. And he was now looking straight at me, in the same way he stared when he crushed the tomato in his big hands.

'Ast...asnoma,' he blurted.

I looked at Sylvie, the blood had drained from her face, she looked petrified.

'Go away,' she said loudly.

He didn't flinch, just continued to stand there, ignoring Sylvie, directing his hate at me. He jerked his head. 'Astynomia,' he suddenly blurted, pointing his finger at me, and I realised with a jolt, he was saying police in Greek.

I almost fainted at this. Why was he calling the police on me, what did he *know*?

'Please go away!' I cried, my whole life seemed to be imploding, and now a suspected murderer was threatening *me* with the police.

He obviously didn't understand me, and continued to breathe raggedly, while staggering about the terrace, deranged, confused. Sylvie had her hand over her mouth, her eyes wide open like they might pop out any minute. She looked as terrified as I felt. There were two of us, but physically he could overpower us both, and we were on a terrace with a drop of twenty feet, with a very low wall. Was this the end of my story?

FORTY

'If you don't go away *now*, I will call the police,' I warned him, trying to hide the fear in my voice.

Sylvie finally dragged her hand away from her mouth to say, 'What do you *want*, Dimitris?'

At this he extended his arm and pointing his finger directly at me. He was trying to say something, but he couldn't get the words out. He put his hand down the back of his trousers.

'Oh he's being gross,' Sylvie groaned.

I continued to watch him, and realised he was trying to take something from his back pocket. Eventually he pulled out a rolled-up piece of paper, and threw it on the table. It landed just by my hand. He was nodding at me all the time, seemingly gesturing for me to open it up. So, holding my breath I picked it up carefully, unfurled it very, very slowly, almost knowing before I saw it, what was on the paper. I groaned as the faces of the missing women emerged. He'd copied them all onto one sheet, some faces I hadn't seen before, but *she* was there. Was he taunting me?

'Are you telling me I'm next?' I asked. I heard the tremor in my own voice, against the rasping of his breath.

'Go away!' Sylvie was yelling at him, but he seemed oblivious to her as he reached into an upper pocket of his shirt, and retrieved another rolled-up piece of paper. Again, he seemed to be urging me to look at the paper in his hand. He was holding it out to me, beckoning me to him when Sylvie tried to snatch it from him. But he lifted his fist at her, and she leaped back, whimpering. This was horrific, there were two of us, and only one of him, yet he was controlling us, trying to bring me towards him and pushing Sylvie away. Realising I had no intention of going near him, he placed the piece of paper on the table beside me, then walked a few paces back. I reached out and unfolded the piece of paper. I looked from him to Sylvie and back again.

'This is the house I'm trying to buy... how does *he* know about it?' I said to Sylvie, who shook her head slowly, glaring at him. All the blood had drained from her face, she was terrified.

I stayed where I was, clutching the piece of paper as he gesticulated towards it. I glanced at the printed picture, the details of my beautiful town house in Corfu. I just kept looking at him, saying, 'What?' But unable to speak English, and clearly having problems with his speech, he just kept pointing at me. He presumably wanted me to read it and was becoming very agitated, I didn't want to make him angry and had to keep everything calm. So to appease him, I pretended to read what I thought I'd already seen. I skimmed the price and square footage and all the usual estate agent details, and was about to put it back on the table, when something caught my eye. There was no Adonis estate agent's heading as there had been on the printout I'd been given by Clio. There was no price either – but there *was* a price per night, as the house was available to rent on Airbnb, which the owner had told me. But what was *Dimitris* trying to tell me?

He was now walking towards me, but before he could touch me, Sylvie had leaped on his back. Her arms were wrapped around his neck and she was screaming at him and dragging him backwards across the terrace.

'You   BASTARD!!!'   she   was   yelling.   'YOU MURDERING BASTARD!' She'd obviously taken him by surprise, and this had given her the opportunity to overpower him. She was yelling and heaving him across the floor, but once he'd orientated himself, he managed to squirm free from her grasp.

Dimitris was clumsy. He staggered, but he was bigger than Sylvie and just by pushing himself at her he'd knocked her down. She was now on the floor and from the corner of my eye I saw her reaching for the stone statue standing on the terrace. She used it to heave herself to her feet, and once she was stable, she somehow managed to lift it from its stand. I'd always assumed the statue was bolted to the ground, but Sylvie just picked it up, and with a loud, guttural cry, ran at Dimitris. To my relief and horror, he crumpled and fell to the ground with a heavy cracking sound. Sylvie had also fallen, and landed facedown. She was now trying desperately to get to her feet. But the blood on the decking was slippery, and she was sliding around on her stomach, screaming. It was all so quick, I must have been in shock, and stood, frozen to the spot.

I couldn't help her, I was triggered by the blood, and back in the supermarket on Valentine's night. I'd seen Della pregnant, I'd been devastated, and now I remembered Dan's cruel remark that he'd finally found a *real* woman to have his baby. I'd screamed at him and in my distress, tried to leave, and pushed him out of my way. He hadn't expected this, and had tripped, landing hard, and falling behind a shelf stocked so high with boxes of valentine's chocolates, that he was hidden from the CCTV. But what I hadn't realised, was that the CCTV in my brain *had* recorded and stored everything, but buried it deep. I stared ahead in shock, as my mind played everything second by second. And as Sylvie struggled on the floor, and Dimitris' blood trickled across the pale wood floor, my memory relayed to me what had happened that night. And as Sylvie rose from the ground, covered in blood, I saw Dan *get* up and slowly rise to his feet, and when I saw his fury I froze, waiting for the inevitable blow. His face was red with embarrassment and rage and he raised his fist. It was all too clear now, as my memory continued to roll like film through my head. But as I braced myself for the blow, *someone* – not me – reached into my bag, took out the bottle of wine and whacked it hard across Dan's head, knocking him to the floor. All unseen on CCTV. But I saw it, I saw it clearly. She'd seen what he was about to do, and instinctively, she'd stopped him. She couldn't watch him deliver one more slap, one more cruel remark, or one more beating. It wasn't *me*, it was *Della* who'd killed Dan.

FORTY-ONE

I stared at Dimitris' blood seeping onto the decking. I was crying, tears were streaming down my face. I'd stored what happened in my memory, refusing to look at it. I'd done what I always do, and run away. And then I'd run away from the police, even though I was innocent. Heather was right, I should have stayed and fought.

Sylvie was now shouting at me, and I came to, suddenly aware of the present, and realising what had just happened. 'I think I've killed him,' she was saying, standing over Dimitris, sobbing, she was covered in his blood.

I immediately crouched down and touched his face, then held his wrist to check for a pulse. 'There's something faint, yes, there's *something*,' I said hopefully. 'He's not dead. Thank God! Get some paper towel,' I barked, and Sylvie immediately ran down to the kitchen and back in seconds, carrying the paper towel and a big bottle of bleach.

'We need to call an ambulance,' I said, as I wrapped the kitchen towel around his head.

She was scrubbing at the wood of the terrace floor with

bleach, and suddenly stopped. She looked up. 'You're kidding, right?'

'No. We might be able to save him, Sylvie!'

She kept on wiping the floor, harder and harder. 'He's dead, and if he isn't he soon *will* be, I gave him a really hard whack.'

'But we can't leave him like *this*!' I was horrified, trying to press my hand onto his head wound to stop the blood I couldn't reach for my phone.

Still on all fours, she kept on scrubbing like a woman possessed.

'Sylvie!' I yelled to get her attention.

She suddenly seemed to be aware of me, and sitting up, dropped the bloodied paper towel to the ground.

'Hello? You're on a *murder* charge,' she said. 'You can't risk being involved in this, you'll be sent home and they'll throw away the key.' She picked up the paper towel and went back to scrubbing the floor vigorously; her hands looked red raw.

'No... Sylvie, I didn't kill Dan, I know what happened now, I just realised.'

'Convenient?' she muttered in a voice I didn't recognise as hers.

'But he's not dead,' I said again. 'No one murdered him, if we can call an ambulance...'

'He'll be dead soon enough, and then you're involved in another murder.'

'I may be involved, but I'm not responsible.'

'Well it wasn't me.' Her head was down, she was still scrubbing at the blood manically.

'I don't know what you're saying, Sylvie, but I'm your witness, you hit him with the statue in self-defence.'

'Semantics,' she announced. 'Our priority is to get this place cleaned up and get him out of here.' She continued to scrub, her face so close to the ground her blonde hair was trailing in the blood.

'We need an ambulance!' I yelled. In my panic, I was sobbing, my tears splashing on his face as I held his head in my hands.

Sylvie was now muttering to herself while wiping bleach everywhere on the terrace, her cleaning obsession triggered by what had just happened. I searched for my phone, but couldn't see it.

'Sylvie, call the ambulance,' I yelled again, as she opened the door that led to our bedroom, and went straight to the small nightstand where two glasses were kept. I watched with incredulity as she opened the doors of the nightstand, took out a glass, then went into the bathroom. Seconds later she returned with a glass of water.

'What are you *doing*?' I asked.

'Drink this, it will calm you down, while we work out what to do. I can't lose you, Alice, I can't let you go to prison, he's dead.'

'But I *told* you, he isn't, and if we just tell them the truth about what happened here, there's no problem. You hit him with the statue in self-defence—' I repeated.

'Yeah we can *tell* them anything, but you can *see* how it would look. British woman runs to Corfu escaping a murder charge, then she's involved in *another* murder.' She was still holding the water out to me. 'Now come on, drink this, you need to stay calm.' I pushed it away. '*Alice!*' she said between gritted teeth, as the water spilled everywhere. 'You stupid bitch!' she yelled, and dropped the glass. It smashed into a million pieces all over the terrace, and in the dim light I looked up at her face, covered in blood and sweat, and I didn't recognise her.

I suddenly spotted my phone on the table, so stood up, dashed to grab it, and dialled 112, the number for emergency services in Greece. Sylvie suddenly realised what I was doing. 'No you *don't!*' she hissed as she tried to grab the phone from me, but I moved away quickly just as someone answered. I was trying to fight her off while shouting, 'Ambulance, ambulance,' into my phone. But the operator didn't understand and before I could say anything else, she'd knocked the phone from my hand. It landed close by, and I covered it with my foot, thinking about Heather's instructions.

'I told you NO AMBULANCE, he's DEAD!' she yelled in my face.

I gasped. Unable to speak, I just stared at her, unable to comprehend what had happened to my lovely friend. We glared at each other in stunned silence over Dimitris, as his life ebbed into the wood grain of the decking.

'I don't understand.' My voice was shaking, and I had tears all over my face. I wiped my nose with the back of my hand.

'Why the tears, Alice? You *hated* him. You were always complaining about him, you wanted rid of him, and now he's gone.'

'But I didn't want *this*.'

'I thought it was your solution to all your problems, you got rid of your ex-husband and now him. Anyone else you'd like to confess to while we're here?'

'Sylvie, you aren't making *sense*. We don't have to lie. You hit him in self-defence.'

'No, you're the murderer, Alice. And once the Greek

police have finished with you, the UK police will extradite you back home. *Two* murders that we know of, you're a one-woman killing machine!' She chuckled at this. She sounded unhinged and obviously scared.

She didn't want to be blamed for Dimitris' death, so was throwing the nearest person under the bus instead. Me!

'Nik's lawyer helped me to get a Greek passport, and as a Greek citizen, I *can't* be extradited from here.' I was bluffing of course. I'd realised by now that I was as likely to see my new Greek passport as I was my new Greek town house.

'Oh you mean the passport organised by legal eagle Christos, the sad old am-dram queen who'll play any part for a few quid?'

'I knew it, I bloody knew he wasn't real!' Then I stopped for a moment. 'But how do *you* know Christos?' Then I realised what she'd said just a few minutes ago. 'How do you know Dan died?'

She laughed at this. 'Nik told me.'

'When? I don't understand,' she barely knew Nik, why would he be talking to Sylvie about me?

'Oh, Alice, there were moments when I thought you might just have twigged, that you might be that bit brighter than the others. But when it comes right down to it, us women are all the same, aren't we? From CEOs to bankers to doctors, we all become dumbos when faced with a good-looking, charming guy who tells us we're beautiful.'

'What are you talking about?' I suddenly saw Dimitris move. 'Look, I don't know what you're saying, Sylvie, I'm not even sure who you *are* right now. But we need to get this man to hospital.' I leaned closer to him and heard a faint rasping breath coming from deep, deep down in his chest. 'Christ,

Sylvie, a man's *dying* here,' I cried out, feeling the life flowing from him.

I looked at her, searched her face. 'How did you know the statue wasn't bolted to the ground?' I asked.

She didn't even look at me, just took her vape pen from her pocket, put it to her lips.

'You knew where the glasses are kept in the bedroom too, you went straight to them.' An idea was forming in my head. An idea I didn't want to let in. 'When have you been in our bedroom?'

'Oh chill out, Goldilocks, I haven't been sleeping in *your* bed, not for a while anyway. We've been using the other bedrooms since *you* came on the scene.'

'I don't understand... Are you saying you've been sleeping with Nik?'

She nodded.

'Are you joking?'

'Why would I joke about something like that?'

'How long has this been going on?'

'Oh don't play the wronged wife, I've been sleeping with him long before you even *knew* him.'

'You... and *Nik*?' was all I could muster.

She nodded, vape smoke streaming from her nostrils. She looked like a dragon. 'Before, during and after he's been with you to be precise. And sleeping with him in the room next door adds to the excitement on the nights you've gone to bed all peaky after you've drunk too much wine.'

I suddenly realised why I'd been feeling tired and sick with brain fog, it wasn't perimenopause, or the tannin in Kouris wines. 'You drugged the wine, didn't you?'

She smiled. 'And your cups of tea. In fact, whenever you were annoying, which was quite a lot.'

I couldn't take this in. 'I can't, I just can't.' I was shaking my head, hoping I could shake it all away.

'Oh, love, I'm not the other woman, *you* are. Nik's *my* husband.'

'What?' I groaned.

Talking to Heather earlier, I'd guessed about Nik and Dimitris, that one was the brains and one was the brawn of the racket. But Sylvie? No, *not* Sylvie. It didn't make sense.

'How could you bring *me* into your lives, pretend to be my friend, let your husband pretend to marry me. How could you *do* that?'

'Money.'

'Jesus!' I gasped, unable to take all this in. I wasn't legally married to Nik, she was, and the two of them were in this together. 'So you both what? Go out hunting at night for single female travellers to rob?'

She considered this for a moment, as she sucked on her pen. 'We aren't animals. You had a nice little nest egg from your divorce. It's not a huge amount, we've had better – heiresses and millionaires actually. You're small fry, but it's been a quiet season, and we have to keep our heads down because the police have been sniffing around ever since the wedding.'

I shuddered to think how I'd fallen for him, agreed to marry him, and gone through with it when I really wasn't sure.

'I'm not completely surprised about Nik, I knew something wasn't right.'

'It took you a long time to work out, we're obviously good at what we do,' she said this with a smile. I wanted to smack her face.

'We used to do the predictable old life insurance scam,

you know he'd marry someone, or I would, then we'd insure them, then they'd have a *tragic* accident. But everyone's doing it now, and being the recipient of a lot of money when someone dies accidentally is like having GUILTY tattooed on your forehead.' She laughed at her own little joke.

'No, getting the women to buy property is much cleverer,' she continued. 'Of course they don't actually *buy* any property. As I think you realised earlier today, we seduce the women into putting all the money they have into a property. They meet Christos who tells them buying property is the only way to stay with their new husband, and Nik says, "It's an investment, darling." Then the stupid women are given the Estate Agent's account number to pay into, in your case Adonis – we have lots of different accounts, we move the money around the world.'

'The name Adonis on the shop was just a temporary sign...?'

'Yes, as you saw, the whole shop was just like a film set, we hire shops as pop-ups, and turn them into estate agents for a couple of days, just long enough to get the money.'

'It's so elaborate, so horribly planned.'

'Yeah well, it has to be. When you're dealing with wealthy people, professional women sometimes men, the scam has to be good. We do two or three a year. Greece is a great place, but our best years were Rio, we cleaned up there and plan to go back. Everything's so corrupt in Rio you just pay a few reals and the right police officer will turn a blind eye. Sad really, the poor are really poor there, but the rich are *extremely* rich and deserve to be rinsed.'

I was still in shock. 'So where does Dimitris fit in? Do you use him to scare people?'

'Dimitris?' she scoffed. 'He's an irritant, he gets in our

way, it was him who told the police on Nik. Bastard. He's another reason we're leaving Corfu, he ruined it for us. Always poking around. The sooner he's properly dead the better.' She looked over at him lying in his own blood, while she was covered in it.

'Where the hell is Nik?' she murmured to herself, as if I wasn't even there.

'But you called him a murdering bastard?'

'Oh that was just for show, I wanted you to think it was him, I always did.'

'So Dimitris has nothing to do with this?'

She shook her head and sucked on the vape, the air was acidic with chemical citrus.

I couldn't believe it, I'd got it all so wrong, even Heather had assumed he was in on it with Nik. But Dimitris had turned up that night because he *knew* I was in danger? He gave me the poster of the missing women and the house I'd bought that wasn't mine. All this time Dimitris wasn't *threatening* me, he was *warning* me.

FORTY-TWO

Fused images of the missing women fizzed in my brain. Heather said to ask questions, killers love to brag, she'd said, so the questions I'd had for Nik, I was now using on Sylvie. She was the mastermind behind all this.

'So, the women, they are all around forty to fifty. All holidaymakers, all single, all untraceable. How did you find them?'

'Lots of different ways, we meet them in bars, find them on social media, it's incredibly easy to find out the relevant details about someone these days. In your case though, we got your details from Martha, the woman you rented your fancy apartment from when you first arrived here? We paid her a few quid to let us know about any rich, single women renting one of her high-end places. We gave her a vague profile of the kind of women we're looking for, she thinks we targeted you to sell wine and Greek tours around the bay. Same with Zara at the boutique, but she had a bit more about her, soon realised we were doing something far more interesting than bloody wine tasting. So we had to come to an arrangement, and I would take the brides there for clothes, she'd overcharge them and we'd split it.'

'I spent 600 euros on a pair of trousers and a top,' I murmured, shaking my head.

She chuckled at this, 'yeah but the real sting was the two grand for the wedding dress.'

'That wasn't real either? It hadn't been shipped in from Italy?'

'Was it hell, those pearls weren't real nor were they sewn on by hand,' her face was beaming.

'So *you're* like a pimp, or a madam,' I said. 'You find rich women for him, then he marries them and takes their money?'

Sylvie raised her eyebrows. 'I wouldn't call myself a pimp, I'm the bloody brains behind this, I have a little more class than that. And like all the other women, you have to have some sense of responsibility, he didn't exactly drag you screaming to the altar, did he?'

The stench of fake lemons filled my nostrils, mingling with the sharp bleach and the metallic tang of blood. I wanted to be sick.

'We love the needy ones like you, all messed up and desperate, we knew you were hiding something from the beginning. You wanted to be invisible, and we helped you.'

'So your beautiful car, the clothes, the apartment, all bought with stolen money. And the property, the passport, Christos, Clio?'

'All friends of ours,' she said. 'Cheeky bastards won't do it for nothing though, and Christos takes the piss how much he charges. But worth it to take the money out of the open hands of women with more money than sense. As for the properties, we choose an Airbnb and print the details out on headed paper.'

'Like the one Dimitris showed me before.'

'Yeah we just rent them for a day or two, and show the women round pretending they're for sale. They, sorry – *you* are so gullible it's unbelievable.'

I moved away from where she was standing, I didn't want her too close.

'Nik's first wife, Elizabeth Brown, where is she?'

'That was funny, we laughed about that, Nik and I. You thought he'd killed her, didn't you?'

'My sister did, I thought perhaps Dimitris…?'

'Your sister needs to mind her own business, she's as clueless as you! Elizabeth Brown doesn't exist, he made her up.'

'That's where you're wrong, she does exist, she has a website…'

'Yeah, Elizabeth Brown Interiors, it took me a couple of hours to make that website. If things don't work out in my current career I might just go into that, creative, wasn't it?'

I didn't answer her. I hadn't so far had the courage to ask her what I really wanted to know, but I had to ask her now before the police came. 'What about the young girl? She doesn't fit the profile.'

'Who? Oh yeah, you mean Freya, the girl whose picture you're fixated on.'

'Yes, Freya.'

'Nik was stupid to keep a photo, he can be really thick sometimes.' Her face looked hard and mean, I'd never seen her like that before. 'We made a big mistake with that one, nearly got us caught. Nik met her in a bar, started chatting to her, I wasn't keen, she was too young, but Nik found out she had a huge trust fund worth millions.'

'He *married* her?' I asked, horrified.

'Well, that was the plan, but when her parents found out they went spare and wouldn't speak to her. So with them off the scene, it should have made things easier for us. But what I hadn't reckoned on was him, the idiot, falling for her. Our best payday ever, and for once, it wasn't about the money for him, and he started to make mistakes. So when, one night as I lay in the next room, I heard them planning to run away together, I had to put a stop to it. Not only was he cutting me out of the deal to run off with his richer younger woman, I was jealous, I still loved him you see. I'm his only real wife, and it will always be that way. None of the other marriages are legal, but the brides, sometimes grooms don't know that – everyone plays a part, from the celebrant to the guests, are all paid to show up on the day.'

'But Freya... what happened?' I asked, desperate to know.

'Oh it turned out that her estranged parents didn't want to be estranged anymore, she told me they were on their way to Corfu to see her. By then she was no use to us, we depend on the women being single and without any close family who might start kicking off if they go missing.'

I shivered at this.

'So, I took her aside, told her Nik was stringing her along, didn't find her attractive, only wanted her money, and certainly didn't love her. Then I ended it by saying he was married – to me!' She said this with such delight, I wanted to hit her.

'Was she upset, what happened?'

'She burst into tears, and yelled at me and called for Nik and...' For a brief moment Sylvie looked sad again, then turned to me. 'I didn't mean for it to happen, she was young and stupid and hysterical. I should have put the Xanax in her drink before I told her, but I hadn't, so I put some in her glass of water and told her to drink it.' I stood open-mouthed in horror.

'I only wanted to calm her down,' she continued defensively. 'I would have just sent her packing, I wouldn't have done her any harm, she was young and...'

'What *happened*?' I asked, not really wanting to know.

'She was slight and in my panic to shut her up, I hadn't measured the drug, just threw it in when she wasn't looking,' her voice was quieter now, 'she went to sleep and didn't wake up.'

'*You* killed her,' I murmured.

'I didn't mean to. Yes I wanted her out of our lives, out of *his* life, but not like that. I never wanted *that* for any of the women.'

'Where is she now?'

'Her body, you mean?'

I was unable to respond, as heavy tears dropped down my cheeks. I had to hold on to the table to stay upright.

'She's with the others.' She nodded in the direction of the vineyard.

I went cold. 'You killed them *all*.'

'Yeah, once we'd got their money, what else could we do? Leave them to go and tell the police, or in *her* case, her rich parents. She knew too much, she was a ticking time bomb, they all were.' She paused, and thought for a moment. 'You really freaked out when you saw her poster, didn't you? Kept going on about him having a type and you looking like her, I thought you'd realised, I thought you might go straight to the police, but all you were scared of was that if he had a type, you might be next.'

'No, I was scared something bad had happened to her. The girl in the picture is my daughter.'

FORTY-THREE

It was my sixteenth summer when I got pregnant. It was just a couple of years after losing my parents, and I'd gone wild for a time, raging against my lot and taking it out on myself, sleeping around, drinking too much. When I missed several periods, I was in denial. My lifelong pattern of fleeing from trouble started then, and I ran away, not in the literal sense, but from what was happening to my body. I hid my burgeoning bump under loose clothes, and went through life in a fog, not dealing with it, hoping that it would 'sort itself out.' But just like the police investigation, and later when I lost touch with my daughter – these things don't sort themselves out, they *need* to be addressed. At eight months, Heather walked in on me in the bedroom and screamed. Until then, everyone thought I'd just put weight on, including my sister. It was too late for a termination, and we made the decision together, that I'd have my baby adopted. The birth was traumatic. I cried out for my dead mother. And when she was born, for the few, precious hours I was allowed to have with her, I named her Freya. She had the bluest eyes.

I'd bonded with her, she was part of me, and you can't change that, but the adoption was agreed, and despite pleading with Heather to keep her, I couldn't. She could barely make ends meet for the two of us, and at twenty-two was too young to take on any more responsibility, I was enough.

I grieved for years after giving her up. Her birth had been the most wonderful, terrible thing that had ever happened to me. And when I lost her, I never felt whole again, and spent the next eighteen years waiting to meet her. On her eighteenth birthday, I made an application for access. I couldn't wait, the longing to see my child, to touch her was physical, visceral. I longed to see her, hold her, make up for everything we'd missed, I was thirty-four years old, I'd barely lived my life, taking jobs to make ends meet, never really committing to anything or anyone. Since I'd given her up I'd felt like the other half of me was missing, so when she rejected my request to meet, I was devastated. It was as if I'd lost her all over again. So, I grieved for her for four long years, then I met Dan and decided to try and commit to him, and hopefully have another baby. I knew that baby could never replace her, but I respected her desire to move on, and tried to do the same. But then the year she turned twenty-three, she made contact through the adoption services. Out of the blue I received a letter from her, not a message, or a reach out on Facebook, but a proper old-fashioned letter, signed *Freya*, her adoptive parents had kept her name. I was so touched to receive the letter, she'd given me something of herself to hold and to keep and to press against my face, knowing she'd held it in her hands. She told me lots about herself, gave me her phone number, said she was spending the summer on Corfu teaching English, and to call her if I'd like to.

I didn't tell my husband, he'd never known of her existence, I'd always wanted to keep her to myself, and now was no different. I was straight on the phone, and though I cried throughout most of the call I remember every word, every moment, I always will. We stayed in touch for months, I'd never been so happy. It turned out we had a lot in common, the same sense of humour, same taste in food, clothes and music. She told me she'd felt like a piece of her had been missing all her life, and she'd always dreamed of meeting me, but when she was eighteen her parents had been against it, so she'd had to reject my request.

Now she was a little older, she'd had a minor rebellion, escaped from a strict upbringing ruled by class and money, to the laid-back Island of Corfu. Contacting me at the age of twenty-three had probably been part of that late teenage rebellion, but it was leading her down other paths too. One day she called me to say she'd fallen in love for the first time, she was giddy and silly and happy, and I was delighted that she'd chosen to tell me before anyone else. I'd missed so many milestones, it was a privilege to share in the heady excitement of my daughter's first love. However, it soon became apparent that this guy, who worked in a bar, was older, a lot older than her. All she'd say was that he was in his forties, I expressed my concern at this but she insisted he was 'the one.' She hadn't told her parents because they'd try and stop it. She said they'd always been strict, and overprotective, but in just a few months' time she was about to come into a huge trust fund, and they were probably trying to protect her. 'He's asked me to marry him,' she'd said excitedly.

I immediately saw red flags. A bartender over twenty

years her senior, with no money, living on an island like a teenage backpacker? And the only child of very rich parents who was about to inherit a multi-million-pound trust fund? It bothered me. A lot. And I hated myself for bursting her bubble, but I had to say something. So I told her I agreed with her adoptive parents, that she was vulnerable and needed to be careful. She was immediately on the defensive, the conversation escalated quickly and she said I was just like her parents, no one understood her, and she slammed down the phone.

I never heard from her again. She didn't respond to any of my calls or texts, I was devastated and angry with myself because I'd handled it so badly. Until that point, I'd been like a best friend. I thought it was easy being a mum, but I failed at the first test. I never forgave myself for not being gentler, kinder, cleverer, because that's what mums have to be, what good mums *are*. I tried to get in touch with her so many times, and when I knew I had to leave the UK I came back here, to Corfu, I was desperate to find her again.

She would have been twenty-eight by now, and since she'd been born, I'd written her a birthday card every year. I kept them in a box in my suitcase, hoping that we'd finally meet on Corfu and I could give them to her, I wanted her to know I'd never forgotten her. How could I? She was part of me. And now I'd found her, but it was too late.

The man she'd met was Nik, and from that moment, her destiny was sealed, and in the hands of those two evil killers, her death was inevitable, as perhaps mine was now too? And a part of me welcomed that, because at least I'd be with her, and the screaming would stop.

FORTY-FOUR

Sylvie had been pacing the terrace until I'd revealed that Freya was my daughter.

'Shit,' she murmured under her breath, taking her vape pen from her pocket. 'Did you *know* it was us?'

'Not you, Sylvie, I never guessed for a moment. But Nik... when I found her photo in the bedside drawer where he slept, I *knew* he was somehow involved. Before we married, I had an uneasy feeling that he knew more than he was saying about the women, but it was easier to tell myself his involvement was more about covering for Dimitris, instead of himself.'

'Yeah, well, it was easier if I told you Dimitris was weird and creepy. We had to plant that seed so you never listened to him, or went near him. The last thing we needed was you two finding a way to communicate,' she said.

I could feel her opening up, the acrid scent of lemons emanating from her mouth as she spoke.

'Well it worked, I really believed that Dimitris was the killer, but he's the one who's been trying to tell everyone.'

She nodded. 'He was the one who called the police, tipped them off months ago apparently, and they'd been watching Nik, waiting for him to do something. Dimitris told them he thought we were running a scam, he'd been suspicious for a while, but after Magda and the millionaire they realised we were running a business.'

'Magda and the millionaire? Which one of them were you scamming?'

'Well, let's put it this way, Mike the millionaire bought a yacht for three million euros a week after the wedding. He's still waiting for it to be delivered. Oh and Magda has just put in for a divorce, but Mike's kicking up a bit of a stink, so Nik and I are disappearing, we might take a couple of years off,' she smiled, 'after all we have plenty of Mike's money.' She smiled to herself at this.

'God, you really are evil, both of you. And poor Dimitris was the only one who saw it!'

'Yes unfortunately. After Mike and Magda's wedding he went straight to the police and told them he thought it was fake, we had a feeling the police had been following Nik, but after that they upped their surveillance,' she raised her eyebrows. 'Dimitris and his big mouth, that's why Nik was arrested on your wedding day.'

'That wasn't *my* wedding day,' I hissed. 'I'm glad he had Nik arrested, I wish they'd kept him in, thrown away the key.'

She smiled at this. 'Well they didn't, because I got him out. I knew if Nik was left there he was likely to drop us in it, like I say, he can sometimes be a bit thick and say stupid things. So, while you were playing Miss Haversham downstairs in your veil, I popped to the kitchen to make your special tea...'

'Containing sleeping pills?'

'Something like that – and while that kettle was boiling, I called the police and told them Dimitris had sexually assaulted one of my staff.'

'What? But he didn't.'

'Did he hell, since his stroke a few years ago he can barely walk and talk, let alone...'

'So his difficulties communicating, heavy breathing, his strange gait? They are the after-effects of the stroke?'

She nodded. 'Luckily for us, Angelina will say anything for a few quid, probably *do* anything too,' she added as an afterthought. 'I offered her money to go to the police and tell them he'd sexually assaulted her. Obviously there was no physical evidence so it was her word against his, and it didn't stick.'

'So you lied to me about the police suspecting Dimitris was the killer?'

'Yeah. But as nosy old gossips say, "there's no smoke without fire," so his legend continued. I also lied to you about calling the police. That 'conversation' I had with them on your wedding day was fake, there was no one on the end of the phone. But you were so out of it by then on wedding drama and Xanax, I could tell you anything.' Then she chuckled. 'Mind you, I could tell you anything without drugs and you'd believe me.'

'Like the lie that Dimitris had killed the missing women? Pointing me in the direction of Facebook to see all those posts and comments?' Then I realised. 'Did *you* put some of those lies online?'

'Yeah,' she said almost proudly. 'I was Kate from Kalami, and Eleni from Corfu Town,' she added with a smirk. 'Initially all fake accounts, but it didn't take the trolls long to smell blood and pile on, and soon he was the Corfu Killer.'

Now I understood why Dimitris was haunting the vineyard at night – he wasn't *digging* graves, he was *searching* for them. Like me, the man was being driven mad looking for answers, knowing in his heart that Nik was involved, but not being able to prove anything.

'So Dimitris' physical issues all fed into your horrible narrative.'

'Yeah, it worked for us, we couldn't believe our luck when the vineyard advertised for a manager a few years back. Nik was working the bars in town.'

'The Aphrodite?'

'Yeah, that's right. And I was making what I could with work here, work there and a few dodgy deals. Anyway, Nik went for the job with a pimped-up CV and got it.'

'So Nik only *works* here, he isn't the owner, and they aren't cousins?'

'No, Dimitris is, he's Kouris wines, that's why we had to say they were family, so Nik could be a Kouris too.'

'Nik just works for him?' I never expected that.

'Yeah, he's his right-hand man. When he had the stroke he was incapacitated, he has no kids to look after him, just a brother somewhere near the coast. Dimitris is the oldest brother and inherited the vineyard from his father, it's sad really because when he dies his bloody niece will get the lot. She doesn't even live here any more. We had all these plans, hoping he'd see Nik like a son, or brother, thought he might leave us this place in his will. But we couldn't get him to change it, old Dimitris is surprisingly astute, one of the few people we haven't been able to con,' she said this half-admiringly. 'Anyway, our vineyard dream is over, thanks to him blabbing to the police we're going to have to leave the island now.'

'Where will you go?' I asked.

'We've got tickets to Rio,' she looked at her watch, 'hope Nik isn't too late, we don't want to miss the flight.'

'How can you talk about Dimitris' money and flights to Rio, when he's lying there,' I cried.

'Yeah, it breaks my heart, but it's too late to change his will now,' she half-joked. 'Nik tried to be the son he never had, but he was too old and cynical, never trusted Nik from the beginning, and the old sod treated me like dirt.'

'What a shame for you, all that money tied up in the vineyard and you couldn't get your filthy hands on it.'

She shrugged. 'With more time we could have worked something out. Damn him,' she cursed.

'You beguiled vulnerable, innocent women, you stole all their money, and then you killed them and buried them here, in Dimitris' vineyard. What kind of animals *are* you?'

'Clever ones,' she said defiantly, without a trace of shame. 'It was a great cover, Nik the amiable, attractive owner, single and quite a catch. He was the widower, the divorcee, the man who'd never been able to commit until now. We had a few different characters for him. Our wedding service was bespoke, I'd first find out *who* the women were looking for, and Nik would become that man. Not many wedding planners can do that!' she chuckled to herself.

'I don't know any wedding planners who are sick enough to *want* to,' I spat, but she didn't hear me, she just kept talking. She told me proudly how she had a talent for spotting rich, single women, how she'd bump into them in shops and bars, and make friends with us all. Then she'd filter out the ones with family, the ones who didn't have enough money, the ones who weren't quite so vulnerable.

'But I have family, I have my sister,' I pointed out.

'Heather?' she laughed at this. 'She's just an irritant who harasses you all the time, you came here to try and get away from her. Besides, she's no threat, she's flaky as fuck.' Little did she know.

She went on to brag proudly at how throughout Nik's so-called courtships and weddings, she'd lived in the shadows, secretly staying overnight, often in the next room. She would slip through doorways at dusk, move swiftly upstairs, hide in corners and doorways, watching, always watching. She was consumed by jealousy and obsession, but what drove her was the money, the end game.

I was horrified, the familiar laugh, the smile I knew so well, but here in front of me was a very different person.

At one point, she lowered her voice and came up close to me. 'Oh yes, I know everything, Alice, the way you begged Nik for sex, stripping for him and pleasuring yourself like a sad whore,' she snapped viciously.

I gasped, horrified.

'I'd scared you so much about Dimitris you thought it was him spying on you from half open doorways, but all the time it was me. And just to mess with your mind, Nik played the loyal cousin and defended him so you'd think your soon-to-be husband was a good, kind family man. You liked that, didn't you? It played into your need for someone you could trust. Meanwhile, was Dimitris a killer or a scapegoat? Was he? Or wasn't he? You were never a hundred per cent sure about anything, were you, Alice? And that's what we do, we mess with you. Of course the sleeping drugs in drinks help too, we can't take *all* the credit.'

I was beginning to understand. Sylvie had made a lot of money from all this, it was her career, her life, she knew no other way. But she was consumed with jealousy, she hated Nik being with other women, even if it was fake, because what if sometimes it wasn't? This was her way of humiliating his so-called brides, when she finally told them the truth, hurt them, made them pay for falling in love and marrying a stranger – this was her therapy. But she could only tell them when she knew there was no possibility of them going to the police.

'You're telling me everything, because you're going to kill me, aren't you?' I said calmly. 'You're just waiting for Nik to get here.'

Her mouth tightened. 'If he ever does. God knows what he's doing.'

She glanced at her watch, I could see she was anxious concerning Nik's whereabouts, she obviously wasn't comfortable dispatching me without him. Presumably that was his forte? But watching her twitch and fidget, I suddenly saw a way in.

'I reckon he's with Angelina, they're probably gazing at each other now across a candlelit table in Sidari,' I said. And before I could continue, she reached out and smacked me hard in the face with the back of her hand.

'Bitch!' she spat, then immediately composed herself, and murmured into my ear. 'If that's the case, he can dig *two* graves tonight, and she can join you.'

I trembled slightly at this, but tried not to let her see.

'Look, you think you have the upper hand, but Nik's taken the piss out of us both. He's used you like he's used all the other women,' I declared. 'Can't you see it? He's with Angelina, he's always looking for someone better to come along. It's who he is. After emotionally devastating women, he kills them, he must hate them, why are you any different Sylvie. He hates us all.'

'Oh fuck off with your tin pot psychological tricks,' she hissed.

'But some women are different, they are younger, more pliable, and far more his type. Look what happened with Freya,' I continued, hating to even utter my daughter's name in her presence, 'he kept her photo in whatever bedroom he was sleeping in, he might have finally believed he'd found what he was looking for, and you killed her. Do you really think he can forgive you any more than I can for ending her life?'

'Shut up, shut UP!' she yelled. Still stinging from the last surprise slap, I was braced for another, but ploughed on.

'Sylvie, the police are on their way,' I said quietly. 'My sister has called them, she knows everything.'

'No she hasn't.'

'You're making yourself a sitting target for the police by hanging around here waiting for Nik. Meanwhile he's in the back of his car with the gorgeous, young and very willing Angelina.'

'He isn't, he isn't!' she yelled, then turned to me, eyes of fire, and said, 'But if he *is*, I'll *kill* her with my bare hands.'

I believed her.

We glared at each other across the terrace, the sun had gone down, the night was coming and Dimitris' blood had congealed on the wood floor.

'If you kill me, the police will come after you, Heather will make sure of it.'

'Yeah? Your Heather really needs to get a life if she's calling the Greek police from Britain to report something that *might* be happening to her sister.'

I stood up to walk towards the stairs. What Sylvie didn't know, was that earlier, when she knocked the phone from my hand, I'd discreetly called Heather on FaceTime. I hadn't walked into this trap blindly, my sis and I had cooked up a plan on the phone while I'd waited outside the estate agent's that afternoon. The idea was for me to get Nik's or/and Dimitris' confession, we had no idea about Sylvie, even my armchair detective sister would be surprised at this twist. Heather said she would listen in, then after the confession, but *before* I was in any danger, she would call the police. 'They always confess, criminals and murderers love to brag about their work,' she'd said, 'you won't have any trouble getting a confession.' And she was right in Sylvie's case. I just hoped to God we were still FaceTiming, and she was recording, and the police were on their way, because things had taken a sudden turn. And I was now going to try and walk away.

Sylvie didn't make a move, and as I turned my back I didn't know if she was watching me leave and letting me go, or waiting to pounce any minute. Then I felt it, the whack on the back of the head. The statue already covered in Dimitris' blood had been used to hit me.

'I'll say you fell,' she was muttering to herself. 'Even your helicopter sister can't prove it wasn't an accident.' She dragged me out to the edge of the terrace and even in my dazed state, I was knew the low wall was the only thing standing between me and death.

I made a vain attempt to scratch Sylvie's face, to leave scars and have her DNA under my nails – all part of

Heather's sage advice. Her hours watching TV detective dramas hadn't been wasted. So I tried hard to scratch and scar and gather her under my nails. I drew blood, and she became really, really angry. What still shocks me to the core, is what she did in retaliation to this. Sylvie punched me. Hard. In the stomach. My friend. The woman with whom I'd laughed, drunk cocktails, shared my story – the woman I'd trusted. The woman who had killed my daughter.

I kicked out, hoping for bruises, leaving something for Heather when I'd gone. I also wanted revenge for Freya. Each weak, but hopefully painful kick was for my girl. My hate and hurt was overwhelming the dizzy effects from the whack on the head, and I grabbed at her eyes, scratching and kicking, making her scream as I snatched great chunks of her hair and pulled as hard as I could. I found some comfort in those final minutes, thinking of Heather and how she would take on the fight after I'd gone. Sylvie was a fighter, and so much stronger than me. She'd punched and kicked me until I couldn't fight anymore, and she was pulling me by my feet to the low wall. Clinging like a limpet to the bricks, my nails bled as I tried hard to hold on. Even in that terrified, dazed state, I was hoping and praying the police would get there in time, but I heard no sirens, no noise, just her breathing and muttering and cursing. The woman who killed my daughter was now about to kill me. I could hear the women's screams in my head, my voice joining theirs in a crescendo of agony and fear. Then everything went black.

EPILOGUE

I lift my heavy suitcase onto the conveyor belt. It's filled with my clothes, my toiletries and my secrets. I surrender it reluctantly as the uniformed woman slaps on security stickers and points to 'Airport Security' with a sulky nod. I nod back, saying nothing, not wanting to attract attention to myself in any way.

So far, so good. I step outside for a quick vape before returning and heading for security – my tomato-red Hermes handbag on my arm, my mouth dry as sand. Stale heat gathers around the homebound tourists with sunburn and sad faces, all queueing to go home when they don't want to. I keep my eyes downwards, don't engage with anyone and after too long, I finally see Border Control.

Walking on wobbly legs towards the serious man waiting behind glass, I cast my mind back to when I first arrived here. The person who came to this paradise island is very different from the one who's leaving. I came in search of something, someone, and I found them, but now I have to go again.

I hate to leave this beautiful place, where the sun shines

all day and the cocktails flow all night. But if you look closer, there's a dark side, and friends, lovers and murder, are just a whisper apart.

The border guard is looking at me from behind glass. He doesn't smile, but I do.

'Are you going to Rio de Janeiro on business or pleasure?'

'Pleasure.' I lean forward slightly and lick my lips suggestively; straight away, his eyes are on my lips. He hands me back my passport, and I try not to look too relieved. Or too guilty...

The flight is due to board soon, so I call Clio, the estate agent. 'Darling, there's been a slight change of plan,' I start. 'Alice is gone, as planned, but sadly, the police arrested Nik in Sidari, he was having dinner with his young mistress, I'm devastated. It's awful, and the vineyard's now crawling with police looking for bodies or something. But the really bad news is they know all about the money Alice paid into the Adonis account for the property.'

'Oh shit,' Clio murmurs.

'Right? Anyway, I'm leaving the country, and as Nik's in police custody, that leaves just you. And your fingerprints, metaphorically speaking – are all over that half a million.'

'But I don't know anything about it. Shit, Sylvie, I just do what Nik tells me, I only get ten per cent, it isn't worth going to jail for. I don't want to be Clio the estate agent anymore, I'm Clio the actress really.'

'I know, I know, and I'm sure you'll soon be a big star, but think of it as the ultimate in method acting.'

'If you try and pin anything on me, I swear—'

'Calm down,' I say. 'I wouldn't *dream* of dropping you in

it, that's why I'm calling you now, because I have a solution. My oldest and dearest friend in the UK is going to take the heat out of this for us. I just need for you to do exactly as I say, and you'll be clean as a whistle.'

'Okay?'

'You must take out *all* the money from Alice Evans, or Alice Kouris or whatever she was calling herself, and deposit it into another account.'

'Will it go away then?'

'Yes, but only if you do it ASAP, because the police have a list of names, and I'm sorry, but your name's on it,' I lie. That money is hot and linked to poor, dead Alice and I'm the only one with the contacts to get rid of it. But if you dump that money now, they'll have nothing on you.'

'What about my ten per cent?'

'Oh for God's sake, Clio, as soon as it's safe I'll get your ten per cent to you,' I lie again. 'Do you understand how serious this is and what I need you to do?'

'Yeah, I understand. So give me the name and bank details of where you want the money to go.'

'Sylvie Brown,' I start, then give her all the information she needs. Her bank details were in the Hermes handbag, and for a con artist, her password was easy to guess. I've practised her signature, but as most banking is online now, I doubt I'll need it.

'Probably best if we don't see or speak to each other again,' I say to Clio. 'Have a fabulous life, and I hope you get your big break, my love.'

Then I call Heather.

'It's me.'

'Oh, thank God, you're later than I expected. Is everything okay?' I can hear the excitement in her voice.

'All good.'

'Any news on Dimitris?' she asks.

'Sadly, despite the best efforts of the medics, he passed.'

'Ahh. He died trying to save you love. I'll never know where he got the strength from.'

'Me neither,' I reply, recalling the moment when Sylvie was about to push me off the terrace. I'd blacked out, but came to slumped over the wall as she struggled to push my dead weight over it.

'Poor Dimitris, he must have found the last vestiges of strength to save you, and push her.'

'Yes, she hit the ground, died immediately, but he was so weak he fell *with* her. I feel bad about how I was so scared of him. He was just trying to warn me, and follow me to make sure no one hurt me. We were the only witnesses, we were on the same side, but because of my prejudices, my closed mind, I didn't look beyond what I saw. I hadn't realised that the man I thought was trying to kill me, was actually trying to save me.'

'Be careful, love,' she says.

'Thanks for your crazy idea about FaceTiming everything.'

'I'm just relieved it bloody worked,' she said. 'I was having a heart attack here waiting for the police to arrive, I can still hear the sounds of her punching you, I felt every blow.'

'I know you did, Heather, you've felt everything for me all my life, you've felt my pain like no one else. Thanks for always being there, for saving me when Mum and Dad died, and for keeping us together. It used to annoy me that you always asked me where I was, and what I was doing, always worrying – but now I realise that's what family is all about.'

'Yeah, love and worry,' she says with a sigh.

'If those women had someone worrying about them like I have you, they might still be alive. Thanks for missing me.'

'I do, I miss you so much, Alice, and I always will wherever you are in the world. I just wish I'd helped you to keep Freya in our family rather than insist she was adopted. I will regret that until the day I die.'

'Don't, we were both young and we did what was right at the time. We couldn't have given Freya the life she'd had, however short it turned out to be.'

I'm about to go, when I remember. 'Heather, just one thing, I meant to ask – when they... find her, will you make sure she gets a head stone, and take flowers on her birthday?'

'Of course, I'll be there, and I'll take her cousins with me.'

'Love you, sis,' I say.

'And be careful, don't do anything dangerous or stupid, you know how I worry.'

'You? Worry?' I smile.

We say our goodbyes not knowing if or when we'll see each other again. I feel like I might cry, and don't want to draw attention to myself, so take out my phone to distract myself and calm my nerves, and when I look up, someone is standing over me.

For a moment, I don't recognise her. 'Angelina?' I'm horrified, and finding it hard to conceal that horror on my face. 'What are *you* doing here?'

She sits down next to me. 'More like what are *you* doing here?'

'I'm... I'm going away.'

'I don't blame you.' She looks down at the tomato-red Hermes bag on my knee. 'You still like her style then?'

I am mortified, I can hardly explain that I'm travelling on Sylvie's passport and ticket because I'm wanted for murder in the UK. Angelina would drop me right in it, just my luck to bump into her at this moment, it could ruin everything.

I always loved this handbag, and when I found it in my bedroom at the vineyard where she'd left it, I opened it and inside the lining was her passport, credit cards, bank details and over five thousand euros. I presume this was in case she needed to make a quick getaway, which I'm doing now. It was the universe handing me a plane ticket, a couple of weeks' grace before I find a new job, and a fabulous, tomato-red designer bag.

I glance nervously at Angelina. 'Are you here to make sure I leave Greek soil?' I ask nervously. 'Or are you going to threaten me again? You don't need to, I'm going. And Nik's in police custody, we were never married by the way, it was all a big scam set up by him and Sylvie – his *real* wife.'

'I know all about it.'

My heart thuds, and I notice Angelina is wearing chinos and a blue shirt, a world away from the frilly, low-cut tops and miniskirts she usually wears.

'Alice... I have something to tell you...'

I hold my breath. I can't imagine what fresh hell *this* is.

'What?' I say weakly. Can I take any more?

'My name *isn't* Angelina,' she starts, 'it's Eleni Doukas, and I followed you here.'

I groan. 'Oh no, you're *one* of them too? You were just pretending, like Christos and Clio and...?'

She shakes her head. 'No, I'm with the police here on Corfu.'

What the hell kind of game is she playing *now*?

'No you're not,' I say dismissively, but I'm flushed and

panicking. She's probably winding me up, but in the unlikely event that she's telling the truth, I need to get on my plane and get the hell out of here.

'I am, I'm a detective. I feel I owe you an explanation. I know you went through a lot and you deserve to know what happened.'

'I'm very confused,' I say, mesmerised. She has no make-up on, and her hair is tied back in a ponytail. This is Angelina, yet it isn't. Perhaps she *is* telling the truth?

She offers me her ID card, which looks legitimate to me. 'Bloody hell, I don't understand.' My head is a mess, nothing and no one are as they seem.

'The recordings you made of Sylvie confessing are invaluable to us. I know she's dead, and beyond justice, but we have all the information we need to prosecute Nik Kouris – real name David Mills.'

'David Mills – so he isn't even Greek?'

'I'm afraid he and Sylvie were just creations, neither of them were who they say they were. Everything they told you was a construct to hook you in, they've been doing it for many years. The problem has been tracking them down because they never stay in the same place for long, they operated throughout Europe and the Americas. They have millions stashed all over the world from their fake marriages. Thing is, we have no idea of the body count,' she adds regretfully.

'Yeah, I had a feeling this was just the tip of the iceberg. Sylvie mentioned Rio de Janeiro.'

She nods vigorously. 'I reckon that's where they did some of their "best work," and sometimes, in some parts of the world the authorities turn a blind eye. The police take bribes, and money takes precedence over justice. Sadly, we don't have the resources to cover their past crimes, but what we can do, is make sure we get justice for *our* victims here on Corfu.'

'Oh God. The poor families. Sylvie said they had no one, but everyone has someone. The not knowing is almost the worst part of losing someone you love.'

She half closes her eyes, acknowledging my pain. 'I heard about your daughter on the recordings. You were very brave to come here, to try to find her. I hope you take some comfort knowing that thanks to you, Nik – David Mills – will be in prison for the rest of his life.'

'I guess it's a crumb of comfort that he can't kill any more women and destroy any more families. It's the mothers,' I say, tears in my eyes. 'If the mothers don't *know*, how can they ever find peace?'

'Remains are being recovered now, and we will make sure that the families of the women who lost their lives here will *know*,' she said gently, 'as will you.'

'Thank you. How long had the police here been watching Sylvie and Nik?'

'Dimitris Kouris alerted us he'd been suspicious for a while, he'd been working with us. And when he saw them homing in on you, we soon made the connections with the missing women.' She's sitting with her legs apart, elbows on her knees, leaning forward, close enough so only I can hear her.

'I was drafted in from Athens to work on the operation, but these two were so slippery the decision was made for me to go undercover.'

'That's when you became Angelina?' I try to take in what she's telling me, but my mind is racing. I wonder fleetingly if I can ever trust anyone again.

'Being undercover, I had to play a part.'

'You played it well, a little too well if you don't mind me saying? I didn't like you at all.'

'Yeah,' she smiles. 'Sorry about that, but I couldn't get close to you, I had to just make sure we had enough evidence.'

I suddenly feel sick; 'Talking of evidence, you may have heard on the recording that I have an issue back home? My ex-husband died and...' I start.

She shakes her head. 'I don't remember anything about your ex-husband, it must have been lost,' she says with a half-smile.

'Thank you,' I can finally breathe again. I'm still wanted for murder in the UK, but at least I know the police here aren't going to tell them where I am.

'When did you realise about Nik?' she asks.

'Looking back, I knew something wasn't right on my wedding day. I didn't know exactly *what* was going on, but I began to feel uneasy. Until then I'd thought it was Dimitris working alone, then I started to look at Nik slightly differently.'

'You were right to feel uneasy. At first we thought it was Nik working alone, it was only a few months ago we realised he had an accomplice, but Sylvie stayed under the radar. We were aware they were connected, we just weren't sure if it was romantic, friendship, or criminal. I actually told her that I'd seen Nik with one of the missing women – it was a test to see how much she knew. But when I told her she said it doesn't mean he did anything *wrong*. Then she told me off for saying things like that.'

'I remember overhearing that conversation, I thought you were talking about Dimitris.'

'Poor Dimitris,' she sighed, 'he came to us a while ago saying he was suspicious that Nik was somehow involved in the disappearances of some of the women. The irony was that Nik was the weak link, Sylvie was the real mastermind of their nasty operation. Once I was inside though, it only got darker, and when you were identified as the next potential victim, we knew we had to work hard to keep ahead.'

'I heard you arrested Nik in Sidari?'

'Yeah, he really thought I was into him, and when he offered to take me there we realised it was a way of keeping the two of them apart. Your sister had called us that day and told us you were heading back with Sylvie but she was worried about Nik. What we didn't tell her was that by then we were more worried about you being on your own with Sylvie. So we arrested Nik late that afternoon, confiscating his phone to stop him from letting her know we were onto her. But meanwhile, you pulled a master stroke and got her confession, the details and everything else we needed on your FaceTime to your sister. I heard that your sister was at the other end and one of your nieces was recording it from her phone?'

'My sister's idea. She's amazing.'

'She is, it was quite ingenious, and it's given us everything we need.'

'Something that's puzzled me, I saw you with Dimitris at one of the weddings, he was really close, whispering in your ear. You looked really scared,' I said.

She nodded. 'He was telling me that Nik had been in the orange grove with you, that you'd kissed. Dimitris had followed you, and he was worried you'd seen him. I was horrified. I knew then that they'd chosen you as their next victim, and you were in danger. I looked scared because I was terrified for you.'

'Wow! I like to think I understand people, that I can read them. My sister and I used to think we could solve crimes, two armchair detectives,' I say, shaking my head. 'But this was going on in front of me and I missed it.'

She shrugs. 'These people were professional scam artists, and clever too, they really studied their victims, using psychology and body language. They made it their business to know your weaknesses, your needs, your desires.'

'Yes, that's exactly it, as Sylvie said, her weddings were bespoke.'

'They sure were, that's why we had to match them, to out-scam them. I had to be flirty and friendly with them, to play my part. I needed to get Nik onside so he'd tell me everything, and he did. Meanwhile, my priority was keeping you safe while keeping you at a distance – that's where my bitchiness came in,' she smiled. 'You might remember I actually told you not to trust *anyone*.'

She stands up, opens her arms and for a moment I don't understand what she's doing, until she hugs me. It's so unexpected, I don't respond. 'Sorry, I still see Angelina, and that bitch would *never* open her arms to me,' I joke, going back in for a hug.

'Oh don't worry, Angelina's gone, like Nik and Sylvie, and sadly Dimitris. No one is left. And now you're leaving too, but going to a better place I hope.'

'Me too,' I say, and suddenly remember someone else. 'What about Maria?' I ask.

She smiles. 'Ah you mean Lieutenant Helen Loukanis? She did a great job, she's very young, but one day she'll run this force, a brilliant policewoman.'

I am still trying to take it all in as we say goodbye and as she leaves she turns and waves at me. For the first time I actually feel sad to be leaving this lovely place, what a shame I can't ever come back here.

I now need a drink, so order a cosmopolitan. As I wait for my flight to be called, I sip my drink, and decide to take care of final business before I leave. So I message Della on Instagram. It will be in breach of the injunction, but it doesn't matter anymore, in a few hours I'll be Sylvie Brown in Rio and Alice Evans won't exist anymore, so I type:

Hi Della, I know what you did. And I won't tell. I'm not taking a mother away from her baby, so I'm going away, and I won't be coming back to the UK. So live your life, all I ask is that you love your baby girl, and keep her close.

Less than a minute later I get a notification.

I couldn't stand by while he punched you. I'd been there too many times myself. I'm sorry I tried to blame it on you, but I had no choice. I'm a lawyer, I knew if the truth came out I would go to prison for manslaughter at the very least. I couldn't leave my baby, but I didn't give you the credit you deserve for understanding that, and sacrificing your own life. I'm glad you know, and I won't tell if you don't tell. But if ever I can help in any way, please ask me, I owe you so much. I was so worried I might have to leave my baby girl. I'll never forget what you've done for me. If ever anyone finds you, and you need legal help, I'm your lawyer. Sending love from both of us. Xxx

PS. I never wanted compensation, that was something Dan talked about straight after the accident, I went along with it for a while. He thought it was you who'd hit him, and I told him no different. I'm sorry.

PPS. I hope this wasn't your way of tricking me into a written confession?

I assure her it's all good, and click off my phone, tears in my eyes. Then I message Heather. The money for the divorce settlement will soon be in Sylvie's account, which of course I have access to now I have her cards. Her pin number was as easy as her password, and worked first time I tried – 231067 – Nik's birthday, she really was crazy about him, well as much as any psychopath can be crazy about another. It's been three days since she died, and so I have a small window to put money through before the bank is notified about her death. Heather is completely across it, has access and is now waiting for the money to drop into the account from Clio. She's then going to withdraw everything in there, which is quite a lot. She'll send some to me once I have a new bank account in a new name, so I can start a new life. Then I want her to put some in a trust fund for her girls, and also for Della's baby. The rest of the money is Heather's, but it can't just turn up in her account, so I've told her to stick it under the mattress. I've also asked her to try and find Freya's adoptive parents, they are elderly, and there's a chance they might still not be around, but if they are I want them to know. I couldn't bear to think of them not knowing what happened to her, because that's the worst part of all this.

Once the police have identified Freya, I've asked Heather to take her girls on holiday on Corfu, go out on a boat one sunny day and scatter her ashes. Perhaps then I will be able to sleep again, knowing where she is?

I wish I could join my family to say goodbye to my daughter, but I can't risk it. I can't return here as there'll always be a chance that the police on Corfu might discover some discrepancies in my story. On the night Sylvie and Dimitris died, events didn't happen in quite the way I told them. Dimitris *did* try and save me, he clambered up and hurled himself at Sylvie while she tried to push me over the wall. But unfortunately, he was very weak, and she moved quickly enough for him to fly past her and hurl himself to the ground. This gave me a few precious seconds to get up, and left the two of us to face each other again. I was terrified. In those few moments, I blacked out and seeing the faces of all the women whose screams had lived inside me for so long. And then I heard Freya's laugh, that tinkling sound I'd heard so often on the telephone, but never in real life. And when I came to, I focused on the woman in front of me, who'd killed my daughter, had stopped her laughter and taken her life. And my hurt and fury flared up like scalding flames, out of control and headed only in one direction, making me roar like an animal, and push her over the wall. Sylvie was dead on impact.

Fortunately, the FaceTime shows none of this, my phone was lying on the floor, facing the night sky. But there *is* audio, and if any keen officer were to take the time to listen, they could perhaps put two and two together. So it's best for now that Alice Evans disappears, and Sylvie lives – for now.

My flight's called, and I pick up my hand luggage heading for another life in another country under another name. I needed somewhere far away, where no one knows me, and I can grieve for my daughter, perhaps even help other mothers, sisters, daughters? Sylvie and Nik spent some time in Rio, she told me they made the most money there, which means there were victims, and where there are victims, there are mothers like me looking for their daughters. Once there I'll start asking a few questions, as my sister always says, someone, somewhere always knows something. And in time I hope to help those mothers find their peace too.

As the plane takes off, I open Sylvie's red handbag, and take out the photo of Freya.

People go missing every day, and the ones who are left behind are faced with the loss, and the pain of never knowing. I miss her, I've missed her since she was taken from me at just a few hours old. I've lived with that agony, that loss, but just knowing she was here on earth for a brief time, makes me happy. And wherever I go, I know she's with me. I carry her in my heart, and always will.

The photograph is all I have, but it's everything. I need her light more than ever after the darkness. Just looking at her smiling face in the sunshine, with flowers in her hair, blows away the cobwebs of my mind, and stops the sound of screaming, for now...

A LETTER FROM SUE

Thank you so much for choosing to read *The Wedding Day*. If you enjoyed it, and want to keep up to date with all my latest releases, just sign up at the following link. Your email address will never be shared and you can unsubscribe at any time.

www.bookouture.com/sue-watson

This book is essentially about people who go missing, and the ones they leave behind.

The initial idea for *The Wedding Day* was sparked when Helen, my editor sent me a news cutting about a wedding that wasn't what it seemed. Wedding days are supposed to be the happiest days of our lives, so what if, for one half of the happy couple, love *isn't* in the air. And what if this wedding isn't about white lace and promises, but money and murder?

I set the book on the Greek island of Corfu, a beautiful holiday setting where the sun shines and the sea sparkles – but no one sees the glint of danger lurking under that big blue sky, and when they do, it's too late.

The idea led me to think about what happens when someone goes missing far away from home, and about the loved ones waiting for news. I can only imagine the pain they go through wondering what happened to the person they love, did they leave of their own accord and find another life, or are they suffering, or worse? They say it's the not knowing that's the worst, and among many other things, this book is about how someone can disappear without a trace, and the not knowing.

I hope you enjoyed *The Wedding Day* and if you did, I would be so grateful if you could write a review, it doesn't have to be as long as a sentence – every word counts and is very much appreciated. I love to hear what you think, and it makes such a difference helping new readers to discover one of my books for the first time.

I love hearing from my readers – so please get in touch, you can find me on my Facebook page, Instagram, and Twitter.

Thanks so much for reading,

Sue

www.suewatsonbooks.com

facebook.com/suewatsonbooks
twitter.com/suewatsonwriter

ACKNOWLEDGEMENTS

Huge thanks to my fantastic editor Helen Jenner who provided the inspiration when she sent me a news story. After a long, exciting discussion, we just knew this book had to be written.

As always, my huge thanks to the wonderful team at Bookouture who are far too many to mention individually, but without them my books wouldn't exist.

Big thanks to my Canadian friend and reader Harolyn Grant who reads through my work, untangles it and translates for Canadian and American readers. I'm in awe of her ability to really see the detail, and spot what I've missed, and so grateful for the time she takes out of her own busy life to save my books.

Big love to Sarah Hardy for doing a great and insightful first read, to Su Biela for beta-reading, and to Anna Wallace who did a great and detailed final read. I don't know what I'd do without all these ladies!

For several years now, a wonderful lady, Ann Bresnan from Alabama, has beta read my work, and I've relied heavily on her opinion, her insight, and her eagle eye. I've also enjoyed our friendship, our chats about our daughters, American politics, our shared fears during Covid, and her wonderful sense of humour. But it's her dedication that astounded me, an example of this was an email I received late one night when Ann was doing an early read through of one of my books.

'*Sue, I wanted to get back to you tonight in case I lose power. As you know I'm in Alabama and we have a hurricane breathing on our neck right now. Raining since last night and the wind is really starting to pick up. Lights have flickered a couple of times.*'

Worried for her safety, I immediately emailed her back telling her to forget about the bloody book and make sure that *she* was okay. But being Ann, she was totally committed, and continued to send me her notes on each chapter throughout the night as the hurricane raged. Ann had agreed to read my book, and she was damn well reading it. Nothing stopped her!

But sadly at the end of November 2022, lovely, unstoppable Ann died unexpectedly after a short illness, and I feel her loss keenly. Ann was a one-off, a very special lady, and I can only imagine the impact of her death on those lucky enough to have had her in their lives. I was privileged to know her for just a few years, and my heart goes out to her family, especially her daughter, Shay, who was everything to her.

Of all the brilliant things she brought to my work, what I miss most about Ann is her brutal honesty, which is something every writer needs. She never sugar-coated it, and would tell me in no uncertain terms when something wasn't working, but always wrote in capital letters when it *was*!

I just hope wherever Ann is, she's read this book, and approves – in CAPITAL LETTERS!

Manufactured by Amazon.ca
Bolton, ON